While studying Elizabethan and Jaco[...] Oxford University, Victoria Lamb h[...] [...]s of novels about Shakespeare's 'Dark Lady'. Now a busy mother of five, she has finally achieved that ambition. Along the way, she has published five books of poetry under the name Jane Holland and edited the arts journal *Horizon Review*. She is also the author of a series of Tudor novels for teens. Victoria lives in a three-hundred-year-old farmhouse on the fringe of Bodmin Moor, Cornwall, with her husband and young family. She is currently working on her third novel featuring Lucy Morgan.

You can follow Victoria Lamb on Twitter @VictoriaLamb1.

Also by Victoria Lamb:

The Queen's Secret

For young adults:

Witchstruck

His Dark Lady

Victoria Lamb

CORGI BOOKS

TRANSWORLD PUBLISHERS
61–63 Uxbridge Road, London W5 5SA
A Random House Group Company
www.transworldbooks.co.uk

HIS DARK LADY
A CORGI BOOK: 9780552165280

First published in Great Britain
in 2013 by Bantam Press
an imprint of Transworld Publishers
Corgi edition published 2013

Addresses for Random House Group Ltd companies outside the UK
can be found at: www.randomhouse.co.uk
The Random House Group Ltd Reg. No. 954009

The Random House Group Limited supports the Forest Stewardship
Council® (FSC®), the leading international forest-certification
organisation. Our books carrying the FSC label are printed on
FSC®-certified paper. FSC is the only forest-certification scheme
supported by the leading environmental organisations, including
Greenpeace. Our paper procurement policy can be found at
www.randomhouse.co.uk/environment

Typeset in 10.5/13pt Sabon by Falcon Oast Graphic Art Ltd.
Printed and bound by CPI Group (UK) Ltd, Croydon, CR0 4YY.

2 4 6 8 10 9 7 5 3 1

For A

'Presume not that I am the thing I was.'

William Shakespeare,
Henry IV, Part Two: Act 5, Scene v

'How far that little candle throws his beams!
So shines a good deed in a naughty world.'

William Shakespeare,
Merchant of Venice: Act 5, Scene i

Prologue

Kenilworth Castle, Warwickshire, April 1578

HANDS CLASPED IN PRAYER, LUCY BENT HER HEAD, WATCHING a stag-horned beetle crawl across the rushes. Her knees hurt on the stone floor, its cold striking into her bones through the thin embroidered cushion on which she knelt. They would not have much longer to wait, she told herself. Her mind drifted to the past and she struggled to drag it back to prayer, to the present moment, to this small draughty room high up in the castle keep. Her back ached as well as her knees; her sleep had been disturbed last night. Too many unhappy memories in this place. Perhaps she should not have agreed to return to Kenilworth.

The widowed Countess of Essex knelt a few feet away, her lips moving in more fervent prayer. Her cushion was larger and plumper, Lucy noticed.

A pack of raucous men passed below their window with torches and bawdy shouts. The countess jerked in shock, her hair hidden demurely beneath an embroidered cap and veil. She stared across at Lucy, her only companion during these difficult hours. Her eyes shone in the candlelight. Were those tears?

9

The long wait was over. A moment later there was a hammering at the outer door of the countess's apartments, followed by a hubbub of raised voices. This time Lettice gave a little gasp and crossed herself, shaking her head as though to deny that the moment had finally arrived. Not so calm as she would like to appear, then. Lucy shifted uncomfortably on her cushion. Would she be allowed to rise now?

Lady Mary Herbert, the fair-haired Countess of Pembroke, came to the bedchamber door looking flustered and unsure. 'My lady?'

'What is it?'

Behind the girl's shoulder, Lucy could see as many as a dozen men in livery filling the outer chamber, their faces flushed and intent; she smelt the acrid smoke from their blazing torches.

Lady Mary stammered, 'Th . . . the men are here for you, my lady. They say the hour has come. That you must descend with them and make no delay.'

'Don't fret, Mary,' Lettice Knollys replied calmly, having got herself back in hand. 'You may tell them I am ready and prepared, and must finish my prayers.'

Lady Mary looked nervous, but nodded and withdrew. The thick oak door closed behind her, shutting out the noise and smoking torchlight.

Poor child, oversensitive and scared of her own shadow. Lady Mary Herbert was only here at the request of her uncle Robert, and was clearly not happy to have been placed in such a dangerous situation. Sometimes the Earl of Leicester failed to appreciate how his plans might affect those around him, thinking only of his own desires. The Queen's favourite, he had always been wilful and head-strong; yet Lucy had never felt able to dislike him for it, such was the force of Robert's charm. No doubt he had also charmed his niece into attending tonight.

Lucy watched the Countess of Essex with curiosity. How could she seem so calm? The widow was skilled at hiding her emotions, clearly. She had spent most of her life in high places, after all, and must be accustomed to lying to save her neck. Though tonight would mark an end to her greatest lie of all.

Her prayers finished, still kneeling beside the bed with a Breton lace shawl over her shoulders to keep out the draught, Lettice Knollys rose gracefully to her feet.

'Well,' she muttered. 'It's time.'

She shrugged off the shawl and shook out the heavy skirts of her gown.

'How do I look, child?'

Lucy examined her ladyship with an experienced eye. Even in the dull glow of candlelight the Countess of Essex looked magnificent. The finery of the dress, all silver lace and gold satin, was topped by a stiff white ruff sprinkled with diamonds and pearls. Her slippers were embroidered silver, peeping out from beneath the swaying gown. Her reddish hair shone with a gold net of jewels. There was no sign that this transformation had taken five hours and as many women, pushing and coaxing the widowed countess's too-rounded figure into the costly gown.

'Beautiful as a queen,' Lucy told her, and was rewarded by the countess's smile, her face aglow with triumph.

The Countess of Essex took her hands and kissed Lucy on both cheeks. Her lips felt cool, her kiss somehow perfunctory, yet Lucy was still surprised by the gesture. Lettice had never showed her this courtesy before, much less friendship. But then her ladyship had never stood in such danger before.

'I have not thanked you for agreeing to attend to me tonight, Lucy. I know how much this loyalty will cost you if the Queen should ever hear of it.'

Lucy lowered her gaze, saying nothing. Had she been

given any true choice in the matter she would not have come at all. But it had been presented to her as a summons, not a request. Two hooded servants had accompanied the note, ready to sweep her secretly from court and on to a covered wagon that had trundled and lurched along the roads to Warwickshire with little care for her comfort. She could have refused, of course. But where was the sense in making an enemy by refusing when she might make a friend by agreeing?

Lettice snapped her fingers and Lucy hurried to open the door. They were not friends yet, and she knew her place.

'I have my own women to dress me,' Lettice continued, fiddling distractedly with her silver belt-chain as she stepped outside, 'and Robert's niece to sit beside us at the bridal dinner. Mary is a pretty girl, but only recently married, and still a child for all that she bears the title of countess. I need at least one court lady at my side tonight who knows how things must be done. And who can I trust more than you?'

'You do me great honour, my lady,' Lucy murmured.

She stooped and lifted the heavy silver train of Lettice's gown off the rushes where it was already soiling. The jewels prickled under her fingers; the countess's gown was almost as extravagant and richly made as anything from Elizabeth's own wardrobe.

'Strange to think that in another few minutes I will have stolen the Queen's most prized possession.' Although Lettice laughed, Lucy detected a hint of fear in her voice. 'What will my royal cousin say when she discovers she is too late, that I am already Robert's wife?'

'Best not to think on it, my lady.'

'It is all I have thought on for months.' The countess's expression grew suddenly defiant. Lettice Knollys was only beautiful when she was calm, Lucy realized, and hurriedly lowered her gaze in case the unkind thought

12

showed in her eyes. 'Yet what can Elizabeth do? Throw us both in the Tower for marrying without her consent? She'd never do it. Not to her darling Robert. And as for me, she would not dare such an outrage against her own cousin.'

Lucy thought the Queen capable of any outrage when it came to keeping Robert Dudley close to her. Yes, Elizabeth might baulk at locking up her favourite, but Lettice would be foolish to consider herself safe from the Queen's anger on his account, given how much the two cousins loathed each other. Lucy only hoped the Queen would overlook her part in all this when she did discover what had taken place so secretly here at Kenilworth.

'Come,' Lettice ordered her. 'My bridesmen are impatient for a nuptial, it seems. Let us give them one to remember.'

The countess and her rowdy entourage of bridesmen and -women moved in a torchlit procession through Kenilworth Castle, with the rest of her servants following behind. Negotiating the narrow, low-roofed passages and stairways of the keep, they at last reached the grand staircase illuminated by great flaming torches and guarded at intervals by Leicester's men in their smart blue livery. It was a warm spring evening as they crossed the courtyard under the looming gaze of the banqueting-hall windows, the torches of the bridesmen casting vast dancing shadows about them. One of the great state apartments in the new block above, built in honour of Queen Elizabeth's visit there three years before, had been swept out the previous day, the rushes renewed and the white marbled mantels dressed with flowers newly cut from the earl's gardens.

One of the castle guards was staring at Lucy, his eyes bloodshot from the smoking torches. He glanced away when their eyes met. No doubt the foolish man thought her a heathen with her black skin, come here like one of the devil's own to cast a curse on the company. If only she had some bones to rattle at him, she thought, and suppressed the urge to stick her tongue out.

Nobody in the castle was supposed to know why this room had been prepared. But of course there could be no such thing as a secret wedding when so many servants and villagers had been involved in fetching up armfuls of white spring blossom to decorate the mantels, clearing out the state apartments to make way for the company, and preparing a rich array of dishes for the feast that would follow.

The procession paused outside the open door to the magnificent state apartments. One of Lettice's women fumbled with the countess's gown, shaking out the heavily jewelled skirts so they would catch the candlelight to better advantage.

The groom stood by the vast marbled fireplace with his back to them, talking earnestly with the lean-faced Anglican priest who had ridden over from Coventry to marry them.

Lord Leicester looked almost regal tonight, Lucy thought. She sensed the countess's pleasure as she too paused on the threshold to stare at her husband-to-be. Lucy could hardly believe what she had heard about him, that once he had merely been Robert Dudley, Master of the Queen's Horse; that night he was every inch the wealthy, landowning Earl of Leicester. For his wedding suit, he had chosen a fashionable red doublet and hose of French design, a fine woollen cloak hanging from one shoulder, a gold-hilted sword by his side, his velvet cap feathered and set at an angle on silvering hair.

From within the apartments came the sound of music: a single tabor holding a rhythmic beat against the sweet notes of hautboys and horns. Lucy listened to the slow dignified music of the pavane and let it fill her, suddenly overjoyed for the couple, so very much in love that they would dare the Queen's fury like this.

'I've won,' Lettice muttered, feeding on her bridegroom with her eyes. Her knuckles turned white as she clutched a spray of fresh spring flowers. 'It's happening at last, Lucy. There's nothing the Queen can do to stop us now.'

Lettice swept in and Lord Leicester turned eagerly, only to fall silent at the sight of his bride-to-be in her wedding gown.

Holding up the countess's train, Lucy followed at the same pace, dressed soberly in a gown of russet taffeta. She curtsied to Lord Leicester and the robed cleric from Coventry, then stepped back into place behind Lettice as the couple spoke quietly together for a moment.

The room had been splendidly dressed for the ceremony, the white and yellow blossoms set about with candles, and hanging silks to soften the castle walls. On the sideboard under the window stood the bride cup, dwarfed by two large silver branches of candles. It would be Lucy's duty after the ceremony to fill the heavily ornate gold chalice with spiced wine, handing it to the newly married couple to drink each other's health. A dozen tiny bridal cakes had been stacked up delicately beside the cup, sweetly fragrant and oozing honey. A young pageboy had been set to wave away any flies or moths attracted by the candle flames. The boy looked quite awed by the splendour of the occasion, staring back wide-eyed when Lucy winked at him.

Abruptly, the laughter and talk in the crowded chamber became subdued. The music swelled to a finish. A space was cleared before the stone-flanked hearth, where a low fire burned steadily. The countess turned her head and Lucy gathered up the silver train of her gown. She followed the countess slowly forward to where two velvet cushions had been set for the couple to kneel on, then knelt behind them on the wooden floor.

On either side of their small party stood the bridesmen and -women in the countess's colours of scarlet and gold, some smiling with approval, others solemn. Liveried yeomen stood shoulder to shoulder in front of the door as though to guard them from interruption, and against the walls she could see the servants staring, hands clasped in prayer as the priest turned from blessing the wine and took up his book.

Lucy was smiling too, though inwardly she felt uneasy. She tried not to dwell on what might happen if the earl's niece spilled this news to the Queen and court. Lady Mary would never betray her own blood, she told herself. Besides, it was too late to do anything about it now. More was the pity. The Queen's temper, always violent and uncertain, had grown ever more unpredictable as she had entered her middle years. Surely she would never harm Robert Dudley, her favourite? But what of the rest of us who dared to witness this wedding and not prevent it?

The priest was looking nervous, too. His hands shook as he began to read, 'Dearly beloved friends, we are gathered together here in the sight of God and in the face of this congregation.'

Greenwich Palace, London, late April 1578

Fresh buds on the trees, the love-dance of the peacock shaking the 'eyes' on his splendid blue-green tail, a weak April sunshine on the grassy lawns. These were some of her favourite sights in spring. Yet Elizabeth could hardly bear to stop and admire them as she paced the neatly kept paths and gardens at Greenwich Palace. She bit her lip, rubbed and clapped her gloved hands together, now walking briskly, now standing in a daze like a moonstruck calf. Where had Robert gone? What was he doing that was so important it must keep him from court? She had thought they were growing closer again, this past year. Why would he cause her this new grief?

The Earl of Leicester had come back to court from the country on her summons, then kept mysteriously to his own suite of rooms, claiming to be ill. Now he had vanished entirely, and without asking her permission to leave court. It seemed the earl had been ferried back across the river with his servants to sit out a fever at Leicester House, her spies had told her apologetically. But Elizabeth could tell they were unsure of their information. Shuffling feet, downcast eyes. Hurriedly penned notes that spoke of indecision. *Might be there, Your Majesty. May lately have been seen in the vicinity.*

Idiots! And they dared to call themselves her spies. She should have them all strung up as fools and knaves. Except, as her spymaster, Sir Francis Walsingham, was fond of reminding her, she would then get no information out of them at all, let alone this embarrassed throat-clearing over Robert's whereabouts. What were they trying to hide from her?

It had once again become her custom to walk out with her ladies in the early mornings. It had been another bitter winter, ice remaining on the ground long after it should have thawed, and the stiff green tips of spring flowers frozen where they grew. But now it was late April, and at last Elizabeth was able to enjoy the sweet breeze and the birds calling to each other in the spring sunshine. Such a relief, she thought, to leave behind the choking air of chambers where night pots had not yet been emptied nor soiled rushes swept away. They had been in residence several months now, and it was becoming impossible to mask the stench of the privies with burned herbs or sweeten the odour of unwashed flesh with pomanders.

She turned back towards the palace. 'Speak, what is it?' she asked brusquely, seeing one of her stewards hurrying towards her.

'The Spanish ambassador awaits you in the Presence Chamber, Your Majesty.'

Signor Mendoza! She had forgotten their meeting this morning. She thought of his watchful eyes and the dark oily sheen of his hair, but could not quite find it in herself to dislike the man. He might be reporting every movement she made back to Spain, but at least he understood how to entertain a bored queen with gossip.

'What's that?' she demanded. Something had fluttered slowly down from an open window above their heads. Elizabeth stared upwards, but it was impossible to make anything out against the sunlight. 'Pick it up, man, and give it to me. Is it a letter? From whose window did it fall?'

'Window?' the steward repeated blankly, but craned his neck upwards at her command. 'I cannot tell, Your Majesty. I see no one.'

The letter was not addressed to anyone; it merely held a few lines in a bold hand. Her blood chilled as she read them.

'I do not believe it,' she choked, then crumpled the letter up tight in her gloved hand.

God's blood, could it be true?

Remain calm, she told herself, aware of her women staring. Remember that you are a queen. Reveal nothing.

'Send for Lord Leicester. I would speak with him at once.'

'But, Your Majesty, he . . . his lordship is not at court at present.'

'Then send to Leicester House and tell him I will brook no delay, but must see him this very day.' Elizabeth stared at the trees swaying gently in the spring breeze. How dared he? How dared he? The blood thrummed in her temples. 'No, wait! I shall go myself. Have my barge readied.'

The steward stared at his queen as though she had

turned mad as old King Canute. Perhaps she was mad. Yes, that would explain her look: as if she would snap his neck like a twig if he did not at once carry out her command.

'Your b . . . barge, Your Majesty?'

'Out of my way, fool,' she snapped, sweeping past him in such a rage that she was barely able to make herself understood to her women as she fumed at them to change her walking gown.

She stood impatiently while women fussed about her, stepping out of her petticoats and holding up her arms for the sleeves to be unlaced. She did not stop to wonder who would have thrown down such a letter for her to find. Walsingham could discover that later. For now she must simply determine whether or not it held the truth. Though in her heart she knew it was no lie.

Damn him, damn him!

Elizabeth rode towards the river in the breezy spring sunshine, surrounded by guards and her flustered-looking women, a light wind whipping up sand on the pathway. Was that genuine confusion on the faces of her ladies-in-waiting or had she been the last to know again? Bad enough his flagrant affair with Lettice three years ago, that Elizabeth knew had slowly rekindled after Lettice's husband had died, but this . . .

In the royal barge, she straightened out the crumpled note and read it once more, her heart lacerated by its contents.

R. has been secretly married these past three weeks to Essex's widow, who now holds court with him in queenly estate at Leicester House. A Friend.

Holds court? That was a cunning phrase, right enough, but what did it signify? Did Lettice now presume to become queen in her place? Elizabeth ground her teeth in rage and frustration. She would have this out with Robert

19

today, even if it meant outright war between them. At least surprise would be on her side.

But on arriving at Leicester House, Robert's extensive London residence that opened its gates on to the Strand, Elizabeth found to her great annoyance that a messenger must have ridden hard ahead of their company. The doors to the great house stood open, all the servants down on their knees outside as the cavalcade approached, a litter bearing her from the river.

'His lordship is unwell,' his steward babbled as Elizabeth was helped from her litter, 'and begs for a little more time to prepare himself for your honoured visit, Your Majesty.'

Ignoring the man, Elizabeth strode into the house, past staring servants, and up the grand staircase. Her women began to follow her in whispering disorder, but she barked, 'Wait for me below!', sending them back outside in disarray. Let them stare and make baleful predictions there, she thought. This was one interview they would not be allowed to overhear.

Elizabeth found Robert in the doorway to his bedchamber, wrapped in a house coat, looking very pale – and in truth unwell.

'Your Majesty,' he croaked, then knelt, head bowed, as she met his gaze with utter fury and contempt. 'Forgive me.'

His servant bolted when she turned to glare at him.

'Is it true?' she managed after a threadbare silence, looking down at Robert's bent head. 'Are you and my cousin Lettice wed?'

He looked up then, and she knew the letter had not lied. His dark eyes watched her, eyes that made it impossible for her to order his death. 'Yes, it is true.'

The blood beat in her ears so loud she thought she would faint. Married, married, married. She would kill him. No, she would kill her. Rip her throat out. Toss her liver to the dogs. Stick her bloodied head on a pike for all to see.

Elizabeth counted silently to ten. Better that than launch herself at him with a scream, all claws like a shrew.

'And where is this she-wolf?'

Why did her voice have to sound so shrill? It angered her that she cared what Robert did after all these years. They were not promised to each other, had never been in any way the Council would recognize. This jealous rage demeaned her, lowered her to the status of a fishwife. He was her subject. Nothing more. What did it matter with whom he coupled, so long as he served her? Except this union could weaken her hold on the English crown. Lettice was of royal blood, had some claim to the throne, and Robert might no longer be young, but he was a nobleman now, an earl with vast resources at his command. Resources she had put in his path. Elizabeth cursed herself again for a trusting fool.

'Not here,' he told her. 'I sent her home.'

'Home?'

'To her children.'

She waited. 'You did not seek my permission to wed.' It was a statement, not a question.

'Would it have been given, Your Majesty?'

'That is not the point.'

Her voice nagged at him. Yet she was somewhat mollified by his penitent tone. She liked that Robert was still on his knees, looking up at her like a supplicant. That was his place, that was where he belonged. On his knees to her, his queen.

'My cousin Lettice is the widow of an earl, not a washerwoman. Her remarriage required my signature, as well you know. I should have you both arrested.'

'Arrest me, Your Majesty, not your cousin. The fault is

21

mine. I insisted that we wed without waiting for your permission.' He was sweating and shivering, his discomfort obvious. Hard to counterfeit a fever. 'Lettice is guiltless in this.'

She would have laughed but her anger forbade it. Lettice guiltless? One day, she thought. One day I will make her suffer for this insolence.

'You are fortunate that I am a forgiving queen,' she told him, then hated herself for such female weakness. Arrest them both. Give Lettice a taste of the Tower that would leave her knock-kneed in fear for the rest of her life. Do not let their disobedience pass without right and proper punishment. Yet she found herself saying instead, 'However, you will not return to court. You and your bride are no longer welcome there. Not for any reason, not on pain of death. Am I understood?'

Her favourite nodded, clearly relieved to have escaped a stay in the Tower. He knew what horrors that grim place held. They both did.

'Yes, Your Majesty. I thank you for your mercy.'

He must think her a fool. And with good reason. She struck at him with the only thing she had left. Not her pride. Sweet Jesu, that had gone years ago between them. 'If all goes well, you may yet be permitted to return to court to celebrate my nuptials. Though your wife will never be invited.'

His eyes had narrowed as he watched her face. Elizabeth smiled, knowing that word had slipped between his ribs like eight inches of Italian steel.

'Yes, my *nuptials*,' she repeated, gloating over his dismay. 'For you should know, I have recently been reconsidering Alençon's interesting proposal of marriage, and find we may suit after all. I could not take him seriously as a spotty youth, but now that he is grown to manhood and been made Duke of Anjou . . .'

22

'Marry a Frenchman?' Robert seemed to be choking.

'You have often said I should marry, so why not a French noble? Besides, a union with France pleases me more each time I think of it.' Oh, the steel was in him now, she thought. His eyes were suffering. 'Alençon is still young, yes, but that will have its advantages in the marriage bed. Or so the doctors tell me.'

Excellent, she thought, now he's sweating for quite another reason. As she turned to leave Robert to his feverish imaginings, Elizabeth permitted herself a further sharp thrust, just to make sure her favourite knew she meant it.

'These things always take so long, though, if left to diplomacy alone. I will arrange for Alençon to visit me once he is free of his military duties, and then we shall see if any . . . intimacy develops. I am still angry with you, Robert, but we have been friends such a long time.' One more should do the trick. 'Wish me well with my young French suitor, won't you?'

Part One

One

The Cross Keys Inn, London, autumn 1583

'OUT THE WAY!'

At the hoarse cry, Will Shakespeare flattened himself against the wall of the passageway. Late for his cue again, William Kempe squeezed past in his tattered fool's costume, gripping the wooden neck of a hobby horse. As he dashed on to the makeshift stage, the theatre erupted in cheers and whistles, those seated in the galleries drumming their feet on the wooden boards with a sound like thunder.

'How now?' Kempe called across the heads of the groundlings, then whirled into a crouch with teeth bared and arms wide.

The house fell silent and breathless, waiting for his next line.

Someone came up behind Will, muttering in his ear: 'They were ready to tear the place apart a minute ago. Now they're meek as lambs. How does he do it?'

It was James Burbage.

'He makes them laugh and cry at the same time,' Will whispered, watching Kempe as he effortlessly dominated the scene, 'and they love him for it.'

'Another full house.' Burbage jingled a bag of coins at his belt. His voice held satisfaction. 'God preserve us from the plague and the city magistrates, and we'll be rich men in another year.'

Will looked at the heavy pocket-bag. 'I owe a month's rent.'

Burbage clapped him cheerfully on the shoulder. 'All in good time, Shakespeare. Never let it be said I allow even my apprentices to go short. But think, if I were to pay you now, how much of it would go on saving your family's reputation?'

Will frowned. 'What do you mean?'

'Have you not heard of the fall of the mighty Ardens? Why, man, it's all they were talking about in the Tabard last night.'

'I was busy last night. Making a fresh assault on *The Troublesome Reign of King John*.'

'Excellent. Is the play finished yet?'

'Not quite. It is proving more troublesome than I expected. But if you will give me these ancient plays to rewrite . . .' Will glanced out as another roar of laughter went up from the groundlings: Kempe galloping about with a woman's petticoat over his face. 'So what tale is this about the Ardens? They're not close family of mine, you know. Distant cousins.'

'Aye, that's it, best to disown them.' Burbage tucked his purse out of sight under the folds of his jacket. 'No amount of money could save Edward Arden anyhow. They say his head will be decorating London Bridge soon enough. Yes, and with the rest of the family to follow by Christmas.'

Will stared. 'Traitors? The Ardens?'

'If you poked your head out of your pit more often, Master Shakespeare, you might hear something of the world's doings. Yes, the Arden family were arrested as

28

traitors a week or more ago. It's a rare old tale. Arden's son-in-law is John Somerville. You know of him, surely? Poor fool, they say he was born with his brain cracked. Well, good John sets off for London, ranting at every inn along the way that he plans to shoot the Queen.'

'*What?*'

Burbage grinned, warming to his story. 'Somerville was seized before he even reached the city, of course, and Edward Arden and his wife and daughter were taken soon after, as equal conspirators against the throne. The whole family rests now in the Tower, they say, with Edward Arden himself in Little Ease.'

'Good God.'

Burbage laughed. 'Who would have thought it, eh? Your sleepy Warwickshire risen against the Queen before the North. It seems the Catholic roots run deep there.'

Edward Arden, head of the family, in the grim Tower cell they called Little Ease, where it was said a man could neither lie down nor sit? Will thought of his mother and father back in Stratford, not far from the Arden estate.

'What of the rest of the family?' he demanded. 'How far do these accusations go?'

'Now, don't start dreaming you'll rush home to save your loved ones from the law. Write them to hide their catechisms and get themselves to a good Protestant Mass, and no one will hang for it. If the Queen killed all the Catholics, there'd be no one left to wind the clocks and run the towns. Jesu, man, you're as pale as a sack of flour.' Burbage nodded towards the stage. 'Hurry, now. Isn't that your cue?'

'Aye, aye.'

Blowing out his cheeks, Will stepped from the dark passageway into the draughty hall of the Cross Keys Inn. The floor was lit with chill November sunshine streaming through the unshuttered windows, with lanterns set in brackets on the walls to further light the small playing area before the crowd.

All eyes turned to him as he made his entrance. Will felt again the rush of blood that had so excited him the first time he had ever spoken a line onstage. Then he had been a boy, beardless and still unmarried. It had seemed such a great adventure, playing to the city crowds at Coventry, walking home that night with the unaccustomed weight of coins in his purse. Now it was his work and he could not live without it. He was already up to his ears in debt, with a wife and child at home in Stratford expecting him to support them.

Yet there was still a tingle of excitement on treading the boards, knowing that when he opened his mouth to speak all these folk would stop and listen.

Kempe pretended to slip over, crossing the stage, and Will's first line was drowned out by a roar of laughter from the crowd.

Undeterred, Will raised his voice.

Kempe stumbled back to his feet, his expression rueful. He made a face, then rubbed his backside with both hands. The crowd roared again, delighted by the fool's antics.

Adopting an attitude at the front of the stage, Will folded his arms. He waited for the laughter to die away before attempting to deliver his next line. He suppressed a flicker of annoyance. It was all part of the act; Kempe loved to upstage the other players and raise the temperature of the house.

Will gazed across the laughing crowd of playgoers, those who could not afford seats pressed together near the stage. There was a cloaked woman among them, watching him intently. She was taller than the rest, her face half-hidden by a smoke-grey hood. There was something about the woman that drew Will's attention, and it was not just that her skin was as black as the night sky, and her eyes . . .

30

A shock struck him, like a flaming arrow to the heart, and suddenly Will could not recall his next line.

'Lucy,' he whispered under his breath.

The woman stared back at him. Her dark gaze widened and locked to his.

He had been little more than a boy, a mere eleven years old, the summer he had met Lucy Morgan. Yet he had never forgotten her, nor the marvellous festivities laid on for the Queen's visit during those long, hot weeks.

Had she recognized him?

Kempe launched into a foolish little song-and-dance routine, improvised to cover Will's silence.

'There was a man with half a head,' he began whimsically, and the audience laughed, waiting for the rest.

No doubt believing Will had forgotten it, the prompt called out his line from the side of the stage.

Faltering, Will gave his line, and the next lines too. But he performed them only to the Moorish woman in the hooded cloak, who did not smile at his attention but drew back cautiously into the shade of her hood.

That night at Kenilworth eight years ago, he had climbed the steep bank above the castle wall and seen Tom's bloodied body on the grass, men peering down at his corpse in a ring of flickering torches. It had been his first sight of a dead body. At the time he had assumed that Tom Black and Lucy Morgan had been lovers, and that they would have married if the Moor had lived. Certainly the two had been close.

His father John had dragged Will home before he could discover the full truth of what had happened that night. A plot against the Queen was all he had been told, with never a whisper spoken afterwards. Everyone in Stratford knew the Shakespeares were not the good Protestants they pretended to be, so to dwell on such things could be

31

dangerous. Will had begged to be taken back to Kenilworth to see Lucy, to comfort her over Tom's death. Part of him had worried that he had been to blame, that he had not run for help quickly enough. But he had never seen Lucy again.

Now here she was, a few feet away in the crowd, no dream to vanish at daybreak but a flesh-and-blood woman.

A sudden shriek turned Will's head. A woman had risen from her seat and was screaming hysterically, pointing at a broad-shouldered man in a coarse suit. He had blood on his hands and was stooping over another man, who seemed to be slumped in his seat.

The broad-shouldered man vaulted the wooden rail of the gallery and forced his way through the jostling crowd to one of the side corridors.

Nobody tried to stop him, though several shouted 'Murderer!' as he disappeared into the inn courtyard beyond.

When Will turned back, Lucy Morgan was gone.

Two

LUCY MORGAN SLIPPED OUT OF THE CROSS KEYS INN unnoticed, her hood drawn so far over her face she almost collided with a band of watermen in the street outside. Dressed in leather aprons, the watermen called after her, but Lucy ignored their less-than-polite suggestions. She was more concerned that the expected meeting with her guardian had not gone as planned. Fearing he must be dead, she had been delighted to receive a letter from Master Goodluck recently, still very much alive and suggesting a discreet rendezvous at the Cross Keys Inn that afternoon.

So why had he failed to make their appointment?

Lifting her skirts to sidestep a steaming pile of horse shit, Lucy hurried down the narrow street towards the main thoroughfare. She wished she had taken a litter or brought a manservant with her. But she could not have trusted a companion to keep his mouth shut, and the Queen's displeasure was a more chilling prospect than a few insolent watermen.

That young player on the stage had stared at her so hard, she had felt quite uncomfortable. He must be a country boy, new to London's theatres. She knew most of the regular players in the capital, but could not recall ever meeting that particular one before.

Yet there had been something familiar about the young man's eyes. His face tugged at her memory. Where did she know him from?

She put it aside. It would come back to her. For now she had more pressing matters to consider.

Lucy paused, waiting for a heavily laden cart to trundle past through the mud and stinking debris of the street.

She ought not to fret that Master Goodluck had not met her as arranged, but to rejoice instead that he was still on this earth. He was one of Sir Francis Walsingham's most experienced spies, and no fool. With all the recent arrests, Lucy was sure he must be up to his neck in Catholic intrigue; perhaps he had been unable to make their meeting. Though she feared that one day he would push his much vaunted 'good luck' too far, ending up dead or in prison himself.

'Lucy!'

The hoarse whisper turned her head, then there was a gloved hand on her arm.

'Master Goodluck!'

'Don't look at me and don't say a word.' His deep and familiar voice echoed off the walls of the alley. 'Down here.'

Glancing about to make sure she was not observed, Lucy raised her skirts out of the filth and followed Goodluck down the narrow alleyway. The ancient wattle walls were crumbling to dust in places, and the lane was so tight a squeeze it was not possible for two to walk abreast. Her nose wrinkled. She could not see what was underfoot, but could guess from the stink of urine.

Once out of view, Goodluck turned to embrace her, kissing her roughly on both cheeks. 'Lucy.'

'Goodluck.'

'I can't believe it's been three years. All that time in a stinking Roman prison the memory of your face was what kept me sane. It's good to see you.' He smiled, showing his teeth in the darkness. 'Fine court lady or not, I am glad your skill with coded messages has not deserted you.'

'I had a good teacher.'

A wry laugh. For all his tales of prison, he was in a fine mood, she thought, and smiled back at him. Goodluck threw back his hood. His keen gaze searched hers. 'You found the bag?'

Lucy nodded. 'And brought it as requested,' she replied, drawing the heavy purse out from where she had hidden it as best she could beneath the folds of her cloak. She handed it to Goodluck. 'Come, what's all this about? I've never seen so much money in my life. Are you in trouble again?'

'No more than I'm used to.' He weighed the purse in his hand, and she saw relief on his face. 'Thank you, Lucy. I could not have trusted anyone else with this. Most would have cut my throat and taken the money for themselves.'

She fingered the sharp little dagger hanging from her belt. 'I was tempted.'

'My throat's somewhat hard to find these days,' he told her ruefully, and smoothed down the vast beard that stretched almost to his chest. She could see grey hairs among the dark ones, and noticed the deepening of wrinkles at his eyes. 'And I'm sorry if you soiled your finery retrieving it.'

'Only you could choose a chimney breast as a hiding-place for your gold. I ruined my gown,' she told him, frowning with mock anger. 'And that is not your only sin. Why didn't you meet me at the inn today, as arranged?'

'I'm sorry about that. When I arrived, the entrance to the courtyard was being watched – whether for me or someone else, I couldn't tell. But it wasn't worth the risk of being seen, and I hoped to catch you coming out instead.'

Lucy thought back to the pale-faced woman screaming from the gallery, the man slumped in his seat, covered in blood. 'A man was murdered at the play. I didn't see what it was about. I left before people started asking questions.'

'I wonder who it was.'

'Whoever it was, may God have mercy on his soul.'

'Indeed. Though I'll be spared little enough mercy when it's my turn to meet my Maker, I fear.'

'Don't talk like that. You know I hate it,' she told him disapprovingly. 'Besides, you're hardly in your dotage. You're not even old enough yet to be—'

There was some commotion out on the street, and Goodluck laid a finger on her lips.

Raised voices echoed back along the alleyway. They listened for a moment. But it was only a merchant in the street, arguing with a man and his wife over some unpaid debt.

'Now listen,' Goodluck said urgently, lowering his voice almost to a whisper. 'I had intended to meet Master Twist at the Curtain playhouse tonight and give him this gold. But I've been unable to get anywhere near the place. My face is too well-known, and I can't risk alerting anyone to my return yet. There are agents on every corner between here and Bishopsgate.'

'Walsingham's men?'

Goodluck shook his head. 'I've nothing to fear from that quarter. No, these are Catholic agents who would pay well for news of my presence in London.' With a grin, he indicated his bruised face. 'I had a recent disagreement with a drunken Spaniard. It's a long story, but at least he will not be carrying any more tales to his masters.'

She closed her eyes. 'Goodluck!'

'Some of his Catholic friends saw me arrested for his

murder shortly afterwards. So they won't take kindly to my wandering the streets of London as a free man while Signor Fernandez is stiffening in his shroud.'

'When was this "disagreement"?'

'Four days ago on Bankside.' Goodluck rubbed his bruised face, grimacing at the pain. 'We needed to search his lodgings, and Fernandez came back unexpectedly. Took out one of my men on the door below. I hadn't intended to kill him, but the fool drew his sword and insisted on making it a fight. I called on Walsingham's help after I was thrown in the Clink, and he arranged for my release. But for all our Catholic friends know, I'm still locked up there and awaiting trial for murder.'

'You want me to give the gold to Master Twist?'

He nodded, and handed her a roll of parchment. 'Along with this letter.'

'Will it be dangerous?'

'I'd not send you if it was dangerous. It's only me they're looking for, and I'd trust John Twist with my life.' Master Goodluck shook his head at her expression. 'Come, would I risk my own ward's life? You've known John since you were a small child. The man used to bounce you on his knee, for pity's sake. You are as safe with Twist as you are with me.'

Lucy raised her brows, smiling faintly. 'Is that supposed to comfort me?'

'Rascal!' Goodluck laughed, and pinched her chin. 'It's a sad truth, and not something I am proud of, but I often think I taught you too well. You trust no one, Lucy. Not even those whom you must trust.'

She thought of the endless intrigues at court, the plots within plots, the secret affairs and political wrangling.

'There is no other way to live at court. Once, the intrigues hardly touched me. Now I am too close to Her Majesty. Everyone thinks I have her ear.'

'Don't you?'

She shook her head. 'The Queen has grown cold towards me. Some days I fear . . .'

'That the Queen will cast you off?'

Lucy hesitated. 'That she looks for an excuse to do so, perhaps.'

'Then we must not give her any reason to doubt you.' He drew down his hood again. 'Back to Whitehall with you before your absence from the Queen's side is noted, and be sure not to be seen when you visit Twist.' Goodluck paused. 'Whatever you do, Lucy, keep that letter safe. You are in some danger while you carry it.'

She stared at him. 'You said it was not dangerous.'

'Just keep the letter close until you hand it over to John Twist. You will not be searched, for you will never be suspected of carrying anything.'

Goodluck's face was unreadable in the shadow of his hood, but she heard an odd note in his voice.

'Besides,' he added drily, 'if you find yourself in difficulties, you have only to mention Walsingham's name and you will be restored safely to court.'

'Only by the Queen's men.'

'So try not to get tangled up with any of those tricky Catholics. You promise to be careful?'

'I promise.'

'Good girl.' Master Goodluck kissed her on the cheek, his face suddenly distant. It was like being five years old again, dismissed after one of his fleeting visits with a pat on the head and a new peg doll. 'Now we must go our separate ways. I will contact you again once you have seen Twist.'

Then Goodluck was gone, squeezing out of the alleyway into the crowded street beyond.

Lucy stood a moment, feeling the weight of the bag in her hand. Then she hooked it on to her belt beside her little dagger, folded the letter for John Twist twice over until it would fit in her leather pocket, and wrapped her cloak carefully across both.

She shied away from the idea of meeting Master Twist. It felt like a step back into the cruel and dangerous world she had left behind at Kenilworth eight years before.

But Goodluck would never have asked her to run this errand for him if it was not of vital importance. She remembered John Twist's dry wit and ready smile, the narrow pointed beard that he loved to keep oiled, the way his blue eyes had always watched her with love and concern, and comforted herself with the thought that she had known him since she was a child. What danger could there be in seeing an old friend again?

Three

THE KNOCK AT HIS DOOR WAS SO SOFT THAT WILL ALMOST missed it. He had been writing furiously all evening, hoping to get the fifth act of *The Troublesome Reign of King John* copied out in his best hand before the candle stub flickered out and left him with nothing but firelight to work by. He raised his head and frowned at the closed door as the knock came again. This interruption could cost him dear. If the good copy was not finished by morning, Burbage would not pay him, and he could lose his lodging.

'Yes?' he demanded, flinging open the door.

A tall man in his late twenties stood outside on the London street, hooded and cloaked, his travelling boots stained with mud.

'Now what kind of welcome is that?' the man asked. 'For a weary Warwickshire lad, far from home?'

Will stared, amazed. 'Cousin Richard?'

'Hush, man, not so loud. Do you want all the city's eyes on us?' Richard Arden peered into Will's room. 'Are you alone in there? May I come in a while, maybe take a drink with you? I've only just arrived in town. Not even had a chance to wet my whistle yet.'

'Of course.'

While his cousin prowled about, his lean face watchful, even suspicious, Will hurriedly locked the door and pulled the ragged curtain across that kept out the worst of the draughts.

'It's only a poor room, as you see,' Will commented, feeling the need to apologize for his lack of housekeeping skills. He indicated the good chair to Richard Arden, acutely aware how poor his home must seem compared with the comfortable and spacious houses of his wealthier relations. 'But it's all I can afford on my wages from the playhouse. I send most of my money home to Anne.'

'Aye,' Richard agreed with a sigh, removing his damp cloak and hanging it before the charcoal brazier. 'You always were a good lad, Will. But your wife misses you sorely.'

'You've seen Anne? Spoken with her?'

'Five days ago, just before I left Warwickshire. No, don't look like that. Your wife was in good health when I left, both her and the child.'

'Thank God,' Will muttered. He poured a generous drink of ale for them both, handing the cup to his cousin with hands that were not quite steady. 'When I saw you on the doorstep, I thought . . .'

Richard Arden sat down. 'I'm sorry if I alarmed you. But Anne is well enough, and your baby daughter thrives.'

'Then why have you come to London?' Will realized too late how rude that must have sounded, and corrected himself, his smile dry. 'Forgive me, but I recall you saying only thieves and whoremasters would soil themselves in the filth of this city.'

'Did I say that?' Richard snorted, then took a long draught of ale. 'Aye, well, times change. And we must change with them.'

'So what can I do for you, cousin?'

'All in good time, man. They say city ale is watered

down and tastes like sheep piss, but this stuff's not half bad.'

Will looked at him curiously. There was no point pressing the man for an answer, but for a countryman like Richard to have dared the long journey to London, he had to want something important. Something connected, Will presumed, to the arrest and imprisonment of Edward Arden.

He covered his fresh draft of *The Troublesome Reign of King John* with a clean sheet, taking care not to smudge the ink, and sat down beside the brazier, which was still giving out good heat. The rickety stool creaked beneath him, a relic left behind by some previous tenant.

Richard Arden had not changed much. There were streaks of grey in his beard and a new hardness about his eyes, but Will could have picked him out in a crowd. He still remembered scrumping apples with Richard as a boy, stealing from a neighbour's orchard and being shown which branches were safe to climb by his older cousin. Will's father had offered Richard an apprenticeship once, to teach him a trade as a glover. But he had chosen to be a farmer instead, settling north of Stratford, and his life had not been easy. He was smiling now, though, nodding with satisfaction as he set aside his emptied cup of ale.

'So, Shakespeare, I hear you are a player, and make your living on the boards.'

'I do.'

'Your father is short-handed in the shop, and there are complaints about him in the town. Men say he cannot pay his debts, that he dare not even show his face on market days in case the bailiffs see him.' Richard looked at Will. 'This play-acting is big business, to be sure, and I imagine the whores are good too. But it's time for you to get yourself home to Stratford and do your duty there.'

Will held his breath a moment before answering, not

quite trusting himself to be civil. He emptied his last meagre bag of charcoal into the brazier, and hoped that he would manage to finish the play, and Burbage would make good on his offer of payment in the morning, else he would be going cold as well as hungry. The flames began to lick greedily about the fuel.

'You bring this message from my father?'

'Dear God, of course not. John is a good man and will not stir himself to ask you home, however much he hurts. And who can blame him?' Richard eyed him sharply. 'A father should not have to beg his son's help. It should be given freely and without the asking.'

'What trouble is he in this time?'

'The same as before.' Richard shrugged. 'Nor is he to be blamed for that, either. John Shakespeare has mouths to feed and must make his living somehow. If that means a few pursefuls change hands at the back door, so be it. The laws would pinch a man to death with taxes these days.'

He stared into the glowing embers of the brazier and his voice hardened. 'But the town council cannot turn a blind eye to such back-room handshakes when townsfolk talk of his dealings openly on the street. He has never been one to hold his water, if you catch my meaning.'

'So you've come to warn me?'

'Nothing so dramatic, lad. Just to remind you of your duty to your father as his eldest son, and as husband to a loyal and obedient wife. If you have good work here, well and good. It is a husband's part to support his family. But if you could work as well at home . . .'

'As well, yes, but not aim as high. There is money to be made in the playhouses.'

'Then make it and stop wasting your time.' Richard looked about the room, distaste in his face. 'I've seen cleaner shepherd huts than this place. Aye, and cleaner sheep.'

43

'I am no good housekeeper, it cannot be denied. But if you send word next time you are planning a visit, I'll make shift to clear the place first.'

'Oh, I don't intend to make a habit of putting myself in the way of London's plagues and diseases.' Richard paused, his expression reluctant. 'But if you must remain so stubbornly away from home, floating about the filthy taprooms and whorehouses of London, then I have something to ask of you.'

'I have never . . .' Will did not bother finishing. His cousin would not believe him anyway. 'Go on, what is this request?'

Richard leaned forward, his face clenched like a fist. 'You must have heard of all the terrible doings up in Warwickshire in recent weeks. By which I mean, Edward Arden's arrest,' he muttered, then glanced towards the door.

'We are safe enough here,' Will reassured him. 'My neighbours are actors and they are all out tonight. At the whorehouses, I should expect.'

'Well, and why not?' Richard spat on to the hearth, regarding his saliva on the hot stones with satisfaction. 'A young man should know how to stir a pudding.'

Will covered his snort of laughter by poking the brazier noisily. He threw the iron aside with a clatter. 'I'd heard that Edward Arden had been brought to London, yes. But his arrest will come to nothing. A few months in the Tower, perhaps. They would not dare to proceed with any trial without strong evidence. And what can they prove? That his son-in-law John Somerville is mad, and anyone in Warwickshire could tell them that.'

'Stark staring mad, the poor lad,' Richard agreed. His shrug was fatalistic. 'But that will not stop Leicester from prosecuting the law to its fullest extent. Don't forget, it was Edward Arden who called him a whoremaster before

44

the Queen the summer she came to Kenilworth. Aye, and refused to wear his livery and take his orders that year, and all but publicly named the Countess of Essex as Leicester's mistress. A man as powerful as the Earl of Leicester does not forget such insults, however many years may have passed since they were thrown at him.'

Will nodded. He had some vague memory of the scandal, though what he chiefly remembered from that summer at Kenilworth was Lucy Morgan's dark face and eyes.

Richard slapped his knee. 'I knew you would understand, that you had not forgotten your roots.' He lowered his voice. 'And here is where you play your part, Will. The family needs to know what is being said here in the city about the Ardens. We are so far away in Warwickshire, we have little warning when danger threatens.'

Will stared, frowning. 'I don't understand.'

'Sniff about the city, see what you can glean of our troubles. If Arden is to die, we cannot help him if we are unprepared. And if there are any here who would support us in a fight, send us their names. Not too openly, though, in case the letter should be intercepted.'

'So I am to spy for you?'

'For God's sake, hold your tongue!' Richard looked furious. 'Spy is not a word to be used aloud. Do you know nothing of discretion? You will make enquiries on how opinion swings in the city and send back reports. You are a player, Will. Hundreds pass through your theatre doors every day. You must hear all the latest gossip, whatever is being said on the streets and in the taverns. You are no spy in this matter, merely a friend to the Ardens.'

Will looked down. 'Aye,' he agreed reluctantly. 'I will keep my ears open whenever I can.'

'Good lad. I knew the family could rely on you.'

Richard eased back in his chair and accepted another

cupful of ale with sincere thanks. They warmed their feet at the glowing brazier and spoke for another hour of homely matters – the seasonal tide of rural Warwickshire life – the conversation easier for both of them when it concerned sheep and local politics rather than treason. The Watch called out the hour in passing at eleven o'clock, and Richard finally sat up, stretching sleepily.

'Eleven? Sweet Jesu, I did not know the hour was so advanced. I've a place commanded at an inn a few streets shy of the city wall, and I'd best not disturb the landlord too late.' Richard frowned. 'I'll be spending this winter at the farm. Send any correspondence there. But write circumspectly. Say nothing that could be misread if intercepted.'

'And if I discover nothing?'

'Not possible.' It was a threat and both of them knew it. Richard stood up and reached for his cloak. He shot Will a look from under straight brows. 'Your mother may have married a Shakespeare, but Arden blood runs in your veins. You are one of us – one of the old kind. And while you remember that, the Ardens will remember the wife and child you've left behind. They will come to no harm in our care.'

Will wondered how much longer the Ardens would be a name to conjure with in Warwickshire. But he said nothing, merely showed his visitor politely to the door. The powerful Edward Arden and his family in the Tower, the old Catholic families of Warwickshire held in the greatest suspicion, their houses ransacked, their livelihoods under threat. The whole thing was a bloody mess, whichever way it was looked at.

Wrapping his long cloak over one arm, Richard paused in the doorway to embrace Will. He gazed balefully around at the neighbouring houses, their slatted walls cracked and daubed with mud and dung. Somewhere a baby was crying for its mother, and three young men were staggering past from the ale houses, singing loudly with no fear of the Watch calling them to order.

'This is a stinking place,' Richard commented at last.

'But cheap,' Will murmured. He raised his hand to one of the drunken young men, an actor friend and a neighbour of his. 'Parker!'

'Will Shakey Speare!' his friend replied cheerfully, and sketched an unsteady bow. 'I'm drunk as a horse.'

'Best get yourself to bed then, ale head, you've a rehearsal in the morning.'

'Who's your friend?'

Richard Arden drew his hood close over his head and frowned warningly at Will.

'No one.'

'Someone from the country, by the vile look of his hose.'

Parker gave a violent hiccup and staggered to his door, waving goodnight to his friends. 'Goodnight, goodnight!'

There was a burst of hysterical barking from within Parker's lodgings. Then the door banged shut behind him, the two friends lurched drunkenly on, and the street fell silent again.

'If I need to send a letter, can I reach you at this address?' Richard asked Will, his look disdainful.

'That depends on whether I get paid tomorrow. I owe several weeks' rent on this place.'

His cousin fumbled at his belt, releasing a small leather purse. 'Here,' he muttered. 'Use that to keep yourself off the streets. You can pay me back when you come home.'

Will took the bag reluctantly, hearing the clink of coins inside. He knew what it signified. 'Thanks. But you're sure you won't stay the night? I'll be working late on the play, you can have the bed.'

Richard shook his head. He pulled his cloak tight and

stepped over the stinking sewer. 'Thank you, no. Keep yourself well, cousin. God be with you.'

'And also with you.'

Will shut the door on Richard Arden's retreating back and leaned against it, swiftly counting the contents of the purse. Enough to pay the rent he owed, and some left over for a good supper. Several suppers if he chose the establishment wisely.

A goodly amount. The price of a man's integrity.

Four

ELIZABETH SAT IN STATE IN THE PRESENCE CHAMBER, surrounded by the decaying tapestries and archaic glory of Whitehall. She sighed, resting her chin on her hand as the courtier on his knees before her droned on ad nauseam. Some dreary dispute with his neighbour at court, a matter of no importance whatsoever. Elizabeth tried not to look as bored as she felt, examining the Presence Chamber with a jaded eye. Whitehall had been her father's most flamboyant city palace, and Cardinal Wolsey's before that, but she had been unable to spare anything from the royal coffers for its upkeep, and its age was beginning to show. The gilt ceiling murals were flaking, moths had made holes in the magnificent tapestries, and the large private apartments stank of sewage all year round, not helped by an all-pervading stench of mud and ordure from the nearby River Thames.

Perhaps if she had agreed to marry Alençon, the French duke's coffers might have paid to clean this place and the stinking city streets beyond its arched doorways. The little Duc d'Anjou with his curly black hair and muscular body had come closest to being her husband, after all; she could not deny that giving herself to a man like Alençon had seemed an attractive proposition in those first grim years after Leicester's marriage. But the game had rapidly grown stale. Public flirtations, secret messages and assignations, the gorgeous little gifts they had exchanged . . . and the kisses. The anger of her people had only served to make her more determined to marry him. How dared they seek to sway her mind with seditious pamphlets and rebellious mutterings?

And Leicester's grief had been a rich reward for those nights she had indiscreetly allowed Alençon the freedom of her chamber. Yet she had flinched from his offer in the end. Marry at last, after all these years, and bow her head to a Frenchman's will? So she accepted the fading splendour in which she was forced to live. It was one of the prices she had paid for her freedom.

London had grown filthy in recent years, the river almost solid with black slurry in places, the narrow city streets teeming with disease and foul air. Every now and then, the plague would sweep through it like wildfire, killing thousands of her people, their diseased corpses cast into plague pits without name or ceremony beyond a muttered prayer for their souls.

Some nights Elizabeth woke hot and sweating, fearing herself sick with the plague, and would cry fitfully into her pillow once the physicians had gone, not relieved by their reassurances and wishing herself safe in the country. But her people liked their queen to reside here a few months of the year, to show her face and walk among them on holy days, dispensing alms as her father had often done or healing the sick with just the touch of her hand. So it must be the palace of Whitehall now and Richmond later, or perhaps Hampton Court; she could not recall which of her residences would be ready for the court first.

'Your Majesty,' someone murmured, and Elizabeth came to with a start, realizing that the droning courtier

50

had finally stopped talking. He was still on his knees, waiting for her to pass judgement on his complaint. She glanced about the crowded Presence Chamber and the assembled courtiers discreetly averted their eyes.

Had she been on the verge of sleep? Well, if these fools would bore her.

'Where is Lucy Morgan this morning?' she demanded, noticing that the young black singer was not among her ladies.

No one spoke. Several of her women glanced at each other, though. Such malicious smiles. What were they hiding? She heard rumours about Lucy from time to time. But the girls who brought them to her ears never seemed sure of their veracity. And yet . . . Well, she suspected that Lucy Morgan had been involved with Robert's secret marriage, but she had little proof of it and would not make a fool of herself by pursuing the matter.

One day the truth will come out, Elizabeth thought bitterly. Then she would have her revenge. She would make Lucy suffer for aiding her rival to marry where Elizabeth could not. Meanwhile the wretched girl was not in attendance on her – why was that?

'Find Lucy Morgan and bring her to me,' she instructed one of her pages, who jumped to his feet and scampered off through the courtiers. She looked about the chamber restlessly while she waited for him to return, searching for Robert's dark head in the crowd. 'And where is the Earl of Leicester these days?' she demanded of her ladies. 'Is he missing from court too?'

Now she was not imagining the smiles. Well, let them smile. It had been a mistake to allow her old favourite out of exile so swiftly, barely a few months after his marriage. She knew that. She was weak, that was the truth of it. And Robert still had the power to amuse her. Besides, there were so few men left at court whom she could trust. The doughty old noblemen who had surrounded her during her first years on the throne had died, one by one, and the youths with their pointed beards and lavish doublets who had taken their places were not of the same character.

She could no more ask advice from such boys than she would order her hunting dogs to sit on the Privy Council.

Robert had gone home to his wife again without permission, no doubt. Why did no one obey her any more? Was she grown so toothless, so ancient, that her courtiers mocked her behind her back and did precisely as they chose?

She sighed and leaned her cheek upon her gloved hand again. They were the gloves Alençon had given her. Perhaps she ought to have accepted him. She could be married now, and with a son of Tudor blood to inherit her throne. What was left to her instead but this tiresome parade of complaints, and the same old songs, for the rest of her life?

A tall, silver-haired courtier in russet threaded through the crowd and sank stiffly to his knees before her. What now, she thought wearily, what now? As he looked up and their eyes met, she realized it was Robert.

But how old he looked!

'Your Majesty,' Robert murmured. 'You called for me?'

Did *she* look that old? She baulked at the thought. Yet they were the same age. Fifty years. Fifty years old? It was hard to believe she had now been on the throne half her life. Once, it had seemed such an impossible dream that she would ever wear the crown. First had come her poor brother Edward. Then Northumberland and his treacherous plot. Poor little Jane had paid the price for that, sweet child but too weak to save herself from ruin. After that, her sister Mary. That nightmare had dragged on and on until she had thought she would die in the Tower before she was ever queen. Yet here she still was, clutching at a crown that constantly threatened to be snatched away if she so much as blinked.

'I am glad to see you at court, my lord Leicester.' Elizabeth moved upright in her seat. Her body was stiff, her skirts rustling. I am not old yet, she insisted to herself. Slowly, she thought back over the particulars of the man's complaint. 'Let the baron be fined for his lack of consideration, and let him leave court until . . . until . . .'

'Michaelmas?' Robert suggested.

Elizabeth nodded, trying not to let her gratitude show on her face. She had not yet forgiven Robert for marrying that woman. Perhaps she would never forgive him. But she did feel weary today.

'Is that the last this morning?'

'Yes, Your Majesty. Though there is that other matter that needs to be heard. Sir Francis Walsingham awaits your pleasure in the Privy Chamber.'

Thankful, Elizabeth rose and allowed her old court favourite to help her down from the low dais. She did not need his help, nor the velvet-topped cane her steward shuffled forward to offer her and that she waved impatiently away. But after sitting so long, her legs were always a little stiff and her knees liable to give.

She gripped Robert's velvet sleeve. 'We missed you at court last week, my lord. I do not recall giving you leave to return home. Not so soon after your summer visit there.'

'Forgive me, Your Majesty.'

Never. She stiffened and her lips thinned, but she said nothing. There was nothing more to be said on that score.

In the terrible weeks after she had heard of his marriage, she had wept so bitterly she had thought she would die of a broken heart. Toothache, her old complaint, had come back to haunt her, like a physical reminder of the pain she was feeling inside. She had sent away all her women, smashed priceless ornaments in her private apartments, spent long, cold hours alone, planning how she would avenge his betrayal. Oh, how she had wanted to punish them both, to see them on their knees before her! Nothing short of the headsman's axe would do for that she-wolf, that thief of men, Lettice Knollys, so shameless in her crime. But for Robert?

There, she had been hazier in her plans. Even in the white heat of her fury, Elizabeth could not quite bring herself to take his head. Not Robert's darkly beloved, treacherous head.

Yet the punishment she did impose – Robert's exile from court – had not lasted as long as she had intended. Time had dragged without his presence, and his letters of humble contrition had touched her heart. And so within months Robert had been back at her side, paler than before, less outspoken, but still the companion of her youth. Later, a son had been born to the she-wolf, healthy and strong, but Robert had not dared raise the subject in Elizabeth's hearing, and she had never spoken of his heir. His marriage was still a wound in her side, a vicious thorn no amount of talking would pluck out.

Elizabeth raised her voice. Let the court hear her reprimand, she decided. They must know her favourite to be still unforgiven for his secret and imprudent marriage. Elizabeth Tudor was not weak and womanly like her cousin Mary Stuart, Queen of Scots, whose husbands had always played the tune to which she'd danced so foolishly. She would have the respect of her people, even if, as she constantly feared, she did not have their love.

'You will not leave court again without our permission,' she told Robert coldly. 'We have need of you here. Is that clear?'

'Yes, Your Majesty.'

The richly dressed courtiers fell to their knees on either

side as she passed, murmuring 'Your Majesty' in suitably respectful tones. Among their downturned faces were one or two young noblemen who eyed her eagerly and with a little too much impudence. She ought to have reprimanded them, too. But to own the truth, it was entertaining to see their boyish smiles in the court, and to dangle intimacy in front of them whenever she wished to hurt Robert. Today though, she could not spare the time for such pleasures.

Gripping Robert's arm more tightly, she walked steadily past the kneeling courtiers and into the Privy Chamber, followed by two of her noblewomen. She could guess what awaited her behind the splendid double doors, and drew herself up, not wishing to hear more bad news but knowing such blows to be an inevitable part of government. It seemed there was always one more thing to be faced before she could make her throne secure. If it could ever be fully secure, which she was beginning to doubt.

Damn Catholics, always scheming for her death.

In the first years of her reign, she had set her heart on a smooth transition back to a Protestant country. She had intended no burnings, no torture, no lengthy or unwarranted imprisonments, and a tacit pardon for those willing to forego their Roman Mass for the plainer truths of the Anglican church. But Elizabeth had not reckoned on the stubbornness and absolutism of these religious fanatics, on their determination to drag her from the throne rather than live peaceably in the new and more tolerant England she had built.

Walsingham and her treasurer, Robert Cecil, Lord Burghley, were waiting for her in the Privy Chamber, two black figures on either side of the fireplace; vying with each other, it seemed, as to which should look more sober and plainly dressed. They bowed as she entered with Robert, and she waved them to their seats. She had no time for ceremony today. Her head ached, and her bad leg was throbbing. The physicians would need to tend to it again before tonight's feast for the visiting Swedish ambassador and his entourage.

She allowed Robert to lead her to her seat at the head of the table, and settled herself there heavily. Lady Helena Snakenborg stood to her left, arranging the jewelled folds of Elizabeth's gown. Lady Mary Herbert, a heavy-jawed young woman with yellow hair set in ringlets, poured her a glass of wine and set it at her right hand, then smiled prettily across at her uncle, Robert. The girl had been away from court for months, nursing her baby son. However, it was unlikely she would stay for long before returning to Wales, as her husband Henry, Earl of Pembroke, was apparently eager for yet more offspring. Being a man of advancing years, Elizabeth thought sourly, he was no doubt fearful of dying before he could secure the Pembroke line by means of his young wife.

'Let us not waste time in pleasantries,' Elizabeth said sharply.

'This might be better heard alone, Your Majesty,' Walsingham suggested.

She sighed, but indicated that the two noblewomen should leave the room. When the door had closed behind Mary and Helena, she turned to her spymaster again.

'Well?'

Walsingham bowed, and slid a sheet of paper across the table towards her. 'This was intercepted at Dover yesterday, Your Majesty. It is a letter from one Thomas Dooley, a Catholic priest. He writes from the seminary at Rheims to one of my agents here in London, thinking him a Catholic too. This Dooley lays out plans for how the English court may be infiltrated by Catholic priests disguised as porters and watermen.'

Elizabeth barely glanced at the letter. It was always the same thing these days. Plots, plots, plots.

'What, am I to be threatened with incense burners and a three-hour Mass as they row me across the river? Tell me you have something more substantial, Walsingham. I have a headache.'

'Your Majesty, Signor Mendoza is mentioned several times in the letter as a courtier to be trusted and approached for funds.'

She paused then, looking narrowly from him to Cecil. 'The Spanish ambassador?'

'The very same, Your Majesty,' Cecil agreed. 'And it is not the first time we have intercepted letters of this kind, naming Mendoza as a contact for incoming Catholics. I'm afraid there can be little doubt that the Spanish ambassador is no friend to us.'

'Mendoza is friend only to those who would bring England back to the old faith, we have long known that. But to be named in a coded letter . . .'

She drank some wine and fell to brooding on her many enemies. Would she never be safe on her throne? 'Though our Englishmen are little better. What of this Master Arden whose lunatic son was to have shot me and stuck my head on a pole, or some such nonsense?'

'We have Edward Arden and his son-in-law safe in the Tower, Your Majesty. And their wives too.'

'Their wives? Why, were these women to have cooked up my bones in a broth when their men were done murdering me?'

Cecil looked uncomfortable. 'Arresting the wives along with their menfolk seemed the wisest thing to do, Your Majesty. The Arden family have long been rebellious and worked against your reign in Warwickshire. They are hardened Catholics, and would be pleased to see your cousin on the throne and England restored to the Roman faith. These arrests make an example of the entire family and may suppress further rebellion in the Midlands.'

She indicated the letter. 'Walsingham, when we spoke earlier, you said there might be a link between these disguised priests and the Arden boy's lunacy. What did you mean by that?'

'I cannot say for sure, Your Majesty. But there is a link between the Arden family and Mendoza. Arden's son-in-law, this John Somerville, has spoken several times of the ambassador under torture. Not coherently enough for an arrest, but it seems Signor Mendoza may be involved in some movement against you that stretches as far as the Midlands, and possibly into the North too.'

Cecil's expression was cautious. 'This is dangerous territory, sir. The boy may have heard some idle talk against the Queen through a keyhole, and decided to do the great deed himself. That he knows Mendoza's name does not mean the Spanish ambassador was involved in some Papist conspiracy. Let us not forget the boy is a lunatic.'

'That has not yet been proven,' Walsingham reminded him softly.

'Then prove it,' Elizabeth said with a snap, and stood up from the table. 'And don't come back to me with any more of these wild conspiracies until you have harder evidence. This is not one of our own, but the Spanish ambassador we are talking about. We cannot accuse Mendoza on the strength of a single coded letter and the ravings of a lunatic. We must be certain of his guilt first. We must be sure beyond all doubt. Do I make myself clear?'

Cecil bowed and removed himself from the room. She looked at Walsingham. He said nothing but reached for the incriminating letter, his grey head bent.

She raised her eyebrows. 'Well, sir?'

'Edward Arden,' he murmured, 'is not guilty of conspiring with his son-in-law to assassinate you, Your Majesty.'

'So release him.'

'It is not that simple, Your Majesty. He is guilty of . . . other crimes. He is a Catholic and a supporter of Catholics. This is not mere rumour, but cold truth. They have found a Catholic priest in hiding at one of the Arden houses, and various documents suggesting links with Catholics abroad. Arden is a dangerous man, and I have long wished for an excuse . . .' Walsingham smiled and made a gesture with his hand, '. . . to squeeze and question him.'

'You want my permission to torture Master Arden?'

'To torture him, yes. But also to execute him for treason. And any of his family who may reasonably be suspected too. Including the young man who would have killed you if he'd had the chance.'

'The women too?'

'Why not, if they are guilty?' Walsingham shrugged, and tucked the letter inside his severe black coat. 'The creature who tried to assassinate you at Kenilworth was female, and no weaker than a man for that task.'

'True, but these country wives may have had no knowledge of their husbands' treachery. I would not have them go to the gallows if their complicity cannot be established.' Elizabeth mused. 'Well, do what you must. You have always made your own path anyway. I shall not refuse to support your actions if whatever you do is done for the good of England.' She shivered. The fire was getting low. 'Now I am tired. Send in my women as you go.'

Once her court ladies had come rustling into the Privy Chamber, bearing fresh wine and chivvying the servants to make up the fire, Elizabeth looked about their cheerful faces searchingly.

'Is Lucy Morgan in attendance yet?'

The ring of women parted, and Lucy came forward, sinking to her knees in a rustle of silk, her head bent, her

59

coarse black hair teased and combed back with chaste white ribbons.

'Forgive me, Your Majesty. I was sick.'

Elizabeth regarded her broodingly. The memory of that dreadful night at Kenilworth eight years before still weighed on her heart. She had grown to find Lucy's dark beauty tiresome, and distrusted the way the younger courtiers constantly complimented the African singer and followed her about the court.

But it was true that she owed Lucy her life for her part in thwarting the Italian plotters that night. Perhaps she had been hasty in her recent snubbing of the young singer, favouring other court entertainers and refusing to allow Lucy any new gowns from the royal wardrobe. Lucy Morgan had not shown herself wanton with any of the young men, after all. To be admired was not to be wanton, or else she herself would stand accused of that failing ten times over.

She gestured for Lucy to rise. 'You are fully recovered?'

'Yes, Your Majesty, I thank you.'

'Why were you sick? Have you spoken to a physician?'

She eyed the girl's belly. Still flat, her breasts small and high. No outward sign of a pregnancy. Yet the suspicion that Lucy was lying about her sickness would not be shaken off.

'It was nothing serious, Your Majesty. A fever that lasted the night, with some sickness when I woke. But it soon passed.' Lucy hesitated. 'I must have eaten some meat that was not fresh, Your Grace.'

Elizabeth settled back in her favourite chair and waved Lucy Morgan into the centre of the room. 'If you are indeed recovered from your sickness, Lucy Morgan, then you can earn your keep and sing for us.'

Elizabeth played with the jewelled rings on her white fingers, turning them round and round. She remembered

Edward Arden's outburst at Kenilworth. She had reprimanded the staunchly Catholic Arden in front of the court and his Warwickshire peers, as she recalled, even threatening him with a public whipping if he persisted with his drunken abuse.

Was that when he and his mad son-in-law had first devised the idea of conspiring against her?

'Give us some sweet country song,' she muttered as Lucy took up her position. 'Something we have not heard in a long while.'

'"Robin, Oh Robin"?' Lucy suggested.

Elizabeth looked at her from under lowered lids. The black girl was sharper than she liked people to think. Or did everyone at court know which way Elizabeth's mind swung today? Oh yes, sometimes she would pout and think of the Duc d'Anjou. Sometimes she even wore the jewelled frog he had left her as a parting gift, or wrote him poignant letters which Cecil wisely refused to send. But her heart belonged to Robert. It might as well belong to a stone, of course. But she was a woman as well as a queen. She could not help her foolishness.

'A good choice,' she agreed drily, and took a sip of wine. 'Come, then, Lucy Morgan. Entertain me.'

Five

THE NARROW LANE OUTSIDE THE CURTAIN THEATRE WAS noisy and chaotic, crowded with playgoers and street sellers. Lucy was jostled on all sides and wished she'd thought to bring her maid Mary with her. Then at least she could have sent the girl for help if there was trouble.

Two coarse-voiced beggars arguing near the theatre entrance collided with her painfully. One called out a curse, making a grab for her arm.

Lucy staggered on and kept walking, her head down, face hidden by her hooded cloak. She could not afford to draw even the slightest attention to herself, not while carrying out Goodluck's errand. Such men would cut her throat for a ring, let alone a bag of gold.

It was a chilly November afternoon. A brazier glowed at the back door to the theatre, putting out a feeble heat. Lucy stood across the lane, waiting for her chance. Players came and went, unchallenged by the scarred man on the door, but she did not see Master Twist among them.

At last, the scarred man moved away to speak to one of the older whores plying their trade among the playgoers. Despite his disfigurement, the woman greeted him cheerfully enough. Leaning against the wall of the theatre, she dragged her revealing bodice even lower, her toothless smile inviting.

Lucy hurried across the lane and slipped through the unguarded doorway.

Backstage was no quieter than the street, crowded with players practising their cues or complaining about their ill-fitting costumes. But at least the narrow passageway behind the stage was dark and concealing, the infrequent windows so small as to admit almost no light at all. Wall lanterns had been hung at intervals so that players could read their cue sheets, but their light was inadequate, leaving deep pools of shadow through which Lucy was able to pass almost unnoticed.

'Now, mistress?' a voice at last hailed her. 'What are you doing back here?'

She turned. It was not Master Twist but someone she had never seen before. Balding and a little corpulent, his leather jerkin straining over his belly, he had the air of a man used to getting his own way. She guessed at once that he must be one of those in charge of the daily running of the theatre. She had known several such men as a child, growing up among players and theatricals. When she did not immediately reply, he stroked his beard, looking her up and down impudently.

'Well?' he demanded.

Lucy knew a moment of trepidation, then stuck her chin out. If she could deal with the daily insolence of courtiers who believed her dark skin meant she would be happy to act the whore for them, then she could certainly handle a common man of the theatre.

She put back her hood and looked him in the eye. 'I'm looking for Master John Twist,' she said briefly, giving no further explanation. 'Do you know where I can find him?'

The man turned his head and shouted hoarsely down

the passageway, 'Twist! How many times have I told you not to bring your whores backstage?'

A dark, crookbacked figure disengaged itself from the shadows at the far end of the corridor and began limping towards them. She stared. Could this be Master Twist? She had known him since childhood, and he had always been in good health, tall and sturdily built.

'Get rid of her, Twist,' the man added impatiently. 'The show's about to start. You can tup her in the interval if you must. And leave some for me this time, will you?' He leered at her as he turned away. 'She's a tasty piece.'

He disappeared back along the corridor. Lucy gazed at the crookback's face. This was indeed her old friend.

'Goodluck sent me,' she whispered, seeing his look of surprised recognition. 'Is it safe to talk here? I have something for you.'

Taking her by the elbow, John Twist steered her into a low-ceilinged, unlit corridor that seemed to lead even deeper into the inner workings of the theatre. Safely away from the curious eyes of the other players, he embraced her roughly, then held her at arm's length, searching her face.

'Lucy,' Twist muttered, his lips thinning as he looked her up and down, no doubt taking in the costly court gown under her cloak.

She examined him too, not caring if he thought her rude. Twist looked older than she remembered, his face toughened and wrinkled, his hair coarser and streaked with grey. That was no surprise, of course; she herself was no longer the soft-faced child she had been during that summer at Kenilworth, though the court had saved her from the worst ravages of city life. And Twist must be in his late thirties by now, almost past his prime. Yet he still possessed the sharp self-assurance she remembered, his blue eyes watching her narrowly without giving anything away.

'What's this about Goodluck?' he asked in a low voice. 'I thought for sure he was . . .'

'Dead?'

'Never coming back, perhaps. It must be several years since I've heard his name.' Twist smiled down at her grimly. 'But it seems the man has nine lives.'

'Yes, and is going through them rapidly,' she agreed.

'I'm glad to hear he is alive and well.' He hesitated. 'What are you looking at? The hump? Never mind that, it's for the play. I'm still the same Twist underneath.' He squeezed her hand in reassurance. 'But you said . . . You have a message for me?'

'Here,' Lucy said, glancing cautiously about herself before handing over the purse and letter that Goodluck had given her. 'He wants to meet you. It's urgent.'

'With Goodluck, it's always urgent.'

Twist took the purse with a slight smile. He shook it, raised his eyebrows at the weight, then clipped the purse on to his own belt and carefully arranged the folds of his costume over it.

He grinned at her expression. 'I had better hope no one grapples me too firmly on the stage, for I shall have no chance to put this away before my part.'

There was a sudden burst of muffled applause and a drumming roar close by. The walls and wooden frames around them shook as though the theatre was being besieged. Lucy jerked at the noise and gave a little cry, her nerves already stretched. Belatedly, she realized it was only the performance starting. The enthusiastic playgoers in the gallery seats must be stamping their feet on the wooden boards, the noise reverberating through the theatre like a thunderstorm.

Twist did not seem to have noticed. He was staring down at Goodluck's letter, a frown on his face. He did not break the seal to open it, but weighed the parchment thoughtfully in his hand.

'I have to go soon or I shall miss my cue. The play has begun.' He looked at her. 'Perhaps you could stay and we'll talk later?'

'I'm sorry, I can't. It's too dangerous. If the Queen discovers that I have left court without permission, I will be punished.'

'Of course, forgive me.' John Twist broke the seal and quickly scanned the letter. He nodded. 'Are you able to give Goodluck a reply from me? Will you be seeing him again?'

'I'm not sure. Perhaps.'

'If you see him, tell him to meet me at the Dun Cow by Bishopsgate the day after tomorrow.' He rolled up the letter and slid it carefully inside his shirt. 'Between six and seven o'clock of the evening. By then, I should have what he requires.'

'And if I don't see him?'

'Then I shall enjoy two or three tankards of ale, and go home that night a merrier man.' He smiled and held out his hands to her. 'Come, kiss me and get yourself safely back to court. It was dangerous to come this far north of the city. The theatre is no place for you.'

'I was brought up among players,' she protested.

His gaze moved over her court gown, an ironic gleam in his eyes. 'I remember it well. But you are too fine a lady for us now. Quick, they have nearly reached my cue.' He kissed her warmly on the lips and Lucy pulled back a little in surprise, lowering her gaze before his. To her relief, he did not seem to notice. 'Don't forget my message to Goodluck. Do you need me to repeat it?'

'I have it perfect.'

Twist laughed, sweeping his voluminous black cloak

over his arm as he bowed. 'Farewell then, Mistress Morgan. We'll make a spy of you yet.'

'I hope not. Spies have short lives. I'd rather not end up with my head rotting on a pike above London Bridge.'

'Such a pretty head too,' Twist murmured, and smiled at her in a way she found rather uncomfortable.

Six

GOODLUCK DRAGGED HIS CLOAK TIGHTER AND SET HIS HEAD against the driving rain, his hat soaked, boots squelching in the muddy quagmire that was Bishopsgate. He was early, and deliberately so. He did not doubt John Twist, but a certain measure of caution was always required when there were others involved in a meeting. The Catholic informant he had asked to meet might have been followed, or even have changed his mind and betrayed them. Either way, Goodluck wanted to look over the place in advance, not least to see whether anyone else was engaged in the same activity.

Lucy's message had been brief: a time and place only, scrawled hurriedly in code, with no signature. Goodluck had recognized both the hand and the code though, not needing to see the name.

The note had reached him via Lucy's cloaked and hooded maid, a frightened-looking girl who had handed it over without a word and then fled, not even glancing at the penny Goodluck had held out to her. No doubt the girl had been taught that players were next to beggars, and as likely to rape her and slit her throat as give her a penny for her trouble. And with some players, he thought drily, she would not be wrong.

Lucy had certainly made some powerful friends since that summer at Kenilworth when she had first come to the Queen's attention. To have her own maid was a mark of the respect and wealthy patronage she must be receiving at court.

Goodluck could not help feeling a little uneasy, though. There had been something brittle about Lucy when they had met outside the Cross Keys Inn. Life at court had changed his ward over the past few years, and not for the better. Lucy was no longer the sweet-faced innocent he remembered from her childhood, that little girl whose smile had lit up his heart. But he was willing to swear she was still untouched, still a virgin.

Goodluck paused outside the Dun Cow, glancing up at the ancient building, which leaned to one side and was so dilapidated it could not be long before it was knocked down to make way for some new hostelry. The mud-spattered door was closed and the narrow front windows had been shuttered against the rain, but he knew the place was open. He could hear the hubbub from inside, and had seen several men staggering away in the rain as he approached, their faces red from too much ale.

Goodluck pushed his way through the smoky taproom. There were several tables still empty. He pulled up a chair and began to remove his sodden cloak and hat.

'Sir?'

Goodluck smiled up at the plump serving girl who had stopped to clean his table. Businesslike, her sleeves rolled to her elbows, she wiped up a spillage of ale with her coarse, dirty apron, and straightened a fallen chair, all the while sizing him up, as though trying to decide how much money he might be carrying in the purse that hung from his belt.

He leaned back in his chair and met her look openly. No

doubt there was more to buy from this girl than ale and a pie, but she was out of luck. He was not in the mood for a girl tonight, however comfortable her ample breasts and belly.

'A tankard of ale,' he ordered briefly. 'And a bite to eat. Something hot and simple will do me well enough.'

'Bread and hot pottage, master? Or salt pork with beans?'

He shrugged. 'Whatever is cheapest and to hand.'

The girl turned away, clearly disappointed, and disappeared into the back kitchen with his order.

Goodluck waited in silence, discreetly examining the men in the taproom. He knew a few faces, but most were unfamiliar. John Twist was not among them. So he had maybe half an hour to kill before the meeting.

Lucy had not always been so wary of men, he thought, remembering the caution in her face when he had called after her in the street. She had fallen in love with that boy at Kenilworth, and what had happened? The young fool had got himself killed defending the Queen. Small wonder Lucy preferred to keep herself aloof these days.

Though that was not all the story, surely?

Goodluck suspected that, despite her striking beauty, Lucy had found it hard to catch the eye of an honest man at court. Her black skin and outlandish hair must set her apart from the other women in Elizabeth's service, making it harder for any courtier to pursue her without drawing both the Queen's attention and displeasure.

He frowned, wondering if she had already had trouble of that sort. Fond though he was of Lucy, Goodluck knew that if a man of noble birth ever looked sideways at Lucy's fascinating black skin and high breasts, it would be for reasons other than marriage. She had neither fortune nor title to tempt an ambitious man, and ambitious men were the only sort who lived off the court. Yet they would be interested, and try to persuade her into their beds.

'Didn't expect to see you here, Master Goodluck,' said a soft voice at his elbow.

Goodluck turned to see who had come in from the rain. It was Master Parry, one of London's most slippery businessmen, a man who was well-known for saying the wrong thing at the wrong time to the wrong person, and yet who always seemed to end up on top. He was in company tonight with a young, curly-haired man Goodluck did not recognize, though by his swagger he perhaps ought to have done.

Goodluck stood and shook hands with Parry. 'Nor I you, Master Parry. You are in good health, I trust?'

'I can't complain, though I could do without the rain.' Parry wiped his face and beard dry with the underside of his cloak. 'God, this weather is appalling. But at least there's a good fire in here, and better company than we had in the Fighting Cocks. May we share your table, Goodluck?' He nodded over his shoulder. 'This is Kit Marlowe, by the way, a young friend of mine just down from Cambridge.'

Goodluck shook the lad's hand. 'Pleased to meet you, Master Marlowe.'

'Kit,' the young man insisted, and smiled, not showing his teeth.

By the look of his pointed beard and slashed velvet doublet, Marlowe was not one of Parry's business associates. He did not look like a poor student either, but more like a theatrical. And for a young theatrical to be in Parry's company meant one of two things. Either he was of the same persuasion as Parry, who rumour had it enjoyed young men the way the decadent Romans used to, or Marlowe was a spy. Possibly both at once.

Kit Marlowe was looking Goodluck over in the same assessing way, his dark eyes narrowed. 'Will you take some ale with us, sir?'

'I've already ordered mine. Here it comes now.' Goodluck could see the plump serving maid threading her way across the crowded taproom with a tray. The girl kept halting to slap away a groping hand or two, though she seemed more amused than angered by the attention. 'I'm just waiting for . . .'

Goodluck hesitated, then thought better of mentioning John Twist. He seemed to remember there was some bad blood between the two men. He did not want to frighten Parry off. Parry was a weasel and a turncoat, everyone knew that. But he had been known to serve Walsingham as a spy from time to time, and he might have some useful information about the latest Catholic plots.

'Well, no matter. Come and drink with me, both of you.' Goodluck drew up some chairs for them. 'It's been an age since we last met, Parry. Lisbon, wasn't it? Before Philip of Spain took it.'

'Madrid,' Parry corrected him.

'Both dangerous cities for Englishmen these days.' Goodluck smiled as the serving maid banged his tankard and supper down on the table. 'Thank you.'

The two men ordered their drinks.

Once the girl had gone, Parry turned back to him with a frown. 'You think Spain more dangerous for Englishmen now? So things will soon come to a head between our queen and King Philip, is that what you're saying? Well, I cannot pretend I'm surprised at the enmity there. Philip very gallantly offered to marry her, you know, after Queen Mary died. They say Elizabeth sent him a lemon, as a token of the bitter hospitality he could expect from her.'

Goodluck sipped at his ale, trying to hide his grimace. The ale tasted bitter too, though not to an unpalatable extent. Some claimed the ale around Bishopsgate was traditionally 'improved' with a little piss. That would certainly explain the taste, he thought. 'Come, these wild taproom stories get us nowhere. You know as well as I do that the English Catholics grow more daring and ungovernable every day,' he said, not bothering to lower his voice.

It was not treason to speak against the Catholics, only to speak for them. But he saw Kit Marlowe's hands clench on the arms of his chair and wondered at it. Was the boy playing both sides?

'Spain has become the seat of their passionate hatred for the Queen,' Goodluck continued easily. 'This is not news. Any fool with half a brain can see that.'

'Aye, well, I know more about that than most,' Parry muttered. 'England shall have war before the year is out. And I say we shall lose if Elizabeth does not marry, and soon. For what country ever won a war with an unmarried woman on the throne?'

'A war between England and Spain?' Goodluck glanced about the crowded taproom to see who might be listening. This was open and dangerous talk even for someone as foolhardy as Parry. 'I would not care to bet on that, Parry. There are those who might mistakenly think I had some special knowledge.'

'And do you?'

Goodluck laughed, and began to tear his coarse bread into strips. He dipped a piece into the steaming bowl of pottage.

'You are a bold man, Parry, and a clever one. All the world knows that, and I should not dare dispute it. But I am not so bold. I have no special or intimate knowledge of Spain, nor of what the Catholics may be planning. I am merely hungry, and my supper is getting cold.'

Parry watched him in silence for a moment. Then he shrugged. 'One day you will come to me for a favour, Master Goodluck. On that day, I trust I may give you a more favourable reply than this you give me.'

'You must forgive me, friend, but there is nothing I can

tell you. I am not the fount of anti-Catholic information you think me.' Goodluck drank deep from his tankard, pretending disinterest. With a shrug, he set to eating his supper again. 'Though it's true that sometimes I hear certain things as I go about the city. If you wish me to keep my ears open . . .'

'Let's just say, you would be serving your country well if you did so.'

Goodluck smiled, and wiped his mouth. 'In that case, Master Parry, you may consider it done.'

'I am glad.' Parry rose, pulling his cloak about him. He tossed a few coins on to the table; one rolled across and fell on the floor at Goodluck's feet. Parry jerked his head at Marlowe, like a man summoning his hound. 'That should cover what we ordered. When the girl comes back, you can tell her we went elsewhere. The ale tastes like gnats' piss here, anyway.'

Once the two men had gone, Goodluck bent slowly and picked up the fallen coin. It was a ha'penny.

Frowning, he turned the small coin over in his hand and stared down at the Queen's head before throwing it back on to the table.

What was Parry up to? Despite his patriotic enquiries, it was clear he was not interested in Queen Elizabeth's fate, nor indeed that of England itself. Philip of Spain had 'very gallantly' offered the Queen marriage, had he? Now there was a man who could happily live once more in a Spanish England, as the suffering English had done under Mary's reign.

Was it possible that Parry, for all his weaknesses and underhand dealings, could be the traitorous mastermind Goodluck was seeking? The man who had helped fuel the assassination plot at Kenilworth in 'seventy-five and was even now engaged in drawing a secret force against the Queen from within her own court?

The round-faced serving maid arrived with the unwanted drinks and stared in dismay at the empty chairs. Goodluck explained the situation to her delicately, handing over the money and leaving out the remark about 'gnats' piss'. If there was one sure-fire way to get your ale liberally laced with urine, it was to complain to the landlord that it already was.

The door swung open and Twist came in at last, wrapped in a dripping cloak and looking half-drowned from the violent downpour lashing the city.

Goodluck waved him over with a sense of relief. 'Here,' he said, shaking hands with his old friend. 'I have a table, and drinks already served. Do you want to eat?'

'I've already eaten,' Twist said, and embraced him. 'By our Lady, it's good to see you.'

'And you.'

'I don't much like this tempest, though. Did you bring it with you from the Continent?' Twist unwrapped himself gingerly. He was wet underneath the cloak as well. 'Look at that. I'm soaked through. But here I am complaining about the weather, when you have been several years in a Roman prison. How are you?'

'Older and fatter, for all my captivity.'

Twist laughed, and leaned back in his chair. 'It comes to us all in the end.'

'Now don't go wishing the end on me. I've a few years left in me.'

'Amen to that.' Twist took a swallow of ale without any sign of disgust. 'This ale is good. Just what I need to take the theatre dust out of my mouth.'

'You're playing at the Curtain, is that right?'

'For my sins, yes. One show today, another tomorrow. Sometimes we play at court. No, don't look so hungry to return. The crowds are huge on a good afternoon and the money is useful, but working in the theatre

75

these days is enough to kill a man. Our masters work us too hard. And then the city fathers accuse players of loose morals, and of keeping a whore in every house between here and Spitalfields.' Twist laughed. He shook out his sleeves, rearranging the frayed lace cuffs. 'I ask you, when am I supposed to sleep, let alone fuck?'

'I haven't had the pleasure myself since returning to London. Though I hear the rate for a clean whore has grown beyond my slender pockets now.'

'Whoring has become an expensive habit of late,' Twist agreed ruefully. He leaned back in his chair and looked at Goodluck. 'So you got out of Rome alive. You were away so long, I was beginning to wonder if I should come after you. What happened?'

'Someone gave me away.'

'You were betrayed?' Twist frowned. 'Do you know by whom?'

'Not yet. But I intend to find out.' Goodluck met his gaze. 'Now to the letter I sent. Did you find the man I was looking for?'

Twist shook his head. 'I'm still asking around the town. But it's difficult. No one is talking. The Catholics are lying so low right now, you could trip over one in the street and not notice. Every day brings rumours of a fresh plot against the Queen. Walsingham's agents are all around, but some of them play both sides of the net, and there's no guessing their allegiances until it's too late. It can be dangerous to draw attention to yourself by asking too many questions of the wrong man.'

Goodluck smiled. 'I learned that lesson the hard way in Rome.'

'Torture?'

'I didn't talk, if that's what you're worried about.' Goodluck called the girl over for another tankard of ale, deciding to make a night of it. 'You're safe enough.'

Seven

Whitehall Palace, London, winter 1583

'IF YOU WOULD ONLY ALLOW ME TO RUB IN SOME OIL OF cloves again, Your Majesty, the pain would abate. I swear it.'

'Fool, your vile oil burns, and I will have none of it!' Elizabeth roared, and knocked the tiresome apothecary away, his tray and bottles clattering to the floor.

Toothache again! The unfairness, the injustice of it. The sunlight hurt her eyes. Why had the shutters been thrown so wide open on her bedchamber windows? She stared about at her women in silent accusation. Was she expected to rise and be dressed and rule the country in such agony? Did nobody care how she suffered?

'Where are my doctors?'

Lady Helena was at her side at once, offering a cup of wine and a fresh platter of lavender-steeped cloths. She at least knew how to treat a queen. 'They await your pleasure, Your Majesty, in the antechamber. You told them to . . . to go hang themselves yesterday. Shall I send them in?'

God's blood, her jaw was on fire!

'Yes, yes, send them in at once,' Elizabeth managed, clasping a dampened cloth to her cheek, where the pain throbbed most viciously. When would this agony cease? God had sent her this repeated affliction as a punishment. No woman was intended to rule alone, and she had been given chances to marry, only to spurn them. Her monthly courses, never easy to predict, had grown strange and difficult of late. Her womb ached some nights and prevented her from sleeping. What other explanation could there be? She should have married and produced a child. Instead her body was beginning to tumble down like an old tower under siege, more broken and ramshackle with every year that passed.

Her physicians came in, dark-cloaked and hatted, with long staffs and impressive wooden chests of medicaments, bowing and making their customary noises. 'Your Majesty, the remedy is simple.' She waited for the inevitable, glaring at them, daring them to say it. 'The tooth is rotten and must be drawn. There is no other cure for the toothache.'

'I will not lose any more teeth!'

She rocked in pain as her tooth throbbed violently, as if a hot wire was being drawn swiftly back and forth through her body. Her spine was on fire, tendrils of flame reaching even to the tips of her fingers. Her body would be left hollow soon, like a burned-out tree, nothing remaining but the pain of this tooth still smouldering in the ashes. Give me a mallet, she thought. A great bloody mallet to smash this jaw into pieces and grant me peace. Let someone drive a stake through the top of my head and pierce the agony where it grips me.

No, no, no. Her mind groped for control. She must preserve what teeth she had left. She would not lose another one. She refused to gum her food like an old woman while the younger courtiers gaped and laughed behind their hands.

'Lord Jesu in heaven, look down and help thy servant in her pain and distress,' she moaned, and crossed herself. 'I cannot lose this tooth. I *shall not* lose this tooth.'

No answer came from on high. The pain continued unabated, swelling and beating her jaw like a drum. It must indeed be a punishment from God, she thought hazily. Is it Thy will, O Lord, that I should wish to throw myself out of the highest tower window rather than live through another hour of this agony? God was angry with her for rejecting Robert, for turning her nose up at so many suitors, for having wriggled out of her written agreement to marry the Duke of Anjou, for never having married. Now she must suffer and feel His displeasure.

'The pain will pass,' she groaned, barely able to form words. 'It always does. Give me something for it. Poppy or strong liquor to help me sleep.'

Her physicians looked concerned. They muttered among themselves while she writhed in agony, clutching her jaw. 'It could be dangerous, Your Majesty. At your age . . .'

'*I am not old!*'

More fearful muttering. More frowning and head-shaking. Old men with moths in their fur-lined cloaks and straw between their ears. Let one of them rule a kingdom, they would soon learn to act swiftly.

A cup was brought to her lips and she drank in tiny thankful sips, roaring each time the foul liquid touched her inflamed tooth.

The room seemed to darken. Elizabeth looked up groggily. Where had the sun gone? Rain beat against the windows in a thrumming rhythm. A fire crackled cheerfully in the hearth, warming her drowsy body. The bed was candlelit. That was when she realized that time had passed. She was lying down, her jaw bound up in warm cloths that stank of some herbal astringent, and Helena, dear kind-eyed Helena, was perched on the coverlet beside her, a steaming bowl in her hands.

'Better, Your Majesty?'

She lifted her head, and the pain shot through her again. Not so intense now, though. A sharp, quick, circular pain that filled her mouth, danced on the bones of her spine a moment, then ebbed to a dull ache. It was nearly over. At least, she no longer felt an urge to strangle her doctors with her bare hands. That was a good sign.

Warily, she sat up. 'A little,' she conceded. 'How long have I slept?'

'Most of the day, Your Majesty. It is nearly nightfall.' Lady Helena hesitated. 'Lord Leicester is waiting in the Presence Chamber, Your Majesty. He heard you had the toothache and came straightaway to see you. I . . . I hope I did right in asking him to wait. I remembered how his lordship always used to sit with you when your toothache came on, and you said you could not have got through it without him.'

He was out there now, waiting while she slept? The thought pleased her, though she felt anger, too, that he had not been dismissed as soon as he had arrived. It was true. Robert knew how to joke and bully her through the pain better than anyone. But let him in now? Into her own private space – her bedchamber, no less? How would he explain that to his wife?

His first wife, Amy Robsart, had died soon after Elizabeth became queen, falling downstairs 'accidentally', the coroner had ruled. It had never bothered her to invite him into her bedchamber when he was married to Amy, nor to allow him to kiss and caress her, a married man, promised to another in the sight of God. But this was different. Lettice Knollys was no meek country girl like Amy, easily neglected and forgotten, easily sidelined from court. Or perhaps it was her own feelings for Robert that had changed. Did she no longer love him? She thought of her love, and saw how it had been dented by his marriage to Lettice, broken and battered like a shield that could no longer hold off its enemies. Robert, Robert. She allowed herself another moment of childish dismay at his betrayals and lusts, then moved on. Her toothache. His presence. The decision.

'Tell him to go,' she muttered. 'I am much recovered and do not need him to . . . Tell him to go.'

Lady Helena's eyes were sympathetic. She was a good girl. Not like some at court. 'Yes, Your Majesty,' she agreed, and removed herself from the room.

As soon as the door had closed, the pain flared up again. Elizabeth's tooth became the centre of her being for one exquisite moment of agony, then the rest of her jaw caught fire. She buried her head in the pillows again, stifling her moans.

If only Robert was here, she thought, to let her squeeze his bare hand. That would help to distract her from the pain. Or he could play thimblerig to infuriate her, switching cups around too quickly for her to remember which one hid the gold coin. Or juggle apples on one leg, laughing, until he sent the fruit rolling across the floor. Or peel and slice the least bruised one, feeding it to her on the tip of his dagger with studied intimacy.

But she must keep him at a distance now. He was no longer hers. It was hard remembering that. And becoming harder with every day that passed.

'I can't thank you enough, Will. I can't be a player short for a court performance, and this part calls for a "handsome young man of Italy".' John Laneham nodded as Will laughed. 'I know, I know! But you were the only player under twenty-five I could find in the city who can carry a line and isn't otherwise engaged tonight.'

Laneham handed over the other shoe and watched critically as Will forced his too-large foot into it.

'Sorry about the tight fit, lad. Gerrard had a smaller foot than you.'

'How did he die?'

'Foolishly, just as the drunken sot lived.' Will looked up and Laneham made a face. 'He fell off a ladder during a performance at the Cross Keys. Snapped his neck clean in two. Don't you do the same, you hear me? I can't afford to keep buying in new players. He was meant to be climbing over a high wall to woo his lady, but if you don't think you're up to it—'

'I'll be careful.'

'Good lad.'

John Laneham threw him a richly embroidered, fur-lined cloak that seemed smart enough until Will looked at it closely. Then he spotted the loose seams and realized it needed a trip to the seamstress. Or else the midden, he thought, recoiling from the smell.

'You have a play roll for me?'

'Here.' Laneham took a battered play roll from the roll bag and handed it across. The parchment was torn in places, and marred by scribbling and greasy fingerprints. 'This was Gerrard's. The lines are simple enough. "I love you, I want you to be my wife," and all that. You could crib them in half an hour, which is about all you've got before the performance starts. You play a young Italian who's sick with love. That can't be too much of a stretch for you, even for a man who's sworn off women.'

Will smiled. 'Alas, my reputation as a happily married man . . .'

'Now don't blaspheme, lad.' But Laneham grinned and clapped him on the shoulder. 'Come to me after the play, there'll be two shillings in it for you. And a jug of ale, too.'

'No wine?' Will glanced about the high-ceilinged room

with its gilt walls and expensively leaded windows. 'I've no wish to sound churlish, but I expected more hospitality from the palace of Whitehall. Is it true what they're saying, that the Queen's coffers are empty?'

'Be content with the ale and the two shillings, lad, and keep your mouth shut around court. You should think yourself lucky to be working here at all.'

'It will be good to have money in my pocket again, not just a promise of it.'

'Oh aye, the money's good for us Queen's Men, for all it's a new company. And I don't doubt there'll be wine aplenty for the fine courtiers, as there always is when we play at court. Rivers of the bloody stuff, from Burgundy or the Rhône or wherever. But the Queen's Men won't see a drop of it. We're players, lad. Too lowly for such costly fare. They'll give us roast pig and a good jug of ale apiece after we've done our work. What more could a man want?' Laneham grinned. 'Except a woman who doesn't mind a jig or two when the candle's out?'

'You'll not find many of those at court.'

Laneham tapped the side of his nose. He leaned in close, stinking unpleasantly of cabbage and unwashed body. 'You leave it to me, young Master Shakespeare. These court ladies may look too fine for the likes of us, but trust me, if there's one here who will fall on her back for me, I'll find her before they kick us back out into the streets. I can sniff out a silken whore at a thousand paces. Yes, and have her too, before the bitch even knows what's been up her skirts.'

Will laughed. 'You are a very devil!'

'It has been said, Master Shakespeare. It has been said many times. Nor have I ever denied it. But only for the ladies, mind. I'm as true and honest a man as you will ever meet elsewise. And here's my hand to prove it.'

Will shook his hand. He looked about in the general

hubbub as the other players began to arrive and pull on their costumes. He recognized a few faces, for the London players were few, and frequented many of the same taverns. But he was only with the Queen's Men for tonight's performance. It would not feel right to mingle too freely with them.

'I'd better find somewhere quiet to learn my lines and cues.'

'I'll send a boy for you when the court's assembled and we're ready to start. We have a prompt, in case you forget your part, but I'd rather you were not forever stuttering and staring before the Queen. She's had the toothache this past month, they say, and her mood is bitter. So learn your part well.'

With a nod, Will took his play roll away down the narrow corridor. He wandered aimlessly for a moment before finding an opening in the wall that led out into a small enclosed garden. There was nobody about. It was chilly and already growing dark, but Will knew he would rather get cold outside than try to read by the light of a spitting torch in some smoky antechamber.

He found a stone seat under a willow and settled himself there to read the play roll, peering at the cues in the semi-darkness to make sure he knew each one. The lines themselves took only a few moments to commit to memory. It was always the cues he had trouble remembering.

Will could hear the sounds of the city outside the walls, still humming with life even at dusk: street sellers packing up their wares for the night, women laughing somewhere nearby, the constant rumble of carts and, a little further away, the haunting cries of the watermen, drumming up night trade or just calling to each other across the broad expanse of the River Thames.

Cursing, he wiped his hands on his too-loose trousers. Why was he so nervous?

Will knew the play well enough – he had seen it performed twice before, at Warwick and Coventry – and he had a good memory for lines. He could only assume it was being in the rarefied courtly air of Whitehall that was making his palms sweat.

That, and the knowledge that if Burbage heard of him taking a part in another man's company, even just for this one night, he could lose all hope of future work in that quarter. Burbage didn't like his men to play for anyone else. It was a matter of honour with him, of loyalty to the company. But then, Burbage didn't have to scrape a living from a few shillings a week, sending home as much as he could to a wife and child he had not seen in months.

Above, shutters were thrown back noisily and a light shone from an open balcony window. Inside he caught a glint of gold and heard the whisper of women's voices, then a rustle of stiff silk.

Shrinking into the shadows – was he even allowed to be here, in this private garden overlooked by what must be the Queen's own apartments? – Will sat perfectly still and gazed up at the woman who had come out on to the narrow balcony.

The woman was turned away from him, looking back into the room. She was wearing a broad-skirted white and black gown decorated with pearls, her bearing very erect. The gloved hand that clutched the stone rail of the balcony bore a large ruby ring. Even in the gloom of dusk he could see that she was tall, stately even.

One of the Queen's ladies, he guessed, judging by the richness of the pearls glinting in her dark hair and on the bodice of her gown.

Then the noblewoman turned to look down into the garden, and he saw her face for the first time.

A shudder ran through him. *Lucy Morgan!*

Will stared hungrily up at the dark face he remembered,

beautifully drawn by the hand of Nature with the high cheekbones and full lips of the African. He had seen her at the Cross Keys Inn, and now here she was again. His whole body shivered. He had chosen to come to court for this night's work, knowing he might see her again in the Queen's company of ladies. But this chance meeting . . .

Not chance, but the hand of God. It had to be fate that Lucy Morgan had come to this very window and looked out over the garden in which he had chosen to sit. What else could she represent but his destiny, clothed in human flesh – and a gorgeous black flesh, at that?

Lucy shifted slightly, and noticed his still figure under the willow tree.

Fixed by the intensity of her dark, brooding gaze, Will found himself unable to move or speak. Perhaps she would think him a statue.

'Who's there?' she demanded, shattering the illusion. When he did not respond, she drew herself up angrily, staring straight at him. 'Speak, or I shall summon the guards.'

Had she always been so tall?

Will frowned, looking again at the black hair that framed her face, bound in a silver net and gleaming with tiny seeded pearls. Pearls were the Queen's favourite adornment, too, a symbol of chastity, of untried virginity. Yet surely an exotic beauty like Lucy Morgan could not still be unmarried? Though perhaps, in the service of the Queen, she had little choice but to remain a virgin too, as her mistress claimed to have done.

He was not tongue-tied, but dazzled. He revelled in being able to say her name for the first time in years. 'Lucy Morgan.'

She stared down at him through the darkness. Her voice was hesitant. Perhaps she feared he was a courtier who would be offended by her questions.

'Who are you, sir? These are the Queen's apartments and you are standing in her Privy Garden. I don't know how you came to be there. But if you are seen, you will be arrested.'

He let the play roll drop and came swiftly to the foot of the wall. The balcony on which she stood was two floors up, but there was a young sycamore tree immediately below it, and a high ledge to one side that he could probably stand on to speak to her. He gazed up, assessing the height. As a boy in Warwickshire, he had been forever in and out of trees ten times the size of this. Leaving the stinking cloak behind him on the grass, Will scrabbled up into the tree, balanced along one of its slender branches – which bobbed and danced beneath his weight like an unbroken pony – and pulled himself painstakingly up on to the stone ledge.

Flattened against the wall, Will turned his head to see Lucy hanging over the balcony, staring down at him. God, she was a beauty. He felt himself harden with desire and was shocked into silence. What had he told Laneham? That he was a happily married man?

Since coming to London, he had seen women running about half-dressed in the streets, and had had young whores sit in his lap, offering him their bodies for little more than fourpence, and had not been moved.

Lucy Morgan was different.

She was shocked that he knew her name, that he had climbed up like a boy to speak to her. It was in her eyes, the way her hands gripped the stone rail of the balcony. Was she Lucy Morgan? Could he have been mistaken? No, hers was the same dark face he remembered, the beautiful woman of his dreams.

'You don't recognize me, Lucy?'

She frowned. 'You're . . . the player from the Cross Keys.'

She did not remember him. Why should she? He had been nothing to her at Kenilworth. Just a local boy. He must make a fresh start with her, make her see him as a man.

'You must look further back than that.'

From the start, Will had been desperate to conceal his rural origins from the London players, renting a more costly room than he could afford, packing away his frieze suits for a more fashionable doublet with slashed sleeves and coloured hose, even shedding his embarrassing country accent. To be thought a country bumpkin had been his constant fear.

Now, though, he made no attempt to hide the soft brogue of his Warwickshire burr, hoping to remind her of the past. 'Eight years back, to a boy who had lost his father in the hurly-burly of a great country castle welcoming its queen.'

She looked at him properly for the first time. Her stiff court dignity fell away. For a moment, she was almost the old Lucy, her voice rising like a girl's. 'Will? Is . . . Is it truly you? Young Will Shakespeare?'

'The very same.' Will bowed as best he could, balanced on the narrow ledge. 'Though not so young any more. I shall be twenty years of age in April. It is good to see you again, Mistress Morgan.'

She was shaking her head, her eyes still wide. 'I can't believe it.' She stared at his face, then at his clothes. 'You look so different.'

'I'm a player now. I've come to play before the Queen tonight.'

'You're with the Queen's Men?'

He wanted to say yes, to impress her. But it would be a simple enough lie to expose. 'For tonight only,' he admitted. 'I am not attached to any company, I work where I am paid to work. They were a man short tonight.

But I would like to join them, yes. If they will have me.'

Her gaze moved to the play roll, lying forgotten beside the bench. 'You were learning your part?'

'Yes.'

Someone called her name in the brightly lit room behind her, and Lucy straightened, something like fear in her face. 'You'd better go before they come out here to find me,' she told him hurriedly, and glanced over her shoulder. 'The Queen must be leaving her chamber. I have to accompany her downstairs with the other ladies.'

'You'll be at the play?'

She turned back, and now she seemed to be smiling. 'Of course,' she whispered. 'But you must go, Will. If you're seen here, you might be mistaken for a spy.'

That was no exaggeration, he thought wryly. The company had been closely searched tonight on entering the palace, their play chests thrown open for scrutiny, even their carts turned over. On the streets of London, the muttered talk on everyone's lips was the continuing ferment of Catholics in England, and the threat of a war with Spain. People were nervous. And in such times, for him to be caught climbing a wall in the Queen's Privy Garden would be tantamount to treason.

Nonetheless, Will could not seem to make his feet move from the ledge. 'Don't go,' he told her, and he reached up as far as his arm would stretch. 'Not yet.'

'I must,' she replied. That half-smile again. Yet she did not move either, looking down at his hand near to hers, so close.

'Lucy Morgan.' He took pleasure in her name, willing her to reach out and touch him. 'Please.'

Her eyes met his, pleading with him in return. 'I can't. If anyone should catch us . . .'

Will said nothing but continued to hold out his hand, his gaze locked with hers.

'Lucy!' the woman called shrilly from inside the room. Her voice was angry now, insistent. 'Her Majesty is waiting! What are you doing out there?'

Lucy leaned perilously far over the balcony. She was tall and must have been standing on tiptoe; even so it was a stretch. Her hand met his for a second, just a brush of gloved fingertips across his. Then she was gone.

The balcony was empty.

Will dropped lightly to the grass, resettled the filthy player's cloak about his shoulders and hurried to retrieve the abandoned play roll. How much time had passed up there on the balcony ledge? His eyes skimmed the lines, but his mind could not seem to take them in. He was so on edge after that strange meeting. Lucy Morgan. The object of his secret desire for most of his boyhood. And he had met her again here in London, still beautiful, still bewitching. Too bewitching for a married man, he thought.

'Master Shakespeare?'

Startled, he looked up from studying his part. But it was only one of the play boys, calling his name up and down the cloisters. He gestured to the boy and quickly rolled up the lines, sticking them under his arm.

Of course, the Queen must have descended by now, which meant the play would be starting. He had no speech until at least fifteen minutes in, but it would be best to get himself behind the screen that would serve as their backstage area in the Queen's audience hall.

Will slipped out of the Privy Garden as quietly as he had gone in. He knew his part. Just as well, too, for all he seemed able to think about was Lucy Morgan, her gaze meeting his as they touched fingertips.

Guiltily, he thought for a moment of his wife. Quiet, slender, pale-skinned Anne.

He had left her back at his father's home in Stratford,

nursing their child at the breast and helping his mother run the household. It was not a happy remembrance. Anne had been furious when he'd told her he must leave, that London was where he had to live if he wished to make his fortune. She could not be made to understand that he had no desire to follow his father into the glover's trade. Whenever Will thought of his father's house in Stratford, he remembered the stench of leathers soaking in lidded buckets along the outside passage or in the backyard, and his nose twitched in disgust.

That was no life for him, a life of tanning and stretching skins. Not when he could live like this instead, paid to step out on the boards and perform to a lively audience day after day. To laugh at the heckles of the crowd and sometimes do a little jig at the end for ha'pennies. He was even paid to copy out and improve the plays from the play chest, for he was no mean copyist and had soon learned a trick or two from watching so many performances himself. One day he would no longer be a jobbing player, working where he could, but a full member of a noble company like the Queen's Men. Perhaps, like James Burbage, he might even be master of his own company.

Leaving Stratford, he had promised Anne he would not lie with the whores and the slatterns, but keep himself clean and faithful only to her. And he had never once been tempted. Not even by the merchants' wives who hung about the theatre doors after the plays finished, disguised with veils or hoods, eager to take players into their beds. The wives were clean and pretty enough, it was true, though faithless to their husbands. He had to confess he had looked once or twice at the younger ones with interest, even if he had never gone with them.

Lucy Morgan was no whore. Yes, she was one of the Queen's ladies now, and some of them were of easy virtue. Will was certain though that Lucy had never played the games that ladies loved at court, lewd games they called Gentlemen's Fingers or Hunt the Lady's Purse back in Warwickshire.

How he desired her! But would a court beauty like Lucy ever consider taking a rough country player as her lover?

Will listened for his cue behind the wooden screen, trying not to think of his absent wife, Anne Hathaway. His conscience pricked him. What of his marriage vows made before God, did they mean nothing?

With difficulty, he pushed Anne's face to the back of his mind. His wife was half a world away in Warwickshire, and he had kept his word to her until now. He still loved Anne. But he was in London now, and what she did not know could not hurt her.

Eight

LUCY GATHERED HER SKIRTS AND HURRIED DOWN THE STAIRS after the Queen's entourage. She caught the eye of her friend Catherine rising from her knees as the Queen passed on through the hall, but had no time to do more than smile. She knew Queen Elizabeth would be furious that she had not been there when the party began to descend, as Her Majesty enjoyed showing Lucy off at these public occasions, the Moorish singer who served now as one of her ladies-in-waiting. Nor did Lucy think the other ladies would have made an excuse for her absence. Most of them hated her, for she was not of the English nobility like them, but descended from an African king. Of course, she had no proof of noble descent. It was merely what she had been told by her guardian as a child, after being orphaned and left in his care. Master Goodluck had barely noticed her as a child, leaving her with his sister's family, all of whom were acrobats and performers, until she was old enough to be around players and theatre men.

And now her attention had been caught – and held – by another player!

For shame, she told herself angrily. Those wild early days with Master Goodluck were long over. She was in the

Queen's service now, and not able to please herself for a husband. The Queen would have her severely chastised if she knew about that snatched conversation in the garden.

Master Shakespeare.

Where was he now? Among the players? She could not see him there. But then, she had only just left him in the Privy Garden. He would be on his way to join them, reading from his play roll, no doubt, their meeting forgotten.

For a moment, she had looked into Will Shakespeare's eyes and remembered every horrific detail of the time at Kenilworth when they had last seen each other. That had been the night of the attempted assassination of Queen Elizabeth, when her beloved Tom had died. They were memories she had shut away in her heart, and seeing Will had brought them all tumbling back.

How old had he been when they'd last met? Eleven?

Lucy herself had been little better than a girl at Kenilworth that year, and like a fool had fallen helplessly in love with Tom Black. Of African descent like herself, Tom had been such a handsome young man, one of Leicester's most trusted grooms.

Tom had loved her too, she felt sure of it. Yet his love had killed him. Trying to protect her and the Queen from death, Tom had met a brutal end himself, mauled viciously by an assassin's bear, then run through with Italian steel and left to die below the castle walls. And for what? Most of the Italians involved in the assassination attempt had never been caught, and the Queen had never mentioned Tom's death afterwards. He had died to save them, yet it seemed to Lucy that Elizabeth had accepted his sacrifice as though it meant nothing to her.

Lucy took up her customary position near Queen Elizabeth's throne and sank into a deep curtsy as Her Majesty seated herself on the high dais.

When she straightened, Lucy looked across at the

assembled players from under discreetly lowered eyelids. She was waiting for Will Shakespeare to make his appearance. She was also aware of the Queen watching her suspiciously, and was careful not to look too eager for the play to begin.

Queen Elizabeth had been in a foul mood for weeks. Her bouts of toothache came and went, sometimes leaving her weak and miserable, sometimes resulting in such a temper that none of her ladies dared approach her for fear of being slapped or dismissed. Dark days at court, and darker still for those with secrets to hide. Lucy never knew what mood her mistress would be in when she was called to sing or dance before her. But one thing was for sure: the Queen could sniff out a secret at a thousand paces. If any of her unmarried ladies appeared late to their duties, breathless, their hair untidy or their gowns awry, they would be immediately questioned under suspicion of ungodly behaviour. Lucy shuddered at the thought of undergoing any such rigorous examination herself, especially if she was ever brought before the Queen's stern spymaster, Sir Francis Walsingham. She had known Sir Francis since her earliest days in the Queen's service, and had not yet earned his disapproval. Yet Walsingham still had the power to terrify her with a single look.

The play had begun. In the gallery, the musicians were playing some soft Italian air. The bearded players strode to and fro, speaking their lines in a stilted fashion and flourishing their swords. A young boy stepped out from behind the wooden screen at the back of the hall, dressed in a long gown, and began to sing.

'Signorina,' came a discreet whisper beside her. It was Mendoza, the Spanish ambassador. He searched her face as she turned towards him. 'You do not smile tonight, Signorina Morgan. Does it displease you, the subject of this play?'

Mendoza. A man to avoid, if the rumours were true. She forced a smile. 'No, Signor Mendoza. The play does not offend me. I do not even know what it is about.'

The Spanish ambassador smiled in return, though he must have thought her a simpleton. His dark hair glistened with oil. He took her hand and kissed it in an exaggerated way, his head bent. 'It is about love, Signorina Morgan. It is a play about lovers.'

Lucy waited a decent interval before pulling her hand away. Horrid man. But she must hide her distaste for him. That was how the courtly game was played. 'Then the play cannot offend me, sir. There is no better subject for a play than love.'

'You would not prefer a history, or a biblical tale?'

'Not at court, sir. This is too intimate a space for such epic subjects. But we must be quiet.' People had turned to stare at their whispered conversation. Her skin crawled. She did not want to be thought his 'special friend'. Or worse, his accomplice. Lucy laid a finger on her lips and moved a little away from him. 'The song is finishing and we will spoil the tale by talking.'

He shrugged and turned to watch the play. Lucy saw Sir Francis Walsingham watching her from the doorway and schooled her expression to reveal nothing. There had been rumours flying about the court in recent weeks that the Spanish ambassador had exceeded his authority and the Queen was not pleased. Little surprise that Mendoza should have turned to her. She too was an outsider, never quite accepted at court. But she had been careful not to smile too long at him, nor too warmly. Even a smile could be misinterpreted as conspiracy when directed at such a man.

Lucy heard Will's voice. That soft Warwickshire burr. He had stepped out from behind the screen, swaggering slightly, wrapped in a long fur-trimmed cloak he had gathered up and thrown over his arm, no trick of her imagining, but as real and solid as when she'd touched his hand in the garden.

It was strange to see Will as a player. She remembered him as a boy, that serious face set above a lanky body and thin legs. He had been as brave as any man twice his age, and intelligent too. Sharp eyes, and a sharper mind behind them. Now there was a neat pointed beard on the once-hairless chin, his chest and shoulders were broadening out, and his boy's high pitch had deepened. All in all, a man.

He had not lost his accent, though his voice was less countrified than the one he had used in the garden. Did Will Shakespeare fear to be mocked for his true self, for the green meadows and hills of Warwickshire that lay behind each word? The sound of his voice brought back Tom's face, his kiss, the way he had touched her one night in Lord Leicester's stables. If she had lain with Tom then, as he had asked . . .

Her eyes were suddenly wet. Lucy lifted a hand to dry them. No one must see her cry. She bent her head as though she had something in her eye, some irritating speck of dust. Not memories of a love she would rather forget.

Will was courting the young boy in a woman's hood and gown, kneeling to declare himself. But his eyes lifted to hers. Locked with them. Made his intentions known. For a guilty moment, she allowed herself to imagine Will Shakespeare touching her, and felt a sharp thrill that pierced her to the belly.

At once she was hot with shame. Tom had died to protect her. Now was she imagining another man in his place?

All her life she had heard women described by men as faithless, and had been determined not to prove so herself. Yet a young man had touched her hand tonight, and already she was dreaming herself in bed with him, her past love forgotten in the time it had taken for a man to whisper her name in the dark.

'Signorina?'

The scene had finished and the court was applauding the players. Mendoza was whispering to her again, his dark eyes keen on her face.

'You do not look well, Signorina Morgan. Allow me to have wine fetched.'

The Queen's voice broke across his whisper, shrill and demanding. Her toothache still paining her, no doubt. 'What is it? Is something amiss, Lucy?'

Danger prickled under her skin. 'Nothing, Your Majesty, I am merely a little warm.' She curtsied very low, not rising until she felt it was safe to do so. 'The room is so close.'

Elizabeth was not easily satisfied, of course. But she seemed to let it go, her eyes darting from Lucy's face to Mendoza's. 'Signor Mendoza, come and speak to me. Not to my ladies. Tell me what you think of this play. These lovers seem too young and unruly, too ready to ignore their parents. It displeases me. This scene takes place in Italy, we are to believe. Tell me, would such a free courtship be permitted in Spain?'

The Queen fell into rambling Spanish. The ambassador moved swiftly to her side, bowing and complimenting Elizabeth on her command of his language with many eloquent gestures. He was a player himself, Lucy thought drily. The theatricals stood frozen, glancing uncertainly at each other. They could not continue without the Queen's permission. The court held its breath and watched to see what would happen, some turning to consider Walsingham, who was still blocking the doorway, others looking for Leicester, who seemed to have drawn a little way off with the Captain of the Queen's Guards.

Her Majesty waved Mendoza silent with an impatient

hand. 'Yes, but when a rule has been laid down, and it is wilfully broken, what would the punishment be in Spain?'

'It would depend, Majesty, on whomever had made the rule.'

'If it was . . .' Elizabeth hesitated, and there seemed to be cunning behind her words, and malice too, her small, dark eyes narrowed on the ambassador's face, '. . . the King of Spain, let's say, who had made this rule, and it was broken, what then would be the punishment?'

Mendoza must have felt the trap tighten about him, for he looked uneasily around the court. His gaze lighted on Walsingham first, at the door, then moved slowly through the assembled courtiers until he had found both Lord Burghley and Lord Leicester. He hesitated. 'I am not sure what the punishment would be, Your Majesty.'

'Death, perhaps?'

A bead of sweat rolled slowly down the ambassador's face. 'It would . . .' He cleared his throat and began again. 'The severity of the punishment must depend on the severity of the crime, surely?'

Elizabeth pretended to ponder this. 'You believe so?'

'A great prince is always merciful, Your Majesty.'

She nodded, and played thoughtfully with her ostrich-feather fan. 'You think exile would be the answer, then, rather than imprisonment and execution? Dismissal from court?'

He knew he was in deep now. The fear on his face could not be hidden from the court, and nor could his guilt. Lucy looked from the Queen's easy cruelty, playing with him as a cat plays with a mouse before she deals the final crushing blow, to Mendoza's tense, sweat-riven face, and almost felt sorry for the man. But she too was afraid. For whatever the Queen's spies had found out about Mendoza, for Elizabeth to destroy the Spanish ambassador in so public a manner could mean only one thing. She intended war with Spain.

Mendoza broke. He bowed stiffly, pretending to be in pain and clutching at his stomach. 'Forgive me, Your Majesty. I would not offend you but I am taken ill. May I crave your leave to depart?'

Elizabeth's lips tightened to a thin line. But she did not deny his request. Her hand cupped her jaw, rubbed at it rhythmically. Toothache again? 'You may leave us, Signor Mendoza. Only do not stray far from your rooms. Sir Francis Walsingham has some small matter he would speak to you about when you are in better health.'

Still bowing, Mendoza walked backwards from her presence, only straightening when he reached the door, which was still blocked by Walsingham's dark figure.

The two men looked at each other, one in fury and terror, the other calmly and with intent. Then Mendoza pushed past with a muttered apology, and Walsingham turned to watch him go. The Spanish ambassador's two swarthy servants hurried after their master, bowing to the Queen and the court as they left, one losing his cap in his hurry to escape.

Walsingham looked up at the Queen on the dais. He did not smile, yet Lucy knew that he was satisfied – perhaps even amused – by Mendoza's reaction. Elizabeth gave the slightest of nods, and Walsingham bowed deeply, then left the chamber himself.

Lord Burghley struck the floor with his cane. Another player. 'Let the play continue!'

The courtiers, who had been holding their breath throughout this fascinating exchange, began to shift and whisper among themselves, a noise like the Thames rising at flood time along the banks. Accompanied by this agitated hiss of voices, the players sprang into movement, like living statues released from a spell. The scene was hurriedly changed, and Lucy found herself looking at Will Shakespeare on his knees in a dark cell, pretending to weep as he cradled the head of his 'dead' lover on his lap – though the boy twitched and rolled an eye at the audience, so that even Elizabeth laughed, the pathos of the scene ruined.

After the play was done, and while the players were still bowing under the court's applause, the Queen summoned Lucy with a crooked finger.

'Deliver this to Lord Leicester after the court has dispersed,' Elizabeth whispered behind her fan, leaning over to hand Lucy a folded slip of paper. There was a slight flush on her white-painted cheeks and she seemed excited. 'Discreetly.'

'Yes, Your Majesty.'

The players were still bowing. Lucy met Will's intent gaze as he straightened, and looked quickly away. She did not want Elizabeth to sense an intrigue where there was none. She had known Will once, and loved him like a little brother. Now that he was grown to a man, there was no longer any room in her heart for him. Not if she wished to continue in the service of the Virgin Queen.

'Enough!' Elizabeth barked, and the court fell instantly silent, watching her.

The Queen rose from her throne, gripped Lucy's shoulder, and began to make her way down from the dais. The court fell to its knees before her in a rustle of silk, heads respectfully bowed. Elizabeth swayed slowly to the door, an odd grimace on her face, her narrow lips drawn back from her teeth, and Lucy knew that her mistress was in pain. Not only her old foe, toothache, but now a terrible ulcer on her leg.

Her ulcer pained Elizabeth more and more these days, and there seemed little her physicians could do to alleviate her suffering. Still, she liked to try and dance most evenings, gamely attempting the volta and the galliard. Lucy did not enjoy watching. It felt cruel.

At the door, Elizabeth released Lucy's shoulder. 'Lady Helena!' The red-haired woman hurried forward and took Lucy's place as the Queen's support. Elizabeth's sharp voice echoed along the torchlit corridor towards the stairs to her apartments. 'What did you think of the play, Lady Helena? Those are the Queen's Men, I am told. A stout company who seek to carry my fame about the country like a banner. What do you say to that? Shall we kick them down the stairs for their bad playing, Helena, or put them in the stocks? "The Queen's Fools" is a better name for them. They would make better fools than players. As you saw, even Signor Mendoza's stomach was turned by their antics. And Spaniards are famed for their strong stomachs the world over, so the dish must have been very much to his disliking.'

The court began to follow the Queen, filing out of the room as the sound of her laughter floated back towards them. Lucy turned, expecting to have to deal with young Shakespeare again. But the players had vanished, the screen and scenery already being dismantled by sturdy men in rough clothing who whistled as they went about their business.

The paper was still in her hand. It was as well Shakespeare had gone, she told herself. She had no time to think about men. Nor would she wish to drag Will into danger by encouraging his smiles and meaningful looks.

Lord Leicester had stayed behind to speak to Lord Burghley. She caught his eye, and soon he left the elder statesman and came over to where she was waiting.

'Mistress Morgan,' he said, and bowed his head. She saw a flicker of unease in his face and knew he was uncertain of her news. 'I saw you in conversation with the Queen.'

'She charged me with this for you, my lord,' Lucy murmured, and passed him the slip of paper.

The Earl of Leicester unfolded the note, read the Queen's short message at a glance, then slipped the paper into the leather purse on his belt. He drew a sharp, exultant breath, and Lucy could see relief in his face. 'Tell your mistress, "Yes."'

'"Yes", my lord?'

Leicester nodded, and laid a hand on her shoulder. Lucy could feel him trembling through the thick silk of her sleeve, and looked up at the earl in surprise.

Then she remembered Elizabeth's excitement, more like a young girl's than a middle-aged queen's. Whatever hurts Leicester had done her in the past, Queen Elizabeth still looked to him for counsel and friendship, and Leicester seemed to feel the same. He had aged rapidly in the last few years, while so frequently exiled from court for his marriage to Lettice Knollys. Indeed, it was difficult to reconcile the grey hair and the lines on his face with the powerful man in his prime that Lucy remembered from her first years at court.

'It's good news, Lucy,' Leicester whispered in her ear. 'She asks me to her chamber tonight. Elizabeth must have forgiven me at last.'

That seemed unlikely. But Lucy managed a smile. 'I am glad to hear it, my lord.'

He straightened and his gaze met hers directly, not flinching from the raw truth of his situation. There was pain and hesitancy in Leicester's face, along with an optimism she recognized, a rekindling of the youthful ambition many considered he had laid aside when he chose to cross the Queen by marrying her rival.

'Lettice must not know,' he reminded her urgently. 'If it should come to my wife's ears that I have visited the Queen in secret . . .'

'I shall say nothing, my lord,' she assured him, and allowed him to draw her aside as two noblemen of the court passed them in velvet doublets and lavishly fur-trimmed robes, their curiosity obvious.

Lucy had come to realize in her time at court what a fragile thing reputation was, and how easily it could be lost – overnight, in some cases. Those who had the Queen's ear could do anything, it seemed, and escape unscathed. But those who lost her confidence were quickly shunned and cast out beyond the brilliant inner circle that surrounded her. It seemed the earl was willing to sacrifice even his wife's trust in order to regain power.

'Come to the west door later and I will let you into her rooms unseen, my lord. There are always guards, but they'll hold their tongues.'

'Thank you.' He moved swiftly away before their conversation became too conspicuous.

Hurrying to relieve herself, she left the room. Rounding a corner in the cloisters, darkened between torch brackets, she stopped. What was this? Signor Mendoza at the end of the corridor in whispered conversation with a cloaked man. Remembering the Spanish ambassador's rage earlier at the Queen's snub, she flattened herself into the nearest doorway and waited for him to move on.

Mendoza was nodding, his head bent. He accepted something from the cloaked man, glanced at it briefly, then hid it away under his own cloak.

A letter?

Lucy held her breath as the ambassador's head swung, questing up and down the poorly lit corridor. He did not appear to have noticed her.

The two men spoke, their voices so low she could not catch what was being said. Then she heard someone coming the other way, their footsteps loud in the echoing cloisters.

Mendoza turned without bowing and hurried up the stairs to his right. The cloaked man continued along the cloisters towards her. He passed without comment, perhaps not even seeing her in the alcove. His hood was drawn down, face hidden from view, even his hands gloved as he grasped the edges of his fur-trimmed cloak. She peered at him as he passed, but could not tell who he was.

Whoever had been coming passed into a chamber further along the corridor. The door clanged shut. She was alone in the flickering torchlight.

Lucy stared in the direction of the now-vanished cloaked man. There had been something naggingly familiar about his walk, the way he held himself. But with the cloaked man's head and face hidden, Lucy could not think what had made her suddenly so certain she knew him.

Nine

ELIZABETH WAITED AS THOUGH FOR THE CALL OF AN executioner, back straight, propped up in the cushioned chair by the fireside. She was beginning to regret having decided to see Robert tonight. It was chilly, although the flaming logs kept out the worst of the draughts in this old palace, and she was in pain. To see Robert tonight would only remind him of the difference between her and Lettice. His red-haired wife – waiting at home with their babe – was so much younger than Elizabeth. It was a comparison she could not bear to make herself, and would never have voiced to him or any of her women. Yet how could she avoid it? Lettice was younger and therefore more desirable than she was.

Elizabeth's hands curled into fists, her nails cutting into her palms. How she longed to flay Lettice's face with them until she screamed for mercy! But she was a queen and must bear this pain in silence. To act upon her jealousy would be to lower her in the eyes of the people, who remembered only too well the tyrannies of her father.

What would her father have done? Elizabeth considered the axe lovingly, then shrugged the temptation away. To execute Lettice she would have to execute Robert too, and that she could never do.

Not her old friend. Not the man she loved.

She sighed and looked about the high tapestried walls with a creeping sense of horror. She remembered Whitehall from her childhood as a place of lights and music, of astonishing bustle and colour. Now Cardinal Wolsey's once-grand palace was falling apart, its court apartments degrading as the years rolled by. That was how her body felt, too.

She must ask Cecil about renovations to Whitehall. It was absurd to let the place go like this. Though they could hardly spare the money from the royal coffers. If there was a war with Spain . . .

The door to her chambers stood open. Lady Helena was in the doorway, staring at her.

Elizabeth realized that she had fallen asleep. She stirred groggily and wiped her mouth, at once on the defensive. 'Yes? What is it?'

'You cried out, Your Majesty.'

'Nonsense.' Elizabeth straightened in the chair, and signalled her lady-in-waiting to fetch her cup from the table. 'Yes, give me wine, I need to wet my throat. The fire is smoking badly tonight. Are the other women abed?'

'Yes, Your Majesty.'

'Good.' Elizabeth drank deeply, suddenly filled with a roaring thirst, then handed the cup back to Helena. She smiled. Felt her jaw with her hand, gingerly. 'My toothache has gone. Quite gone. A miracle. Do you believe in miracles, Helena?'

'I believe the Good Lord provides, Your Majesty.'

'You may be right. I am not so sure. But the pain has gone, nonetheless. See that I am not disturbed again tonight. Whatever you may hear. Is that clear?'

'Yes, Your Majesty.'

'I will call for you when I wish to be readied for bed. Now leave me and shut the door behind you.'

Lady Helena curtsied and backed out of the room, her head bowed. Then she stopped at the door with a startled expression, turning back. 'Your Majesty . . .'

Elizabeth found herself irritable again. 'What now?'

Helena moved back against the wall to allow Robert to enter the room. 'The Earl of Leicester, Your Majesty.'

He came in bowing, splendid in a silver doublet and black hose, his feathered cap in his hand.

Elizabeth suppressed a smile. So he had come. A married man with a young son at home, and he had come visiting her after midnight!

When Lettice heard of this visit – and Elizabeth was convinced the new Countess of Leicester must have her own eyes and ears at court – she would finally understand how poor Amy Robsart had felt. The forgotten wife left at home in the country, never permitted to set foot at court, while Elizabeth enjoyed her husband's company freely.

Still, it would not do to indulge him. Whatever he might have been to her in the past, Robert was her servant now and must know his place. Or be taught it.

'You may enter,' Elizabeth told him unnecessarily, for the saucy man was already on his knee before her, and the door had closed discreetly behind Lady Helena.

'Your Majesty,' he murmured, kissing her outstretched hand.

'Robert.'

She waited until Robert was beginning to look uncomfortable, then gestured him to rise. 'You have news for me? Some business that would not wait?'

Now that he had her attention, Robert seemed to hesitate, standing before her awkward as a boy in his stiff court finery, a gold-hilted dress sword by his side. These days he looked every inch the statesman, perhaps aware of how his reputation had been tarnished by his ill-advised marriage to Lettice Knollys, her husband, Essex, barely dead a year before he took her for his bride. And with a sword boldly at his belt? Before the Queen, no less. Not so whipped and cowed as some would think, then. Perhaps she would do well to send Robert to Ireland or some other heathenish place, where he would get the chance to serve her as a soldier, not merely a courtier. He would need to remain abroad a year or two, of course. Such a lengthy absence from court would hurt. But it would hurt his wife more.

'Your Majesty, I wish to beg your forgiveness and throw myself on your mercy.'

Elizabeth felt her hands clench into claws again. She forced herself to relax them. She was his queen. She must not allow him to witness such emotion.

Let's hear it, then. Her smile was careful. 'Indeed?'

'It is the matter of my marriage to the Countess of Essex that brings me here tonight, Your Grace.'

'Ancient history,' she replied with a shrug, pretending to dismiss the whole affair as a matter of no interest to her.

'Yet it haunts my every step at court. I know you hold it against me still,' Robert insisted doggedly, and met her gaze at last. 'Elizabeth . . .'

'You forget yourself, Lord Leicester!'

'Forgive me.' Robert dropped to one knee again and bowed his head. 'Your Majesty.'

An unexpected show of deference. Humility, even. Mollified by this, Elizabeth settled back in her chair and tried to regain some composure. So her one-time favourite had not come here tonight in a spirit of sulky defiance. She listened to the spitting crackle of logs in the fireplace, and heard the guards being changed in the antechamber. For a few moments there was the scrape of feet on the stairs, followed by a rumble of male voices through the wall.

What was that smell? Logs smouldering or horse dung on his boots? Even now, elevated to an earl, he still smelt of the stable.

'Tell me how Mendoza does,' she ordered him. 'And stand up. You look ridiculous down there.'

Stiffly, Robert straightened. There was humiliation in his face. Good, let him learn his lesson well. She signalled him to draw up a stool, watching as he lowered himself to it, for all the world like a small boy.

'Sit yourself down and speak to me of this damn Spanish ambassador. We will talk of your affairs later. For now, the only matter that properly concerns me and England is Spain. That, and the miracle of my toothache vanishing.'

'I am glad to hear it,' he murmured. A sudden twinkle in his eye. 'Except that you will not need me to hold your hand against the pain.'

A tacit reminder of how close they had been in the past. Perhaps not as humbled as she'd thought. Or the saucy knave considered himself a forgiven man, and was heading straight back to where they had left off.

'Spain?'

Robert smiled at the tart reply. He spoke of the investigation against the ambassador while she watched him, noting the shadows like bruises under his eyes, a new tension about his mouth. So fatherhood had not served him as well as he had supposed. Perhaps his wife was neither obedient nor malleable, and forever irked his heart out, demanding to be back at court. Such were the rumours she had heard. But to hear his dissatisfaction with Lettice from Robert's own lips, that would be gratifying indeed. Not that she was likely to wring any such confession from him. But it was a happy thought to entertain.

He stirred from his stool, rising to stoke the fire. I did

110

not tell you to stand, she thought irritably, staring at the back of his grey head, but said nothing.

'We cannot arrest him, of course. Not the Spanish ambassador.'

'But we can humiliate him. Mendoza will be expelled from court and escorted to Dover by a troop of soldiers. He and his men will be put on a boat for Spain. His disgrace will be assured on his return there.'

'There will be a war with Spain. King Philip only waits for such an excuse. You understand, Your Majesty?'

'I am not a fool.'

Robert smiled, coming back to his stool. He settled there drily, glancing up at her as if to say, 'Yes, I am your dog.' She knew such humility would not last. But it was a start.

'Indeed you are not, Your Majesty.'

'I have wanted to avoid war, yes. Struggled and fought for years to avoid it,' Elizabeth admitted. 'But conflict with Spain is unavoidable. I see that now. I am reconciled to it. What bothers me is that our shores are not yet proof against invasion.'

He nodded sombrely. 'It is a problem.'

Elizabeth played with her ruby ring. She frowned, watching the dark red gemstone flash in the firelight. 'They tell me Spain has many great warships, and to spare. We have our own fleet, yes, but what if they should fail? England must be able to defend herself against the invading Spanish. There must be some way for those along the coast to give the alarm if even one enemy ship should be sighted. And if they land before the army can reach them, what then? Every town and village between London and the south coast must be defended by stout burghers ready to die for England. Aye, and their sons too.' She looked at him. 'Though how such a thing can ever be achieved, given the weakly state of our coffers, the Lord only knows.'

'Do you wish me to put these issues before the Council, Your Majesty?'

'Not yet,' she decided. 'Let us dispose of Mendoza first. Philip will bluster, no doubt, and we can deal with that. Then it will come to war.' She hesitated, glancing at him. 'Perhaps I should not leave the city this summer?'

'And risk the plague?' He shook his head urgently. 'Let me counsel you against such a dangerous course. England needs her queen safe and well. There are other matters first, before Spain, that need our attention. The Catholic cause grows stronger every month. Priests trained to avoid our searches are coming over in droves from France and the Low Countries. This threat is not an idle one. Each priest that enters England will convert others to their cause, sow the seeds of rebellion among the Catholics already here, and drag us closer to an open and bloody war against our own people.'

Her mouth twitched. She remembered only too well the burnings of Protestants that had taken place in market towns throughout England during her sister Mary's reign. She did not wish to make an enemy of the common people as her sister had done, yet how else to control these Catholics? They were like a disease spreading through a healthy body and destroying it before her eyes. Left to thrive and multiply, the Catholics would bring England to her knees, and not in prayer.

'I will not have us brought to civil war.'

'You may have no choice in the matter, Your Majesty. But there will be a war, even if it does not come yet. Spain is not afraid to engage us in conflict. It only waits to make its position stronger. Meanwhile, the greatest threat still lies at home.'

'Meaning?'

Her sharp question brought his wandering gaze back to her face. 'Mary Stuart, Queen of Scots. You hold the most important piece in this game, yet you hesitate to use it against your enemies.'

Elizabeth stiffened. 'My cousin is a queen anointed, as I am. To execute her would be to condone the disposal of a prince from her throne.'

'Begging your pardon, Your Majesty, to execute Queen Mary would be to make England safe from the nearest of these Catholic plots.'

Elizabeth stared into the fire, which was dying now. The heat of the red-gold embers seemed to mock her chilled body. 'She is my cousin, Robert.'

He nodded without speaking, then stood abruptly. He swung the cloak from his own shoulders and laid it about her own. 'The room grows cold. Shall I call for more fuel?'

'No, I must get to bed and sleep.' She looked up at him, still leaning over her. His face was haggard, wearing his years heavily. 'But what of you?'

'I shall retire soon, Your Majesty.'

'I meant, how are you? You are so often from court these days.' Elizabeth hesitated, then forced the difficult words out, her smile thin. 'Marriage and a comfortable home in the country suits you better than bouge of court, perhaps?'

He was surprised. Then wary. 'Not at all, Your Majesty. I am content to serve you and England as Your Majesty decrees. If I am away too often, I pray you forgive the duties of . . . of a new father.'

She waved him to sit down again on his stool. Robert complied, the silence between them awkward. He looked once more like a schoolboy in fear of a reprimand from the schoolmaster, crouched on the stool in his fine silver doublet, playing with the hilt of his sword, his face averted.

'I have heard of this child,' she managed, then cleared her throat. 'You call him the Noble Imp?'

Robert looked up eagerly at this. There was a new brightness to his eyes that no talk of Spain and the execution of princes could have put there. Elizabeth thought of a hound's head going up at its master's whistle, and almost smiled.

'Yes, Your Majesty.'

'And,' she ventured, 'the mother does well?'

'In good health, Your Majesty. The child, too. Little Lord Denbigh will make a fine boy and a good servant to Your Majesty.'

Her eyes met his, and she saw him break. His face changed, just for an instant, and she almost put out a hand to him, so clear was the pain on his face.

'Robert?'

He buried his face in his hands, his voice muffled. His feathered red velvet cap fell to the floor. 'Forgive me. I beg you to forgive me.'

She did not move, could not speak. She had never seen him so broken. All her anger evaporated, leaving nothing but a terrible sadness in its place.

'Y . . . Your Majesty, it was wrong of me to marry Lettice w . . . without your consent . . .' His stammering lurched to a halt. 'Elizabeth . . . please.'

He looked up, and his eyes met hers at last, bloodshot. His words were half-excuse, half-apology. 'She gave me a son,' he whispered.

Her hands were shaking. She laid them in her lap, not looking at him any longer.

He was crying. God in heaven, he was crying like a boy! Elizabeth tried to think of the last time she had wept so passionately, and could not remember. There was only a chill numbness inside where womanly tears had once been. That was the price of kingship.

Robert came to his knees before her, and laid his head in her lap like a supplicant, nudging her hands.

For a moment Elizabeth said nothing.

Then she placed a hand on his head and stroked his silver-streaked hair. 'I know,' she murmured gently. 'I always knew she would.'

Ten

WE ARE BETRAYED. MEET ME UNDER THE SIGN OF THE wool merchants, River Lane, sundown.

Goodluck tucked the coded note back inside his jacket and peered out into the rain. The needle-thin alley in which he had taken up position was opposite the entrance to the old, high-gabled wool merchants' building. The sky was gloomy, the sun on the point of dropping below the horizon. Most of the wool workers had gone home for the day, only the turnkeys left behind to lock the shutters and secure the gates for the night, shadowy figures moving occasionally in the interior. Rain had been falling heavily, and the mud-riven streets were all but deserted now, only a few determined souls braving the sluice of open ditches to reach their single-storey makeshift dwellings along the waterside. This close to the river, mud slides were common in bad weather, the bankside lanes too treacherous to attempt at night.

Receiving the note that morning, Goodluck had recognized the hand at once. The thick slanted flourishes belonged to Sos, the little Greek with whom he had been working since returning to London.

The code was good. Even their new pass sign had been

sketched on one corner of the note, leaving him in no doubt that it was genuine.

We are betrayed.

For the first time since returning to English shores, Goodluck experienced a flicker of fear. The Catholics were not this organized. Or never had been before. This was something new. It felt personal, aimed solely at him and his men, as though he himself had been identified as a target.

Up at the east end of the lane, a handful of rain-sodden men wearing the Queen's livery gathered under the hunched, mossed column of an ancient stone cross, sunk so far into the mud at an angle that it looked more like a milestone. One of the men was giving orders, pointing the others towards the nearest buildings.

Gloomily, the bell of a nearby church began to toll the hour. Through a darkened haze of rain, Goodluck saw a familiar cloaked figure approaching from the west end.

It was Sos.

The short, wiry Greek was staggering through the muddy sluice as though drunk. His hands were held out before him, his face hidden by the deep cowl of his hooded cloak.

For a moment, Goodluck hesitated, fearing a trap.

Then the Greek's voice, muffled but still recognizable, called out, 'Goodluck!'

Goodluck stepped out of the alleyway to greet him, but the laughter died on his lips when he saw that his friend's wrists had been bound together with frayed rope. Below the drenched hood, Sos's face was contorted with pain. There was blood on his lips, and the whites of his eyes were showing.

'Sos!'

Gargling blood as he struggled to speak, Sos plunged forward, just missing Goodluck's outstretched arms and falling face-first into the mud. That was when Goodluck saw the black-handled knife between his friend's shoulder blades, buried up to the hilt.

There were shouts from the top of the lane. The Queen's men must have seen Sos fall. Goodluck saw three running towards him, pikes held out at a threatening angle.

Goodluck turned away at once and slipped through the open gateway to the wool merchants' warehouse. It was dark inside, only one man in sight, keys in hand, preparing to lock the gate.

'Hey! What do you think you're doing?'

Ignoring the man's shouts, Goodluck ran through the warehouse, keeping low behind stacks of untreated wool as he made for the light on the waterside.

Near the back of the warehouse, a row of high-sided wooden vats rose out of the darkness, blocking his way. Goodluck threaded a path between them, choking and covering his mouth with his sleeve. The acrid stench of the wool treatment stung his throat and eyes.

He grieved for the Greek, but there was nothing he could have done. The wound had been mortal.

He heard shouts behind him in the warehouse. Crouching lower, Goodluck hurried towards the gloomy patch of light coming from the waterside door.

If he was taken, it could take days for Walsingham to give the order for his release. Assuming the Queen's spymaster would even do so. Goodluck had not been received with much grace on his return from Italy, as though his story of capture and incarceration was considered suspect. It was a risk he did not wish to take, having only just escaped from a long stretch in an Italian prison.

To his frustration, there was an old man standing guard over the back door to the warehouse when he reached it. No doubt hearing the shouts and sounds of pursuit, the old fool had armed himself with an ancient pike. His grey beard swam up out of the gloom, his face pale but show-ing determination to do his duty.

'Hold fast there!' he called in a quavering voice, and shoved the pike in Goodluck's face.

'I've done you no harm, sir,' Goodluck murmured, opening his hands to show that they were empty. 'And I'm not here to steal. Just let me pass and there'll be no trouble.'

Even in the dim light, Goodluck could see hesitancy in the old man's face, and guessed he would prefer not to use the pike.

Then the damning cry went up behind him, 'Murderer!'

'He's back here!' the old man called out, then lunged at him with the rusty old pike, ripping Goodluck's cloak and almost catching him in the shoulder.

Cursing, Goodluck felt for the long dagger at his belt. But he did not draw it. He knew the odds were against him succeeding if he made a fight of it. His pursuers would be upon him before he had a chance to use the dagger. Flight was his best option. Hurriedly, he took advantage of the old man fumbling to pick up the pike, and ran past him to the open doorway on to the river.

It was almost dusk, and rain was still falling heavily. There were no boats tied up to the entrance, nowhere to jump to as he had hoped. Again, he cursed under his breath. There was nothing for it but to go down into the water.

Standing on the lip of the waterside doorway, Goodluck glanced down for an instant, trying to judge the height of the drop. The river lay at his feet, a dark mass rolling sluggishly under the constant pelter of rain, maybe twenty feet or more below.

He looked up and out across the River Thames. He knew how to swim, thank God, but it was a daunting stretch between him and the nearest spars of the south

119

bank. A few small craft bobbed at anchor in the distance. Rather closer to hand, drifting slowly under the nearside arch of the bridge, was an ancient river barge. Battered, and listing badly in the current, the barge looked as though it had seen service in old King Henry's time. Through the dark haze of rain, Goodluck could just make out a squat figure, wrapped up and hunched over the tiller. There could be little hope of help there.

'Murderer!'

Half-turning on the ledge at that cry, Goodluck felt something thrust between his shoulder blades with a terrible burning pain.

His knees crumbled as the cold metal twisted in the wound it had made, then was brutally withdrawn. Too late, he realized the old man was not as frail as he had looked.

With an agonized cry, Goodluck launched himself into mid-air and fell, quick as a stone, into the dark current below.

Eleven

Whitehall Palace, London, spring 1584

LUCY SANK TO HER KNEES BEFORE THE THRONE AND WAITED for the Queen to snap her fingers so she could rise. She enjoyed singing the English country songs best, for they suited her voice, but the old French ballad requested by the Queen for tonight's masque was also one of her favourites.

'Now for some dancing!' the Queen announced. She straightened her gold-fringed mask and clapped her hands at the bemused courtiers, seeming to forget that Lucy was still on her knees before her. 'Come, let us hear something livelier!'

Leicester bent to her ear, and Elizabeth made an angry gesture at his whisper, then rose to dance.

'Sir Christopher, I wish to lead the revels tonight,' the Queen said, and held out her hand to an elderly courtier in a stiff doublet of black and silver. Sir Christopher Hatton bowed low over it before guiding her down from the dais.

Hurriedly, the court musicians struck up a tune with horns and flutes, one single drum note keeping the beat, and the Queen began to dance. She raised her heavy skirts with one hand until a gold-encrusted slipper appeared,

121

tapping to the beat of the drum. Hatton bowed slowly, turned, and lifted her hand between them in a high salute. She swayed back and forth in the dance, finally allowing Hatton to lead her round the circle of admiring courtiers, rather like a horse at market being shown off to prospective buyers.

Cautiously, her knees aching on the cold stone, Lucy raised her head and peered through the slanted eyeholes of her mask at Lord Leicester.

Leicester gave a shrug. She could not see his expression under the black mask, but his fist was clenched in anger on his sword hilt. He glared across at the Queen, who was apparently too busy dancing with Hatton to notice, and gestured Lucy to rise.

Staring at the dancers, Lucy wondered what she could have done now to incur the Queen's displeasure. She tried to school her expression not to show her concern, but it was impossible. Her friend Catherine sidled up through the crowd and squeezed her arm.

'Don't pay it any mind,' her friend whispered in her ear, leading Lucy away from the dancing. Reaching the back wall of the chamber, she stopped to adjust Lucy's mask, which did not seem to fit properly and kept slipping off. 'Gossip has it that it's not just the toothache that irks her these days. Some say the Queen's been bleeding for weeks and is in a foul temper. Soon she'll be too old for child-bearing, and that'll bring an end to all the handsome young foreign princes coming to court her.'

'Hush, Cathy,' Lucy cautioned her, though she could not help smiling at her friend's wicked gossip. 'Someone might hear you.'

'No one can hear us.' Catherine pressed a cup of wine into Lucy's hand. 'Look, drink this and cheer up. You've been gloomy for ages. What is it? Still dreaming of poor dead Tom back in Warwickshire?'

Lucy drank some wine. It felt heavy and strong, tingling against her tongue. 'No,' she defended herself. 'I was thinking of my guardian, Master Goodluck. I sent him a letter two weeks ago, asking his advice, and he has not written back.'

Guiltily, she realized that she had not thought of Tom Black for ages. Not since that strange night when she had seen Will Shakespeare in the Queen's garden. It was as though seeing the boy again – a man now, and grown more handsome than she could have imagined – had erased Tom Black from her mind.

'Good,' Catherine said pointedly. 'It's about time you stopped mourning poor Tom. It's been years since he died, and you've never even looked at another man since. As for Master Goodluck, he'll be in some scrape or other, and will no doubt send you word once he's out of it. Besides, I've something exciting to tell you.'

Lucy looked at her suspiciously. Her friend's eyes were glittering oddly behind the mask.

'What are you up to this time?' she demanded, then lowered her voice at Catherine's instinctive protest. It was always important not to be overheard at court. 'Come on, what news is this? You've been planning something for weeks. I can always tell when you've some new mischief in hand.'

'It's Oswald.'

Lucy sighed at the name. She had never met Oswald, but had heard of him often enough from Catherine. He was the eldest son of one of her father's neighbours back in Norfolk, and completely besotted with Catherine, by the sound of it. 'Not Oswald again.' She shook her head. 'It's no use trying to see him, you only just returned from Norfolk. You'll need special permission to leave court again so soon, and you'll never get it, not with the summer progress so close at hand.'

Catherine grabbed at Lucy's hand and drew it to her belly, which felt curiously hard and rounded under the folds of her skirts. 'I won't need permission now,' she hissed in her ear. 'Feel that bump? Oswald wrote me yesterday. He knows about the baby and says we're to be married at once. I'm leaving court tomorrow and going back to Norfolk to be with him.'

Lucy was aghast. 'A child? Out of wedlock? But you'll be punished once they find out.'

'They won't find out,' Catherine said, and smirked from beneath her little white eye-mask. 'I've told the steward my father is dying and I've to go home at once. Once there, I'll be married straightaway and that'll be that. I'm not like you. I'm not important. No one will miss me or care if I never come back to court.'

'I'll care,' Lucy said thinly. 'You're my only friend here.'

Catherine hugged her. 'I'll write every month.'

'It won't be the same.'

'It can't be helped. Not now.' Catherine kissed her on the lips. 'You must see that I have to marry him.'

Lucy closed her eyes. 'Oh, Cathy.'

'You must come and visit me in Norfolk once the baby is born. I'll be bored to death in the country. Promise me you'll visit next year.' Catherine gave a little cry, squeezing Lucy so hard she could hardly breathe. 'I don't know how I'll survive not being at court. Not dancing every day. Not singing for the Queen. It feels like I've been here all my life.'

'You belong here.'

There was some noise and commotion behind them. The horns and flutes had stopped. From the sudden burst of laughter and applause, Lucy guessed that the players had entered the chamber. She glanced over her shoulder and saw lithe men in striped yellow and green tumbling and jumping on each other's shoulders. They reminded her of the young

124

Italian acrobats she had seen at Kenilworth, she thought, and the memory was like a knife to her heart.

'Who is it?' Catherine asked, staring.

'The Queen's Men, I think,' Lucy whispered back into Catherine's ear. Her friend was holding her by the waist. 'They're to play a short comic piece before the Queen. Do you sing later?'

Catherine nodded. 'With the others.'

The play started and the crowd about them thinned, moving to watch the players.

Catherine took another drink of wine and looked about the chamber. 'Everyone is so stern these days,' she whispered. 'I heard the Spanish ambassador was escorted to the coast under guard in the New Year, and all his servants with him. Will there be war with Spain now, do you think?'

'Yes.'

Catherine's unbound fair hair shone in the torchlight as she shuddered. 'I'm not sad I shall miss that. Though Oswald is so stupid sometimes. He talks of going to war at his father's side if it comes. I've told him he can't. Not once we are married, and he is a father himself. But he refuses to listen. Oh, Lucy, how shall I bear it if he is killed?'

'He's too young. They wouldn't take him.'

'Oswald's not a boy any more. He's almost twenty-five years of age.' Catherine giggled at Lucy's amazed expression. 'He has a full beard!'

Lucy stared, then shook her head. 'I forget, sometimes, how long we've been at court. The years fly so quickly.'

'Then let that be a lesson to you to get yourself a man and marry before it is too late.'

'It's already too late.'

Catherine pinched her arm. 'Don't talk nonsense. You are still a young woman.'

'Her Majesty would never give me permission to marry. She made me swear, years ago, to stay a virgin.'

'She makes all her unmarried ladies swear that! It doesn't mean you have to obey.' There was a burst of laughter from the crowd as the fool slipped over, making some jest at his own expense. Catherine dragged Lucy nearer to the door before releasing her, and lowered her voice. 'You want to grow old and wrinkled and barren like the Queen, is that it? You want to sleep alone every night and never know the pleasure of a man inside you?'

Lucy laughed, though she was in truth a little shocked by her friend's directness, and shook her head. 'Well, if that's how it must be—' she began, and looked up to meet the intense stare of Will Shakespeare.

The words dried in her throat and Lucy stumbled, putting out a hand to support herself against the wall. She glanced at him briefly, then away, suddenly unable to trust herself even to look at him without revealing her thoughts.

Will was bare-headed, his short dark hair slicked back. He was cloaked as though dressed for the street, where it had been raining most of the day. Underneath the cloak he was dressed in the green and yellow stripes of the company, his mask dangling unused in his hand.

'What's the matter?' Catherine asked, then turned and saw Will herself. Her smile broadened as she gazed from Lucy's averted face to Will Shakespeare's, no doubt sensing some intrigue between them. 'Who's this?'

'Madam, my name is Will Shakespeare and I bid you good evening.' He looked directly past her at Lucy. 'I do not wish to be uncivil, but may I have a word alone with Mistress Morgan?'

Catherine ignored Lucy's urgent protest, and curtsied. 'But of course you may,' she said at once, annoying Lucy. 'You are not uncivil, Master Shakespeare, though you are

126

perhaps a little rough in your ways. My friend Lucy may not like such stableyard manners.'

'I am from Warwickshire, madam. My countrymen are all like this, or worse.'

'I am from Norfolk myself, so I shall not chastise you further.' Catherine smoothed down her fair hair, still smirking. 'Indeed, I am very glad to go, and must take my leave anyway. If the players have finished, I have to go and sing for the Queen.'

'Another songbird,' Will murmured admiringly, and bowed again as Catherine disappeared into the noisy crowd. He turned back to Lucy, his eyes alive with determination. 'Shall we walk together, mistress?'

'No, we shall not. I'll be seen!'

'Unlikely. Everyone is looking at the Queen, you see, and the Queen is looking at the players.' To her horror, he pulled her by the hand through the open doorway, past the grinning guards, and down the corridor away from the noise of the masque. 'Hush now, and stop struggling. I won't hurt you. I have paid good coin for a few moments alone with you in a room set apart, and I intend to have them.'

'*What?*' Lucy's eyes widened in astonishment. Paid good coin? 'You bribed the guards?'

'It didn't seem a very surprising arrangement to them. I'm guessing it happens quite often at court. Ah, here we are. They said this was a popular spot for such meetings.'

Will pulled her into some kind of low-roofed storeroom and shut the door behind them. The place was chilly, but a flaming torch had been thrust into a high sconce, lighting the room with its rows of wooden chests and barrels. There Will pushed her against the rough stone wall and smiled into her eyes.

'Not as comfortable a place as I would have liked for our first meeting alone, but it is at least private.'

127

'You must be mad.'

'Mad with love, yes.' He took her hand and kissed her fingers, one by one. 'Mad with desire. Mad for you.'

'Madness will be no defence when we are caught here. You will be whipped, and I . . .' She shivered, imagining the Queen's fury at hearing of this loose behaviour. 'Please let me go.'

'Not yet. A moment longer.'

She said nothing, watching him. He touched her face gently and wonderingly, as though he had never seen a woman before, lingering over the contours of her mouth. A feather's touch, a stroke of warm air against her skin. He closed his eyes, then opened them again on a sigh, staring at her. Such dark eyes, she thought, and was suddenly a little fearful. She could lose herself in them.

He murmured in her ear, 'Do you feel nothing for me at all?'

'No, nothing.'

'Liar.'

His hands were at her waist. 'No,' she insisted, a little flushed now, and pushed him away. 'You have mistaken me for another woman.'

'Impossible thought.' His eyes found hers again, pinning her back against the wall. She found she could not move, caught in the silence between them. The longer he held her, the less able she was to remember why she should not be there. It was a trick. A spell. He was a player. He understood how to charm and flatter with a look and a word. All this was false. 'You are Lucy.'

She tried to speak, but could not.

'What is my name?' Was he a conjuror? Surely he must have her in some kind of spell? Her skin seemed to prickle with his nearness, her senses dazzled by the dark narrow space between them. 'What is my name, Lucy? I want to hear you say it.'

'Will,' she managed hoarsely.

His eyes closed and he breathed slowly. 'Again.'

'I cannot!'

He moved his hands to either side of her head. Eyes still closed, his head dropped, his mouth came close to her throat. Her mind leapt to the sinewy leopards, all claws and teeth, that prowled the tapestries at court. What was wrong with her? How had she allowed this to go so far?

'Indulge me,' he whispered.

'Will.'

'Oh, my lady,' he whispered, and touched his lips to her throat.

She inhaled sharply, scenting ale on his player's costume, her whole body tingling. Was he drunk?

'Stand still,' he told her, and turned his head, finding her mouth.

Lucy had thought Will little more than a charming boy before. Now as he touched her she realized he knew the world better than she did. Certainly he knew more about passion. If this was desire, her love for Tom Black had been little more than girlish adoration, for she had felt nothing like this when Tom had kissed her in the stables at Kenilworth. Will leaned against her, trapping her against the wall so that she felt her own helplessness, and his tongue invaded her mouth. He groaned against her lips, kissing her deeply.

'Lucy,' he muttered. 'I always knew you would taste this sweet.'

His fingers stroked her throat, trailing down to the cleft between her breasts. Then he slipped a hand inside the bodice of her gown and stroked her skin, his mouth on hers. It was an intimacy that excited her. No, he was no longer a boy. And she would find no distaste in becoming a woman beneath him. His hand cupped her breast, brushed her stiffening nipple. She found herself imagining what might follow, the unknown pleasures of surrender, and her mind shrieked at her to escape before it was too late.

'Please don't,' she managed to tell him, and after a moment's hesitation, his arms dropped away.

He watched as she prowled the small, torchlit room like a wild animal looking for a way to escape the trapper's cage. 'What is it, Lucy? Have I misunderstood the signs? You do not want me?'

There was no useful answer she could give to that question. Her mouth still tingled from his kisses. The truth would only make her appear light in his eyes, and she did not wish to lie.

'We should not be here like this,' she compromised, trying to keep her distance from him in the cramped space between barrels, though in truth they could never be more than a few paces apart. 'Not in the heart of the court. It's too dangerous. I am one of the Queen's ladies. Have you no sense?'

He grabbed her hand and drew it to his lips. 'Not where you are concerned, it seems.' His smile was swift, almost boyish, reminding her of the young Will Shakespeare she had known in Warwickshire. 'My body is on fire for you, Mistress Morgan. I would risk even my poor neck to pursue you. No, not only is my body on fire, but my heart, too. I am in love with you. I think I may have been in love with you ever since I was a child and first saw your beauty. Looking at you is like staring into the sun. You leave me blinded. Will you not let me show you the depth of my love?'

'The Queen—' she began carefully, but he interrupted her.

'The Queen is not here. In this little room, it is but you and I, and the heat that lies between us. Do not lie to

130

yourself and turn cold, Lucy.' His voice seduced her. 'Be warm and true with me.'

Will pulled her close and kissed her again. This time Lucy did not protest but closed her eyes, daring to enjoy the heat and pressure of his body against hers. Many of the court ladies took lovers behind the Queen's back. It was a dangerous game – but a highly pleasurable one, she had been told. Would it be so terrible to let herself feel for once? Her body craved his, of that she was sure. She had been locked up in darkness and isolation for so many years, clinging to her memories of a dead man, a love she had long since outgrown. Why not let the past go?

Will had sensed her acquiescence. His kiss deepened, his hands grew bolder. Lucy allowed this madness too, her eyes still clamped shut, not wanting to see even the dark outline of his head, to remember who this man was and where they were, hidden away only a few steps from the Queen and her court.

'You want me?' he muttered in her ear.

'Yes,' she admitted. He had felt the heat on her skin. She had matched his kisses. Why bother to deny it now?

But when he dragged at her skirts, pulling them up past her stockings to expose bare thighs, she pushed them down again.

'No, Will,' she whispered. 'I cannot.'

'I thought you wanted me, that we were agreed. Now you tell me no. Must I court you over again?' Will Shakespeare stared down at her for a moment, his features barely visible in the dark room. His chest rose and fell as though he had been running. 'Are you promised to another man? Is that it?'

'I am promised to no one. Nor am I likely to be, for you must know the Queen's ladies are required to stay maids until Her Majesty gives them permission to marry, which she does not like to do, being fixed as a virgin herself.'

'So, what then? We part and never see each other again?'

He was still so young, so passionate, she thought. He fancied himself in love with her, but she could not bring herself to believe in such a violent passion. If she let him take her, calling it love, that passion would blow itself out like a tempest in the night, and she would find herself pregnant and alone at first light.

Lucy came at it from another direction, struggling to make him understand her fear, her hesitation. 'This is just too sudden, Will. Your love is too violent, and I cannot take it in. One minute you were a boy in my memory, now you are a man and want to be in my bed.'

'At least I am an honest man, then.'

She did not laugh with him. 'My head is spinning. I cannot think with you so close.'

'What is there to think about?' Will demanded, and kissed her throat hotly. His hand stroked beneath her skirts again, bold and invasive. 'Come, I shall give you more pleasure than you have dreamt of.'

She pushed against him, but her heart was not in the struggle, and they both knew it. The temptation to give in to his seduction was too strong.

'How can you know what pleasures I have dreamt of?' she began to ask, but was interrupted.

The door creaked open and one of the guards stood there, peering round the room, a smoking torch in his hand. The guard winked at the sight of Lucy and Will together. 'Begging your pardon, young master. But your time here is finished, unless you have more coins in that fat purse of yours. The Queen calls for her lady.'

'Another minute, for pity's sake!'

'Another shilling for another minute, master. And another again for our silence.'

Will groaned, and dropped Lucy's skirts with an angry

laugh. In his frustration he turned cruel. 'My purse is as empty as hers, so it seems we must all go begging.'

Another shilling for another minute? How could he laugh when the man might as well have called her a whore and had done with it?

Lucy tidied her dishevelled skirts and dragged the back of her hand across her lips. Her desire had fled, replaced by fear and a burning sense of humiliation. If the Queen should hear of this, she would be dismissed from court as a slattern.

'You have shamed me, Will Shakespeare,' she managed in a low voice before turning to the door.

Will followed her to the doorway. The fire and passion seemed to have died out of him now, his eyes intent on her face.

'I did nothing shameful. Nothing you didn't want me to do.'

What a fool she was! If she had truly wanted him to stop, she could have done it with a single blow. Goodluck had taught her once how to defend herself against men if she had to. A pity he had not taught her some defence against her own desire!

Now Shakespeare thought her a whitewashed whore, one of those self-righteous court ladies who professed virginity and chastity while sweating under a different courtier each night. And who could blame him, after the way she had encouraged him?

She must put him off with insults. It was the only way. He must not be allowed to come seducing her at court again.

Lucy drew her skirts about her and squeezed past the sneering guard in the doorway, head held high.

'Lucy, wait!'

'Pray do not bother to pursue me, Master Shakespeare. I have no taste for young men. I shall be on progress with the Queen soon enough, and beyond your reach. But do not despair.' She swept away down the corridor. 'There are plenty of whores in London who will scratch your itch for a shilling.'

Twelve

GOODLUCK BECAME AWARE FIRST OF A GENTLE ROCKING motion, like being carried on a litter, followed by an unpleasant smell of river mud that seemed to pervade everything.

So he was not dead. Not yet.

Behind the rocking and the stench was pain, beginning to throb in slow waves throughout his upper body. It hurt even to take shallow breaths, which could not be a good sign. The pike – or whatever it had been – must have buried itself deep enough in his back to be mortal.

He wondered dimly how long he might have left. Minutes? Hours?

Goodluck clung to that comforting darkness for a few more minutes, then reluctantly opened his eyes.

He was lying in a rough, narrow cot, under a horsehair blanket drawn up to his chin. The low-ceilinged space in which he had been laid was cramped and piled high with sacks, barrels and other debris. It was lit by one gloomy lantern that swung slowly from a central hook, creaking along with the timbers that surrounded him. Between the cot and the lantern, a small brazier with a makeshift chimney gave off enough heat to make the room feel pleasantly warm. A short man sat huddled on a wooden bench opposite, watching him in silence. His thick, coarse-haired coat steamed in the heat from the brazier. That was the source, Goodluck suspected, of the nostril-twitching stench of river mud.

From the constant rocking, he guessed he must be on board a river vessel. Goodluck shifted, trying to look down at himself, but the nausea he felt at the pain in his chest persuaded him to lie still again.

Despite the warmth in the smoky little space, and the horsehair blanket over his wet clothes, Goodluck found that he had begun shivering violently.

Another bad sign.

The man's gaze held his for a long moment, a pair of not-unfriendly hazel eyes peering out from between the turned-up collar of his steaming coat and the pulled-down woollen cap that all but obscured his swarthy face.

Goodluck suddenly remembered the squat figure at the tiller of a passing river barge. 'You were there,' he managed hoarsely, 'when I fell.'

With that, the rattling agony in his chest overwhelmed him, and he sank back into oblivion.

By the time Goodluck came to again, the lantern had been lifted from its hook and set on top of a barrel next to his cot. The fire in the brazier was burning more fiercely, lighting up the narrow space below deck. The man in the woollen cap had risen and was bending over him, peeling back the horsehair blanket with careful hands.

Goodluck's instinct was to push the man away, yet he could not seem to move his arms. He was shivering once more, his teeth chattering.

'Try not to speak again,' the bargeman warned him. His voice was muffled by the thick folds of his coat, pulled up high over his mouth, but he spoke with the coarse brogue of the Thames watermen. He tucked the horsehair blanket back under Goodluck's chin and straightened, so short he hardly needed to bend his head under the low ceiling. 'There's a hole in your back big as a man's fist.'

A hole in his back?

The likelihood was that he would die soon. Goodluck examined the idea hazily and did not find it too disturbing. At least death would bring an end to this pain.

Nonetheless, Goodluck took the bargeman's advice and did not make the mistake of trying to speak or examine himself again. He set aside his questions for the moment and focused instead on the struggle to control his shivering. Every movement, however slight, jerked another white-hot bolt of agony through him. If he could manage to lie still for a few minutes, he told himself, the pain might become manageable.

Despite his efforts, Goodluck must have passed out again, because he slowly realized that the lantern was once again swinging from its hook and he was alone. The bargeman had left him lying there on the cot, one bare arm dangling over the side. He tried to lift his arm back on to the cot, and cried out at the wrenching pain in his chest.

He lay panting for a while, grimacing as he fought against the desire to faint.

There was a bitter taste on his lips, and a tankard of some dark liquid beside him on the floor. Had the bargeman given him something to drink before he'd left? Goodluck had no memory of it.

His mind wandered, but kept returning to Sos, the lively Greek he had left for dead in the mud under the sign of the wool merchants.

We are betrayed.

By whom, though, and to what end? Someone who had known he would be meeting Sos there at sundown, and had carefully arranged matters to make it appear as though Goodluck himself had murdered his friend. That would be how it must look to the Watch, and no doubt his name would have been given by now as the murderer by whoever had plunged that knife into the poor Greek's back.

Goodluck had begun to shiver again. He stared into the glowing heart of the brazier, willing his sluggish body to warm up.

If he survived this wound, it was clear that he would be unable to show his face in London until he had managed to clear matters up with Walsingham. Unless it was Walsingham himself who had ordered this? He did not wish to consider that unsettling possibility, and put it aside, like his questions to the bargeman about how he had been pulled from the river and where he was now.

The important thing for the moment was the sure knowledge that he represented a serious threat to somebody. The same somebody who had betrayed him and his team, or else who had bought the loyalty of one of his men.

His eyelids flickered. He felt drowsy now, and wondered if the bitter taste on his lips was a drug he had been given.

Could the traitor on his team have been Sos? The only one of them not born English and raised a stout Protestant from the cradle?

Or was that precisely the lie he was supposed to believe?

Thirteen

Stratford-on-Avon, Warwickshire, June 1584

THE PLAYERS' CARTS HAD BEEN ON THE ROAD SINCE DAWN, trundling through narrow country lanes bordered by woods and fields lush with thick grasses and the tall, bright spikes of meadow flowers. Cutler, in the lead cart, pulled on the reins as he reached the crossroads – which was marked only by a weathered wooden cross set at a drunken angle into the soil – and the whole cavalcade creaked to a halt.

Will glanced behind him. Apart from those driving the carts, the rest of the company seemed to be asleep, dozing in the June sunshine with their caps over their faces. That was how he preferred it, though: slipping away quietly without any long goodbyes, especially since he owed one or two of the players a handful of shillings that he was unlikely to be able to pay back before the end of the year.

He slung his bag over his shoulder and jumped down lightly from the cart.

'Thanks, Cutler,' he told the cart-driver, a large-bellied man whose unkempt beard was constantly tucked into his shirt, apparently to save it falling in his ale. 'I'll catch up with the company in a month's time, as agreed.'

'We only play Warwick for two nights at best. So don't come late.' Cutler looked down at Will's threadbare shoes. 'If you miss us, it's a long walk back to London.'

Will grinned and reached up to shake Cutler's hand. 'I know, I've walked it before. I'll be there. Have a good journey up north.'

'It's not too late to change your mind and come with us, Will. We're playing some of the biggest houses in the North this year. Think of the wages you'll miss.'

'I am thinking of them, trust me. But I can't go. Not this time. I promised my wife I'd come home for a few weeks this summer.'

Cutler snorted. 'I promised my wife fourteen years ago that I'd come home. She's not seen hide nor hair of me since. Though I believe my absence hasn't stopped the old whore producing a child every few years. Better count your children once you're home, and be sure they're all yours. Wives can be funny like that.'

Will stepped back with a laugh and waved him on. 'Get on with you, villain. I've only one daughter, thank God, and a faithful wife. When I've as many children as you, I'll be sure to count them. Until then, I'll keep my promise and get to sleep in a comfortable bed for a few weeks, instead of a damp field or some nobleman's stable.'

Cutler tapped his nose. 'Aye, and then you'll have more mouths to feed this time next year, and wish you'd not stopped at home so long this summer.'

The company rolled by in the early sunshine, three cart-loads carrying players and props up towards the northern counties for their summer tour. For all Cutler's jokes, Will knew he would not fail to rejoin them as they came back down through Coventry and Warwick in July. His reserves of money would be all but exhausted by then, and another season in London would be beckoning. For now though, he thought happily, breathing in the familiar country air he had missed, he was in Warwickshire and almost home.

A family of speckled wood thrushes were singing gloriously in the hedgerow as Will took the narrow lane at the crossroads that would lead him in a few miles to Stratford. He had not been home for about a year, he realized. The last time he had seen his little daughter Susanna, she had been a tiny scrap of flesh, her red face screwed up in fury, mewling and stinking out the bedchamber.

He grimaced at the memory, and wondered how Anne had managed with the baby on her own all this time. Though she had his mother to help, of course. She would never have been properly alone, not sharing his parents' house in Stratford. Guiltily, he remembered promising Anne a place of their own as he left for London. But so far his wages as a player had not allowed him to make such an extravagant gesture. One day, perhaps . . .

The small ford at the next crossroads was almost dry, just a trickle for him to step across. The lane swung round to the left. Above the sprawling hedgerows, hot sun beating down on the back of his neck, Will caught a glimpse of a shining spire, then the thatched roofs of timbered houses clustered together in the heart of the town.

He recalled Richard Arden's visit to London, and the trouble facing their family after Edward Arden had been executed for treason. Catholic families everywhere were under suspicion, it seemed, even those who had turned publicly to the Queen's Protestant faith.

His travelling bag was heavy on his shoulder. He shifted it to the other side, beginning to sweat in the sun.

Will tried to imagine his stiff-backed father agreeing to his house being ransacked, their possessions turned over by soldiers and the Queen's officials in search of illicit Catholic reading matter. It was an impossible thought. His father had always been such a proud and private man, a respected tradesman who had sat on the town council for many years. To be held up in public as a suspected criminal must have eaten away at his dignity.

Will quickened his pace, and could soon smell the sweet and muddy River Avon on the air.

Almost home!

Walking through the straggling outskirts of Stratford, Will passed several townsfolk that he recognized, and paused to shake their hands and exchange a few words. He felt their curious stares on his back as he continued on towards the market. It was a small town, and everyone who stopped to speak with him seemed to know where he had been.

London! There were few in Stratford's quiet streets who had ever visited that great city, let alone lived and worked there as Will had done.

At his father's house on Henley Street, the workshop window stood open, the counter pulled down to invite passing customers. Will bent his head to peer inside, his nostrils twitching at the familiar, burning stink of the treatments his father used to strip animal flesh and hair from the skins, a mixture of urine and cow dung that left them smooth and supple.

Inside, the workshop was warm, the air stifling. Pushing aside a row of finely stitched kid gloves hanging in the window, Will saw a lanky young apprentice in the doorway to the yard, bent over a vat of skins and holding a long-handled stirrer. The boy was coughing violently, his eyes bloodshot, trying to keep his apron up over his nose as he stirred the vile mixture. Closer by, at the workbench, Will's father was stretching a freshly cleaned skin to fit the glove mould, whistling beneath his breath as he worked. His father had lost a little weight since Will had last seen him. His hair was thinner and showed more grey, too. But there was no indication from his face or bearing that he was in any kind of trouble, as Richard Arden had suggested.

Will cleared his throat. 'Father,' he said loudly through the open window, trying to suppress the exuberance inside him.

John Shakespeare looked up in surprise, frowning thick-browed, and their eyes met.

His father left the workbench and came to the window, staring. 'Will!' he exclaimed, wiping his brow. 'I can't believe it! The prodigal son returns! But why didn't you send word you were coming home?'

They shook hands through the window, his father's large palm damp with sweat.

'I did send a note a few weeks back. Perhaps it went astray.'

'Well, it's good to see you.' His father nodded him towards the locked passageway into the backyard. 'I'll have to unbolt the gate. Wait a moment.'

Stepping into the cool, shady passageway between the house and the workshop, Will threw down his travelling bag and embraced his father properly. He had forgotten how tall his father was, and the thick burr of his Warwickshire accent. Like a child, he rested his cheek against his father's familiar-smelling jacket for a moment – surprised by how achingly sweet it felt to be back home in Stratford – then straightened.

'How is the family? My brothers and sisters?' he asked, releasing him. He was embarrassed to hear a boyish choking in his voice. 'And how are you?'

'Oh, we are all well enough,' John Shakespeare told him, his own voice a little muffled, then threw open the doorway into the house and called out, 'Mary! Anne! Come quickly! See who has come to visit us at last.'

Will glanced at the apprentice, who had closed the lid

on the vat and was leaning against the wall, watching him with a vaguely resentful expression. 'You have new help in the workshop, I see.'

'Aye, this is Edward Bowden,' his father said, and Will nodded at the lad, who did not move but continued to stare at him. Perhaps he feared Will was back home in order to take his job. 'I took him on at Michaelmas for the winter rush, and he's proved useful about the place. There's never as much trade in the summer, except for the ladies' gloves, of course. But your mother sends him on errands for the house most days, and I'm even teaching him how to stitch now. He's not bad, either, though he'll never make a master glover. Too clumsy for the close work.'

Will's mother came out into the passageway, frowning and wiping floury hands on her apron, and gave a sharp cry at the sight of her son. 'Will!'

He kissed her on both cheeks and she laughed, staring. 'It's the way a Londoner kisses a lady,' he explained, then embraced his mother properly. 'I've missed you.'

'Come, I know someone who has missed you,' his father said meaningfully, and pushed him into the doorway to the house.

Anne stood in the shadows just inside, her blue eyes very wide, a small child balanced on her hip. She looked at Will blankly, her fair hair straggling from under a white cap that sat askew as though it had been too hurriedly pinned in place. There was a streak of soot on her cheek from the oven, and he could smell fresh bread baking in the kitchen behind her.

'Will, you're back,' she managed faintly, then looked away from him as though dazzled, into the tender, round-cheeked face of the child, also staring up at him with the wide blue eyes of her mother. 'Susanna, this is your father. Say "Hello, Papa."'

The child gurgled something, and he stroked her cheek wonderingly. So soft.

'Hello, my little daughter,' he said gently, then rather wretchedly wished his child was not there, that someone would take her away, so he could kiss his wife properly. He looked at Anne's pursed lips, her downcast eyes, and knew she was furious with him.

Will frowned and hoisted his bag on to his shoulder again. He was struggling through the various possibilities, confused by what he sensed as his wife's simmering anger, her lack of a proper greeting. Did he not merit a kiss? He had come home, and this was his welcome. A cold face, and a child in the way of his kiss.

'How was London?' Anne asked, following him into the house, where he threw down his heavy bag and settled himself at the table as though in expectation of lunch.

'Busy.'

She played with the child's fingers, her head bent. 'It must have been,' she agreed quietly, 'for you to have forgotten about us so completely this past year.'

'D . . . did I not write you letters?' he asked, and heard himself stammer as he had once done as a boy. It made him angry. 'Send money home whenever I could? Provide for you and the child?'

'You know I cannot read. It is not enough to hear my husband's words read out to me, like a sermon on Sundays. And I thought you would call us to London too. I kept a bag packed for the first few months. Then I realized you had no wish to bring me and Susanna to London, that you had abandoned us here.'

Taken aback by the sudden sharpness of her tone, Will was not sure how to answer. His father disappeared discreetly back into his workshop, and his mother signalled their serving girl to take up his bag and bear it away next door, to the little adjoining cottage his father had given them for their own. His mother followed in the girl's wake, issuing orders about the freshening of linen and rushes.

They were alone in the downstairs of the house, just him, Anne and the child. He stared at the child's downy cheek and could not quite believe she was his. Susanna had been so tiny when he had left; now she had a thatch of dark hair and a few small white teeth that he could see as she beamed at him, waving and gurgling. He remembered Cutler's jibe about asking his wife who had fathered their children, but set it aside in a second. Anne was not that sort of woman. Fierce and passionate she might be in private, when no one but Will could see, but she was not a whore.

'I could not have brought you to London. I cannot support you there. London is no fit place to house my wife and child: the streets are full of whores and cut-throats.' He shook his head. 'I need to know that you and little Susanna are here in Warwickshire, safe in the heart of my family.'

She raised her head and met his gaze frankly. 'It is the whores I worry about most.'

'Anne,' he began, shaking his head, then paused, and felt a little frown tug at his brows. Lucy Morgan.

Will squirmed against the memory of his attempted adultery, like a fish caught on a hook. He tried to tell himself that the overriding lust he felt for Lucy Morgan was no threat to his love for Anne, and that for a married man to want a mistress was not to disown or dishonour his wife. Such backstreet dealings went on in every town in England, and they were the smooth and easy lies on which most lives were built.

But when he looked into Anne's strong and stubborn face, he knew his wife would never agree with him. Her belief in the sanctity of marriage was a cliff against which such neatly thought-out arguments could only ever dash themselves in vain.

She had seen his hesitation, and her thin brows arched in a question. 'Well?'

'You have nothing to fear from that quarter,' he finished flatly, and stood up. 'Now, I'm tired and need to sleep. Does Susanna still cry at night?'

'A little. But I can keep her quiet on the breast.'

'She is not yet weaned?'

'She likes the breast,' Anne said simply.

Surprised, his gaze dropped to her breasts. They pushed high and firm against the bodice of her gown, their milk-bloated swell not quite hidden by the cloth she had draped about her neck like a shawl. He wished then that he had not looked at her like that, nor thought of her breasts when she was unclothed, for suddenly he was filled with a desperate urge to make love to his wife, to see her naked once more and feel her body press against his.

The women had stopped moving about upstairs and the house was suddenly quiet. The silence felt strange after the restless hubbub of London, where no one was private and there could never be a moment of complete quiet, even in the long watches of the night.

Hurriedly, he closed his mind to thoughts of London. He would not allow himself to think of Lucy Morgan's dark beauty and quick, light-footed grace. Not here in Stratford, and not in their bed.

'Will you come upstairs with me?'

Anne stared at his question, then hot colour ran into her cheeks.

'The child,' she whispered.

'My mother can take her for an hour or two, surely?' He dropped his voice, knowing that when the house was still like this, every word that was spoken could be heard from one end to the other. 'I must lie with you.'

147

'Cannot you wait until tonight?'

'No,' he said decisively, and saw her eyes widen. He had never spoken to Anne like that before – as a man speaks to his wife, rather than as a boy pleads with his older lover – and he could see that she was surprised and, he hoped, at least a little impressed. 'It has been too long since we were last . . . intimate. I am impatient to remind myself why I married you, Anne. Now give the child to my mother and come to bed with me.'

Later, watching his wife undress with her back to him and the shutters drawn against the sunlight and the noise of the street below, he commanded her to turn and face him. Anne obeyed, but with an uncertain look on her face, as though she was no longer sure who he was. Methodically, she unpinned and combed out her long fair hair while he waited. She laid her gown and cap neatly on the clothes chest for when they had finished and she would have to get dressed again. Then she climbed into bed beside him, wearing only her thin shift and stockings, and the old bedstead creaked comfortably about them as they looked at each other through the shadows.

'Your parents can hear us,' she muttered. 'The walls are thin.'

'Then they will have to close their ears,' Will told her, a little more sharply than he had intended.

Trying not to hurry, though his need was now urgent, he stroked her hair, which fell almost to her breasts. 'It has grown,' he remarked, and ran his fingers through the smooth fair tresses, which seemed brighter and more shining than he remembered. Her hair was like sunshine, he thought, and at once could not help comparing it with Lucy Morgan's tight black curls, so strange and yet so fascinating at the same time. He suddenly felt angry. He did not want to be in bed with his wife and thinking of another woman.

'Kiss me,' he told Anne abruptly, and was relieved when she obeyed that order too, despite her surprise, placing her lips against his very lightly.

Will pressed her back into the fresh sheets, ignoring the creaks and moans of the bed supports beneath the mattress. She whispered his name, and he kissed her throat and breasts. He turned her face away from his after that, covering her eyes with her hair, twining its thick length about her throat. Anne gave a tiny cry which she tried to stifle, and he knew she was frightened of him for the first time in their marriage, of his sudden, unexpected return, and the urgent desire he was making no attempt to conceal.

He pushed between her pale thighs a moment later, entering her with a groan of relief that reminded him of the first time he had lain with her, that incredible surge of triumphant lust.

When he pulled out, not wanting to spill his seed inside her, Anne hissed under her breath, then covered her face with a sob.

Will rolled away from her in the darkness, his skin suddenly prickling with annoyance. What on earth did Anne expect of him? Did she wish for another baby, knowing he would be away most of the year in London? Wouldn't that be like giving birth to a stranger's child?

No wife could want that, surely?

The baby's cries through the wall stopped abruptly. Will stretched out his legs to the low-burning fire and closed his eyes. Susanna must have been put to the breast, he reasoned, greedy little thing that she was.

Yet even with the baby's insistent cries, the silence of this place was a godsend after London's restless stir and hubbub. It was good to be back home for a space, away from the noise and filth of the capital. His lodgings in

London with the narrow cot and soiled rushes seemed to belong to another man, a chaos somehow unimaginable in the order of his mother's household.

It was quiet upstairs, even his younger brother Edmund asleep, a stout, restless child of four years who loved to run about, shouting in a high piping voice. Will had carried the boy up earlier, then watched him prayed over and put to bed by their mother. Next to Edmund in the bed lay Dick, ten years old now and an intelligent enough lad, for all he rarely spoke.

Outside, Henley Street had fallen silent too, only the town Watch still going about their business, sometimes calling out the hour as they passed. Will's younger sister Joan peered in at him on her way to bed, shaking her head: 'Don't set fire to your boots.' Yes, life was peaceful here with its steady routines, its lack of surprises.

His father came in from the workshop, hung up his cap and sat down beside him on the tall-backed wooden settle. 'Well, William,' he said heavily.

'Father.' Will nodded.

'I'm glad you're home.' His father sat for a while in silence, staring into the fire. Then he shifted his buttocks uncomfortably on the settle, and also stretched out his feet to the warmth. 'It's not been easy without you this past year. Anne helps your mother about the house, but she is busy with the child, too. Your wife struggles, having another mouth to feed.'

'I've started making a little money now from what I write. I'll send more this winter, I promise.'

'It's not just about the money. Your brother Gilbert is a steady lad, but he's not often here these days, and I miss having another man about the house. All that trouble we had last year.' John Shakespeare frowned, shaking his head. 'John Somerville marching on London to assassinate the Queen! That was a bad time for us. Twice, men came

150

to search the house that month. They even took away our family Bible, and we've not had it back. We were afraid to set foot outside the house at one time, in case we were arrested.'

Will thought of his father's books and documents, the ones he always kept locked away for fear of discovery. 'They searched the house?'

His father smiled grimly. 'Aye, but found nothing. We had word they might be coming and hid what was necessary under the eaves. The carved statue of St Ignatius was too large to hide, so I had to burn that, and the little wooden crucifix that your sister made for your mother.'

'Bastards.'

'I needed you here that day, for sure.'

'Forgive me.'

His father shrugged. 'You are a man now, William. You must do as you think best for your wife and child. Just as I have always done. Though your mother suffered terribly when we heard the full tale of the Ardens' disgrace. You know how proud she was to be one of their blood. She cried for hours when she heard Edward Arden had been executed.' He sighed. 'A man of his rank and distinction, brought low by an idiot.'

'I know, I heard it all.'

'Did you go out to Smithfield to witness his death?' His father spoke in a lower voice so that the women, moving quietly above as they prepared for bed, would not hear through the cracks in the floorboards. 'They say his head was stuck on a pike on London Bridge afterwards for all to see.'

'I did not watch Edward Arden executed, no. There was much strong feeling against the Ardens at the time, and I did not want to run the risk of being recognized in the crowd at Smithfield. But I did glimpse Master Arden's head once or twice on the bridge.' Will hesitated, recalling

151

the grisly sight of his kinsman's severed head stuck high on a pike above London Bridge, blackened lips curled back in a perpetual grin, his eyes long since plucked out by birds. 'They leave traitors' heads to rot there for months. Hard to miss when you live in the city.'

His father nodded. Folding his arms across his burly chest, he looked not at Will but at the floor. 'While we are talking of troubles, I believe you had a visitor come to see you in London last year.'

Will frowned. 'You mean Richard Arden?'

'I do.' His father glanced at him out of the corner of his eye, just a quick flash, then stared again at the dark knots in the floorboards as though he had never seen them before. 'Richard came to see me on his return. He said you had agreed to write if there was any news we should know back here in Warwickshire.'

'I did, yes. But happily there was never any news to send home.'

'Did you make a hard push to find out the talk on the streets, or is that the truth?' his father asked quietly.

Will felt uneasy and sat up straight. 'I am not a spy,' he replied with some irritation, though speaking carefully in a whisper. He was uncomfortably aware that his mother overhead might be able to hear what they were discussing. Through the cracks in the ceiling, he could see light from her candle as she moved about. 'I told Richard I would listen to what was being said in the inns and theatres, and if there was any news which concerned the Ardens, I would write to tell him of it. Yes, people talked. But it meant nothing. It was just idle chatter. There was never any threat, not once Arden's head was on a pike on London Bridge and his son-in-law's alongside.'

'That poor boy was a fool,' his father muttered. 'He should never have been allowed to do what he did.'

'It was never about Somerville,' Will pointed out, 'though

his mad rantings against the Queen started the affair. Arden made too many enemies, that was why he had to die. And those who wanted him publicly shamed and executed got their desire. Once the head of the family was dead, and the Arden name disgraced, the rest of us were unimportant. I did not write because I am not a spy and there was nothing to tell. Not because I wished anyone in Warwickshire harm. I was relieved to hear that they released his wife and daughter though.'

John Shakespeare got up and prodded the fire with an iron. 'Well, I shall not go on about the matter. I just wanted to be sure. But all's well that ends well. We survived that month, and things seem to have died down for now. Your Arden cousins still live undisturbed, albeit less wealthily than before, and your mother need not fear for our lives as she once did.'

'I am glad.' Will loosened his belt, not used to eating so well as he had done that evening at his father's table. Another reason to be glad he was home, he thought wryly, was the quantity of simple, fresh food served up at dinner. 'But what of you, Father? My cousin Richard told me there had been some trouble in the town.'

'Did he, now?'

'Some matter of an unpaid debt.'

His father grunted. 'I have more unpaid debts than I have gloves for sale in my workshop. Yet at least these are honest debts. The fines are worse. For not attending church when I should. For selling wool when I should not. Next I shall be fined for breathing in the street and for making merry when I am sent to court again.'

Will laughed reluctantly.

His father continued, 'But yes, it was a bad year, and this one has been little better. Your cousin did not lie. I should wish you home again, but you have your own life now. Do they treat you well, these theatricals?'

'As well as they treat anyone.'

'Did you know that Anne talks of travelling down to London to live with you there?'

Will stiffened at the suggestion. He shook his head. 'London is no place for a decent woman to live. Nor a young child.'

'I have no doubt of that, Will,' his father said heavily. 'I know how it goes when a young man takes himself off to a city. But your wife will not listen to reason.'

'You think I visit whores and spend my nights drinking?'

'Do you not?'

'I may be young, but I am no fool. Listen, Father, London is dangerous. Plague is rife in the summer, and even the beggars will not venture within the walls while it is raging. I cannot allow Anne and Susanna to come to me there. It would be like signing their death warrants.'

His father nodded with satisfaction. 'I knew you would not. Besides, none of us want that. Your mother would miss Anne terribly if she left Stratford. And the babe, too. When you first made the match, well, we thought Anne too old for you, and too high above herself. But she is a good mother, I will give her that. Though she pines for another child.'

Another child? Will sat a moment in silence, unsure whether to tell his father to mind his own damned business or explain why such a thing was impossible. Then he shook himself and stood up, stretching his back out. 'Time for bed. Will you damp down the fire or should I?'

'Leave it to me, you must be tired.' His father stood, too. He laid a quick hand on Will's shoulder. 'Forgive me if I seem to interfere. But Anne is a good wife, and you are away so much. Another child would at least give her some comfort. And your mother, too.'

Will managed a smile and said goodnight. He let himself through next door and up the narrow, creaking stairs to the chamber he shared with Anne and the baby. He had not brought a candle and had to feel his way in darkness. He stood before the chamber door a moment, brooding on what his father had said, then opened the latch and slipped inside.

Fourteen

ONE EVENING, GOODLUCK OPENED HIS EYES AND WAS astonished to find he was still not dead. Nor did the room spin around him as it had done for days. The stale air in the cabin seemed fresher, as though the trapdoor had been left open on to the river, and the hanging lamp glowed rather than glared, swinging softly with the motion of the barge. He was even able to turn his head to look at its steady flame without burning out his eye sockets. Goodluck had been left to lie propped up on his side for more days than he could remember, but now at last could feel his back beginning to mend. He was stiff and still in pain, but he was no longer aware of the agonizing edge of mortality, where the slightest movement had left him close to sickness and fainting.

It was surely a miracle that he was still alive. If the man's thrust had not done for him, the river would have finished the job. Yet here he was, still breathing.

He struggled to recall exactly what had happened that day on the riverfront. But all he remembered was the agony of steel entering his body, then a long fall into water, the icy shock of it slamming into his body like stone.

When the heavily cloaked boatman came shuffling

down into the cabin an hour or so later, Goodluck made an effort to raise his head from the pillow. Outside, he could hear an insistent pattering of rain on the wooden deck, then the softer fall on to water beyond.

'Who are you?' he questioned him. The boatman, as usual, made no answer. He really was a taciturn fellow, Goodluck thought irritably. He tried again, though in little expectation of a reply. 'Where are we? Still on the Thames? Come, man, how long have I been here?'

The boatman came over to examine his back. From what Goodluck had guessed by glancing gingerly over his shoulder whenever this was done, his injury had been swathed in cloths that stank of some grisly ointment. The boatman grunted over the wound for a long while, each poke drawing a hiss of exquisite agony from Goodluck's lips. Then he peeled away a few of the stiff, bloodstained cloths and tossed them aside.

'Your back's healing well,' the boatman muttered in a gruff voice as he worked. 'I thought you were sure to die at first, but it missed your heart. Go about things carefully, and you could be on your feet in a few days.'

'I am glad to hear it, and I thank you for saving my life. But wait, answer me this,' Goodluck insisted, grabbing at the man's arm as he turned away, 'are we still in London? And how long have I been in bed? What day is this?'

'We're moored on the Thames three miles downstream from Richmond, and the month is June.' The boatman shook him off with an unexpected vehemence, his voice rising oddly. 'Now lie still before you burst your wound again and die of a fever!'

The man's hood had fallen away in his anger, revealing swathes of filthy, matted hair. Goodluck caught a glimpse of a swarthy face beneath the hair, but no beard, nor any sign of one, and no moustache either.

157

The boatman saw him staring and hurriedly went to cover his face, but it was too late.

She shrugged then, and bent to poke the stinking cloths into the brazier with a long iron. 'Aye, so I'm no man. What of it? You don't touch me and I won't tip you overboard. And don't think I can't do it, however big a man you may be,' she added fiercely, and turned to brandish her hot iron at him. 'There's more ways than one to leave a boat, my fine master.'

Goodluck watched his strange companion in silence, disliking the disturbing revelation that he had been under the care of a woman these past few weeks. He could not doubt her skill as a healer, for the stab wound in his back – which he had thought surely mortal when he had received it – seemed to be mending well enough. Yet this woman must have stripped him naked while he lay in his delirious fever. How else could she have cleaned and dressed his injury?

'What is your name, mistress?'

'I do not go by that title, nor any other. I need no title. I am plain Jensen.' She sat down opposite him, still wrapped in her thick hooded cloak, and fixed him with the bright eyes he remembered from his first night aboard her barge. 'Jensen was my father's name, and his father's name before him, and it is mine, too, by right of descent.'

'I do not doubt it,' Goodluck agreed solemnly.

'As is this barge, which you shall not take from me.'

He nodded, hearing the fear behind the stubborn will that must have kept this huddled man-woman still working the river long after her father and grandfather had departed this earth.

'Understood. The barge belongs to you. I have no designs on it.'

'Spit on it!' Jensen insisted, nodding at his hand.

Goodluck raised an unsteady hand and worked a small

amount of spittle from between dry lips. This he placed on to his palm, then held his hand out to Jensen. She rose, spat heartily into her own palm, and seized his in a firm grip, pumping it up and down as though her life depended on the handshake. Which, he supposed, it did.

'I'm glad I fished you out and you didn't die, master. You've a good look about you.' Jensen scratched her nose, sitting down heavily on the bench opposite. 'Who was it wanted you done for, anywise?'

He had to decipher this question slowly, having lost most of his strength in the handshake, and feeling drowsy again. 'I have many enemies,' he managed in the end, not feeling up to a lengthier explanation.

'So have I,' she commented sagely, and lay down to sleep on the bunk in her wet boots. 'They won't be finding us on this stretch of the river, though. Not for a good while yet.'

Fifteen

'MY STRIKE!' ELIZABETH DECLARED MERRILY, WATCHING HER hawk land with its white dove. She threw her gauntlet to Lucy Morgan amidst applause from her ladies and courtiers. 'Give that to the falconer.'

Elizabeth walked her horse slowly across the flat green lawns around Richmond Palace, enjoying the sunshine. She must not stay out in such strong light for long, or her complexion would suffer for it. Yet there was a certain pleasure in the touch of the sun's heat on her face. It made her recall other moments of heat, moments of recklessness.

'I win again, Sir Christopher,' she said, glancing at him, then back at Lucy on her neat brown mare. 'Did you see how my hawk flew, Lucy? How she turned in the air? That is how a dancer should move, with the same economy and grace.'

'Yes, Your Majesty,' Lucy agreed.

'I am on fire today,' Elizabeth continued, and pulled her riding gloves back on. 'But Sir Christopher, you look downcast. You do not like to be beaten by a woman, is that it?'

'You are the finest falconer in England, Your Majesty,' Sir Christopher Hatton told her as he followed respectfully, his horse two steps behind her. His own hawk had failed to make its kill, and was hooded again now, sulking on his wrist, dragging fretfully at its leather jesses. 'No man would be such a fool as to deny it. I fear it is hard to compete with your skill.'

Elizabeth clapped her hands in delight, and her ladies followed suit. 'The finest in England?'

'And the fairest, Your Majesty.'

She smiled, turning to him. The blue skies were suddenly less bright, though the sun remained undimmed overhead. 'I had heard you thought another lady held that honour, sir.'

There was a silence among the surrounding courtiers. Even those ladies who had followed the horses on foot stood still under the trees, a light breeze rustling the silks of their skirts.

'Your Majesty?'

Elizabeth looked back at Sir Christopher Hatton, her eyebrows raised haughtily. 'Sir?'

Hatton was stout now, sombre-faced and with a neatly trimmed grey beard, no longer the handsome young man she remembered from her early years on the throne. He sat bewildered on his horse, glancing from the courtiers to her as though hunting for clues, his expression nervous and perplexed.

Yet there was guilt in his eyes, too.

He stammered, 'I . . . I do not know to what you refer, Your Majesty.'

'By *Mary*, do you not?' Elizabeth demanded, stressing the hated name of her enemy, and saw Sir Christopher Hatton flinch. 'Why, now he remembers!' she exclaimed. 'A man's mind is a marvellous instrument, that plays a song one moment, then forgets it the next. Sir, there is a lady by that name whose claim on your admiration is greater than mine, or so rumour tells me.'

'Not a whit,' Hatton replied earnestly. He dismounted and knelt heavily on the grass before her, down on both knees, his head bowed. 'Your image is always and for ever in my heart, Your Majesty. No other lady could hold my admiration, and this I will swear on my sword and by any other oath you might devise.'

'Then rumour lies?'

'Or is most grievously mistaken, Your Majesty,' he insisted, head still bowed. His voice grew more dogged. 'The lady of whom you speak must herself have put these untruths about, out of very spite for being your inferior in every case, but most in beauty. She is like a candle to the sun, a dim star to the full moon. She has no claim on any Englishman's affections, but can only usurp one through lies.'

Suddenly impatient, Elizabeth waved him to his feet. 'Put up, sir,' she told him as he began laboriously to draw his sword. 'There is no need for you to swear an oath. This Mary wearies me, for all your swearing that she is not my rival. I shall listen to no more gossip about who among my courtiers is in her favour, or out of it. Shall I send her back to Scotland, do you think, or on to France, where she may make a pact with my enemies?'

'Neither, Your Majesty,' interrupted Walsingham, who had approached on foot with his customary stealth. 'A caged bird may sing too loud at times, but at least it cannot fly.'

Cecil was two steps behind him, frowning. Her treasurer bowed, addressing her with unusual severity. 'Do your hawks fly well today, Your Majesty? I am glad of it. But we must spoil your sport with bad news, I am afraid.'

'Come to darken my summer's day with your clouds, Lord Burghley?' Elizabeth was laughing, but Cecil's unsmiling expression told her the news he brought was in truth bad. If so, it was not for the ears of the common court. She dismissed the courtiers, and signalled her ladies to depart, too. 'Not you, Lucy. Nor you, Helena. I may need comfort after these gentlemen have had their say.'

She spoke lightly, but her heart weighed heavily inside her. Was this some new blow to her person?

A death, perhaps?

If only it could be news of her cousin's unexpected death that Cecil brought, she thought with a sudden flare of temper. But she knew better than to hope for such a reprieve. Whenever a prisoner represented some threat to her throne, it seemed they must live for ever unless poison or an axe should intervene. And much as Elizabeth hated her flamboyant cousin Mary, she was loath to dispose of her as her father had her mother.

To execute a queen anointed was to set a poor precedent. For who knew that her own head would not be on the block soon after? It seemed the Catholics were intent on removing her if they could, and execution had always been the quickest way to dispose of a queen, to sever her royal head from her body and call it justice. One more swift uprising among her nobles, and Elizabeth herself could be in the Tower, and thence to the block.

Elizabeth dismounted and handed the reins of her horse to a page to hold while they talked. She preferred to receive bad news on her feet, standing in the green shade of a young oak, her hands clasped demurely before her.

'Well, my lord?' She signalled Cecil to speak directly. 'I am prepared to hear this grievous news you bear.'

Cecil held up a state letter, its broken seal that of the French court. 'It is my sad duty, Your Majesty, to inform you that Alençon, Duke of Anjou, is dead.'

Her lips parting in shock, Elizabeth shook her head. Not little dark-haired Alençon!

Her voice sounded like a piece of wood cracking. 'Alençon? It cannot be true.'

'I fear it is, Your Majesty.'

Dearest Alençon. Dear little François. She thought of how they had met on his visit to England, his sweetly animated face, narrow as a boy's, and his high-pitched laugh, so droll, so infectious. They had sat together in her bedchamber some evenings – mainly to annoy her nobles, but also in the hope that word of her indiscretion would reach Robert – and he had held her by the waist while she ran her fingers through his dark young curls. '*Tu m'enchantes, mon amour*,' he had murmured in her ear, his compliments delighting her, a different one to accompany each kiss, '*ma reine, ma joie, ma belle, ma petite fille*.' It had been the most delightful ten days of her life, that first visit, and even though she had sadder memories of his second visit, nonetheless she could not forget how they had exchanged gifts and promises.

'Marry me,' he had whispered, and she had consented, captivated by the thought of such love at her age, a muscular young man in her bed. It was surely no sin to have enjoyed the thought of what Alençon might bring her as a husband. To have tasted a little of such delights as they lay together on her day bed in the drowsy afternoons . . .

'No,' she managed, and staggered, her knees giving way.

At once, Helena was at her side, supporting her. Dear girl. Dear, sweet girl. Elizabeth steadied herself, gripping Helena's shoulder. The two men waited in silence, their heads discreetly bowed. Let them wait. Hateful men with their hateful news.

Alençon.

If she had known her little Frenchman would never return, that he would die so young, would she have said yes to his suit? For the carnal pleasure of such a marriage, yes. But for her country, too, and the great line of Tudor. She might have borne the duke a son before he

164

died, a child to rule both England and France after they were turned to dust, a legendary king of kings. Now neither of them would enjoy such bliss. The dream of uniting their two countries must be laid aside, as the hope of their marriage had been put by once Elizabeth saw how the English hated her for contemplating it.

Her bones ached. She was too old now for a marriage. Too old for anything. 'Where is Robert?' she asked plaintively.

'He is at Wanstead, I believe.' Walsingham spoke quietly, always a discreet man, even when imparting difficult news.

'Wanstead? With *her* and the child?'

'Yes, Your Majesty.' Walsingham did not offer to send for Robert, she noted sourly. 'You have received unhappy news today. Your ladies-in-waiting should attend you at once. Shall I call for the others, Your Grace, and for wine to be brought?'

She looked from his swarthy face to Cecil's paler, more noble countenance. Cecil was watching her closely. He was nervous, she realized, and almost smiled in grim recognition of his fear. He had considered her love for Alençon a weakness, and her desperate pining for him after he had left England a mere affectation. Now he feared she would crumble at this news, would tear her hair like any woman of the streets, and be unable to attend to the affairs of state until the madness passed. But what did Cecil know of loneliness, a man who spent his private hours surrounded by his family? He did not know, nor could ever understand, the terrible solitudes of the night, the knowledge that one could never be a whole woman, a wife and mother, never live out one's life as other women did, in obedience to a man. Once she had thrilled at the idea of such obedience even as she had loathed and rejected it. Cecil was a man. A good husband and father, but a man. What could he know of her fears?

'Yes,' Elizabeth declared. 'Let red wine be brought for us to drink to the Duc d'Anjou's memory. And order black clothes for every lord and lady of the court. I shall wear a veil in his honour, and to hide my red eyes. There will be no dancing, but only Mass heard and songs for the dead. Send out a decree.' The pain would consume her. How could she survive this latest blow? Yet she must, she was the Queen. She did not allow her voice to break again, but felt her body tremble. 'Now leave me.'

Cecil bowed gravely, and Walsingham followed suit. Both men turned and made their way back to the palace in the sunshine, Cecil's secretary scribbling notes as he hurried behind.

Elizabeth sank on to the grass under the oak tree and buried her head in her hands. Helena and Lucy sat beside her, murmuring words of comfort that she could not hear. *François is dead.* He who had courted her for so many months, and with whom she had shared kisses, long into the night, in open defiance of court gossip, delighted to see Robert burn with fury and despair at their closeness. She wondered how he had died. Some sickness, or an accident? He had loved hunting. Perhaps he had fallen from his horse. What did it matter? Alençon was dead, that was all she needed to know.

He will come to visit me no more.

How could such a man have died so young?

He had given her a golden flower, decorated with a tiny jewelled frog, as a parting gift the last time they'd met.

Memento mori.

Her heart was broken and she would die of it! She had only loved two men in her life: one was Robert, the other Alençon. One had been snatched away from her by another woman, and now the other had been taken by death. Yet she was a queen as well as a woman, and must bear her grief with fortitude.

'Sing for me, Lucy,' Elizabeth choked, and dragged a hand over her face as the young black woman rose to her feet. 'Sing one of those sad French ballads you love so much. Let me dream of Alençon once more.'

Sixteen

WILL WAS WOKEN BY THE SOUND OF HAMMERING AT HIS father's door. He opened his eyes, dazed. He was half-sitting, half-lying, next to Anne in bed, snug in the cosy little cottage that adjoined his father's house. Beside their bed stood a sturdy wooden cradle which he recognized as his own, and his brothers' and sisters' after him, in which now lay his own child, Susanna. His daughter was awake and gurgling happily, sucking on her fingers.

Groggily, Will swung his bare legs out of bed and looked down at her. She stared up at him cheerfully from the cradle, her blue eyes wide, utterly unafraid of this stranger who was now 'Papa'.

The hammering had stopped. Now voices were being raised. He recognized his father's authoritative tones, angry and strained. Men replied, down in the street, equally angry. Then the hammering on the door began again. Somewhere a dog was barking, too. It seemed the men were determined to get in and find whatever they had come for.

Susanna, no doubt upset by the noise and their early stirring in the bedchamber, began to cry lustily, her face soon wet with tears.

Anne climbed out of bed and snatched up the baby from

the cradle, clutching Susanna against her breast as she tried to peer down through the gaps in the shutters.

'They've come back,' she muttered, and he was surprised at the fear in her voice. 'I knew they would in the end.'

'Who are they?' Will did not waste any time getting dressed. He took two steps to the clothes chest at the foot of the bed and threw it open. Before he'd left, he'd buried the old theatrical sword he'd used for history plays in Warwick and Coventry under the blankets and clothes in the chest, hoping it would be safe there until his return. He rummaged down under the horsehair blankets and rough, clean linen, searching for it. 'Magistrates' men? The ones who came last winter and searched the house?'

She shook her head, hurriedly putting her bodice aside and sliding Susanna on to the breast with a practised movement. 'Traders. Your father owes them money. They came just after Easter, and John told them he'd pay what he owed when you came back from London. I imagine they've heard you're at home again now, and that's why they've returned.'

Will glanced up from the clothes chest. The child clutched at the round white globe of her mother's breast, her small fists opening and closing, her eyes shutting with pleasure, her cheeks suddenly flushing a soft pink as the milk began to flow.

'What are you looking for?' she asked, puzzled.

'My sword.'

'It's under the bed,' she told him, then stared. 'What do you need a sword for?'

Will did not reply, but knelt down in the rushes and felt under the bed. Sure enough, his sword came to his hand, still wrapped in its bundle of old leather, and he drew it out. Then he went to the stairs, glancing back at Anne as she began to follow him.

'No,' he said firmly, 'stay here and look after the baby. This is a man's quarrel, not any business of yours.'

Once downstairs, he threw open the door and ran out into Henley Street in nothing but his nightshirt, for all the world like a poor madman. His bare feet stumbled over the stony potholes, sword in hand as though he intended to do battle for England. His palm fitted snug into the ornate, twisted handle glittering with false gemstones, for this was the sword of King John from two seasons ago in Coventry, and he had wielded it on many occasions that year, in return for a few pence a show. Will had always intended to hand it back to the company after the Coventry play season had finished. Yet somehow King John's sword had found its way into his belt on that last drunken night, and then into their clothes chest at home.

'Get away from the door!' Will shouted as he burst among them, and the rough-looking crowd of men gathered like hungry dogs around the barred door to his father's house stared and fell back. 'Take to your heels, you filthy whoremongers. Save yourselves while you still have legs to walk. Or I swear I shall spit you where you stand and wear your eyeballs for tokens!'

It was a speech he had given on stage, and seemed to suit the moment well. Some of the men drew their daggers but did not move towards him, their faces uncertain. The others stood together, staring at his sword and then, more perplexed, at his bare legs.

Some of their neighbours had stirred at the early-morning ruckus, and were now approaching from the row of thatched houses and shops opposite. The sun had only just risen, and a few of the men looked angry, rubbing their eyes and yawning.

Will's father had thrown back the shutters above and was leaning out of the window, his nightshirt more soberly covered with a cloak.

One of their neighbours called out, 'John, when will you learn to pay your debts? You bring shame to our street with these disturbances.'

Will took another step forward, the sword outstretched. 'There is no need for you to involve yourself, Master Fletcher,' he said, recognizing one of his father's old rivals on the town council, from the days when John Shakespeare had still been a name to reckon with in Stratford.

'Young Will back from the big city, is it?' Master Fletcher replied, and snorted in derision at the sword. 'A plaything in a boy's hand. That won't last three strokes against a proper blade.'

'Try me,' Will muttered.

John Shakespeare called down to the angry men below, his voice hoarse. 'I've told you, there's nothing in the house for you. Let a man earn an honest wage before you come to him for your money. Thomas, for the love of God,' he appealed to the ringleader, a stout man in a well-trimmed doublet and hose, his fleshy face red with fury, 'you know I'm good for it. Times have been hard for all of us. No one is buying except the gentry. But it will soon be summer's end, and then everyone will be wanting new gloves for winter.'

'That makes sense, Thomas,' one of the older men exclaimed, and tugged on the leader's arm. 'Look, we've woken half the town. Short of breaking Shakespeare's door down, we'll not get our money today. Let's go in peace and come back in the autumn, when he can pay us.'

'Double,' Thomas said, stabbing an accusing finger up at the open window where John Shakespeare stood, his wife at his shoulder. 'He'll pay us double what he owes, for making us wait.'

'That's usury!' John Shakespeare exclaimed, a hard flush in his face. 'I'll pay what I owe, as is only fair under the law, and an extra two shillings a head for your journey here today.'

'That's a good offer, Thomas,' the man muttered, and gestured the others to follow him. 'We'll come back another time. If he can't pay then, we'll demand his arrest and his possessions forfeit and sold to the cost of his debt. That's owed us under the law.'

'Aye, we'll be back after the summer.'

One of the men spat on the ground, as if to seal the deal, then followed the others as they walked back to the carts and horses which had brought them into town.

The stout ringleader did not seem to believe they should have given up the fight so easily.

Nonetheless, he glanced at Will with his outstretched sword and reluctantly followed his friends back to the carts.

'Next time, Master Shakespeare, you had better have your debt ready to pay, and the right money too, or I shall not answer for my anger.' The man swung himself up on to a covered wagon and slapped the horses' reins. 'Walk on!'

Above them, John Shakespeare closed the shutters about his bedchamber window with a bang.

Their neighbours were still staring from windows and doorways, most in nightcaps and gowns. Will looked about at their wide-eyed faces, daring any of them to pass comment on his attire, then made his way back to his own snug little house.

Anne stood waiting for him on the doorstep, dressed now in her day clothes. Susanna, perched on her mother's hip, brightly gurgled at his approach and held out a chubby hand to him.

Will bent to kiss her hand, which made the child gurgle even more, her little face delighted, then he led them both inside. The room was chilly, the hearth still dirtied with last night's cold ashes. Once the door was closed he stood his sword against the wall and turned to Anne.

'I told you to stay indoors.'

'You are my husband, Will. I was worried for you.'

He tried to keep his tone light, his anger under control. He did not want to raise his voice in front of the child. 'I am not a boy, Anne. I do not need my wife to watch over me. It was nothing. Those men were full of bluster, that is all. Wind and bluster. They blew themselves out.'

'Is that why you took the sword?' She was busy tidying the child's rough smock, cleaning her face with a wetted finger. 'Because it was nothing?'

Will drew a breath and let it out again. 'You are a woman. You do not understand how these things work. They needed to see the sword to know that I was serious. Next time they come for their money, they will be more polite about it.'

Her blue eyes lifted to his face. 'Or they will come with swords and pikes, and kill us in our beds.'

'That will not happen. This is England. We are at peace with our neighbours.'

'Will—' she began, and he silenced her with an angry look.

'That is enough. You have said your piece, Anne, and I have said mine. That is an end to it. Now I must get dressed and speak with my father. He will expect it.'

Will stooped slightly to enter his father's house, finding his sister and his brothers sitting at the fireside, taking some porridge to start the day. They called out to him joyously, their little faces bright with enthusiasm. 'Will! Will!'

His sister Joan came to kiss him on the cheek, her smile entertained. 'My fiery brother! Where is your sword? The little ones want to see it.'

'I've put the sword away,' he admitted, grinning over

173

her head at his younger brothers. 'But I'll get it out again later and show you a pass or two I've learned at the play-houses in London. Once I even had to die on stage. I made a good death,' he added, and clutched his belly, staggering about the small kitchen as though mortally wounded. 'But then I could not move until the end of the scene, and a fly lighted right on the end of my nose.'

The children gaped in delight and astonishment at this, then begged to hear more about the kinds of plays he had acted in.

'Later, later,' he told them, laughing at their insistence. He kissed his mother on the cheek and sat at the table. 'First let me take a bowl of that porridge, if I may. It smells so good!'

But after he had eaten, it was time for Dick to set off for school. Will watched him go, then shut the door and went to sit by the fire, his conscience pricking him uneasily. He was a married man and this was his family. This was where he belonged. He should never have risked all this by pursuing Lucy Morgan. What would his father say if he knew the extent of his involvement with another woman?

Will was burned up with lust for her beauty. Her face haunted his sleep. But his soul was in jeopardy, and he knew it. He did not want to be a Jack-the-lad like most of the other players, who boasted of their conquests and held it a triumph if they managed to hoodwink one mistress while sleeping with another.

When he returned to London, he would make no further attempt to seek Lucy out again. This constant wish to betray his wife was a sin, and unworthy of his vows to her. He must conquer his lust for Lucy Morgan, or else give up the stage and become a glover here in Stratford like his father. Anything less was unworthy.

Seventeen

THE PALACE OF NONSUCH HAD BEEN BUILT BY ELIZABETH'S father, and bore King Henry's lavish but undoubtedly male touch in its marvellous octagonal turrets and panelled royal chambers. While the outer courtyard was plain enough, the inner one looked more like a Roman temple than a hunting lodge, its walls heavy with stucco gods and goddesses, and many of the doors and fittings in the palace itself gilt as befitted a king's residence. The grand tapestries in the halls were faded, though, some in dire need of repair, and all looked as though they belonged to her grandfather's generation rather than her father's. Everything about the place seemed larger than she would like, the furnishings and even the rooms themselves somehow awkward and unsubtle, the ceilings too high and the bedchambers draughty.

She enjoyed her visits the most in summer, when the formal gardens were at their best and she could walk beside the cooling fountains. In the winter, there was an air of gloominess that hung over Nonsuch Palace and made her long to be elsewhere. Though even in broad sunlight, on a long hot summer's day, Elizabeth could sense some unspoken menace about the place. Walking in the gardens with her ladies in the mornings, delighted by the butterflies that played so daintily about their heads, she would look back, and it would seem as though the turreted palace was frowning at her.

A foolish idea, but one she had never quite been able to shake off.

Now, though, she stood alone with her closest advisers in the Rose Room, beneath a high and marvellously intricate ceiling of red-emblazoned stucco roses, that dizzied her whenever she looked up at them. Elizabeth laid aside the letter she had been reading from her Scots cousin Mary, closing her eyes in sudden, bitter fury.

'Why does my cousin still live?' she demanded of Cecil and Walsingham, aware of the peevish note in her voice but too frustrated to care what they thought. 'Mary is never comfortable. She complains of her jailors. She complains that her bed is too hard. If a meal gives her the stomach ache, she suspects poison. She asks why, if I love my cousin, I should allow her to suffer these indignities, and does not speak of the troubles she causes me simply by being on God's earth. Why can Mary not be like any other mortal and die of the ague, or the pain in her bones, or whatever new sickness plagues her body whenever she writes to me?'

'It could be arranged, Your Majesty,' Walsingham murmured discreetly, and passed her a silver dish of sugared almonds.

She opened her eyes to glare at him. 'I am no murderer, sir. I do not ask for her food to be poisoned by one of your agents. I ask why God in his mercy does not rid me of this woman, this bitter thorn in my side. Every day now, it seems, you come to tell me of some new fanatic who would see Mary crowned in my place, or the thousand Catholic priests who swarm on to our shores each year to spread civil disobedience along with their Roman faith.

My own nobles whisper my cousin's name behind my back, saying she is more beautiful and more devout and more fit to be Queen than I am.'

'Your Majesty, I cannot believe—'

'Do not look at me with that long face, my lord, and say you cannot believe such things,' she told Cecil in a waspish tone. 'Not when your friend Walsingham whispers daily in my ear of secret revolts, and intercepted letters between conspirators, and courtiers who meet after midnight in the darkest corners of my palace.'

'Not in your own palace,' Walsingham corrected her gently. 'Even those who wish for new governance would not be so bold.'

'New governance?' she repeated scornfully. 'To put a whore on the throne of England, and watch her tear this land apart with her ignoble lovers and her divorces and her open murders? Is that the new governance of which you speak?'

Cecil cleared his throat. 'It shall not happen, Your Majesty, for the remedy lies in your own hands. If you would only agree to what we have discussed, there could be an end to these constant plans and plottings, and peace secured for England.'

'Order Mary's execution?' Elizabeth demanded, and shivered just at the sound of those heretical words. 'On what grounds?'

Walsingham arched his thin, dark brows. 'We have evidence enough to condemn that lady ten times over, Your Majesty. I hold in my own custody men who have admitted to carrying letters of rebellion against Your Sovereign Highness, and some of those letters are either addressed directly to your cousin or signed by Mary in full knowledge of her treason. If you would allow me to read you one or two of these secret letters, I could soon point out the fault.'

Elizabeth made an angry noise at this, and Walsingham bowed, yet continued with his argument undeterred.

'I am convinced you would be less averse to ending this dance of plot and counter-plot if you would but agree to read her treason first-hand.'

'I have told you before: I shall not budge on this point. I grant you, gentlemen, my cousin Mary is a whore and a traitorous conspirator against my throne. But she is still my cousin, an anointed queen whose Scottish throne has been usurped. I shall not spill a drop of royal blood, no matter what the provocation.'

She had spoken passionately, with a fiery heart, but knew her head to be clear on this point at least.

Her councillors stood silent, their grey heads bowed in deference to her orders, though no doubt thinking her a foolish woman with no more sense than a peahen.

Exasperated, Elizabeth threw down Mary's infuriating letter of complaint and consoled herself with a sugared almond instead. Yet even that was a mistake. Her skin prickled at the taste as she remembered Robert feeding her sugared almonds once, in the intimacy of her bedchamber.

'Has Robert returned from Wanstead yet? I have written to him twice, demanding his immediate return, and still he does not come.' Angrily, she pushed the dish of nuts aside and stood up. 'Am I no longer Queen? Am I some dairy-maid to have my orders flouted? To be mocked by men who would rather visit their wives than travel with my court in progress?'

Walsingham excused himself with some muttered comment she did not catch, and Cecil, Lord Burghley, was left to placate her. 'Your Majesty, I believe his lordship returned to court last night.'

Her heart jolted at the news that Robert was here at the Palace of Nonsuch. Elizabeth drew breath to steady herself, willing her blood to remain cool. If she wished to be treated as a queen, she must act like one.

She walked to the windows of the Privy Chamber and looked down at the green lawns of Nonsuch. Peacocks strode to and fro across the grass like miniature blue emperors. One bird screeched in the sunshine. Seconds later another answered its call. Wild and imperious creatures, she thought, and gazed past them at the soft red climbing roses entwined with holly bushes and privet along the edges of the lawns, the rows of strawberry beds with their luscious fruit, then the elegantly arched gateway into the formal gardens beyond.

Why had he not come to visit her yet? The question snagged like a thorn, would not let go.

'I wish to see Robert at once,' she said with control, though she knew there was little point hiding her feelings from Cecil. Her most trusted councillor had known her too long to be deceived. 'Send for him.'

Cecil bowed and withdrew without comment.

She did not have to wait long, though by the time Robert came cap in hand to her door, Elizabeth was seated in the high-backed chair that stood below the heavily ornate mantel, her hands folded sedately in her lap. Above her head the Tudor rose design sprawled across the ceiling in testimony to her family's power and magnificence. If she liked anything about Nonsuch Palace it had to be its extravagance, the knowledge that it had been built in great style by her father, not sparing his purse but spending lavishly, the sheer expense of the place intimidating to those who walked there.

Head bent, Robert sank to one knee before her. 'Your Majesty.'

His hair might be silvered, but he still looked much younger than she did, Elizabeth realized with a sudden touch of irritation.

'You ignored my letters,' she said petulantly.

179

'I came as soon as I could, Your Majesty. I apologize for having kept you waiting.' He hesitated, then added unwillingly, 'My son was unwell.'

'I see.'

His son by *her*!

She asked stiffly, 'Your son is recovered, I trust?'

'Not quite,' he admitted, and did not meet her gaze. 'But I am told his health has much improved, Your Majesty.'

He had left his home at Wanstead before his beloved child was fully recovered, she realized with a shock. Her hands could no longer lie idle in her lap, but gripped the arms of her chair in a sudden burst of triumph. He had ignored both his wife's command and his son's illness, and returned to court in deference to her will. Pleasure throbbed through her, and she smiled down at him, magnanimous in victory.

'I hope your son regains his strength soon,' she told him kindly. 'If he falls ill again, you must seek advice from one of my own royal physicians, here at court. There are none better in the land.'

'I thank you, Your Majesty.' Robert smiled and bowed his head, but she sensed that he was still concerned over his son's health. She had never been a mother, so could not be sure how it must feel to fear for a child's life. Yet she had often fretted when Robert was away from her side, and so could understand how sharp the sting must be when one's own flesh and blood was in danger.

He stood at her gesture and seemed to set the matter aside, his voice brisk. 'Cecil tells me there has been another letter received from our Scottish prisoner.'

Wearily, she indicated Mary's letter on the table. 'My cousin is fast becoming the bane of my life.'

Robert read the wretched letter in silence, then laid it aside. He thought for a moment, fretting his lower lip between his teeth. 'All these letters and complaints mean

180

nothing when we cannot be sure what is truth and what is the imagination of a desperate woman. Forgive me for speaking plainly, Your Majesty, but it seems to me that someone more trustworthy than her jailor must review Her Highness's circumstances in person, and make a full report to the Council.'

'I heartily agree.'

'Do you wish me to go up there and speak with her myself, Your Majesty?' Robert asked directly, and looked at her.

Elizabeth froze, staring back at him. Again, her knuckles gripped the carved arms of her chair until the skin whitened.

Was he truly aware of what he was suggesting? That the most powerful man in her kingdom should leave court and meet with her greatest enemy?

'Go yourself?' she repeated slowly, and for a space pretended to give the idea serious thought. 'Mary is our royal guest, detained at my pleasure and for her own security. These tales of sickness and squalor do not sit well with her position. Certainly someone should go and view her conditions on the crown's behalf. A man of rank whom my cousin will respect and confide in. But I am not sure that I can spare you for the task, Robert.'

Her heart struggled like an animal in a trap. All her instincts screamed at her not to allow him within a foot of her beautiful cousin, who by all accounts had captivated almost every man she had ever spoken with. Not only did Robert belong solely to *her*, to Elizabeth Tudor and not that Scots pretender, but if Mary Stuart were ever to ally herself with the Earl of Leicester, already too frighteningly close to Elizabeth in power, England itself might be at risk.

Robert's thin smile cut her, and she stared. He had known before offering what her response would be. He had been playing with her, mocking her weakness. How dared he?

He did not argue but bowed his head. 'As you wish, Your Majesty. Should I appoint someone else to go in my stead?'

'No, you must remain at court in case I need you. I shall instruct Cecil to make the arrangements,' Elizabeth insisted, and experienced a small jolt of satisfaction at seeing his brows contract. Always she had been able to play him off against Cecil. The fear that she trusted the older statesman more than Robert was a stick Elizabeth liked to poke him with whenever he angered or frustrated her. Like an irascible old bear, Robert might growl and show his claws from time to time. But underneath that show of rage he was impotent. She was his queen, and there was nothing he could do to prevent her from tormenting him.

Except marry and get with child another woman behind your back, her mind jeered at her.

Silly old fool, she told herself fiercely. This man does not love you. You may be the Queen, but he loves the she-wolf who lies with him at Wanstead, and who has given him a son and heir to raise.

He came to kneel at her side. 'What next, though?' he asked softly, and carried her hand to his lips, no longer one of her sombre Privy Councillors, but plain Robert again, her horseman, her dark-eyed gypsy. 'Her constant complaints about jailors and ailments are a distraction from her true activities, nothing more. What will you do if Mary will not drop these plots against your throne?'

'She is alone. She cannot succeed in her treason.'

'Mary has a following of stout-hearted traitors, do not believe otherwise. I have seen Catholics tortured who have refused to give up her secret plans. I have spoken to men who have sworn with their dying breath to honour Mary

Stuart above you, their rightful queen, so the Roman faith might come again to England.'

Elizabeth looked down into his face. 'You think me wrong to keep her alive?'

'I think you are merciful beyond your cousin's deserving.'

'If one day it proves to be God's will and in England's interests that my royal cousin Mary should die, then I hope to act with the fortitude of a prince in ordering her execution. Until that day, I shall continue not to act.' She thought his expression betrayed impatience and frustration. 'I would remind you, Robert, that it is also princely to be merciful.'

'Then may you live not to regret your mercy,' Robert murmured, and she smiled at the warning in his voice.

'Don't fret, Robert. I am safe enough from Mary's childish plots.' Elizabeth played her fingers along his jaw and cheek, delighting in his presence back at her side. 'It is good to see you at court again, though I have still not forgiven you for refusing to come back as soon as I commanded it.' She looked down at him through her lashes. 'Fetch wine. And the chessboard. Now we are alone together, let us play a game.'

Eighteen

LUCY WALKED A FEW STEPS BEHIND HER MAJESTY, HOLDING her book and ostrich-feather fan. Two of the Queen's white dogs ran past, knocking Lucy aside as they bit and snarled at each other. A young page came dashing after the dogs with an upraised birch switch, lashing out at their thin flanks as he scolded them. Queen Elizabeth laughed at their antics and turned to Lord Leicester, who was walking beside her, his head bowed in thought. 'You see that? No manners at all. Those curs are like my English nobles. They need a whipping to teach them obedience.'

Leicester was staring at the dogs, seemingly distracted. 'Which nobles are those, Your Majesty?'

'I leave the names to my sombre Walsingham. He is an expert in these dark matters. Though sometimes he shows me letters, signed by names that pain me. Names of great men whom I have trusted, that now turn their gaze and their allegiance to my cousin Mary.' The Queen grimaced, her back very stiff. 'What is the world coming to, Robert? My authority flouted, my nobles in secret dispute over the throne. And now we hear that Prince William of Orange has been murdered. Is royal blood no longer sacrosanct in Europe?'

Leicester did not answer, his head still bowed.

'What, do you find my company so tedious?' Queen Elizabeth snapped her fingers furiously. 'No, pray keep your head low, I shall find it easier to strike off!'

Leicester looked up then, and stared at the Queen as though he had indeed just woken from sleep. 'I beg pardon, Your Majesty. I was thinking of . . .'

He glanced over his shoulder at Lucy. With compassion, she saw that Leicester's eyes were bloodshot, as though he had not slept well. Lucy knew at once that he was still concerned for his son's health, which, by all accounts, was not much improved since Leicester's hasty return to court.

'I crave Your Majesty's forgiveness for my poor wits. Pray do not disturb yourself over this recent murder of the Prince of Orange. Such a heinous act cannot happen here. Your subjects love and honour you as their rightful queen. There is not a man in England who would not die to protect you.'

'So you say,' Queen Elizabeth murmured drily, yet seemed mollified.

'Your dogs do not obey you,' he continued more smoothly. 'If you will permit me to take their training in hand myself, Your Majesty, they will soon be walking behind you as pretty and docile as Mistress Morgan.'

The Queen turned to look at Lucy in an unfriendly way. She glanced at her other ladies, walking some distance behind, then sniffed loudly, her lips pursed. 'Lucy,' she remarked coldly, 'I had forgotten you were still there. You walk so quietly . . . like one of Walsingham's *spies*. Tell me, have you learned the steps to that new Italian dance yet?'

Lucy hesitated. 'Not yet, Your Majesty.'

'Then you must do so at once. Give those things to one of the other ladies to carry, for it seems none of *them* have anything to do but look pale and bored today, either.'

Lucy stood bewildered, unsure what she had done to displease the Queen. She glanced at Lord Leicester and then wished she hadn't, for he winked at her behind the Queen's back, and might have made her grin if she had not been quite so apprehensive.

Queen Elizabeth glared at her furiously, her small, dark eyes narrowed against the sun. 'Back to the palace with you, Lucy Morgan, and without delay. I do not spend a fortune each year to keep you at court so you can look "pretty and docile". I wish the Italian ambassador to see you dance after dinner tomorrow. I have promised that he will be amazed at your skills. Go now and make sure of it.'

Lucy curtsied low and hurried away.

She had not gone more than ten paces through the gardens towards the palace when she stopped, hearing her name being whispered hoarsely from behind a hedge.

'Mistress Morgan!'

A young boy in ragged clothes was peering at her round the hedge with eyes as bright as a magpie's.

She glanced over her shoulder, but the Queen and her entourage had already moved on into the formal gardens. There was nobody else about.

Lucy looked at the ragged boy. He was holding out a folded piece of paper. Her heart began to beat hard. Was it a message from Master Goodluck at last?

'Is that for me?' she asked him.

The boy nodded without speaking and came forward a few steps, but did not pass her the letter. Instead, he held out a filthy hand in a begging gesture. Lucy fumbled in her purse for a penny and dropped it into his palm. Pocketing it, he pushed the letter into her hand. Her eye was immediately caught by a familiar symbol scribbled lightly across the fold: a narrow twist of corn or barley, interlaced with a sloping T.

Master Twist!

Lucy turned to the young messenger with questions on her lips, but the boy had already vanished.

Driven by a caution that seemed to have become second nature to her now, Lucy walked on a little further, then turned aside into the shade of some plum trees. There, unobserved, she opened the letter.

Meet me at the ruin they call Saxon's Tower as soon as you can get away. I have grave news. T

She read Twist's message over several times, startled and uncertain what to think. She knew the place he meant, a tumbledown tower on the northern edge of the Nonsuch estate that had stood even before the palace was built. As far as she knew, the rough shepherds who tended the royal livestock slept there in times of poor weather.

But Master Twist was here in person?

I have grave news.

She dreaded to think what that could mean. Why else would he have come to Nonsuch unless he had news of Master Goodluck? Bad news, at that.

As soon as you can get away.

The plum trees buzzed with wasps and bees above her head, their yellowish fruit sweetly fragrant as it ripened. Warily, Lucy stepped out of their pleasant shade and glanced about herself. The sunny gardens were empty of courtiers, only a few men in leather aprons tending the lawns with edging tools and barrows. From behind the privet hedges into the formal gardens she could still hear the barking of the Queen's dogs. She could slip away and walk across to Saxon's Tower now. With the Queen still at her morning walk, Lucy would not be missed for a good hour or two. There was still the new dance to perfect for the ambassador tomorrow, but it should not take long before she had the steps right. It must be now, or else she might miss her chance.

Lucy hurried across the sunlit lawns and through into

woodland, thankful for the dappled shade. It was a hot July day and her heavy skirts made walking a penance. Every few minutes she glanced over her shoulder to be sure she had not been seen.

The ruined tower leaned perilously at the edge of the forest, more a tall circular heap of stones than a tower, cracked and mossy with age. A rough wooden door had been set into its base, and the gaping holes in the roof where tiles had fallen in were covered with a kind of rough thatching of twigs and moss.

As she came close, Lucy saw that the door stood ajar.

'Hello?' she called, pushing it open.

Someone moved within, then Master Twist loomed up out of the darkness. He caught her by the hand and dragged her inside. His face was haggard, blue eyes blood-shot as he stared out of the door behind her. 'You came alone?' he pressed her. 'No one saw you leave the palace? You were not followed?'

'No,' she assured him, bewildered.

'Well done,' he muttered, and closed the door behind her. He hurried away in the glimmering darkness of the interior, then she saw the warm glow of a lantern spring to life as he removed the cover. They were standing in a little stone cell at the base of the tower, just a rough mud floor underfoot and one window slit that had been blocked up, presumably in an unsuccessful attempt to keep out the tiny black flies that were everywhere. She batted several away as they tried to land on her face. But at least it was not hot and stuffy, like the interior of the palace, which lay most of the day in full sun. This place was cool and damp, and smelt mustily of animals. A heap of matted fleeces lay in one corner, serving as a bed, and above it a crumbling flight of steps led away into darkness. She imagined the top floors were blocked off, too, for they could only lead

188

to the open air now that half the tower had tumbled down.

Master Twist looked as though he had been sleeping rough for several days. His hair was tousled and his shirt soiled, and he was wearing the breeches and plain jerkin of a mercenary soldier, a short dagger stuck in his belt. He seized Lucy by the waist and kissed her fervently on the cheek. Then his kiss touched her lips, and she took a step backwards, startled by his sudden intimacy.

'Forgive me,' he said at once, and released her. His smile seemed strained. 'I'm so glad to see you, Lucy. I have a flask of wine if you're thirsty. Will you sit down?'

Lucy looked about the stone cell. There was only a rough three-legged stool to sit on, or the filthy bed of fleeces. She shook her head, frowning. 'What if we are discovered here?'

'No one will come until tomorrow morning. I gave the shepherds a shilling apiece for the place. It's rough, but it will suffice.'

'I was so afraid when I saw your note. You said . . . grave news. Does it concern Master Goodluck?'

Twist took her hands in his and squeezed them. His face was grim. 'Yes.'

She stared at him, terror in her heart. 'For pity's sake, tell me what has happened. I knew that Master Goodluck was missing, that he might be in trouble again. He hasn't replied to my letters for months now. But I thought perhaps an assignment in France or Italy . . .'

'My dearest Lucy, I wish I had better news for you—' Twist began slowly, but she interrupted, unable to wait.

'*Tell me!*'

'Master Goodluck is dead.'

Lucy heard the words she feared most in the world, and shook her head in speechless anguish. She dragged herself free from Twist's hands and backed away, coming up against the filthy wall of the shepherds' cell.

Her guardian dead?

It could not be true. She thought of Goodluck's black beard, his intelligent eyes, the way he nearly broke her ribs whenever he hugged her in welcome or farewell. He was a part of her. It was not possible that Goodluck could be dead and she had not felt it, had not already known in her heart.

'Another mistaken report,' she whispered. 'It wouldn't be the first time he has been thought dead.'

Twist was shaking his head too. 'With my own eyes, I saw him die,' he replied simply.

Her eyes widened, and she looked a question at him. '*Saw*?'

'It was an ambush. One of our men was murdered in the street. Goodluck ran. The murderer gave chase and killed him, too. I was just behind, but couldn't shake off my own pursuer.' With a grimace, Twist stared at the lantern as though seeing Goodluck's last desperate fight in the flame. 'We were at the back of a merchant's yard by the Thames. It was pouring with rain. There was mud everywhere. I saw Goodluck stabbed through the body. Then he fell into the river.'

'No!'

'I'm sorry, it's true.'

Lucy's voice was husky with tears. 'Yet you escaped?'

He could hardly have missed the accusation in her tone, but he did not choose to comment.

'Barely.' Twist rolled up the sleeve of his shirt to display an ugly scar from a sword slash, the skin still red and puckered as though only recently healed. 'I got this pretty keepsake on my way out. But at least I survived. For once, I was luckier than Goodluck himself.'

Lucy ran a fingertip along his scar. Her hand was shaking. 'This looks recent. Three, maybe four weeks old?'

He shrugged, not meeting her eyes. 'I lay in a fever

afterwards. There's a woman who looks after me from time to time. She took me in and tended my wounds. But yes, it cannot be more than a month since he died.'

'But I wrote to Goodluck. At the start of the summer, before the Queen took us on progress. I wrote several times. He did not reply.'

'It was a difficult time. We were followed so closely.'

Lucy frowned, trying to understand his words, though her head was throbbing with pain. How could such a horror be true? Yet she must accept it. Her guardian was dead and she would never see him again.

She remembered the last time she had feared he was dead, her terrible grief then and how she had wept for weeks, only to discover that he still lived. But no, this time it must be true. Master Twist had seen Goodluck stabbed through the body, he had seen him fall into the River Thames and drown. There could be no doubt.

'Did you ever recover the body?' she asked suddenly. 'Give him a good Christian burial?'

Twist hesitated, then shook his head. 'I'm sorry, Lucy. By the time my fever had broken and I was able to rise from my sickbed, it was too late even to bother looking for him. The river currents are strong. They can bear a man's body many miles downstream in the space of a few days, let alone twenty.'

'Then he could still be alive?'

'Impossible.'

'Do not say so!' she exclaimed bitterly, feeling her last slender hopes falling away even as she said it.

'Lucy.'

As if to comfort her, Twist put out a hand to stroke her cheek. She flinched from his touch and he frowned.

'Even if the wound had not been mortal,' he continued, 'the water would have done for him. It had been raining hard all that day, and the river was swollen higher than

I've seen it since. A strong swimmer would have struggled against that tide, and this was a seriously wounded man. I'm sorry, but he would have drowned within a few minutes of hitting the water.'

His words had the weight of hard truth behind them. Lucy held her breath, willing the trembling light in her eyes not to quiver and humiliate her with weakness. Yet still the tears came, spilling down her cheeks.

She wept, hiding her face in her sleeve. The rich fabric scratched her face.

'Hush,' Twist said, drawing her into his arms. 'Take comfort, it was a kind death. Goodluck was a great man and a master spy. But even great men must meet their makers eventually. I have known you since you were a baby in the care of his sister, and he always bade me look after you if anything should happen to him. Trust me, I intend to fulfil that promise.'

He tilted her chin up and kissed away the tears as though she was still a child and had skinned her knees falling over.

'I want you to think of me as your guardian from now on.' His hands tightened about her waist as he spoke, his voice hoarse in her ear. 'You will not find me any less a man than Goodluck.'

She looked at him and did not like the expression on his face. 'Master Twist,' she whispered. 'You're hurting.'

He loosened his grip, but did not release her. Even in the soft glow of the lantern, she could see that he was staring at her mouth. 'My beautiful Ethiop,' he muttered. 'Such full lips. I have dreamt about you, and what lies beneath your courtly gowns. Did Goodluck ever discover the dark treasure hidden there?'

She was shocked. 'What are you saying?'

'You understand me well enough.' His gaze narrowed. 'I would watch the two of you together, and could not

192

believe he would leave such a delicious peach unbruised. Tell me the truth! When did Goodluck first have you? How many times did he enjoy you?'

She was suddenly scared, seeing the lust in his face, thinking back over his description of Goodluck's death. Twist claimed to have *seen* Goodluck stabbed. To have seen him fall to his death in the Thames. But what if it had been Twist himself who had stabbed Goodluck and pushed him into the water?

'Come, Lucy, you will not find me a hard master to please.' He began to drag her by the wrist towards the pile of fleeces. 'Or you *will* find me hard, but you should enjoy it.'

She fought him, but Twist was stronger. He threw her back on to the fleeces as though she weighed nothing, and scrambled on top of her before she could roll away, pinning her body down into the filthy stench of the wool.

'You were always breathtaking, even as a child. To think that Goodluck was enjoying free access to your body . . .' He shuddered, kissing down her throat, jerking her bodice aside so he could touch her breasts. 'That left a bitter taste, I can tell you.'

'He never touched me! Goodluck would never— '

'Don't lie to me,' he snapped, and slapped her so hard across the face that her ears rang and her eyes blurred with tears.

Twist pushed up her skirts, touching her just as William Shakespeare had done. Only this time she felt nothing but fear and disgust. She suspected now that Twist must have killed Goodluck himself, or at least assisted in his murder. Certainly by his own admission he had made no attempt to save his old friend's life.

Now he intended to rape her – and probably murder her afterwards to hide his crime. Her body sickened at the thought of such a betrayal.

'I know Goodluck must have had you,' he continued unsteadily. 'You were never just a daughter to him. I believe he enjoyed you as a woman. As I am about to do.'

She felt his weight ease off her. The yellow glow of the lantern was behind the dark mass of his body and it was hard to see clearly. But she could just make out Twist fumbling impatiently with his breeches, the thick gold ring on his little finger glinting as it caught the lamplight.

She drew up her knee with as much strength as she could muster, catching him full in the groin.

Clutching himself in agony, Twist rolled away from her. 'You bitch!' he managed hoarsely as she scrambled to her feet and ran for the door. 'I'll see you die for that!'

Outside in the blinding July sunshine, Lucy picked up her skirts and ran for the safety of the Palace of Nonsuch. She ran like a wild animal, strong-thighed and sweating, and did not stop even when briars caught at her sleeve in the woodland and tore the fine lace edging.

She did not look back. That would be to invite capture. *Never look back when you are being pursued, not until you are sure of a safe vantage point.* Goodluck's advice echoed in her mind as though the man himself was still there, whispering in her ear, running beside her.

Rounding the west wing of the palace, Lucy almost collided with a nobleman hurrying in the opposite direction. She recognized him and stopped short, panting and hanging her head, her legs trembling now from the unaccustomed effort of such prolonged running.

Only then did she dare to glance back over her shoulder. But the palace lawns and gardens were empty. There was no sign of Master Twist.

Leicester put a hand on her shoulder. 'Lucy? What is it? What's the matter? Forgive me, I cannot stay. Are you hurt? Let me call for someone to assist you.' He turned and shouted at one of the groundsmen, who was tending

194

the rosebeds, 'You, there! Fetch help for Mistress Morgan, she is unwell.'

'I am not hurt, my lord,' she managed between breaths. She looked up then, and saw with a shock that he had been crying. 'My lord?'

'It is my young son,' he said simply. 'My Noble Imp, Lord Denbigh.'

'Has he sickened again?'

'He is near to death, my wife writes.' Leicester's voice choked on the words and he fell silent. 'I've called for my horse. I must ride for Wanstead at once. I do not even have time to take my leave of the Queen. Her Majesty is taking her midday meal alone and has refused admittance even to me.'

He hesitated, falling back a step to look at her. 'Will you speak to her for me, Lucy? Explain to her why I had to leave court without begging her permission? She will surely understand.'

'Of course, my lord,' she whispered, while her heart wrenched in agony for him.

Someone was shouting behind her. It was a pageboy, pointing and calling, 'Your horse, my lord!'

Leicester clasped her shoulder briefly, then was gone.

Her back against the palace wall, Lucy allowed herself to slide down to the ground. Her legs would no longer support her. She closed her eyes and let a reddish-black wave of exhaustion swallow her. Goodluck was dead. Twist most probably killed him. Now he would kill her, too, for what she knew and what she had just done to him. Better if she had allowed him to rape her, perhaps, and fooled him into thinking she was no threat.

She heard voices and hurrying footsteps, then her own maid was bending over her, and men were helping her back to her feet.

195

'What is it, mistress?' her maid asked anxiously, tutting over the torn lace of her gown. 'Are you hurt?'

'No,' she said, lying instinctively.

Never tell the truth when a lie will serve you better. Goodluck again, whispering in her ear. *Remember: if a woman cries rape, she is thought as guilty as the man who dishonoured her.*

Lucy decided against telling Sir Francis Walsingham about Master Twist, even though he was at court and might have helped her, for she was unsure whether Master Twist was also working for him. If he was, Goodluck's death could have been ordered by Walsingham himself.

When the court returned to London at the end of the summer, she would seek out those who remained on Goodluck's team. They would know what to do, how to act against a man as dangerous as Twist.

'The sun is hot today,' she told her maid, and did not meet her curious gaze. 'I should not have walked so far. Fetch me a drink of wine, and something to cover this torn lace. I must speak with the Queen as soon as possible. Lord Leicester has been called away urgently and has charged me with a message for Her Majesty.'

Nineteen

As the barge pulled alongside the bank on the strong tidal currents, Goodluck jumped off, nearly fell backwards into the water, then steadied himself. He turned to raise a hand, but the barge was already moving on. 'Thank you, Jensen,' he called, and the hunched figure at the tiller raised a hand in reply as the barge rolled away with the currents. 'I shall not forget this.'

Wrapped in a light cloak despite the warm evening, Goodluck limped at an easy pace through the narrow streets until he reached Southwark and the inn known to some as the Angel on the Hoop. There he ordered ale and a small fish supper, and stretched out his legs to the fire. It was September, and the first time he had been ashore since the night he had taken a pike in the back and fallen into the swirling black Thames.

The wound in his back had healed some weeks before, but his mind had taken longer to set itself to rights. Some nights he would wake in a cold sweat, thinking he was being attacked by a hooded man. In the dream, he would throw back the hood and find nothing underneath. Just the mockery of shadows. They were only nightmares,

Goodluck told himself sternly, and he was no longer a child, to be frightened by phantoms in the dark. Yet the fears kept him from falling asleep at night.

Jensen had suggested he retire from the spying game, and join her on the barge instead, the two of them working the river together from Richmond to Southwark and back, carrying passengers and cargo, whatever paid the best. The idea had tempted him at first, but then, as his strength returned, Goodluck had found himself becoming restless. He had grown sick of the endless confinement aboard ship, the rocking of the barge day and night, and the filthy stench of the river and its slimy weeds. So he had put his fears aside and determined to seek out Twist and Ned, and discover whether they knew anything about the men who had murdered Sos.

Goodluck sat by the fire in the Angel for a few hours, watching the door open and close as travellers and regulars trailed in and out. He felt tired but alert. He ordered more ale occasionally, and once slapped the serving girl's bottom when she brought it, knowing himself to be under observation from the other tables. She shrieked but did not call the landlord, and Goodluck tossed her a penny when she came back with a bread pudding.

To any who might be taking a note of his behaviour, he would appear to be making a play to get the girl in his bed later, a good reason for a man of his years to be sitting about in a taproom all evening and not be drunk out of his skull.

At last, his patience was rewarded. He heard Hannah before he saw her, laughing incontinently as she pushed through the Angel's door. Her gaze lighted on him as she looked hungrily about the room, but if the large-breasted blonde had recognized him, she gave no sign of it. 'Who will buy me ale?' she called, and no one stirred, though a few laughed.

Some young fool in an apprentice's robes pulled her gown, so that one of her breasts popped out of her bodice and everyone in the room clapped and stared. She turned and kicked him away like a dog. The boy swore and dragged himself to one side, clutching his groin.

Hannah shrugged and continued to hunt about the room for someone to buy her drinks, gazing at each customer in turn with her sharp blue eyes. One got up and left the tavern, another pretended to sleep under the tilt of his hat, few dared look her in the eye. She was a big woman, and knew how to hurt a man.

He felt sorry for the girl. Under the ingrained dirt and fading bruises on her pockmarked face, Hannah was young enough to be pretty, probably less than twenty years of age, and still had most of her teeth. He had known her for some five years, working the streets and alleys of Southwark as a whore – and occasionally a pickpocket when business was slow. Yet she was still passable in a low light, not ruined and broken like most of the girls of her trade once their first bloom was gone.

Eventually, she reached Goodluck's table. 'Pay for my ale and I'll sit on your lap, traveller,' she said with a lopsided grin.

He raised his head and looked her up and down, as though considering the matter. 'How much to sit on something a little harder?' he asked gruffly, disguising his voice.

'If it's hard enough to stand to, a pint of ale and six shillings for my labour. If it's more than an hour's work, though, the price goes up as long as you do.' Several men laughed. This time Hannah laughed with them, playing to her audience. 'Don't look so worried, old man. You'll reach the goal, even if it costs a little more. I've a trick or two that would turn Noah himself into a randy old goat.'

He felt a stab of annoyance. Old man, indeed! Though it was true that, under this ancient hood at least, he must look grey and bedraggled after several months below deck on Jensen's barge.

'You have a room? I'll not do it in the alley,' Hannah declared, swinging herself over the stool opposite him and sitting with her legs akimbo, skirts draped over her knees, which were still shapely, he noted, though a little scarred and dirty. Perhaps she had spent too much time on them in alleys, he thought.

'I'll talk to the landlord when I've finished here,' he said, and took a leisurely draught of his ale. 'Order your ale and put it on my slate. I'll bear the cost later.'

'Aye, that you will,' she replied, with a crude gesture, but called out her order to the passing girl. 'And make sure you pay for the room yourself. It's not coming out of my six shillings.'

The other men looked away, most losing interest now that business between the traveller and the whore seemed to have been concluded.

Carefully, Goodluck allowed his long sleeve to draw back from his hand as he set the tankard down, and heard her gasp. When he looked up, she was staring at the distinctive scar on his wrist. Then her sharp gaze searched his face more slowly, taking in the beard, the crooked nose, the dry smile on his face as he saw she had recognized him.

'Goodluck?' she whispered.

He shook his head, his frown signalling caution. 'Not here. Later, in the room.'

Hannah finished her ale in a few greedy swallows, then waited impatiently as he arranged with the landlord for a room for an hour or two. This done, he led the way upstairs with a candle, finding the appointed room without difficulty and bolting the door so they could be safe from interruption. It was cramped and barely furnished with two stools, a table and a rough cot. He closed the small window, which looked out over Long

Southwark towards the river, and pulled the shutter across to muffle the noise of evening revellers below.

'There.' Goodluck tossed six shillings on to the table in advance of their talk. He did not intend to bed her, but he knew Hannah would still expect payment for her time.

Besides, it would be unfair to leave the whore out of pocket on his account. From the rhythmic creaking and groaning in the rooms on either side, it seemed quite a popular inn for the plying of a whore's trade.

'I thought you were dead,' she said warily, making no move to collect her fee, but watching him instead.

He discarded his hood and cloak, and drew up a stool to the low table. The room was very dark, with only one candle to light it, and there was no fire in the small grate.

'So did I, at one stage,' he admitted, indicating that she should sit opposite. 'But there are many gates to pass on the way to the grave.'

'Does Twist know you're still alive?' she asked bluntly, remaining on her feet as though ready to run for the door.

'I don't imagine so.'

Her eyes glittered in the candlelight. 'I think Twist might be quite surprised. May I tell him when I next see him?'

'No.' She stared across at him, her mouth slightly open, and he continued, 'Not unless you wish to feel a knife in your back one night.'

He raised his eyebrows at Hannah's prolonged silence, content to play the villain if it got him the result he wanted. Besides, he was not entirely sure whose side Hannah was on. He knew she had been close to Twist in the past. She had even lived and worked in Twist's lodgings from time to time, and passed on her earnings to him in return for protection from the worst of the scum who used her. But it had been a few years now since Twist had turned her out on to the streets, preferring to find his pleasure with younger women instead.

201

'What?' he asked her lightly. 'You do not believe me capable of murdering you to keep my secret?'

Hannah shivered and sat down on the stool opposite. She collected up her shillings and dropped them inside the leather purse at her belt. 'You don't need to threaten me, Goodluck. I won't tell him if you don't want me to.'

'Good,' he said, and smiled. 'You are too pretty for such an unpleasant fate.'

Hannah looked at him from under her lashes, and he felt a stirring of desire. It had been a long time since he had enjoyed a woman's company, and she was not un-attractive. He liked big women who knew their own minds and pleasures, and would not lie passive in bed. But there was more important business to conduct tonight.

'I need information, Hannah. Can you help me?'

She tilted her head to one side and regarded him cautiously. 'Why me?'

'Because you work the inns up and down Southwark. Because you see things, and you're not stupid.'

Goodluck pulled off one of his gloves and passed his palm slowly over the candle flame, testing the heat against his skin. He was tired, and he knew it. But the burning pain helped him to think, to remain alert.

He asked her, 'Where's Ned?'

She was staring at him. 'He's dead,' she whispered. 'Like I thought you were.'

Ned had been one of his friends in London for years, a theatrical turned spy. His fists clenched. 'When was this? How did he die?'

'A few months back,' she said slowly, thinking. 'Must have been just after Eastertide. They say he hanged him-self, poor bastard.'

Goodluck's gaze shot to her face. 'He took his own life? Why would Ned do that?'

'He owed money, I think. That's what they were saying

in the taverns, anyway. And that he'd been drinking heavily before he ... before he died. Keeping bad company, they said.'

'Who's "they"?'

'Just people.' She bit her lip, watching him. 'I'm sorry. Ned was a friend of yours, wasn't he? A bad end, too. The priest wouldn't even give him a decent burial, so I heard, because he killed himself. I saw his wife follow the coffin out through Southwark, and his five children too, one only a babe in arms.'

He passed his hand over the candle flame again. Several men dead from his old team of theatrical spies. And deaths that could hardly be considered natural.

Who was left?

Only Master Twist and Goodluck himself, whom Twist thought safely dead, stabbed and left to drown in the River Thames months ago.

How Twist must have rejoiced at the old man's boldness, running Goodluck through with his pike as he stood staring down at the river! No need for Twist even to sully his hands with his blood.

'Where's Twist now?'

Hannah looked at him with a wary expression, but said nothing, too quick-witted not to have understood the gist of the conversation so far and realized the danger to herself.

'Tell me, Hannah,' he said, as persuasively as he could. He rattled the purse at his belt. 'There's another few shillings in it for you.'

'Out of town,' she said at last.

'For how long?'

'I don't know. I'm not his whore. I work for myself now.' She licked her lips, and he saw fear in her blue eyes. 'If I tell you where he keeps his lodgings these days, will you let me go and say nothing to Twist about me? Nor anyone else? If he finds out that I talked to you, he'll kill me.'

That was true enough.

'I'll tell no one.'

'Swear it,' she hissed, and drew a battered silver crucifix from her purse.

He stared at it, then at her. 'You could be whipped for possessing that. Hanged too, if they think you're a Catholic.'

'What do I care for that? It was my grandmother's. Now hold the cross and swear that you'll never speak a word to Twist about me.'

It irked him to do so, and was dangerous, besides, if anyone happened to be listening at the door. But the old ways still meant something to the girl, so he held the Catholic crucifix in his hand and swore in Christ's name never to mention her to Twist, nor any other man, then handed it back.

'Satisfied?'

She hid it away in her purse and nodded, a smile on her lips. 'You know the Saracen's Head?'

He nodded. A tavern with a dubious reputation, it stood off a narrow lane a few hundred yards down Long Southwark.

'Three doors down from the inn, there's a green gate across an alley. His place is the first on the left inside the alleyway. Go up a flight of steps. The key's kept under a loose floorboard at the top. His mark's on the door, though you won't see it in darkness.'

'And he's away from London, you say?'

'I saw him a few days ago. He said he was travelling into the country for a while, down Surrey way. Something about a girl he had to see.'

'I wish him joy of her,' Goodluck said drily, and stood up. 'Surrey's not far, though. I'd better search his place now while he's away.' He felt in his purse and gave her two more shillings.

'He won't come back into the city after dark, though, will he?' she pointed out, putting the money away. She stood up too, knocking the stool over, her head almost equal with his. Then she smiled at him knowingly and began to unbuckle his belt. 'John Twist's either there now or he won't be back until dawn at the earliest. Which gives me a good while yet to earn those six shillings you gave me earlier.'

'To earn them?'

Hannah folded her long legs beneath her to kneel at his feet. She reached out to massage his groin with an expert hand.

He stopped her. 'That's not necessary.'

She looked up at him, surprised and perhaps a little hurt. 'You don't want me?'

Goodluck smiled regretfully. 'Of course I do, Hannah. But that pleasure will have to wait for another time. My errand tonight is too urgent.'

Following Hannah's directions, Goodluck swung himself over the green gate into the alleyway near the Saracen's Head, and up the short flight of steps to the left. His back was hurting again, but he tried to ignore the pain. Jensen had said she thought it would improve with exercise, and so he must hope, too. The top stair rattled underfoot and he paused, remembering. It took only the blade of his dagger, twisted in the narrow gap between boards, to prise it loose. Beneath lay the key to Twist's lodgings, which he removed gladly. The door was of surprisingly thick oak and would have been difficult to shoulder open; no doubt that was why Twist had chosen this place. Silently, Goodluck traced the mark on the door. Master Twist lives here, it announced. He listened, but there was no sound from within.

The door unlocked, he crept inside, his dagger in hand. The room lay in darkness, an added danger as he tried not to collide with furniture on his way to the window. He fumbled with the shutters to let in the moonlight, then found a candle and tinderbox. To his relief, and as Hannah had rightly predicted, there was nobody home.

By candlelight, he set about a careful search of Twist's scanty belongings, trying not to make it too obvious that anyone had been there. If Twist was the traitor he had been looking for – and he felt pain at the very possibility – then it would not do to alert him that his betrayal had been discovered.

Twist's clothes and book chest revealed nothing out of the ordinary. But it did not take Goodluck long to find, by knocking along the wood and listening to the hollow reply, a false back to the alcove cupboard where Twist kept his candles and tinder. He reached into the dark space and drew out an oblong tin box hidden there. Even its intricate French-designed lock did not last long against the thinnest of Goodluck's lock-pickers.

Inside the tin box, he found various seals and lists of ciphers, an alphabet key, and a bundle of letters secured with a black ribbon.

Goodluck unrolled one of the letters and took it to the candle flame. He stared down at the signature, but could not make it out. It had been marred soon after writing. The letter was more clearly addressed, however, to Philip, Earl of Arundel, a suspected Catholic and one of the Queen's own courtiers. It was dated June twenty-seventh, and made some uncertain references to 'faith', 'the need for secrecy' and, once, to 'Her captive Grace'.

He frowned, studying it for a moment. Either the letter had not been sent to Arundel for some reason, or else this was a copy, made by Twist himself – or perhaps sent on to him by whoever had penned the original.

Either way, the matter to which the letter referred would seem to be treasonous in the extreme. 'Her captive Grace', he read again with foreboding. That could only mean one person: Mary Stuart, the exiled Queen of Scots, who was being held as a royal prisoner by her cousin, Queen Elizabeth.

Was it possible that John Twist had involved himself with the very Catholics they had been working together to uncover? That he was, in fact, one of their number himself, and sympathized with the cause of the Scottish Queen?

Goodluck found an inkwell and quill on the table, tore out a page from one of Twist's books, and copied the ciphers and the alphabet key as swiftly and accurately as he could. If still in use, they might unlock the secrets of other coded messages that fell into his hands. He also took a brief note of the seals, and of the names and substance of the letters he had found, suspecting they could be of interest in the future.

Then he replaced the contents of the tin box exactly as he had found them, locked it and pushed it carefully back into its hiding place.

Sir Francis Walsingham must know of this hoard. Goodluck had thought it too dangerous to visit Seething Lane before – though a coded note had informed Walsingham he was not dead, but in hiding. Now that he was sure of Twist's complicity, to take news of these letters to his spymaster was his only possible move. He only hoped it would not be seen as a double bluff, intended to reveal Twist's guilt while concealing his own.

If Walsingham had ever suspected him of treachery, this find could help to clear his name. Either that or condemn him to a traitor's death.

Twenty

Whitehall Palace, London, December 1584

ELIZABETH SAT UP EVEN STRAIGHTER IN HER CURTAINED BED and stared at her spymaster through the flickering firelight, not quite able to believe what he had just relayed to her.

'Parry said *what*?' she demanded stiffly.

Walsingham looked apologetic. 'That our new law against the Catholics and Jesuits was unjust and would prove injurious to England.'

'And this insolent judgement was declared in the Houses of Parliament in which my generosity placed him only this year?'

'I fear so, Your Majesty, yes.'

'Then you must arrest this man at once.'

Walsingham bowed, a little smile on his face. 'It has already been done, Your Majesty. Sensing the ugly mood of the Commons, and fearing a riot if he was not taken straightaway into custody, Sir Christopher Hatton made the arrest himself, there and then. Even as he was being escorted out of the Commons under guard, Parry attempted to continue with his inflammatory speech to any who would listen.'

Elizabeth shook her head in disbelief. 'What was Parry thinking of, to be speaking so dangerously and against our express will? Was the man drunk?'

'No, Your Majesty. I have examined him myself, and he genuinely considers himself to be in the right. He feels that we do Catholics an injustice by treating them as traitors and driving the old faith underground.'

'Does he indeed?'

'I begin to think he may be a madman.'

'A madman?' she repeated, staring at him rigidly. 'This is the same Parry, is it not, who has spied for you in the past? Who has carried letters for me of a most private and delicate nature? Good God, man, this creature has been allowed access to my person on your own recommendation. Master Parry has come into my Privy Chamber late at night with tales of assassins and high treason and Catholics landing unseen on our shores – and now you tell me he is a traitor to the throne?'

'An error of judgement on my part, Your Majesty. But one I am working to rectify.'

She sniffed at this, unconvinced.

Walsingham continued, 'I have released Parry and set men to watch his house. We have little evidence at the moment, and a false accusation would merely lose us valuable information. If Parry attempts to make contact with anyone we know to be in league against you, he will be arrested again and tried for treason.'

'Very well,' she said, frowning impatiently as the door to her chamber opened. Helena stood blocking the doorway, as though to prevent someone from entering. 'What is it, Helena?'

'Lord Leicester wishes to speak with you, Your Majesty.' Helena's face was grave and unsmiling. She disapproved of Robert's marriage to Lettice, and had never made any show of hiding her feelings. But then, her loyalty to Elizabeth was beyond question, and she objected to anything that might upset her queen. Her Swedish accent was most pronounced tonight. 'I have told him it is very late and you will not wish to be disturbed, Your Majesty. But he would not listen and is insisting that I announce him.'

Robert? Come to see her so late at night?

Elizabeth experienced a flicker of girlish excitement she had not felt in a long time, and saw Walsingham's dark, intelligent gaze narrow on her face.

She steadied herself and tried to look unconcerned. Robert was a married man again now, just as he had been in the first years of her reign. It would not do to encourage the same vicious old gossip by allowing him free access to her chamber late at night. But just this once would not do any harm.

And if it should come to his wife's ears that he was visiting the Queen at night again, so much the better.

'Very well,' she said coolly, and nodded to Helena. 'You may invite his lordship to enter.'

Robert strode to her bedside. His appearance was still as haggard as it had been ever since the death of his little son in July, she noted, and surprised a sympathy in herself for his loss. Yet it was six months since the boy had died. Was he never to recover from that blow? But then, Lettice must be too old to bear another heir to the earldom, and so his line would be broken. His grief must be bitter indeed.

Robert went down on one knee, his cap in hand. When she gestured him to rise, he kissed her hand and muttered, 'My queen!'

Walsingham's eyebrows rose. He cleared his throat, and Robert looked searchingly in his direction.

'What, you here too?'

With a slight bow, Walsingham nodded. 'My business is almost concluded,' he reassured Leicester, then turned to

Elizabeth. 'All that remains to be said to Your Majesty is that I have decided to bait a trap for our Catholic friends. It may take some time to lay the foundations for this trap, and it will be costly. There are men to be paid, and travel arrangements, and other sundry expenses. But if I could be assured of remuneration . . .'

His voice tailed off meaningfully. She transferred her stare from Robert to Walsingham, suddenly realizing his true purpose in visiting her tonight. 'You want more money?' she demanded. 'Already? What happened to the last expenses I granted you?'

'I . . . erm . . . expended them, Your Majesty.'

'I see.' She sighed. 'Well, who are these men that must be paid? I presume the execrable Parry is not among their number this time? For I am beginning to doubt your skill in knowing a loyal spy from a turncoat.'

Walsingham's smile was thinner than ever. 'No, Your Majesty. This is a most trustworthy man whom I am sending abroad to find and follow your enemies. He is highly skilled and has worked for the good of England many times.' His gaze slid to Robert's face, his voice suddenly smooth and empty of all meaning. 'Indeed, he is the self-same man whose skill and daring helped to foil the assassination attempt at Kenilworth almost ten years ago.'

'Then he did not work alone,' Robert pointed out. 'As I recall, my own people also helped to foil that plot. Several gave their lives to protect the Queen that night.'

'Indeed, I had forgotten the small part played by your own men.'

'And by Lucy Morgan,' Robert threw in for good measure, his frown very dark.

Elizabeth watched the two men, amused by their sharp exchanges and posturing. 'Come, sirs, let us not lose sight of the point. Exactly how much am I to lay out for this . . . what is the brave fellow's name?'

'Master Goodluck, Your Majesty,' Walsingham supplied, turning back to her with a sombre smile.

'Ah yes, I remember his name. How much am I to give you for Master Goodluck's mission?'

'I shall draw up a list of what is required, Your Majesty. I merely wished to be sure it would be agreeable to you if I sent spies back into France to discover these English Catholics who have made their homes there.'

'It is most agreeable to me, and Leicester there will be your witness to that effect.'

Walsingham bowed, his look very earnest. 'Thank you, Your Majesty. It is by measures like these that we shall curb Catholic plots once and for all, and settle your throne in peace.'

'Yes, and you had better do so quickly,' Robert remarked, seating himself on the edge of the Queen's bed with an impudent grin in her direction, 'for now we have all signed the Bond of Association, there may be rich lands and goods up for grabs once certain English noblemen have been proven to be traitors.'

'Robert!' she reprimanded him, but could not help laughing as Walsingham took himself away with a hurried bow. 'You are incorrigible.'

'This latest suspicion, that the Arundels are involved in some plot to put your cousin Mary on the throne, seems to depend on a letter of dubious origin. More's the pity, for I'd be glad to see them all executed, if they have indeed conspired against you.' He looked at her with a wry smile, and she had a taste of the old Robert, the one before his unwise marriage to Lettice, before the tragic death of his young son. 'I have no love for these great Catholic families who sit through our plain service with pained expressions, then rush off to their gilded family chapels for a less-than-secret High Mass.'

'Nor I,' she agreed.

'Yet if treason could be proved, who would take their lands under the terms of the Bond of Association?'

She smiled, and answered him as coolly as she could. 'What, are you hungry for yet more wealth and status, Robert? For more land and the power it brings a man when he owns most of England?' He sat up, stiff-backed, instantly on his guard. Her eyes warred with his, only half-joking. 'Sometimes I fear you mean to become more powerful than your queen.'

'If you believe that, Your Majesty, strip me at once of my lands and possessions, and send me begging on the streets of London.' His face was passionate. 'I am still your most loyal subject, and would be even then, as a filthy beggar at your feet.'

'As a filthy beggar at my feet,' she pointed out, 'Walsingham or Lord Burghley or one of my guards would soon have you dragged away by force. Yes, and put in the stocks for daring to approach the Queen!'

He seized her hand and kissed it again, this time more lingeringly, reminding her that they were alone together in her bedchamber.

Elizabeth sat there in her curtained bed, in a nightgown and lacy cap, and looked at Robert sitting next to her, as intimate with her as a husband, just as he might have done if she had agreed to marry him.

'Stay with me tonight,' she whispered daringly, and felt his lips still on her hand.

Robert looked up at her searchingly, and she realized that he was still not himself. His eyes were dark with pain, with a desperate longing she had long since forgotten if she had ever experienced, and there was an anguish in his face that left her in no doubt of his suffering.

'Elizabeth,' he began haltingly, then closed his eyes. His hand clenched on hers compulsively. 'Your Majesty, you honour me too much. I . . . I regret that I cannot stay. I came to beg your permission to leave court for Christmas, to spend a few days at home and return for the New Year festivities as always.'

She stared and could not seem to breathe. Robert had not come here tonight to make love to her, to tell her that everything was back to how it had been before his marriage to that she-wolf Lettice, the woman whose name she could hardly bring herself to speak. He had come instead to ask if he could return to his wife's bed for Christmastide, and she, like a doting fool, had believed his smiles and kisses tonight were for her alone, for his beloved Elizabeth.

'Get out,' she managed hoarsely, and turned her face away so he would not see the tears. She heard Robert go quietly to the door and stop there, still hesitant, still waiting for her reply. She gave her permission wearily, closing her eyes to shut out the glare of the firelight. Her voice rang hollow in the great bedchamber. 'Not a day later than New Year.'

Twenty-one

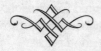

WALSINGHAM GLANCED UP FROM THE LETTER HE WAS writing and, seeing who was at the door, put down his pen. 'Master Goodluck. Yes, do come in.'

Goodluck bent his head to enter the low-ceilinged, dark-panelled study in Walsingham's house, and stood waiting, his cloak and jacket still drawn tight against the chill January weather, his travelling bag slung over one shoulder. Below, he watched a groom saddling a horse in the small yard that backed on to Seething Lane.

Walsingham got up stiffly to unlock a box on the table behind his desk. He took a small pouch out of the box, then closed and locked it again.

'Thank you,' he told his personal secretary, who was still hovering in the doorway, 'that will be all for tonight.'

When they were alone, he gestured Goodluck to sit. 'You're ready to leave tonight?'

Goodluck nodded. 'I have everything with me that I'll need.' The fire in the study was still burning brightly, and the room was warm after the wintry chill of London's streets. He stripped off his gloves and laid them carefully across his knee. 'The ciphers and alphabet key I brought you in the summer, have they proved useful yet?'

Pouring wine into two glasses that stood on the table by the window, Walsingham nodded thoughtfully. 'Indeed they have. Wine?'

Goodluck accepted his glass of wine gratefully, for he felt on edge tonight and needed something to steady his nerves. He was more used to ale these days, and to the stink of common taverns, but red wine was a pleasant alternative. The taste of expensive wine always reminded him of his long-gone youth, in the halcyon days before his father had been executed for treason, his family disgraced, and he himself disinherited and left to wander the country penniless and lost to good sense.

Taking the other glass, Walsingham sat down behind his desk again and rummaged among his scattered papers. 'Here,' he said in the end, and handed over a sheet of strange scrawlings and symbols which would have meant little to most men, but to Goodluck meant a coded letter. He studied it while Walsingham continued, 'Interesting, isn't it? This was taken from a man landing at Dover three nights ago. Using the alphabet key you brought me, I was able to decode it with very little effort. And what do you suppose it is?'

Goodluck raised his eyebrows, waiting.

'It is a set of instructions,' Walsingham told him coolly, 'on how to separate the Queen from her guards in broad daylight and bundle her away to a private place of execution. It even includes details on which prayers should be said before and after that heinous act. Good Catholic prayers, one need hardly add.'

Goodluck was deeply shocked. He looked at the coded sheet in his hand and felt his skin creep with horror. He knew how desperately some of these disenfranchised Catholics desired to regain England for the Roman faith, and how self-righteous would-be assassins of the Queen were when captured. Even so, he could not conceive of how such a letter could be sent in cold blood.

'To whom was it addressed?'

'It bears no name, nor closing signature. Which tells me that its writer was a cautious man, for all his boldness in setting forth the art of royal assassination.' Walsingham accepted the sheet back from Goodluck and, after glancing through it once more, threw it back on to his desk as though it meant nothing. 'It also tells me that he knew we might intercept it.'

'And that there may be others like it out there which were not intercepted, and have found their targets.'

'Indeed,' Walsingham agreed grimly. 'Which brings me to your part in this great comedy. This past year, I have begun to compile a list. On that list are the names of various courtiers suspected either of having dealings with men like the writer of this letter – those who would rid England of Protestant rule for good – or who are themselves the instigators of such treacherous schemes and plots.' Walsingham paused, his expression troubled. 'It is not as short a list as I hoped at the start. But some of the names may appear there in error, and some, perchance, may be persuaded to turn against their fellow conspirators in return for the Queen's pardon.'

'And my part, sir?'

'Your task is to befriend the men whose names are in the paper I am about to hand to you, along with this purse, which is frighteningly heavy and should suffice to buy you priestly vestments and other necessary accoutrements of a Catholic priest, as well as pay for your passage into France. When you encounter these men, as I say, you will persuade them not only that you are a Roman priest, but that you are privy to many plots against Her Majesty and are keen to put them into action.' He smiled. 'You will need to trim your famous beard for this mission, I fear. My apologies.'

Goodluck's mouth twitched. 'In the Queen's service, anything.'

'I want you to send me reports whenever you are able to do so without rousing suspicion. I want names and intentions. I want to know who is involved at the English court. I want to know details and timings of any assassination attempts you uncover. And I particularly wish to be informed if the Queen's Scottish cousin is ever mentioned as having given her consent or blessing to these plots.'

'Sir?' Goodluck stared at him, only now realizing the enormity of the task he had been assigned. His discovery in such a role would almost certainly mean his death. 'How long am I to stay in France and make these reports? Six months? A year? Longer?'

'Here, too,' Walsingham said, ignoring his query, and passing Goodluck the purse and several papers, 'is a pass allowing you to enter and leave any English port at will, no questions asked. Also a note that you may produce in case of arrest. You will see my mark on the paper there. That should get you through most difficult situations.'

Weighing the purse in his hand, Goodluck frowned. 'So I am to pose as a Catholic priest, sir?'

'I hope your Latin's up to it.'

Goodluck grimaced. '*In nomine Patris et Filii et Spiritus Sancti*?'

'Amen.'

'Amen, indeed, if I muddle my declensions.'

'Don't worry. A few days' study and you can begin baptizing the faithful.' Walsingham nodded irreverently at Goodluck's untouched glass. 'Talking of the blood of Christ, you had better down that and be on your way before this conversation becomes redundant.' He turned to consult a book that lay open on the table, its pages covered with tiny crabbed print. 'According to my almanac, the next tide leaves at eight in the morning, and you must go with it to France.'

'Yes, sir.'

Goodluck stood and drained the wine glass. He set it down carefully on the table, admiring the delicate fluting of the stem, the tiny bubbles in the coloured glass.

'Why me, sir? You must have other, more educated spies to choose from, ones who could more easily pass as a priest in a Catholic seminary.'

'Because your French is excellent, your Italian almost perfect, you're quick-witted, and you're skilled at living in disguise for many months without discovery.'

Goodluck's eyes narrowed on Walsingham's face, having sensed a slight hesitation. '*And*?'

Walsingham smiled wryly. 'And you're already dead, Goodluck. Such a convenience to have a dead spy who can still move about unsuspected.'

That had not been the true reason for his hesitation, Goodluck knew instinctively. But it was the only answer he would get tonight.

Tucking the heavy purse inside his jacket, Goodluck turned at the door. 'Sir?' he asked, determined not to leave England without discovering what he had intended to find out for many months now. 'How is my ward? How is Lucy Morgan? I know you must see her at court from time to time.'

'Lucy is very well. A little quiet these days, but that is only to be expected.'

'She will think I'm dead.'

Walsingham inclined his head. 'I'm sorry about that, truly I am. But it's safer for her this way. And for you.' He thought for a moment. 'I can see how you might prefer not to leave her unprotected, however. If you wish, I shall give one of my men instructions to approach her over the sale of your house in Cheapside. You will not wish to keep it on if you are abroad a year or more, and she may be glad of the money.'

'I had rather she was given the deeds, so she has somewhere safe to live if she ever leaves court.'

'Life at court is a precarious existence indeed. Lucy has long been one of my favourites. It will be my pleasure to arrange for her to "inherit" your property until such time as you are free to return and declare yourself not dead, but very much alive.' Walsingham looked at him drily, not commenting on how unlikely that prospect was, nor needing to. 'Anything else?'

'Have you located John Twist, sir?'

'I am still pursuing that lead, though it is not a matter of any urgency. I understand your desire for revenge, believe me. I am often angry myself when men attempt to have me killed – and it was done so clumsily, too. Master Twist must be held in reserve, however, in case his presence proves useful in some way.' Walsingham smiled. 'To speak frankly, his name has not yet come up on my list of men to be detained.'

Still Goodluck hesitated, not satisfied by this answer. 'Forgive me, sir, you have been both generous and patient, and I thank you for it. But when will I be allowed to tell Lucy the truth?'

Without answering the question, Walsingham poured a little more red wine into his glass, and studied it cautiously. 'This Burgundy goes straight to my head in the evenings, you know. I used to drink no end of it when I was a young man. But now . . . Ah well, I must be getting old.' He looked down at his half-written letter and took up his pen again, dipping it fastidiously in the inkwell. 'I believe you'll find a groom in the yard, with a fast horse saddled and waiting for you. Don't miss the tide, Goodluck. *Bon voyage!*'

Part Two

One

Nonsuch Palace, Surrey, autumn 1585

'YOUR MAJESTY,' LORD BURGHLEY SAID QUIETLY, 'I AM afraid Lord Leicester is right for once. We cannot delay any longer. You have promised to send four thousand foot soldiers and a thousand cavalrymen to relieve those fighting the Spanish in the Low Countries, and you cannot now be seen to be withdrawing that promise of help.'

Elizabeth turned from the window, chin held high as she faced her Privy Councillors. It was a beautiful autumnal day, the gardens at Nonsuch glorious with pink overblown roses and the feathery purple heads of lavender. Yet she would not be allowed to wander through the grounds today, nor pick basketfuls of fragrant lavender with her ladies, for she was beset on all sides by those who would set a date for the English fleet to sail to Brill and Flushing.

'And when Spain declares war on England, who will send men for our relief?' she demanded sharply, examining their faces. Only Lord Burghley had the grace to lower his gaze. 'No one, for we are alone in standing up to Philip of Spain and his obsession with empire. You know my policy here, my lords. War bleeds a country dry, and our coffers will not stand such a conflict. Yes, I promised fighting men to the Low Countries to prevent the Spanish invasion there, and Robert to lead them, for he is so well-known on the Continent.' She hesitated, seeing the sudden light of hope on their faces. 'But I did not say when I would send them.'

Robert slammed his hand against the table in frustration. 'This delay is impossible and cannot be borne! Your Majesty, forgive me for speaking so frankly, but our efforts will be ruined if we do not leave before the end of September. At least set a date for October if you cannot agree on one for this month.'

'But why do we need to hurry?' Elizabeth asked. 'I distrust hurrying. It nearly always leads to mistakes.'

'Because I have sent out marshalling letters as you yourself requested, Your Majesty. I have hundreds of men under my command already assembled at Harwich, or on their way to join the fleet as soon as they may.' Robert looked at her bitterly. 'Good men, whom I can ill afford to offend.'

'Then you must send them home again,' she said calmly.

'At whose expense?'

Haughtily, Elizabeth raised her brows at him, disliking his tone and the freedom of his speech before her. Robert was rather too quick these days to forget the deference he owed to his queen. Perhaps appointing Robert as leader of this military expedition to the Low Countries had been a mistake, for his self-regard was now more marked than ever. If he came back victorious, an army at his beck and call, he might even be a threat to her throne.

'At your own, my lord.'

Lord Burghley cleared his throat. 'Your Majesty—'

'Oh, very well,' she interrupted him impatiently, knowing what he meant to say, and not being minded to hear it. 'I will set a date for the fleet to sail. Let it be in October.

No, that is too soon. Early November. Or else December, if there is any further delay.'

Robert bowed stiffly and left the room without asking her permission. She could see that he was angry and did not call him back. Her jangling nerves felt easier when he was not in her presence, anyway.

She avoided Lord Burghley's gaze. He had been suffering from the gout all summer, and his temper was less steady than usual. 'So that is an answer of sorts. Or the best answer you can hope for today. Remind me, gentlemen, how much did I promise from the coffers to keep these men in the field if the conflict should last longer than a year?'

'The sum of one hundred and twenty-five thousand pounds per annum, Your Majesty,' Sir Christopher Hatton announced, checking back through the stack of papers in front of him.

'Merciful heavens,' she said blankly. 'That is a vast sum.'

'But consider, Your Majesty,' Hatton added diplomatically, 'the inevitable result of not supporting the Dutch against the Spanish threat. If the Low Countries were to fall, and King Philip could supply and launch his ships from the port of Flushing, his war fleet would be upon us within days. Nor are the towns on the east coast as fortified as the Channel ports are. Such a sum may seem vast, but it is necessary and proportionate to our commitments there. To ignore the Spanish encroachment on the Low Countries is to expose England herself to invasion.'

'Who is to take command of Flushing?'

'Sir Philip Sidney will control Flushing,' Lord Burghley told her, 'and my own son, Sir Thomas Cecil, will take the governorship of Brill. Their orders, like those given to Lord Leicester, are not to exceed their authority with open warfare but to lend support only. I am as keen as you,

Your Majesty, not to see this conflict escalate into a war with Spain.'

Waving him to silence, Elizabeth paced the room as she considered the matter. Even in the beautiful and extravagant surroundings of Nonsuch, she felt constantly at risk – the very reason why she had not yet returned to one of her London palaces, even though her summer progress should have finished weeks ago. It had seemed safer at first to remain as far outside the capital as possible. Yet Elizabeth knew there would be no safe place for her, whether in London or the provinces, once she had given permission to Robert and his fleet to set sail for Flushing. Whatever Burghley might say, such a flagrant act of defiance would be tantamount to declaring open war on Spain, and with the growing number of Catholics in England, desperate to remove their Protestant queen from power, she might as well poison her own food and have done with it.

Well, so be it. Elizabeth had grown accustomed to living in fear of attack and assassination.

But did this war have to happen now, while she felt so weak and unsure of herself? Mary on the one hand, and now Robert's wife on the other, by all accounts setting herself up as the next queen, with Elizabeth still on the throne.

'Tell me, is it true what I hear about Leicester's wife?' she asked tartly, pausing to stare at her assembled councillors. 'I am informed that since she arrived in London, she is attended wherever she goes by a liveried train of a dozen servants and outriders, and that she dresses as though she were on the throne herself, not a mere countess.'

There was an awkward silence, then Lord Burghley dismissed the other councillors, waiting discreetly until the door had closed behind the last of them before answering her question. 'I'm afraid it does Your Majesty little credit to be overly concerned with the domestic arrangements of Leicester's wife while our fleet kicks its heels, awaiting your order to sail.'

'But is it true?' Elizabeth persisted, hating herself for the shrewish note in her voice, but driven by a compulsive need to know her enemy.

'I believe it is true in essence, yes. But she is hardly ever at Leicester House these days. Knowing your keen dislike of her, the earl has always advised his wife to keep to her country houses and avoid London while you are in residence there.' Lord Burghley shrugged, moving to the window to gaze out over the formal gardens. 'Which you are not, at present. My own advice, Your Majesty, is that you put aside such trivial matters and come to a decision regarding our commitment in the Low Countries.'

'She is my cousin,' Elizabeth hissed. 'You know some even whisper that her mother was my half-sister by King Henry. Do you not see how Lettice puts herself above me with these tricks and antics? How she manoeuvres for the throne itself?'

'Your Majesty, this train of thought is not worthy of your royal estate.'

'But consider,' she insisted, coming to stand beside him at the window, 'Robert is to command our forces in the Low Countries. He is widely considered the first man of our nation, both at home and abroad. If anything were to happen to me, to whom would the people look to save them from a Catholic reign under Mary, Queen of Scots?'

'Nothing will happen to you,' he murmured, staring out at the gardens. 'Leicester will contain the situation, as he has been instructed, and there will be no threat of invasion by the Spanish.'

But Elizabeth caught the uneasiness behind his words. 'Even you do not believe that any more, old friend.'

'If you are concerned, then name your successor. That at least will make your position more secure.'

Elizabeth turned away, smoothing down her heavy red-gold skirts. The gown had pleased her this morning. Until she had heard from one of her ladies that the Countess of Leicester had been seen in a gown that surpassed even her own wardrobe, being cloth-of-gold with ermine trim. Could no one but she see the danger of allowing this upstart wench to outshine the Queen of England herself? And on what pretext? That Lettice was the second – or third, if Lady Douglas was to be believed – wife of a man who had begun his career as her Master of the Horse, and still had the stink of the stables about him?

Her temper simmered, returning abruptly to her earlier subject. 'The Countess does not seek to follow her husband to the Low Countries, I trust?'

'I do not believe so, no,' Lord Burghley said, almost as curt as Elizabeth.

'Make sure of it. Have her watched.'

He bowed. 'I will convey your orders to Sir Francis Walsingham. Meanwhile, Your Majesty, if we could settle on a date for the fleet to sail?'

'Yes, very well,' she snapped, exhausted by his insistence. 'Lord Leicester may sail for the Low Countries as soon as the full fleet is gathered. Draw up the orders and I shall sign them in due course.'

When her councillor had finally left the room, Elizabeth sank to her knees, no longer able to hold back her tears. She did not wish Robert to leave court and her side. She wished she had never thought of him to lead the fleet. Even if his absence would hurt Lettice too, the violent wound it caused in her own heart was not worth the satisfaction of the other.

It was all madness! Robert was two and fifty years old, and suffered from rheumatism. He was no keen young swordsman like Pip Sidney. Nor was he even an experienced campaigner, like the men she was sending to advise him in the field. Robert was a courtier, born and bred to the foolish, stifling life of the court. He was more accustomed to fighting for her affection than wielding a sword in his own protection. Yet he was childishly eager to leave at once for the Low Countries, to sail forth like a conquering hero with thousands of Englishmen under his command.

'The stupid old fool will be killed in the first skirmish,' she moaned into the silence of her chamber, scratching at her forearms and taking comfort from the vicious red scores in her skin. 'He'll fall from his horse and break his neck, or the fleet will be wrecked in a storm. I cannot bear it. I cannot bear his death.'

With Robert gone, she might as well die herself. What would be left to her? The hollow victory of life?

Elizabeth dragged her red wig from her head and tore at her face in a gasping paroxysm of hysteria. She would never let him leave England. Never! She had lost his body to another woman and now was she to lose his soul, too? *Robert!* She screamed his name silently inside her head, forcing herself not to shout it aloud. *Robert! Robert!*

When her ladies came hurrying in to the sound of her weeping, they found Elizabeth bloodied and inconsolable, doubled over on the stone flags like a woman who has just received the news of her husband's death.

Two

IT WAS STILL A GOOD HOUR SHY OF THE AFTERNOON'S performance at the Theatre and the narrow street was crowded with fruit sellers, potmen, whores, ladies in their finery, horses and carts, soldiers in search of a good time before they had to leave for the conflict in the Low Countries, and a turbulent crowd of commoners come to Shoreditch for their entertainment. This sometimes meant fights, particularly among the young men. Even as Will Shakespeare leaned against a barrel of ale by the playhouse entrance, studying an old play script he had been re-writing, he saw a skirmish break out between two bands of youths opposite his vantage point.

Men with stout staves came hurrying down the street, shouting, 'Order, there! Keep the peace!' and the youths darted at once down alleys and into shop doorways, leaving the street in disarray.

'More trouble?' Burbage muttered, coming out of the theatre entrance to see what the commotion was. It was dim inside the theatre, and he held up a hand, squinting across the street in the autumn sunshine. 'These fights will get us closed down. After last year's riot, they've been making a note of every disturbance outside the Theatre or the Curtain. I tell you, Will, they're looking to shut us down.'

'Now *that* would spark a riot!' Will clapped him on the shoulder. 'You've nothing to fear, Burbage. Look at this unruly lot. Whores, thieves and vagabonds, or young men looking to spill some blood. The city fathers want them out of the streets of London as much as you want them in your theatre. Even if they closed you down for a few days, the clamour for the Theatre to reopen would deafen all of London.'

Burbage laughed. 'You've a silver tongue there, Will. Do you use it on the whores?'

'I'm too busy for whores,' Will pointed out. Drily, he held up the half-finished play script he'd been annotating, heavily scored across with scribblings and arrows. 'Nor can I afford such pleasures.'

'Help me move this inside, would you? It's blocking the doorway.' Burbage indicated the full barrel of ale; together they rolled it gently through the door and into a dark corner inside, then came back out into the sunshine. 'If you change your mind, I've a young girl back at my place who's keen to play two men at once.'

Will grinned. 'I would have thought you'd have no end of takers for that.'

'She asked for *you.*'

'For *me*?' Will was astonished, then amused. 'I hope you told her I'm a respectably married man with children?'

'I don't think she'd care if you had ten wives and fifty offspring, she'd still want to play "ride a cock-horse" with you. Though I have to admit, Will, I forget you're married sometimes. I've never even met this mythical wife.'

'Nor shall you,' Will said fervently. 'Anne's a country girl, born and bred in Warwickshire. I'll not bring her to London to die of the pox within a month.'

Burbage grunted, and wiped the sweat from his brow

with the back of his hand. 'So how many children do you have now?'

'Three.'

The theatrical raised his eyebrows. 'Three? When did you have time to engender so many? You spend most of the year in London, and the rest touring. Or is there some other fine fellow up there in Warwickshire, playing the good husband to your wife and keeping the bed warm for you?'

Will felt his fists clench at the suggestion that some other man might be bedding his wife while he was in London. His temper rose, though he knew it was just one of Burbage's jests. All the theatricals made such jokes, it meant nothing. Burbage was a crude man, with a crude sense of humour, and would have thought little of being cuckolded himself. Yet still Will felt his face go red, and fought to control his anger.

'I had a daughter, Susanna, before I came to London,' he muttered, 'then twin children, born only this January.'

'Two sons?' Burbage asked.

'A son and a daughter,' Will said shortly, and stared down at the play script. He disliked talking about his home life when he was in London. Anne and their little children, Stratford, the cramped and smoky cottage on Henley Street: it felt like another life to him when he was here. It was not real, but more like one of the stories he liked to cobble together as he tinkered with old play scripts. 'Judith and Hamnet.'

'So you have a son now.' Burbage nodded approvingly, and spat on the dried mud of the roadway. 'That's all that matters, Will. A son to carry on your name and protect the family after you are gone.'

'I'm in good enough health, thank you,' Will said sharply. 'And the boy's not even a year old yet.'

'But he'll grow, my young friend, mark my words. A few

years and you'll be wondering where the time went. Aye, and reaching in your purse to buy him his first whore! Now, I'd better make sure the scenery's in place for the first act. Though a cup of ale first will set me up for the afternoon, I think.' Burbage laughed, and turned to go back inside the Theatre. He looked over his shoulder at Will, who was still studying the play script. 'You coming?'

'Soon,' Will promised him. 'I have to finish these changes while they're fresh in my head.'

Burbage shrugged. 'It's good to improve the old plays, but I've told you, write me something new and I'll pay you double. Something the crowd has never seen before. A new play will earn you more than this constant knitting up and embellishing of ancient history.'

Will felt uneasy at the thought of trying to put coherent ideas for new work down on paper. It was so much easier to keep rearranging the history plays that were most popular with the people.

'The crowd like the old plays,' he said stubbornly.

'Aye, that they do, but they're starting to get restless. Everything these days has to be *new*.' Burbage raised his head to the sky and sniffed. 'Can't you smell it? There's a change coming. Did you hear about Philip Henslowe? He's getting money together to build a new playhouse down on Bankside. They're going to demolish some of the brothels to make way for it, then it'll go up in a year or two. And then what shall we do? They already have bear-baiting and a bullring on Bankside, and most of the new brothels seem to be setting up there, too. In another year or two, Shoreditch will be empty and the whole of London will be crowding the playhouse on Bankside instead.'

Will could not deny the truth of that. He had been to Bankside on many occasions, and enjoyed the thriving atmosphere about the dog fights and bear-baiting pits, the brothels with pretty young girls standing in the doorways, and the new building work going up everywhere. It was a natural place for such entertainments, drawing in thousands of visitors travelling into the city from the south, and showing them what the ungoverned fringes of London could offer before they crossed the river. He would not wish to live there, preferring the now-familiar streets of Shoreditch, but he could see its appeal to the crowd.

'So move,' he suggested. 'Take the playhouse across the river.'

'Rebuild the Theatre on Bankside?'

'Why not?'

Burbage ran a hand through his hair. 'This is a young man's game, and I'm not young any more. Well, the ale waits,' he muttered, and disappeared inside the playhouse.

Will returned his attention to the play, but found it impossible to think now that Burbage had set up fears and suspicions in his mind.

Could he be sure the twins were his own offspring?

His father had written to him in London in the autumn, telling him that Anne was pregnant again and the child expected in spring, which fitted the dates when he had been home in Stratford. But then the birth had come early, and it had been the shock of twins, not a single child. He had hurried home at once to see Anne in Stratford and attend the baptism, fearful that the babies would sicken and die before he could reach them, for they had been born so early. Anne had been weak and grey-faced, his mother and a wet-nurse caring for the babies while she recovered slowly from the birth. But the twins themselves had surprised him with their pink skin and robust health, crying lustily all night while he was there – until he began to wish himself back in London.

Was it possible they were not his children?

Seven months between his visit and the birth.

Will stared down at the thick dried mud under his feet, his fist clenched on the play script.

His mother had laughed at his fearful expression as he had gazed at the babies' tiny, swaddling-wrapped bodies, and had told him not to worry, they were strong and healthy enough, that twins were often born early. He had believed her without question. But now, with Burbage's joke ringing in his ears, he was back to counting the months on his fingers again.

Had Anne been unfaithful to him last spring? Could the twins be the product of another man's seed?

Looking back, he remembered how Anne had urged him so often and so persuasively to lie with her, to put another child inside her before he left, that he had eventually agreed, and taken great pleasure in doing so. But could it be that Anne had already known she was pregnant by the time of his visit, and had had to hide her shame by ensuring it could be her husband's child?

And to think he had sworn to himself never to see the beautiful Lucy Morgan again. Never to touch her again, nor any other woman or whore, but to stay faithful to his wife alone.

A memory flashed through his head of his father's new apprentice. The lad had been watching him and Anne sitting together in the little herb garden behind his father's house, a few days before he had left for London. Will had been reading out a poem to Anne as she cradled little Susanna in her arms, a poem he had written specially for his wife, for it played on her maiden name, 'Hathaway'. Reaching the end of the poem, Will had glanced up and seen the apprentice gazing at them, and the lad had hurried back into the workshop.

Now that Will thought about it, there had been something strange in the young man's face. Something akin to jealousy.

His father's apprentice!

A boy steeped in the foul stench of the workshop, barely a man, and to think of such a fool easing himself inside his wife . . .

Will closed his eyes in bitter, shaking fury. Yes, there was a change coming. He could prove nothing, and to make such an accusation in public would only drag his family further into disgrace in Stratford. But he could watch his son as the boy grew, and look for signs that he was not his son but another man's.

Meanwhile, he would do what he had been dreaming about for over a year now and only put off out of loyalty to Anne. He would serve out the rest of this year with Burbage and his company, then try to get a permanent place with the Queen's Men.

It would mean disguising his Catholic roots, of course. The Queen's company was made up of zealous Protestants, eager to travel England bearing a message of Protestant faith and a love of Queen Elizabeth to the people. But if Will could somehow avoid admitting that he was a member of the disreputable Arden family, such a sacrifice would be worth it. For as one of the Queen's own players, he would have better and more frequent access to the court – and to Lucy Morgan.

Three

'The ceiling slopes here, Your Majesty. You will need to stoop a little, I fear.'

'I remember the low ceilings,' Elizabeth replied in a hollow voice, and bent her head.

Walsingham had led her uncomfortably deep inside the Tower of London, far from the sombre but spacious suite of rooms in which she had been kept during her sister Mary's reign. The walls of the corridor dripped with water, and the space between them was so narrow, her gown brushed the damp stones on either side as she walked.

She shuddered at the memory of her own unhappy time in the Tower. Nor could she forget that her own mother had ended her days here, out on the windswept green where the glossy ravens strutted and waited for blood. Today she did not wish to think about the anguish Anne Boleyn must have suffered in those last hours, though she had often considered it in her darker moments. If only she had been older, she might have been able to comfort her condemned mother in some way. But she had been so young at the time of the Queen's execution, only two years of age and unable to understand why her pretty mother was no longer there to kiss her goodnight.

To await one's death in this terrifying place! It was a fate that should be reserved only for the worst of traitors, she thought, and hoped she would never have cause to put a noblewoman to death in such a way.

Elizabeth drew her cloak closer, the hood hiding her face. There were guards up ahead and she did not wish to be recognized. 'What is the prisoner's name?'

'Gilbert Gifford. My spies tell me he is of an English Catholic family, most of whom live overseas, where they plot and talk endlessly against Your Majesty.'

'An old story,' she muttered.

'But a dangerous one. I believe Gifford studied for the Church for a while in Rome, then was expelled for some perceived weakness of character. Undeterred, he travelled back through France and secured a place at the Catholic seminary in Rheims. There he was made deacon, and received letters of encouragement from that Welsh traitor Thomas Morgan, who should by rights have been brought home long ago for his treasonous dealings, but who remains free to peddle his views in Paris.'

'So this young Gifford works for Morgan? Why have you brought him here to the Tower?' she asked, frowning. 'I thought he was not to die.'

Walsingham had stopped at the iron-barred oak door of the cell. He turned to wait for her, holding the torch high. 'Nor will he, if the lad is wise and chooses to cooperate with us.'

'He will not be wise, you may be sure of it. Not if he is a true Catholic.' One of the guards glanced at her curiously, and Elizabeth lowered her voice to an urgent whisper. 'These Catholics are stubborn. They will grasp any chance at martyrdom.'

Walsingham shook his head, his expression grave. 'I hope and pray that you are mistaken, Your Majesty. I have not brought him here to die, but to see what horrors could befall him if he refuses my offer.'

'What offer?'

'His life, in return for his service.' With his customary caution, Walsingham ordered the listening guards to move further down the corridor, then spoke quietly in her ear. 'Majesty, you must forgive me for bringing you here tonight. I know these walls held you prisoner before you were Queen. But it is imperative that we persuade Gifford to turn in our favour. I believe the sight of Your Majesty, coming to him at night in such a terrible place as this, may inspire some last spark of English loyalty in his heart, and convert the man safely to our side.'

A hint of anger flickered in her voice, lit by some memory of fear. 'I am not in the habit of converting souls, sir, and this is a dreadful place for any man, whether he be Catholic or not. What is his crime?'

'We have long known that your cousin Mary yearns to depose you and place the English crown on her own head. But we have never been able to come by any strong evidence of this, nor any letters in her own hand which could link her to such endeavours against your throne. This young priest Gifford landed at the port of Rye a few days back. When he was searched, secret letters were found on his person.' Walsingham looked at her. 'Letters addressed to your royal cousin Mary at Chartley House, from certain exiles in France whom we believe to be mounting a new plot against you.'

'There is no law to prevent them from writing to my cousin, only one to bar her from replying in kind,' she pointed out caustically. 'How does this prove anything?'

'We have been working on a new method of "helping" your cousin to smuggle letters in and out of Chartley, so that we may read them before they pass on to their destination. It has not been possible, before now, to achieve this, since we did not have the cooperation of any of her secret messengers.'

'I see.'

'You must persuade this Gilbert Gifford, Your Majesty, that to serve you and England would be far preferable than to continue serving as raw meat for the hot irons and other instruments of the torturer Richard Topcliffe, who awaits us within.'

'Topcliffe? That monster?'

'I am afraid so, Your Majesty.' Walsingham inclined his head regretfully. 'Master Topcliffe serves you keenly. And though I deplore his methods as barbaric and inhuman, I cannot deny that he brings results.'

He signalled the nearest guard, who drew back the iron bolts and opened the door to the cell. The guard's gaze swept Elizabeth's face, then he dropped hurriedly to his knees. No doubt many came through the Tower in disguise, she thought. And some who came this way would not leave the place alive.

The narrow cell stank of blood and excrement, and was lit by two torches, burning in brackets above their heads. She recognized Topcliffe at once, standing by the brazier, his gloating expression repulsive to her. But Walsingham was right. Topcliffe's cruel methods did bring results, and had already uncovered many Catholic priests who, if left unpunished, would have converted countless more Englishmen to the Roman faith. And since all English Catholics ever seemed to want was a Catholic monarch on the throne, the deaths of such men by public execution had become an unpleasant necessity.

Yet if Walsingham could snare Mary and expose her treason with written evidence, it could mean an end to these endless plots.

The unfortunate young man had been stripped of his clothes, and was now wearing nothing but a bloodstained cloth about his groin. His wrists had been manacled to a bar so high above his head, his thin arms were stretched beyond their natural capacity, and his feet could barely touch the floor. He had no beard, though his chin showed a few days' growth. Elizabeth thought he was tolerably handsome, but for his weak mouth. Across his pale body were red lines and marks where he had been whipped, and where irons had been put to him, still hot from the brazier.

As they entered the room, the prisoner's eyes opened and his gaze moved swiftly from Walsingham to Elizabeth. There was terror in his face, and a lack of hope.

She threw back her hood.

Gifford stared at the sight of his queen, then painfully lowered his gaze to the stone flags, as though the true extent of his treason had only just been brought home to him.

'Your Majesty,' Topcliffe murmured, pushing the long iron back into the brazier. He sank to one knee before her. There were flecks of fresh blood on his stained apron, still brightly scarlet. His ruddy face, sweating from the intense heat of the brazier, was flecked with blood, too. He wore a simple skullcap, and this he removed to reveal only a little hair, his forehead gleaming. 'You honour me with your presence here.'

'No doubt,' she said drily, and gestured him to rise. 'You seem to have gone hard about it, Topcliffe. Has the priest spoken yet? Does he confess his sins against our throne?'

'Not yet, Your Majesty, but he will.'

'Stand aside,' she ordered him, and Topcliffe, his gaze shifting to Walsingham's expressionless face, bowed.

Topcliffe stood against the cell wall, his hands behind his back, his gaze fixed on the prisoner as she examined him. Elizabeth guessed that he had expected more praise for his efforts with these Catholics. But to own the truth, just being in the same room with him made her flesh creep.

The way his narrow eyes had burned on her face . . . If her cousin ever succeeded in stealing the English throne from her, and employed Topcliffe as her chief torturer, he would put the hot irons to Elizabeth with the same vicious zeal he used on all his prisoners, and give no greater thought to her agonies. It was pain he loved; that was his only loyalty.

'Do you know who I am?' she asked Gifford.

'Yes, Your Majesty,' he answered, without looking at her, and she caught a hint of shame in his hoarse whisper.

'My spies tell me you came from France and brought letters with you for my cousin Mary. Are you aware of the content of those letters?'

His gaze lifted now and he glanced in obvious terror at Topcliffe. 'I . . . I do not know.'

'Look at me, sir. Not at your torturer. Those letters were from men who seek to put my cousin on the throne of England, and have me executed as a heretic.' She met his gaze directly now, challenging him to think about his actions, urging him with her eyes to regret them. 'I am your queen and such matters concern me closely. So I ask again, were you aware of the content of the letters you were carrying?'

'Your Majesty,' Gifford replied, his voice shaking, 'I had no knowledge of any such treason or plot against you. I bore those letters into England in good faith, I swear it. They were written by men I admire greatly and to whom I owe my allegiance.'

'Do you not owe me greater allegiance, as you are an Englishman and I am your rightful queen?'

Gifford closed his eyes. A tear began to roll down his cheek. Yet he did not answer her question.

Behind her, Walsingham shifted his feet and gently cleared his throat. He did not think much of her interrogation, clearly.

If only she could leave this filthy hellhole and allow

Topcliffe to get on with his work where she did not have to see the evidence of his cruelty! But she was no coward and she knew what was at stake. Walsingham would never have brought her to this vile place unless he thought her intervention absolutely necessary.

She pressed on. 'Are you a Catholic?'

Again Gifford blenched and looked at Topcliffe, as though these were questions that had already been put to him. 'I . . . forgive me, forgive me. Yes, I am a Catholic.'

'And a priest?'

'Your Majesty, yes.'

He was gabbling now, eager to confess. Perhaps he thought death would come quicker if he gave up the struggle to be brave and just confessed.

'Gilbert,' she said softly, looking up into his strained face as she used his Christian name. 'Do you wish to be tortured at the hands of Master Topcliffe, and then be hanged, drawn and quartered for your treason while you are still alive?'

He broke down, weeping openly. 'No, Your Majesty. No, I do not. I beg you . . .'

'Then you will serve me faithfully from now on, and perform whatever you are bidden to do in my service?'

'Yes, Your Majesty.'

'Whatever letters might be put into your hands by my cousin or her agents, you will ensure they are conveyed to Sir Francis before they reach those to whom they have been addressed?'

His hands jangled against his manacles, and he cried out. 'Yes!'

'Swear by Almighty God.'

'I swear by Almighty God and His son Jesus Christ that I shall be a faithful servant unto Your Majesty from now on.' Gifford sobbed, and there was a kind of relief on his face, as though the poor boy had been playing a part all this while, a part for which his nature had been ill-suited.

'Release him,' she ordered Topcliffe, turning away, 'and do not touch him again. His clothes and possessions are to be returned, and he is to be conveyed to Sir Francis for his recovery. Whatever treason he has committed before this hour, it shall be forgotten. Is that clear?'

'Yes, Your Majesty,' Topcliffe muttered, outwardly obedient, his small leather skullcap in his hand, but she could tell that he was angry at having his victim snatched away before he had finished with him.

She swept from the cell with Walsingham behind her, and left Topcliffe climbing on a stool to release Gifford from his manacles.

Vile man!

The air was chilly, the ground hard with frost. Above their heads, stars lay tangled against the sky like diamonds scattered and sewn willy-nilly on to black velvet. She stared bleakly up at them. How many men like Gilbert Gifford had been caught up in Mary's perfidious net, or Walsingham's net of spies, or, God help her, the net she herself had cast when she became Queen and asked men for their hearts and souls?

'Gifford will make an excellent spy for England,' Walsingham murmured, and bowed. 'I thank you, Your Majesty, and I beg your forgiveness for having brought you to this place. But that young man would not have turned his coat for anyone less than the Queen herself.'

Taking deep breaths of air, Elizabeth tried to clear her lungs of the foul stench of the Tower dungeons. Restlessly, she walked a few feet to the wall and looked down at the glint of the dark river as it rolled past below them.

She wished Robert could be here with her, to advise her and lend a friendly ear to her troubles. But he was still in the Low Countries, enjoying his first taste of power rather more than he should. God send that Robert should return safely from that conflict, and with no dangerous, over-reaching ambitions for her crown!

'Never ask this of me again,' she told Walsingham, pulling her hood forward to hide her face. 'Nor involve me in your work. From now on, I wish to hear only what treasons you have uncovered. Not what methods you used to uncover them.'

Four

Greenwich Palace, London, spring 1586

> *Summer is a-coming in,*
> *Loudly sing, Cuckoo!*
> *Groweth seed and bloweth mead,*
> *And springs the wood anew.*
> *Sing, Cuckoo!*

WHEN LUCY FINISHED THE TRADITIONAL COUNTRY ROUND, accompanied by the other girls from the chorus, she hung her head, waiting for the hautboys and tabors to finish sounding.

In the silence that followed, she sank into a curtsy, and heard Queen Elizabeth clap her hands, followed by the rest of the court.

'You still have the sweetest voice, Lucy, a true cuckoo for our spring,' the Queen murmured as the applause died away.

She looked down at Lucy from her throne in the vast, echoing hall at Greenwich and for a moment there was silence. There was an oddly intent look on the Queen's face, an expression she only wore when about to enact some terrible cruelty on one of her courtiers. It worried Lucy to see it.

'But the time has come for us to hear new voices at court,' Elizabeth continued, 'and new dancers too, and acrobats, and players to liven up the hall at night. With so many of our courtiers and young men away at the war, I fear we are in need of greater comfort than one entertainer can bestow, however skilled.'

Lucy kept her expression carefully neutral. But she was shocked by the Queen's remarks. She was no longer a child, it was true. Yet she was only five and twenty years of age. Was this deemed too old to sing before the court?

Lucy had now been among the Queen's favourite entertainers for more than ten years, and it was regularly said that ten years was a long time to hold the royal favour. Yet she had not lost her talent. Her voice had mellowed and her dancing had become more graceful as she matured. But perhaps she was no longer fresh and beautiful enough to turn the heads of foreign ambassadors, and send them hurrying off to write home of the exotic delights of the English court. Nor to hold the attention of a queen whose favourite, the Earl of Leicester, was even now supporting the fight against the Spanish in the Low Countries.

Queen Elizabeth was looking down at her, smiling. 'Do you not agree, Lucy?'

'Your Majesty?'

Lucy gazed up at her tormentor on the high dais, oddly light-headed. The hall was stuffy and overcrowded, and the day had been unseasonably hot. She felt like a criminal about to be sentenced to death. And by a judge with a cruel, gloating smile.

The Queen had chosen cloth-of-gold for tonight's feast, which had been given in honour of the spring equinox, on the orders of her astrologer John Dee, who was claiming that this would be an auspicious year for Elizabeth. Her gown was embroidered with gold thread, and thousands of tiny seed pearls had been sewn on to her lavish sleeves and hem, her thin waist pinched in even more to make her narrow chest seem bountiful.

At her side stood Sir Walter Raleigh in a plain nut-brown jacket and doublet, freshly returned from the Low Countries with news and dispatches from the conflict there. The Queen appeared much taken with Sir Walter's blunt tongue, and had spoken privately with him that morning, keeping her Privy Councillors waiting in the antechamber for over an hour while they talked.

'You look unwell, Lucy,' Queen Elizabeth was saying, leaning forward on her throne. 'Does she not look unwell, Sir Walter?'

Sir Walter Raleigh considered Lucy, a frown on his weatherbeaten face. 'She looks tired, Your Majesty,' he pronounced at last, in a thick country accent that had half the court smiling behind their hands. 'As though she has not been sleeping at night. But perhaps she is missing some young man who has gone to war.'

Queen Elizabeth's gaze narrowed on Lucy's face. 'Do you have a suitor?'

'No, Your Majesty.'

'For you know I will tolerate nothing but the strictest chastity among those of my ladies who remain, like me, unmarried.' The Queen sat in angry silence, staring at her. Suspicion rang in her voice, turning heads about the hall and quietening whispers. 'Tell me truthfully now, are you still a maid?'

'Yes, Your Majesty.'

One of the younger women standing behind the Queen stifled a giggle, and Queen Elizabeth looked at her sharply. 'You have some evidence to the contrary, Bess?'

The girl blushed, and pretended to look embarrassed, casting down her eyes. 'No, Your Majesty. Only that we heard something about Lucy Morgan and a man last year. Only idle gossip, Your Majesty. You know how girls can be.'

'I do, indeed,' the Queen agreed grimly. 'And what did this idle gossip say, Bess?'

Bess glanced at Lucy, who saw the spite on her thin, sallow face and knew herself to be hated among the younger court ladies. 'That Lucy Morgan bribed a guard so she could be alone with a man last year. Or perhaps the year before. I forget when. But it's said the guard found the two of them together later,' Bess dropped her voice conspiratorially, '*in flagrante delicto*.'

A sudden shocked silence thrummed through the hall. So this was about Will Shakespeare! Lucy thought. Would it make any difference to admit the charge and insist that nothing had happened between them, that she was still a virgin? Or should she throw herself at the Queen's feet and plead a conspiracy against her?

Queen Elizabeth shifted on her throne, looking directly at Lucy. Her eyes held an accusation. 'Do not look so amazed, girl. It is not the first time I have heard this sordid tale. But I dismissed it before as spiteful nonsense. Indeed, Lady Helena argued most fervently for your innocence, and you have never shown yourself by any of your actions to be frequenting with men. Yet several letters have come to my hand in recent weeks, addressed to you and containing love poetry intended to seduce and corrupt. How do you answer that, Mistress Morgan?'

Lucy stared and did not know how to reply. Will Shakespeare must have started sending her poems again – except he had clearly not bribed the servants well enough to ensure the letters reached her, and not her mistress. What was this now, any excuse to get rid of her? Too late, she remembered Goodluck congratulating her on trusting no one, not even those in whom she had to put her trust.

She looked at the ladies gathered about the Queen, their

eyes alight with malice. Only Lady Helena watched her with sympathy.

'I must beg your pardon, Your Majesty. I know nothing of any letters. Or . . . Or any poetry.'

'So you have not ruined yourself with a man?' Queen Elizabeth demanded, but did not wait for an answer. 'No, do not sigh and shake your head at me. I have taken my fill of your weary face and do not wish to look on it again. I have heard many tales of your overly forward and loose behaviour since you came to court, and now I am told you were in attendance at the marriage of Lord Leicester to Lettice Knollys, even though you must have known such a marriage was held without my permission. Do you deny that charge also?'

Lucy was dismayed. Who could have told her? Few people had known of the couple's secret marriage at the time, and even fewer would have risked the Queen's displeasure by mentioning it. Then she saw Lady Mary Herbert watching nervously from behind the Queen, and guessed that Leicester's clever young niece had been her source. She could not find it in herself to be angry with Lady Mary though, for she knew her marriage to the ageing Earl of Pembroke had not always been a happy one, his chief purpose in marrying her being to provide himself with sons. Indeed her waist seemed thicker again now, as though she would soon be due to leave for another confinement. Perhaps the tale had slipped out unawares.

'Your Majesty, please.' Lucy fell to her knees, pleading in earnest now as she sensed the danger ahead. 'I cannot deny it. His lordship asked me to attend his bride and I . . . I did not know how to refuse his request. Lord Leicester had been such a generous patron to me in my first years at court. Forgive my stupidity, Your Majesty.'

'I have not forgiven Leicester for his disobedience in marrying that woman. What makes you think I would forgive you?' The Queen's voice rose in her temper, shrill in her fury, carrying the full length of the silent hall. 'You will leave court tomorrow, Mistress Morgan, and you will not return until I have been satisfied of your virtue. I will not have a woman in my court who is neither maid nor married. And I wish you well in Lord Leicester's patronage, for you will find his lordship a hard man to reach these days.

'There now.' Queen Elizabeth looked about herself as Lucy rose from her knees, seemingly satisfied by this pronouncement. 'It is no tragedy. This is a merry court and we shall not miss Lucy Morgan's dark stare. One of the younger women can sing in her place. And Sir Walter Raleigh shall dance with me.'

'You honour a rough sailor, Your Majesty,' Sir Walter Raleigh murmured, bowing jerkily as though not accustomed to making his obeisance, and kissed Queen Elizabeth's proffered hand as she rose from the throne. Nonetheless, his eyes met the Queen's in a curiously intimate smile, as though they were already bedfellows.

A shocked whisper ran through the court, noting the Queen's answering smile, and Lucy could not help but wonder if this countrified adventurer had already supplanted the absent Lord Leicester. Though, knowing how the Queen loved to play one courtier against another, it was more likely her looks and smiles were for show. Perhaps she hoped such rumours would reach Lord Leicester abroad and sow fear in his heart that his days as her favourite were over.

Left to stand there alone, Lucy smarted at the injustice of her treatment. She had been summarily dismissed from the royal presence in favour of some younger girl from the chorus. And why? Because the Queen, it seemed, was tired of her face and ready to listen to gossip from those who wished her ill.

Pushing her way through the crowds at the far end of the hall, Lucy caught a brief glimpse of a face she had never expected to see again.

Will!

Then he was gone, lost in a maze of faces. She stared about the place, meeting nothing but the curious gazes of the courtiers and their hangers-on. Lucy gave herself a little shake. She must have imagined seeing the young Warwickshire player, that was all. She was distressed and her mind was playing tricks on her.

One of the old jugglers stopped her at the door, asking what had happened. Lucy explained, her head down, her face averted, and the old man advised steering clear of the Queen for a few weeks.

'She will have forgotten this fit of temper soon, then you can return and sing for her again,' he murmured kindly in her ear. 'The Queen has always been capricious in her favours. Though no doubt this latest news from the Low Countries, that Lord Leicester has been crowned Supreme Governor and is to set up his own court there, cannot have helped her mood!'

But she saw his troubled look as the old juggler kissed her farewell. And that was when she knew herself to be in danger. It seemed everyone but Lucy herself had guessed that her disgrace would be permanent.

Where would she go? There was no one left for her now, with Master Goodluck dead and the whole court hardened against her. She would have no choice but to open up Goodluck's house, standing empty at Cheapside, and live there alone. Though how she would survive, she had no idea. She had no family now, no husband, no protector.

'Sir Francis may help me,' she whispered to herself, gazing back over her shoulder at the crush and bustle of the court. Goodluck's master had once promised he would look after her if ever she lost her place. But she could not see

Walsingham anywhere. Perhaps he was not even at court.

Besides, she could not in truth ask such a great personage as the Queen's spymaster to shield her from the Queen's temper. No, she was on her own and must make the best of it.

Yet it was unjust to have been dismissed from court for this. So unjust!

She seized a candle and hurried upstairs to the bed-chamber she had been allotted at Greenwich, so gloomy and cramped that none of the other ladies-in-waiting had wanted to share it with her. It had a rough bed, and a narrow curtained alcove where her clothes chest and other possessions were kept, and little else besides. The chamber might be inconveniently small, but its tiny window over-looked the river and brought a breeze off the water during the warm spring evenings – albeit a stinking breeze at times, for the current ran filthy and sluggish near the bank. But at least when she wished to shed a few private tears of humiliation, there was no one here to laugh at her.

Her maid was nowhere to be seen. Lucy called for her up and down the corridor, then realized she would still be down at supper, for it was the custom for servants to eat the leftovers after a feast.

Lucy set about undressing herself, no simple task. It was only when laying out her creased court gown on the bed, clad in nothing but her shift and woollen stockings, that Lucy noticed the scroll of parchment curled up on her pillow and tied with a red ribbon.

Frowning, she unrolled the scroll and stared down at it. It was a short poem, boldly prefaced with the words, *To LM, my dark lady*:

> *Love is too young to know what conscience is,*
> *Yet who knows not conscience is born of love?*
> *Then, gentle cheater, urge not my amiss,*

253

Lest guilty of my faults thy sweet self prove.
For, thou betraying me, I do betray
My nobler part to my gross body's treason;
My soul doth tell my body that he may
Triumph in love; flesh stays no farther reason,
But rising at thy name, doth point out thee
As his triumphant prize; proud of this pride,
He is contented thy poor drudge to be,
To stand in thy affairs, fall by thy side.
No want of conscience hold it that I call
Her 'love' for whose dear love I rise and fall.

Horrified, she turned the incriminating sheet over, search-ing for a name in the candlelight. The poet had left none, but she knew whose this was. Only Will Shakespeare could have written verses like these addressed to her, so mockingly coarse she felt her blood stir just reading them.

Yet how could the poem have arrived in her bed-chamber? Had Will bribed her maid to bring it up and lay it on the bed?

'It's a sonnet. Do you like it?'

Lucy jumped in fright, then realized where the voice had come from. Furious, she tore back the curtain covering the little alcove. Will Shakespeare was hiding there, perched on her clothes chest in a florid player's suit, feathered cap in hand, smiling up at her.

'Hello, Lucy,' he murmured, jumping down and bowing as though his visit was in no way strange.

She had never had a man in her bedchamber before, and his presence there shocked her. Yet it strangely delighted her, too. Such a charming smile! And the awkwardness of his bow disarmed her. He was still only a boy from the country, after all.

She ought to have been furious with him for having

caused her dismissal from court. But it was the Queen she was most angry with.

'You must forgive my appearance. I've come straight from a performance where I was a gentleman of Verona. A very strange gentleman, I am afraid.' Will came towards her, laughing under his breath as she backed away. 'This is rather a small room for playing Hunt the Thimble, Lucy. Though I'll play if you will.'

'How did you get up here?'

'Ah, those friendly guards . . .'

He seized her wrist and Lucy shook her head, panicking. 'Will, let me go!'

'Forgive me, sweet mistress. I've waited a long time to get you alone again, I'm not about to leave without a kiss.' He pulled her close, his hands about her waist in the thin shift, and she felt his warm mouth on her throat, then the bare skin above her breasts. The shock of such intimacies dizzied her, and she shivered, hardly able to breathe. He saw her weakness and smiled fiercely. 'Oh, Lucy, Lucy. I've wanted you since I was a boy. You must be an enchantress. I am bound by your spell and cannot leave. What is it about you that makes me so hot for your bed?'

'Perhaps you are not used to hearing the word "no" very often,' she muttered, but allowed him to kiss her again.

It felt good to be in his arms. She knew she ought to call for help, have him thrown out. Yet the servants would still all be at supper, and would any of the guards bother to help her? Besides, if she was found here with a man, alone in her chamber, the Queen would never believe her innocent. Not after tonight's accusations.

She thought of how Queen Elizabeth had humiliated her in front of the whole court, and leaned further into Will's kiss. Dismissed as a whore when she had done nothing to deserve such a name!

Since her 'virtue' was already lost in the eyes of the court, what was there to lose by allowing Will Shakespeare to make love to her? Nothing, she thought wildly. Nothing, nothing. She was already lost, already damned. This act would merely confirm it.

His hands moved up from her waist, cupping and stroking her full breasts. Lucy sighed, swaying against him, and felt her nipples tauten under the thin material.

With a quick jerk, he dragged the thin shift dress up and over her head.

'You are beauty itself,' he exclaimed hoarsely, staring at her nakedness. He drew her close again and kissed her on the mouth.

For a moment there was silence between them, then he muttered, 'Yes,' as though she had spoken, and pushed her back on to the bed.

His lips had left her unsteady, her skin already beginning to prickle with that delicious heat she had not felt since the last time he had kissed her. Lucy shivered in the cool air from the open window but did not pull up the sheet to cover herself. Instead, she watched avidly as Will, too, shed his clothes and climbed into bed. His body was strong and lean, a young man's, with dark hair down the centre of his chest and in his groin. He was already aroused, his organ swollen between his thighs.

It was bigger than she had expected. She averted her gaze as he knelt above her. Was it a sin to lie with a man who loved her even though they were not married?

Will had said nothing about marriage. Yet he had an honest face. Surely if he loved her, he would marry her in the end?

Lucy slipped her arms around his neck, and kissed him again. It was all she could think about. His lips were forceful now, his tongue pushing hotly inside, leaving her in no doubt of what he wanted. Her body ached and trembled for him. She had been dreaming about this moment ever since he had stolen her secretly away into the storeroom, constantly imagining how it would have felt to have let him take her that night, to have given herself to him.

'Don't be scared,' he whispered, watching her face as he stroked his hands down her body.

'I'm not,' Lucy replied, almost defiant. Well, maybe a little, she admitted silently, and thought again of what she had seen before he climbed into bed. Would it hurt?

Will laughed and bent his head to her breast, sucking one nipple fiercely into his mouth. Her fingers clenched in his short dark hair and Lucy gasped in helpless excitement, arching her whole body towards him.

This was not how it had been with Master Twist. Then, Lucy had been desperately fighting, repulsed by his selfish and unfeeling lust. With Will, it was more like a dance, a dance where she had not been taught the steps yet somehow knew them instinctively. Lucy moved with Will and not against him, welcomed his touch, moaning under her breath as he shifted his lips from one breast to the other, teasing her into forgetfulness.

If this was the sin of lust, it was how she had always imagined love would feel. It was so all-consuming, it ate away her fears and left no other thought in her head but the need for his body to cover hers.

'You must forgive me for how I treated you when I last came to court,' he muttered, kissing her. 'I had been drinking in the taverns all day. I was half-mad with love for you and could think of nothing but tasting your beauty. Did I frighten you, Lucy?'

'Maybe a little,' she admitted, but stroked his hair. 'You do not frighten me now, though.'

Will raised his head to stare down at her in the candle-light, his body suddenly tense. His eyes narrowed to dark slits as he examined her nakedness, as though looking for some sign that she had betrayed him. 'I do not frighten you? What do you mean by that? Am I not the first in your bed?' He seemed to choke over his own questions, his voice thick with hurt. 'It's a year since I last saw you. Have you taken a lover?'

The flash of his jealousy took her by surprise. How could he think her so light of virtue?

Slowly she shook her head, unable to speak. It was because of him that she had lost her place, and now this . . .

He was not satisfied. 'You are still a maid? Swear to it!'

'I swear that I am still a maid,' she whispered into the stillness between them, and was relieved to see his gaze lose that disturbing intensity. 'Why should you care? Does my maidenhead mean so much to you?'

'It's only that I cannot bear the thought of you lying like this with another man.' He kissed the flat of her belly, then moved even lower, making her gasp with shock. 'I told you, it's a divine madness that I feel for you. I have struggled against it this past year, but cannot control it, nor my jealousy. Promise me now that you will never kiss any man but me, nor let him undress you, nor do this to you.'

He slipped his tongue cleverly between her thighs, working at the flesh there, and Lucy writhed in pleasure. She pulled his head closer, gasping like a spent swimmer against the tide. I'm drowning, she thought helplessly, and heard a sudden roaring in her ears. He's going to kill me. This is the end.

He raised his head. 'Tell me, could any other man bring you to such joy?'

'No, no,' she moaned. Love me. Don't stop to talk.

But Will had other thoughts now. 'Swear on your life that you will never open yourself like this to another man.' He shifted above her, positioning himself so gently between her thighs that she was not at first alarmed. 'Let me hear you swear it. I must hear you swear first.'

'I swear it on my life,' she whispered.

He pushed into her body, groaning with undisguised pleasure at his conquest. Dear Lord, it was agony! She lay still as a board beneath him, her expression wooden, all pleasure gone.

'Dearest, dearest Lucy. It will only hurt for the briefest of spaces, my sweet virgin.'

Does every married woman go through this? After the initial pain had eased, his mouth and fingers slowly coaxed her back into pleasure. That's a little easier, she thought at last. Almost worth waiting for.

Then it was good. Undeniably good. Will stifled her moans with his kisses, stroking and teasing until she was half-mad with excitement. They made love in a kind of trance, her gaze locked on his face, the sounds of the river below washing through her as she lay beneath his labouring body. She had never known anything so intimate nor so physically exciting, though the moment of her own release reminded her of the exhilaration of dancing before the court, its glorious freedom and the pleasure of applause.

When Will finally cried out, shuddering with pleasure, Lucy stroked the damp hair back from his forehead and murmured, 'I love you.'

The truest words. And she meant them at first. Then she was no longer so sure. Did she love Will simply because he had made love to her? Maybe it was her body that loved him, or what they had done together, and her heart felt it must follow the body or be left behind. Suddenly she was in a maze, with the centre lost to her. Was that how love always felt, though?

She got up quietly from the bed after he had finished, to clean herself and lock the chamber door, so her maid returning from supper could not disturb them at their play.

Then they made love again, and this time Will taught her how to please him in other ways, his patience never-ending as she fumbled shyly, trying to follow his whispered instructions.

When Lucy woke later in the night and reached out for his warmth, she found herself alone. Will Shakespeare had left without waking her, the only evidence that he had ever been in her bedchamber an unaccustomed soreness between her thighs and the sonnet he had given her, now tucked under her pillow.

Five

The River Thames, London, 22 May 1586

GOODLUCK STOOD AT THE PROW AS THE *SOLEIL* GLIDED silently up the Thames, nearing the smoky huddle of roofs and towers that was London. The dark waters below reminded him of his long sojourn aboard Jensen's barge; he was glad now of the sea-legs he had developed over those tedious months of sickness. They had certainly been tested over the past few days, sailing up the east coast, buffeted by spring winds, and rolling on the tidal swell as the *Soleil* attempted to avoid detection on its return to England. Goodluck had feared capture at Gravesend, where he secretly knew Walsingham had left instructions for every ship to be searched and its crew questioned. But luck had been on their side, and the port searchers, over-whelmed by the number of vessels passing through at one time, had not seen them slip away in the cloudy light. Now, granted the boon of a moonless night, the intrepid French captain had navigated the Thames almost to the outskirts of London, passing more than one port patrol in the darkness without being hailed.

A rope over his shoulder, a sailor with a full beard jumped

neatly ashore as the *Soleil* came to rest against the wooden jetty. Goodluck stood at the ship rail, his gaze searching the shadowy buildings ahead. But the quay was deserted, and if anyone was aboard the other boats moored along the quay-side, they made no sound.

As soon as the boat was tied up, the bearded sailor set the gangplank in place as silently as he could. The man tested it with his own weight, then grinned and gestured Goodluck to come across first.

The narrow plank wobbled precariously beneath him, but did not fall.

Safely ashore, Goodluck pressed two shillings into the man's palm. It had been a difficult journey from France, and these sailors were risking their lives, sailing so far up the Thames with Catholics on board.

The two priests still on deck hesitated, staring down at the murky swell of the Thames as it rose and fell beneath the gangway.

Impatiently, the sailor snapped his fingers at them. '*C'est pas dangereux. Allez, vite!*'

Ballard cursed under his breath, but hitched up his dark priest's robes and trod gingerly across the heaving plank. Caught and steadied by Goodluck on the other side, he grinned. 'I swear, it's good to be back on honest English soil. I hate boats. My stomach is still pitching like a pregnant girl's.'

'Best not leave these shores again, then,' Maude commented lightly, jumping down behind him with a bag slung over his shoulder. He was a tall man, of a skinny, awkward build and a cynical disposition. Although he purported to be a priest, Goodluck had never seen Maude wear robes. Indeed, he had never seen him in anything but the clothes he wore now: severe black hose below a shirt and sturdy doublet, his cloak once fine, now patched in several places. His eyes seemed to stare above sunken cheeks, telling of too many nights spent sleeping off the ale rather than on his knees. Maude seemed an unlikely companion to Ballard, a man whose fanatical belief in the Catholic faith was second only to his obsessive neatness. But then, all they needed to share was a desire to see Mary, Queen of Scots, on the throne of England, and her heretic cousin Elizabeth thrown down into hell where she belonged. And that prospect, Goodluck considered drily, did not seem to trouble either of these men.

'I shall not need to leave England again,' Ballard reminded Maude sharply, 'if our plan succeeds.'

'Hush, not here,' Goodluck said, and pulled his cap low over his face. 'Let us walk into London and find Master Babington's lodgings first. There we will be able to talk more freely.'

They left the Thames, heading for the place near Aldgate where they had been told a man could climb across the city walls unseen. Once inside, they slipped through the dark streets, past Cornhill and the stocks, some of which were occupied by weary men struggling to sleep with their necks and limbs imprisoned, then past the Watch lolling in a shop doorway at Cheapside, who glanced up from their game of dice but did not bother to stop and question them. An empty bottle of ale lay on the step beside the Watch, a good indication of why they were so lax in their duties. Goodluck said nothing, relieved not to have been stopped, but made a careful note of the constables' faces. Walsingham would be interested to know how slack the Watch had become.

Goodluck kept his head low as he passed his own house, which stood in darkness, and hoped that Lucy was still at court. It had not been possible to let her know he was alive, and he felt the daily sting of his conscience for that deceit. But Walsingham had promised to keep Lucy provided for in his absence. He would have to trust his master's promise and put aside all thoughts of Lucy until the conspirators were safe in the Tower.

Turning south to avoid Ludgate, they trudged through a confusing series of narrow lanes and alleyways, then headed north again, up towards Holborn.

Gloomily, a church bell tolled the hour.

Ballard glanced behind them, checking again that they were not being followed. 'How can we be sure he will be at home?'

'Babington will be at Herne's Rents tonight,' Goodluck reassured him. 'He says so in his letter. And if not, he will be there tomorrow. We can beg shelter for the night from his servants, at least.'

'I hope we won't be sent to sleep in the stables again, like we were in Calais.' Maude shifted his bag from one shoulder to the other. 'I'm tired of this endless travelling. I could do with a comfortable bed.'

Goodluck cleared his throat. 'I just wish to be able to say Mass in the morning, and to give thanks to our Lord for bringing us safely home.'

'Amen,' replied Ballard fervently.

'We are not safe yet,' Maude pointed out, though he added belatedly, 'Amen, though, for all that. The Lord Himself knows the vital importance of our mission, and has guarded His servants well.'

'This is the place,' Goodluck said presently, but held the others back as he checked that the house was not being watched.

As he waited, he caught a slight movement out of the corner of his eye. A hooded figure had withdrawn from a vantage place further along the street, slipping back into the gloomy shadow between two houses.

He glanced at his companions, but they were looking the other way. 'It seems safe enough,' he murmured, and knocked at the door.

After a few moments, they heard the bolts being drawn back and a pale face appeared in the crack of the doorway.

The man stared hard at Goodluck, then at Ballard and Maude behind him. 'Who are you?' he asked sharply. 'What do you want at this hour?'

Goodluck pushed his letter from Babington through the crack. 'To see your master.'

The man took the parchment and studied it upside down by candlelight, clearly an illiterate. Yet he seemed mollified by the sight of his master's signature at the end. That, at least, he could read.

'Password?'

'Brutus,' Ballard supplied, glancing about the street as though fearful they would be overheard.

The door was opened a little wider. 'You'd best come in,' Babington's servant muttered reluctantly. 'Wipe your boots, sirs. The rushes here are fresh. The fire's still alight in the front room, but the master's gone to bed an hour since. If you will wait in there, I shall fetch him down for you, by and by.'

The fire in the front room was dying, barely a flicker from the white-red embers. Goodluck took a log from the box on the hearth and pushed it into the glowing hot ashes, hoping it would catch. Above, they heard voices. Then the creaking of a man getting out of bed.

They stood in the small front room in silence, looking at each other. Goodluck could see a tense excitement in Ballard's face, but apprehension in Maude's swarthier countenance. Perhaps it was only now, back on English soil with the plans for Queen Elizabeth's assassination, that their mission had begun to feel real. Inevitable, even. They were set on a course from which there could be no swerving. And Babington was the last link in a chain which stretched from the Pope to the Spanish King, and from the exiled Catholics in France to young Anthony

Babington, even now stumbling down the stairs towards them.

'Courage, my friends,' Goodluck murmured in Latin, and saw them turn to look at him, their backs slowly straightening. 'Whatever happens to us in the months to come, these Protestant dogs cannot touch our souls. We are apostles of Christ. Let us not lose faith in this, our great mission to restore the one true Church to England.'

Ballard bowed his head, piously making the sign of the Cross. '*Et in saecula saeculorum, amen.*'

'I do not lose faith in our mission,' Maude responded irritably. 'But I sometimes think you trust too readily. Babington is a stout enough soul, and has proved himself in Queen Mary's service before. Yet he is young.'

'What of it?' came Babington's voice from the doorway, and they turned to see him wrapped in a cloak, a white nightgown beneath, his hose still on.

Goodluck had never met Anthony Babington before, though they had corresponded by coded letter over the months since he had been away from England. Covertly, he studied the young man. His dark dishevelled locks were worn long, curling like a cherub's about his forehead and cheeks, and there was a fanatical fervour to his voice as he greeted them.

'My brother in Christ!' Babington clasped Ballard's forearm and drew him close for a kiss on each cheek, Roman-style, then turned to Maude with a similarly enthusiastic welcome. 'How I have missed you both, and was buoyed up in my solitude only by your letters! But I have a letter to show you that will make you weep with joy, I swear it.'

He turned to Goodluck last. 'Sir, you are travelling with the two stoutest fellows in the world, and I am glad to make your acquaintance. You must be . . . ?'

'Father John Weatherley,' Goodluck lied smoothly, and

shook Babington's hand. 'We are not strangers, though. We have several times corresponded on the matter of Her Majesty, Queen of Scots, when I was pleased to share certain information with you regarding the support of the Rheims priesthood for any action, however violent, which might see Her Majesty safely installed on the throne of England.'

'Christ be with you, Father Weatherley,' Babington said, and smiled into his eyes. 'And thank you for your letters, too, which have cheered me greatly in these dark times. I always know at once when I have met a man whom I can trust to the death, and you are such a one.'

'I thank you,' Goodluck murmured, and bowed his head.

'Come, my friends, let us all sit and talk. We shall take Mass together in the morning.' Babington laughed. 'At least there will be no shortage of priests for the service, with three of you under my roof.'

Ballard smiled, casting off his cloak. 'Indeed I long to take Holy Communion, and have the comfort of our Lord's sacrifice in my mouth. It was not possible aboard the ship that brought us. The sea was rough most of the way and we were tossed about horrendously.'

'Did you arrive in London only tonight? But you must be exhausted!' Babington stuck his head out of the door and shouted to his servant. 'Hoxton, fetch wine and food for my visitors. And more wood for the fire!'

They ate and drank, then sat beside the briskly burning fire to warm themselves. Goodluck felt his strength renewed after the long voyage. His senses sharpened, he listened to the three men talk eagerly of their plans, then scanned the letter that was passed to him by Babington, all the while nodding his approval.

'That is a letter from Her Majesty, Queen Mary, herself,' Babington told him. With shining eyes, the young man pointed out the rounded, slightly childish signature that had been scrawled across the base of the sheet. 'You see Her Majesty's beautiful hand, how it flows most royally to form her name? And do you mark the crossed R for Regina?'

'The hand of a woman born to be queen,' Goodluck murmured.

'It is, indeed, my friend,' Babington agreed fervently, and clapped him on the shoulder.

'Then why is she not even now our sovereign?' A frown on his face, Ballard stood and strode across the room to pour himself another cup of wine. 'I am sickened to think that a Catholic queen has been kept prisoner by the bastard child of a whore all these years, and none of her followers has succeeded in freeing her. It dishonours us that we have not yet rid the world of the heretic Elizabeth.'

'It will not be long now,' Babington reassured him, his face flushed. 'Pray sit down, my friend, and set your mind at rest. We shall not suffer Queen Elizabeth to live another year, God willing.' He leaned forward. 'Father Weatherley, the letter, if you please?'

There was ample space beneath Mary's signature to forge a postscript, Goodluck noted, handing the letter back to Babington. Nor was there any cross-hatch scoring as a precaution against later additions to the letter. Goodluck wondered at such a lapse in judgement. Queen Elizabeth would never have signed her name in such a way that anyone could have added an incriminating postscript once the letter had left her hands. It was as though the exiled Scottish Queen was making no effort this time to conceal her involvement. Perhaps Queen Mary had grown desperate to escape her long imprisonment – and desperation had made her careless.

Babington handed the letter across to Ballard. 'So, what news from His Holiness, our blessed Pope?' he asked eagerly. 'You said you had been in Rome.'

Ballard nodded sombrely, smoothing out the letter with reverent hands. 'It took nearly a month, but eventually I was permitted private conference with His Holiness. I bring a message of support from the Pope to all English Catholics who would see Mary on the throne.'

'In writing?' Babington's smile was tremulous.

'His Holiness would commit nothing to paper. Nor should we expect him to. The message I bring from Rome is by mouth only, and it promises special dispensation for any man by whose agency the Protestant Queen is murdered.' Ballard nodded grimly, seeing Babington's eyes widen. 'The Pope himself grants us absolution in advance for her murder. It is what you hoped for, is it not?'

'It is beyond what I hoped for, my friend. That His Holiness should know of our plans and approve of them. This news brings me such joy, I cannot tell you.' Babington dropped to his knees and crossed himself, speaking in Latin. 'Hail Mary, the Lord is with thee.'

They all knelt and joined in, Goodluck also murmuring the Latin words of the prayer along with the other conspirators. If his immortal soul was in jeopardy for this deception, so be it.

When they had finished their prayers, Ballard continued in a low voice, 'I can tell you also that we shall not be alone in our efforts to subdue the Protestants after the Queen's death. It is hoped that the Duke of Guise will lead an army of some sixty thousand troops, promised to us by King Philip of Spain. I spoke with his ambassador in Paris, Signor Mendoza. This army would be ready to march on England at the first news of the Queen's death, to enforce the crowning of Queen Mary if it is resisted by the Privy Council or the people themselves.'

'The people will neither resist nor question Mary's right to rule,' Maude muttered. His gaze slid to Goodluck's face, then away again. He stretched out his boots to the fire. 'I say the English people are sick of bending the knee to a known whore. But the Privy Council are another matter.'

Goodluck studied him thoughtfully. There were times when he did not quite trust Maude. His expression was often calculating, his manner shifty, and he watched Goodluck whenever he thought it safe to do so.

Did Maude suspect him of being one of Elizabeth's spies? The possibility chilled Goodluck. Perhaps he should take some opportunity soon to slip away from them and take his news to Walsingham, before his throat was cut in the middle of the night.

'Was there any talk of when the deed should be done?' Babington asked, and at last he seemed nervous, avoiding their eyes as he rose to stoke the fire.

'August,' Ballard told him firmly. 'Mendoza told me the army would be ready by the end of the summer. September at the latest.'

'It is late May now. That leaves us . . .' Babington turned back to face them, licking his lips, 'hardly any time to prepare. If they wait until she is dead, it may be too late. We shall need military support in London in the days after . . . after it is done. There are too many Queen's men in the south. We shall not be able to enforce her cousin's coronation, not without more Catholics whose loyalty and might we can call on.'

Ballard thought for a moment. 'There are Catholic lords in the north who may help us. Men of property.'

'Then you must ride north without delay. Seek out the Catholic landowners and gain their trust. Do not tell them everything. It would endanger our plans if too much is known before the deed itself has been carried out.'

'No *deed*,' Maude interrupted, 'but an execution. Let us be blunt and call it what it is.'

Ballard nodded, leaning back on the creaking settle. 'Aye, Queen Elizabeth must be executed. Like her mother

270

before her. Both of them whores and traitors to the true faith.'

'How to do it, then?' Babington whispered into the silence that had fallen. 'With an axe?'

'If necessary.'

Goodluck looked from Ballard's stony face to Babington's wide-eyed terror, and wondered yet again at how such an unlikely gang had ever come together to plot the death of their rightful monarch. Maude, he noted, seemed unmoved by the idea of violence against an anointed queen, though he was shaking his head.

'A formal execution seems overly complicated,' Maude murmured. 'To be beheaded, the Queen would have to be removed from all her women, her courtiers, and taken to a secret place where her crimes could be laid before her, and judgement given. Her death to follow instantly.' He looked at Goodluck again in that sly, sideways manner. 'It is how it should be done in a just world. But the chance of our plan being discovered is too high. A select gang, maybe five or six people at the most, that is how you murder a queen.'

Goodluck called his bluff. 'Then what do you suggest? That we creep into the Royal Bedchamber and strangle the Queen in her sleep?'

Ballard laughed. 'No, but Maude is right. We stand no chance of engineering a proper trial and execution, however much she deserves to see her death coming. I imagine it will be difficult to come face to face with the Queen, with all her guards and ladies about her, her simpering entourage.' Ballard smiled unpleasantly. 'But a dagger, thrust deep into the heart, will send a whore to hell as swiftly and efficiently as any executioner.'

Babington swallowed, but nodded. 'Then are we all agreed? When the time comes, one of us must seek a private audience with the Queen, stab her in the heart, and rid England of her heresy.'

'But which of us must wield the dagger?' Goodluck asked.

Ballard made a dismissive gesture. 'Whichever of us is still standing. If it falls to me, I will do it gladly.'

Babington put out his hand, palm down. 'We must all swear it. In the name of our Lord, Jesus Christ.'

'Amen,' Goodluck murmured, and placed his hand on Babington's.

The other two followed suit, each declaring, 'Amen.'

Babington shook off their hands, breathing fast. He sat back and stared at the fire, his face suddenly pallid and sickly-looking. 'So we are sworn to it. The Queen will die. Let us talk no more of this business. In the morning, you and Maude must make preparations to ride north,' he said, glancing at Ballard, 'and I will write a reply to Her Majesty, Queen Mary, letting her know that a Catholic army is ready to fight in her cause. She will be glad of such news.'

Goodluck drained his cup. 'Is it safe to write such a letter?'

With a quick grin, Babington looked back at him and nodded. 'Ah, but there's the beauty of it. I write my letters in a code devised by Her Majesty herself. It is quite cunning, and if the letter should fall by some mischance into the wrong hands, it will be unintelligible to those who do not hold the key.' He yawned, stretching luxuriously. 'Besides, the messenger I send is a resolute Catholic and highly trustworthy in this cause. I have never met a braver fellow. Gilbert Gifford will not fail us.'

Six

Dearest Cathy,

It seems an age since we were at court together. I
received your letter last month and am glad to know you
and your son are in good health. How strange it must be
to nurse a babe in your arms! And is your husband
returned yet from the Low Countries? I keep you all in
my daily prayers. Write again and this time spare no
details, I wish to hear everything.

But I have news for you, dearest friend. You remember
one W. S. who so rudely accosted me at the masque? He
has spoken to me since then, many times, and I was
mistaken in him. In truth, I am in love with him and
hope to be Mistress Shakespeare one day. There, it's out,
and looks so cold and hard on paper. But I do, and my
heart sings for the gentleman. For I swear he is a
gentleman, though a player too, and from the land.

I was sorry to hear you have been lonely with your
husband at the war. I am lonely too, not being at court
any more. Come and stay with me in Cheapside, if you
will, and bring the child with you. I long to see you
again. And keep me in your prayers also.

Yours, Lucy

PS W. has promised nothing, yet I trust him. Am I wrong to do so?

*

'So all this is yours now?' Cathy asked Lucy, glancing curiously about the dark, cramped house in Cheapside. She shifted her young son from one hip to the other, hushing him as he protested. 'Since Master Goodluck's death?'

Lucy threw back the front shutters, and warm sunlight streamed in through the window. 'His body was never found, so it remains Goodluck's property until his death can be decided.' She tickled the child under his chin. 'This one's growing bonny. He must be nearly two now. Does he favour his father?'

'I can hardly remember,' Cathy replied, then managed a wry smile at Lucy's surprised glance. 'Oh, do not misunderstand me. I love Oswald well enough. But I have not seen him in nearly a year, not since he went off soldiering in the Low Countries. What if he never comes back, Lucy? What if he is killed out there?' She shook her head bitterly. 'I do not know how we will survive if my husband dies.'

'Whose command is he under?'

'He is with Lord Leicester's troops.' Cathy hesitated, then giggled, her face suddenly diverted. 'With the great man himself. But you will not have heard the stories. You have not been back to court, have you?'

'Not since the Queen in her wisdom dismissed me,' Lucy agreed, then laughed. 'No, don't look like that. My life here is not so terrible, though it seems you receive news of the court while I am shunned. But I am happy now, for you are here at last and we shall be like sisters again.'

It was good to have Cathy to stay. The weeks since she had left court had been filled with days of loneliness and, later, fear of what lay ahead once her guardian had gone and she seemed to have lost her place at court. She knew ways to earn money in the city, but had so far turned her

274

face against them. She might be a virgin no longer, but that did not mean she should become a prostitute. Instead, she had been gradually pawning her last few possessions from court to pay for the upkeep of Goodluck's house, plus her own meagre needs. Sir Francis had written to her in a kindly manner on several occasions, offering assistance, yet she had felt too much shame in her loss of position to reply. One day perhaps, if she grew desperate enough, she would ask for his help. But that day had not yet come.

Seeing Will from time to time lightened the heaviness of her days. It was a sin for them to lie together outside wedlock, and Lucy knew it. Yet she could not seem to help herself, the passion and urgency were so strong between them.

Perhaps one day Will would ask her to marry him. Sometimes he kissed the tips of her fingers, as though she were at court again, and whispered, 'I love you, Lucy Morgan,' leaving her heart deaf to all warnings from her head.

A fear still lurked inside her that he might be married already, but she dismissed it. Will had never spoken to her of a wife or children, nor had Lucy asked, for she felt sure he could not have given his love so freely if he had already been bound by God's law to another.

Cathy's child began to squirm and protest in her arms. Cathy tutted, dragging down her bodice to put him to the breast. 'Well,' she continued cheerfully, as the child latched on and began to suck, 'I had a letter from Alice at court last week. Lord Leicester is all but king of the Low Countries, it would seem, and the Queen is furious at his presumption. There's talk of his countess sailing over there to join him with an entourage of ladies and a hundred squires in livery. And of course that, if she does, there will be a second English court, only on the Continent. It is said the Queen fears that by the time he finally returns from war, Lord Leicester will want to rule over England as well, and not without cause.'

Cathy fell silent as someone in the street walked past the front window. She continued in a whisper, 'For everyone knows his wife would have a claim to the throne, being the Queen's cousin.'

Lucy carefully said nothing.

'But I did not come here to gossip and complain about my husband!' Cathy told her busily. 'I came to keep you company for a few weeks, my dear gloomy Lucy, and that is what I intend to do.'

'It is very good of you to have come all this way.'

'Nonsense. I was itching to get away from Norfolk, as well you know, and I wanted to see you bravely holding this house alone.' She settled the child more comfortably at her breast. 'Besides, when I read your letter, I knew I had to come as soon as I could. Master Shakespeare has nothing,' Cathy reminded her sharply. 'No money, no reputation.'

'He works as a playwright now for Master Burbage and some others. They pay him to improve the old plays, make them longer and more fashionable. No, don't shake your head, Cathy. Will is a player, yes, but he's no pauper. He's paid well for his work in the playhouse.' Lucy frowned. 'Well enough, anyway.'

It was true that Will had been paid handsomely in the past month, constantly reworking the old plays for a new audience. She had seen him with a fat purse one afternoon, coming from the Curtain Theatre, where he had been play-ing in an old piece about Henry the Fifth, and rewriting another play backstage between appearances – so Will had claimed, boasting of it as he kissed her. Yet his lodgings were still in the roughest part of the city, and she had noticed lately that he never seemed to have enough money to buy himself new clothes, nor pay to have his old ones mended. At first Lucy had supposed that – like most young men – Will must be gambling away his fees on dice games or cards, or at the bear-baiting pits across the river at Southwark, or even perhaps on ale. But she had soon learned that Will barely drank when in company, nor gambled more than he could afford, and showed little interest in the various illicit pleasures to be found on the south bank of the Thames.

'And does Shakespeare love you?' Cathy asked, looking unconvinced. 'Has he asked you to marry him?'

Lucy said nothing.

'I didn't think he had.' Cathy looked at her pityingly. 'If you take my advice, you'll forget all about Master Shakespeare. Oh, Lucy, I was like you once. I thought nothing could be more important than being in love. Being too lax with Oswald, I soon found myself with child. Do you remember? I was lucky. Oswald wanted to marry me, and our families were in accord. But if he hadn't married me, I would have brought shame on myself and my family, and my life would have been over.'

'Will loves me, I'm sure of it.'

'Well, maybe Shakespeare does love you. But if he does, he must marry you. Peace, though, I do not wish to distress you. I shall say nothing more about it.'

Cathy stroked her child's curly dark hair. He had allowed his mother's nipple to slip from his mouth and was sleeping now, his flushed cheek resting on her breast.

'You see my little James here?' Cathy murmured, staring down at her young son adoringly. 'He's getting too old for the breast, yet still he demands it. Men are greedy, and do not care for the consequences. I love my little James dearly and would not lose him for the world, but I miss court life so badly some days.'

'Yet you chose to leave.'

'Because I was foolish and fancied myself in love. Now

I am poor, and have a child to look after and a husband who is away at the war. Believe me, living in Norfolk without any money is worse than being buried alive. Do not wish such a tedious life on yourself. Marry a theatrical player from Warwickshire? You'll end up tending pigs in his mother's garden while he's off on tour with his company – yes, and probably whoring every night and gambling away your children's inheritance while he's at it.'

'I thought you would say no more about it,' Lucy reminded her, growing hot-cheeked as her friend's words echoed her own thoughts and fears about Shakespeare. 'I love him and he loves me. Will must follow his heart in the theatre before he thinks of taking a wife. Promise me you will not interfere?'

Cathy shook her head, lips pursed. 'Oh well, a woman in love will make her own bed and lie on it merrily enough. But if you want to avoid a life of drudgery, take my word for it and don't see Master Shakespeare again. He's too young for you, anyway.'

Lucy raised her eyebrows at that. 'There are but four years between us!'

'Aye, and four years is too long a time when it is the woman who is older. But I promised I should not interfere.' Cathy laid a finger on her lips, smiling at Lucy. 'I was a fool once, too. Now it is your turn.'

Seven

'MASTER SHAKESPEARE!'

Will woke with a grunting jerk, staring wildly about at the sound of his name being shouted about the theatre. He straightened his cap and wiped a trace of drool from his mouth. The hot July sunshine poured through a small window above him.

'I'm busy! Can't you see I'm working here?' Will straightened out the crumpled sheet of paper he had been lying on and reached for his quill. 'What is it?'

It was only Master Fildrew, one of the backstage managers at the Curtain. A small man with a limping gait, he threaded his way through the heaped bric-a-brac of the property room and thrust a note into Will's hand.

'Whore at the back door for you,' Fildrew informed him sharply. 'I told her we were preparing for the afternoon performance, but she won't go away.'

Will read the note and jumped up, knocking his chair over. 'At the back door, you say?'

'Aye, Master,' Fildrew agreed, staring as Will hurried from the room. He raised his voice after him. 'And a fine black whore she is too. Do you know her fee? I would be happy to pay ten shillings for a shot at that.'

It was crowded backstage, as always just before a performance. Will found his way barred by minstrels tuning their instruments in the hallway and a boy actor in an unlaced scarlet and gold gown with his wig askew, weeping because he had grown too fat for the gown to be fastened. The dour-faced Scottish costume master fussed behind him, trying to drag the gaping sides of the gown together and swearing at Will in Gaelic as he pushed through to the back door.

A tall figure in the doorway straightened as he approached, and held out two gloved hands. 'Will!'

It was Lucy Morgan.

He took her hands and pulled her close, kissing her on the mouth. She smelt sweet, of violets and roses, reminding him of a country garden. Her gown was demure, not like the extravagant dresses he had seen her wear at court, but she looked just as edible in it. 'Lucy, how I have missed you! So you have come to see one of my plays at last. It's a poor thing, an old story, but I'm rewriting after every performance, making it better each time it's played.' He nuzzled his lips against her throat, trying but failing to suppress the bitter accusation in his voice. 'Could you not have come sooner? It's been weeks.'

Her smile seemed strained. 'I told you it would not be easy for me to escape. I have had my friend Cathy and her child to stay this summer, and I'm afraid she does not approve of our . . .' She hesitated, not looking at him. '. . . Our meetings.'

'Then you should have turned her out into the street,' Will said venomously, surprised to discover a wave of anger inside him that would not be contained. 'Her and her child too. You are your own mistress, Lucy. You do not need her approval.'

Lucy raised her eyebrows. 'Perhaps not,' she agreed, 'but I do need her friendship. I love Cathy, she is my

280

dearest friend, and I would never wish to hurt or offend her. Besides, I need her skill as a housewife. She has been helping me to tidy and clean out Master Goodluck's old house. There were many tasks I would not have been able to undertake without her advice. And the house must be cleaned before the end of the summer. I may need to take a lodger in the autumn, for otherwise I cannot afford to live.'

He stared at her, remembering Cathy, the laughing, golden-haired girl he had met at Whitehall Palace. 'Why does she disapprove of me?'

'I wonder,' Lucy murmured, looking at his wild hair and dishevelled clothes, the ink stains on his fingers.

Laughing, Will drew her inside the theatre. There, in the thick shadows behind the stage, he pushed her up against the wall and kissed her properly, letting his fingers explore her strong throat, then travel up over her jaw to the full-lipped, sultry mouth and high cheekbones above.

'Promise me you will not listen to your friend,' he whispered against her throat, breathing in the delicious fragrance of her dark hair. 'You and I were meant to be together, Lucy Morgan. Our love was written in the stars. And no disapproving housewife is going to exert her baleful influence over us instead, however many thrifty ways to clean wood and pewter she may know.'

Lucy laughed with him, but he sensed her disquiet and was angry with himself for having made her mistrust him. From now on, he must control his temper. This rage would only grow if he continued to feed it with so much jealousy and frustration. It would get out of hand and threaten the love between them.

He heard a commotion from the front gates, and forced a smile. 'Let us not quarrel, Lucy. You are here now, and I must be satisfied with that. Come and watch the play with me! We can sit on the stage, it's the best view in the house.

But we'll have to hurry, they are already letting the play-goers in.' When she did not move, he seized her hand and squeezed it reassuringly. 'Come! What is the matter? The play will begin soon.'

'You wish me to sit on the stage itself?'

'Why not? You can sit on my lap, sweet Lucy, and feed me nuts and oranges when I grow hungry.' He grinned. 'It is allowed, so long as you do not disrupt the players.'

But Lucy was shaking her head. There was anger in her face. 'Will, what are you thinking? Look at me, I am too easily recognized.'

'So?'

'I may not be one of the court ladies any more, but I do not wish to lose my reputation completely by sitting on the . . . on the very *stage* at the theatre.' Her voice shook. 'You must know only a whore would sit there.'

He stared at her, then realized that Lucy was right. What a fool he was! It had not even entered his mind that she could be disgraced by such a tiny thing. Yet he still wished her to sit on the stage with him and watch one of his own plays from close up, not from high in the gallery where the bolder noblewomen or wealthy merchants' wives some-times sat with their maids, covering their faces with their handkerchiefs so they would not be recognized.

'Come,' he said, and insisted on dragging her along the narrow corridor back towards the room where he had been writing. 'What we need is a disguise.'

'A what?'

As they reached the room, the first drum-roll came, then the minstrels struck up their welcoming music, and Will knew there would be little time before the prologue began. He threw open the lid of one of the theatrical chests, and rummaged about among the oddest collection of objects – a broken trumpet, a doll in swaddling cloth meant to look like a baby, a cracked chamber pot, and a dented crown – until he found something suitable.

Will suppressed his grin and handed a bushy grey beard up to Lucy. 'Here, try this.'

She turned it over in her hand. 'What is it?'

'Well,' he said lightly, 'it looks like a baby badger flattened by a cartwheel. But I believe it's meant to be an old man's beard.'

Lucy looked at him. 'You're not serious?'

'Humour me.'

Her eyes wide with disbelief, she held the bushy beard up to her chin, then waited for his verdict. 'Well?'

'Perhaps a mask would suit you better.'

She threw the beard at him. 'Will you be serious for once? I need a man, not a jester.'

'A jester is both.'

She closed her eyes. 'Will, listen to me. There is still a small chance that I may be taken back at court one day, if Queen Elizabeth chooses to forgive me for whatever I did to offend her. Meanwhile, I must *not* lose my reputation by being seen at the theatre with you. It is too public a place.'

'But you'll sit on my lap in the tavern afterwards?'

'Don't mock me, Will Shakespeare,' she told him, her face quivering with sudden fury, 'or I shall leave and never come back!'

Silently, he turned his back on her, and drew a painted mask out of the chest with trailing laces on either side. He stood and fastened it about her head, his fingers curling round her neck afterwards, revelling in the soft smoothness of her skin.

He whispered, 'I love you,' in her ear, and heard Lucy sigh. He waited but she did not speak. 'I know how difficult this is for you. I did not mean to make a mockery of your feelings. Will you forgive me?'

'Oh, Will, why must you be such a child?'

Stung by that, Will resisted the urge to bend the masked

Lucy over his writing table, pull up her skirts and show her how much he was a man. But that would only confirm his childishness in her eyes. Instead, he must mock himself, play the fool, so that Lucy would not see how much she had hurt him with that question.

He hooked the old man's grey beard over his ears so that it dangled bushily on his chin, then stood up and took her hand. In the gallery above, the minstrels had finished playing. The whistles, applause and foot-stamping died away, and he heard the prologue begin his speech.

'Now we are both in disguise,' he said with a grin. 'Shall we go and watch the play?'

Eight

PERCHED ON THE EDGE OF THE STAGE AT THE CURTAIN, LUCY tried to ignore the impudent stares of the groundlings below her. Will sat by her side, eating an apple as they watched the prologue finish his lengthy flourishes.

Will leaned towards her as the man left the stage. 'It's the chronicle of King Lear and his three daughters. Do you know the tale? Burbage has asked me to rework it for the company. Make something bigger of it, a spectacle. Was the prologue too long-winded? I thought it needed a prologue. But to see it played in such an overblown fashion makes me think otherwise.'

'Hush there!' someone called from the crowd.

Will did not even glance at the man. He threw his apple core aside and pulled Lucy on to his lap. She squirmed uncomfortably and did not know where to look, hearing the coarse laughter and comments from the men below. She was suddenly very glad of the mask which hid her face from the crowd, for there was no more prominent position than here on the edge of the stage, in full view of every playgoer.

'Perhaps I shall lose the prologue,' he murmured into her ear, 'and begin with Lear's division of his kingdom. For me, that is the heart of the play. What do you say, Lucy?'

'I say it is you who are mad, not King Lear.'

'You do not like the play?'

Her back was stiff. 'I do not like sitting in your lap before all these people.'

'I would not have all these people in my lap, I tell you, either before or after you have sat on me.'

One of the groundlings tugged violently at Lucy's gown, and she looked down, coughing as a cloud of sweet-scented smoke enveloped her. At first she thought it was a swarthy-faced man, leaning against the stage and smoking a clay pipe. Then she realized it was a woman, with long grey locks and a filthy gown tucked up into her petticoat to reveal stained hose and a pair of boots tied about with twine. Her pipe was clamped between black gums where teeth had once been – as Lucy saw to her horror when the crone removed it to speak.

The woman pointed a crooked finger at Will. 'Tell your keeper to shut up and watch the play, whore.'

'I'm not a whore and he's not my keeper.' She glared at Will, who was laughing silently behind his bushy beard. 'Shut up and watch the play, Master Shakespeare.'

He mimed sewing up his lips, then turned his attention back to the players. At once, his smile vanished and his face became oddly intent.

The afternoon sun came out from behind a cloud, and was soon burning Lucy's back and shoulders through her gown. She had not stayed in London this late into the summer for many years, and the rising stench of the people around her was almost unbearable in the heat. She knew the theatres would soon be closing until the autumn, for the risk of plague was so high in the summer months that the city fathers had decreed that people should not be allowed to gather in large numbers at plays and bear pits.

It was not long before Lucy herself had forgotten her quarrel with Will, so absorbed did she become in the unfolding drama on the stage. She had seen the play herself, but was surprised to find that the crude retelling by street players that she remembered had been nothing like this one. The story, though, had changed little. King Lear chose to divide his kingdom between his daughters according to how much they loved him. His two eldest paid him the most elaborate compliments, and were rewarded with vast and profitable estates. His youngest, Cordelia, was given no portion of land to call her own, for she refused to flatter her father in hope of gain. Being cruel and spiteful by nature, the older daughters soon turned against the powerless old king and mistreated him, then waged war against their younger sister and her royal husband.

The boy playing the part of Cordelia was dark and slender-hipped, a perfect foil to the brash red-haired viciousness of the two older sisters, Goneril and Regan. His voice was a high-noted reed in the silence of the hushed theatre. When Cordelia was hanged at the end of the play, Lucy felt tears prick at her eyes, and wiped them away surreptitiously. It seemed foolish to cry at a story.

But then she heard sobs and sighing from all around, and looked down to see grown men wiping damp faces on their sleeves or weeping openly among the close-packed groundlings, while one woman called out hoarsely from the high gallery, 'Lord have mercy on your poor sweet soul!'

As the play ended, Will took Lucy's hand and kissed it. 'Are those real tears? You do me too much honour. It is barely my play at all, though the original had Cordelia survive. This ending is better, I believe, with her death. Though it may be more poignant if the old king should die too. I shall rewrite it later. When I have time.'

'It is perfect,' she whispered.

He smiled, but shook his head. 'A rackety old thing, cobbled together like a bad shoe. It will take a few years to make it right. It lacks . . . I don't know what it lacks, but one day I will find it. More men, perhaps. There are altogether too many women in the piece. For now, the crowd are happy and that's all that matters. That, and my fee.'

'Don't try to pretend it's all about the money,' she told him, but let him pull her to her feet. The fine ladies and their servants in the galleries and private boxes had already left the theatre, so she felt safe enough in unfastening her mask. 'I should get back. Cathy is alone with her son.'

'Another hour, my black beauty,' he promised, and pulled her close, his arm about her waist.

Oh, but this was dangerous. Lucy looked into his face, aware of the groundlings still milling about below them, and the handful of players already clearing the stage for the next day's performance. 'I loved the play, Will,' she murmured, then unhooked his false beard and dropped it to the stage. 'But I do not love this.'

'Then I shall only wear it when I wish to frighten you,' he replied, and kissed her on the lips.

One of the players made a vile remark as he swept the stage behind them, but Lucy closed her ears to it and let Will kiss her.

She was hardly able to believe that this coarse young man could have brought all those hundreds of people in the theatre to such heights of joy and despair for the past few hours. It was almost as if there were two Will Shakespeares. The one whose soul bled on to the paper in the likeness of a poet, and the other a wicked creature whose hands strayed about her body until she had forgotten all her protests.

'Two hours at the most,' Will continued persuasively. He helped her jump down from the high stage. 'Players and playwrights must always visit a tavern after the play, did you not know that? It is an old English custom – as old as Morris dancers, or plum pudding at Yuletide. No, I insist that you come too. The playwright and his lovely muse. Where would I be without you?'

Entering the crowded tavern in his wake, Lucy was relieved to see other women there. Though it was not much of a comfort to realize that most were whores, for some were sitting on the men's knees with their skirts drawn up, while two or three were openly allowing themselves to be fondled, breasts spilling from low-bodiced gowns as they kissed and drank liberally from the jugs of ale on every table.

'Kit!' Will cried, and held out his hand to a young man lounging at the bar. 'Still writing?'

'Still rewriting, Will?'

Will laughed and shook the young man's hand, but Lucy guessed he was not amused by the jibe. 'We have just come from *King Lear* at the Curtain.' He pulled Lucy forward, ignoring her protest. 'Look what I've found. This is my muse, Kit. Isn't she lovely?'

The young man met Lucy's embarrassed glance with a steady gaze of his own, and bowed. 'Undoubtedly a jewel among the Ethiopians. Does your black muse have a name?'

'Lucy,' Will told him, and smiled back at her lazily. 'Her name is Mistress Lucy Morgan. She is lately come from court, where she had the run of the palaces and served the Queen herself.'

'A lady of the court? I didn't know you moved in such exalted circles.' Kit Marlowe's voice was oddly sharp. Lucy looked at Will questioningly. But he just raised Lucy's hand to his lips and kissed it, smiling again.

'Lucy, this is Kit Marlowe. Don't trust him, and do not believe a word he says. He is a disreputable playwright, just as I am.'

'No, Will,' Kit corrected him softly, 'you are a player

who tinkers with old plays to make them better. I am the only disreputable playwright here.'

Now there was no mistake. Will's face stiffened with anger. What to do now? She dreaded a quarrel between these two men that might draw even more attention. 'My love,' she whispered in Will's ear, rubbing against him, 'can you find me a place to sit by the door? This room is so hot, I can hardly breathe.'

Will turned to look at her. His fists were clenched, his eyes glazed with fury. She guessed why. His pride as a play-wright had been hurt, and in front of a woman too. Then his gaze dropped to her mouth and he seemed to recall where he was.

'A seat by the door,' he repeated slowly. 'Of course I can find you one. Are you faint with the heat, sweet Lucy? I'm not surprised.'

Steering her towards the door, he inclined his head stiffly to Kit Marlowe. 'I'll talk to you later, Kit.'

The door to the tavern had been propped open. Men had already spilt out into the street with their flagons of ale, some singing drunkenly. One collapsed in the doorway as they approached, sprawled on the dirt, and Will swung Lucy into his arms, lifting her high over the man's prone body.

'Drunken sot.' He laughed, and set her down on the low wall outside. She saw several men glance in her direction, and kept her gaze fixed on Will's face. He smiled, kissing her mouth hotly, then her throat. 'Dearest Lucy. I am so glad to have found you again.'

She cupped his face in her hands. 'And I you,' she whispered.

'I'm sorry about Marlowe,' he muttered. 'That young whoreson bastard thinks himself too good for the rest of us, with his Cambridge education and his political plays. He loves to insult other playwrights. If you had not been there, I would have punched him in the face. Still might, if

290

he gives me provocation. He cannot keep a civil tongue in his head.'

'But that would make me unhappy,' she told him. 'You could be arrested for brawling. Put in the stocks.'

'For you, anything.'

He closed his eyes against the bright sunshine, tracing her mouth and chin with his fingers like a blind man. She had seen him do that before, almost as though he were learning the contours of her face. Like his kisses, it seemed too intimate a gesture for such a public place, and she stirred, drawing back a little.

'I am thirsty,' she said plaintively.

Will laughed. 'Then I shall be your servant and fetch you refreshment, Mistress Morgan. Will you share a flagon of English ale with me?' He made a face. 'But I'm forgetting you were a queen's lady. Would you prefer a cup of wine? I don't know if they serve any wine in this godforsaken establishment, but I can ask.'

Lucy shook her head. 'Ale is good.'

He looked about, then hailed a grey-haired man by the door who was deep in conversation with a band of players, some still in costume. She recognized the man as one of Goodluck's friends from the theatre, a James Burbage, who had once or twice been kind to her when she'd been a curious child, peeping round the curtain into the tiring-room – where the actors disrobed after each performance – while Goodluck was on stage.

'Burbage! Will you look after my lady here while I fetch her ale? There's a cup in it for you, too, if you keep her safe from molestation.'

James Burbage extricated himself from the group and hurried over, his gaze full of frank admiration. 'Such a dusky beauty, Will. I congratulate you on your taste. My lovely wanton, if you ever drop Shakespeare, may I be considered next in line for your bed?'

'I . . . I think we know each other, Master Burbage,' she managed, a little hot-cheeked at his impudence. 'You were friends with my guardian, Master Goodluck.'

Burbage looked at her more closely. She saw recognition in his face, then a look that might have been guilt. He bowed over her hand. 'Forgive me, Mistress Morgan. I am a drunken oaf and should have my tongue cut out. How could I have forgotten Goodluck's lovely ward?' He hesitated, frowning. 'I was sorry to hear of his death.'

'Thank you, sir.'

'So you keep company with young Shakespeare now?' he remarked, and again she was surprised at that strange look on his face when she nodded.

What was it? How had she upset him? Was this embarrassment that she was Shakespeare's mistress? Master Burbage had no reason to think ill of her for such a choice; they loved each other and that was all that mattered. Perhaps it was guilt that he had not offered to help when her guardian died? Yet that was hardly his office, even as an old friend of Goodluck's.

Besides, she was no whore, whatever Burbage or any other man here might think, hanging about the theatres in hope of trade. She still had Goodluck's house and she was looking after herself well enough. Soon Will would look after her too. Once they were married.

Another man had joined them, smiling and bowing. He was tall and slim-hipped, built like one of the male dancers at Queen Elizabeth's court. Under his feathered cap, his hair was slicked back. He reminded her of those courtiers who desperately sought to rise in the Queen's favour, yet had neither money nor rank to recommend them.

'But you must be the infamous dark-eyed Mistress Morgan,' the young man exclaimed. He looked her up and down, one hand resting lightly on his hip. 'And now I see why Will made you the subject of so many

292

lovelorn sonnets. You are a beautiful creature indeed.'

Will introduced them with obvious reluctance. 'Lucy, this is a friend and neighbour of mine. His name is Jack Parker, but I beg you to forget it at once. He is the greatest knave that ever—'

'Pax!' Jack Parker held up his hand. 'I shall say nothing more of your sonnets.'

Lucy smiled back at Jack, whom she could not help but like instinctively. He had such an engaging smile, though his admiration seemed a little mocking. But that was the way of all Will's friends in the theatre.

'Sir,' she murmured, curtsying, 'I share your dismay at Master Shakespeare's sonnets. Yet I cannot seem to stop him writing them.'

Laughing and exasperated, Will left her with Burbage and Parker, and went inside in search of ale. Burbage was soon joined by his other friends, some of whom Lucy also remembered from her childhood – those wonderful, unconventional days spent sitting backstage with her horn book or rag dolls while Goodluck rehearsed or performed – and talk rapidly turned back to the theatre. This was something she could understand, and so did not have to stand with her head lowered, unable to take an interest or discuss her thoughts, as at court when politics or intrigue had become the topic of conversation between courtiers. It was not dangerous here to venture an opinion, whereas a word in the wrong ear at court might leave you isolated overnight and in peril of your life.

Will returned with two brimming flagons of strong ale for them all to share, and bought an ounce of tobacco from a passing street trader. With a grin, he settled on the wall beside Lucy to smoke, pressing a few pinches of dried tobacco down into the bowl of his pipe. Its delicately fragrant smoke mingled with the smells of hot roast pig and pickled herrings as an array of trenchers were brought out to the hungry players, who ate standing up, licking their fingers between courses in the absence of a water bowl or cloth.

The afternoon drifted almost unnoticed into evening, the sun still warm on their faces as they drank, smoked and conversed. It was the first time since leaving Goodluck's care at the age of fourteen to join the court that Lucy had felt truly free; free to drink in this rough company of men, to laugh and speak her mind without fear of censure or ridicule. Early on, she had become used to the company of men, as she had run and played among Goodluck's theatricals, their wit and coarse ribaldry sailing over her head. Now that she was a woman, and more aware of the arts of love, she allowed herself to laugh with them as the ale lifted her mood, not caring what any man might think, seeing her so unrestrained.

Will passed her the pipe and laughed when she drew on it curiously, exploding in a fit of coughing.

'Not so deep!' he advised her, and showed Lucy how the pipe should be smoked. 'Try again, and breathe shallow this time. It is good for the heart. Small puffs; you will soon feel its benefits.'

As they were leaving, Lucy unsteady on her feet, Will's arm tight about her waist, one of the older men swaggered forward to stop them. He wore a pearl earring in one ear, and was more richly dressed than most of the theatricals who frequented the tavern. His face and nose were a blotchy red, though, and not merely from the sun, for she could smell the beer on his breath. Lucy supposed he must be one of the theatre share owners, not a mere player, and lowered her gaze before his bold glance.

'Whither are you bound, young Shakespeare? Back to your flea-ridden lodgings and a straw pallet on the floor?' The man laughed carelessly. 'Come back to my place instead. I've a bed, and we can share your black whore more comfortably there.'

The other men with him were grinning. Will's friends stepped forward, shadowing him. The narrow backstreet – so bright before – seemed to darken, a gloomy dusk coming upon them almost by stealth, the overhanging houses looming above them; even the discordant music from a beggar's whistle echoing round the walls suddenly sounded menacing.

The man shook his head at Will's instinctive gesture towards his dagger, tucked discreetly into his belt at the back. 'Now, sir, don't put that frowning face on. I've had a skinful and I know it. But let us not quarrel over trifles. I've ten shillings in my fat purse says your whore can pleasure us both tonight.'

'Don't,' she muttered, reading the anger in Will's face and fearing what might follow.

A dark flush on his cheeks, Will shrugged off the hand she placed warningly on his arm.

'You are mistaken, Carter. This lady is no whore,' he bit out, drawing his dagger, 'and I shall prove that on your dead body.'

The approaching men stopped, instantly wary. The blade was eight inches long, no boy's plaything but a sturdy weapon. Will held the dagger out towards the man, his gaze unwavering.

'Take back your words, sirrah. I will not stand to hear this lady insulted.'

'Lady!' Carter laughed again, but less comfortably. He took a step back and drew his own dagger, a thick-bladed poignard, passing it from hand to hand. 'But if that is how the wind blows, I'd as soon fight as fuck.'

Burbage came to Will's elbow, muttering in his ear. 'Let it drop, Will,' he told him urgently. 'I have seen this fellow

Carter in a fight before, and he knows his business. The quarrel is not worth your death.'

Will ignored him, pushing Lucy behind him as though to protect her. 'The lady is here with me,' he said stubbornly. His jaw clenched as he raised the point of his dagger towards Carter's face. 'And I will defend her honour to the death.'

Burbage swore softly under his breath. But he drew the sword at his side with a bow and a mocking flourish as though still onstage. 'And I, too. Come, shall we make a fight of it?'

'Defend her honour?' Carter repeated, in apparent disbelief, and his friends roared with laughter. But he looked assessingly at Will's stern face, then at the sword in Burbage's hand, and shrugged. 'Well, well! Such stout protectors. The great Master Burbage himself taking up steel in her defence . . . But then, you theatre folk love to share your goods in common, do you not?' He smiled unpleasantly. 'Perhaps I was mistaken in calling her a whore. You must forgive my error. It grows dark, after all, and the wench is the same colour as the sky.'

Will started forward with a growl, and Burbage caught him hard by the arm. Parker was at his other arm in an instant, both men holding Will back with an effort as he strained to be free.

'I'll rip your throat out, you bastard!' Will choked.

But the man called Carter had already turned away, sheathing his dagger and pushing through his watching friends into the tavern. Slowly, these men followed Carter inside, muttering and shaking their heads as though frustrated that the quarrel had not developed, the youngest even making a brief, obscene gesture in Lucy's direction before hurrying after them.

'Leave it, Will,' his friend Parker muttered. 'He is a fool, and not worth spitting on your dagger. Listen to Master Burbage. Take Mistress Morgan home and enjoy the rest of your evening.' With Will still staring fixedly after the men into the crowded tavern, Parker raised his voice. 'Look to your lady, Will.'

At that, Will turned to look at Lucy. She lowered her head, not wishing him to see the fear in her face.

Will slipped his arm back around her waist. 'Come, Lucy,' he said doggedly, 'let me escort you safely back to your home. The streets of this city are overrun with vermin.'

They walked in silence through the dark streets, Will's arm tightly round her, her head on his shoulder. No longer tired but with all her nerves on edge, Lucy turned the quarrel over in her mind. Even with Will by her side, ready to protect her, Lucy thought she had never felt so alone. Nor so vulnerable.

They came to the door of the house that had belonged to Goodluck. She could see the low flicker of the fire through a crack in the door, and knew that Cathy had been waiting up for her. They had no spills left for light, so the fire had to be kept lit after dark. Lucy felt a stab of guilt, and pulled away from Will's tight hold. She had been gone for hours, leaving her poor friend alone in the house with only her baby son for company. But the delicious lure of time spent with Will and his friends had been too much for her.

'Will,' she asked suddenly, 'why do you not marry me? Is it because of the colour of my skin?'

'What?' Will seemed amazed. He stared back at Lucy for a moment, then demanded, 'How can you ask such a question when I have just risked my life and the life of my friends to defend your honour?'

'A black whore is a fine catch for your bachelor days,' she continued steadily, 'but not good enough for your marriage bed, is that it?'

'You are no whore, Lucy.'

'That is no answer.'

'It is all the answer you will receive from me on this matter,' Will said flatly, then pulled her close and kissed her.

They stood in the doorway a few moments, locked together in silence. His hands caressed her spine through the thin fabric of her gown, his lips warm and persuasive.

'Let me in, Lucy,' he whispered against her throat. 'That braggart frightened you, that is the only reason you are upset. But you do not have to sleep alone tonight.'

Yes, she wanted him in her bed again tonight. Her body craved his. But the nights stretched out, and still no promise of a wedding. If they continued like this, lying together like man and wife night after night, taking no care to avoid a child, he would soon ruin her and she knew it. Lucy turned to unlatch the door. She shook her head when he would have followed her inside.

'You may come to my bed again when I have had a proper answer, Will Shakespeare, and not before.' He might be a player, but she would not be played for a fool. 'No, you cannot come in tonight. My mind is made up. If you can say nothing, then you shall have nothing.'

Nine

ELIZABETH RETRIEVED ROBERT'S LETTER FROM THE TABLE and read through it for a fifth time. It was brutally short, not written in his more habitual flowery or persuasive style. Was he unwell? Angry with her? She looked at his signature and traced it slowly with one finger. Why should Robert be angry with her? There was no more money for Robert beyond that which she had already ordered to be sent to the captains, or not until the armies' muster-books were seen to be in order, at least. And if his anger had a more personal spur, she was the Queen and had every right to demand that his wife should remain in England and not join him at his dubious English 'court' abroad.

Elizabeth threw his letter aside again and limped to the window of the Royal Bedchamber. The ulcer on her leg was a nuisance. Yet she would not sit still. That way lay death. Or decrepitude, which was as good as death. The common people must see her up and about. They were at war. They must believe their queen whole and hale. She leaned her arms on the wooden sill and stared out. Richmond was a fine palace, and she loved to visit it in the summer months when she was not away on progress, but this year it felt more like a prison. The satisfying warmth of an English summer streaming through the glass, reflected sunlight dazzling on the ornamental lake below, and yet she hardly dared venture outside for fear of assassins hidden behind every tree or concealed among the flattering smiles of her courtiers.

Meanwhile, Robert remained abroad, and even Walter Raleigh, whose saucy looks and country accent amused her, had upped and gone home against her command. Another one who would not bow to her authority but must wend his own way. Now there were only old men and boys at court to play chess or dance the volta with her.

The war must be won. They had poured too much of England into it. The royal coffers had been depleted to pay the soldiers the hugely inflated salaries Robert had insisted upon. And still the English and their allies lost battles they should have won, and made little headway. Yet to call Robert home would be to admit defeat. She must be brave and hold her nerve, however bad the news.

One of her ladies sighed, sitting on a cushion on the sun-lit floor, and she glanced back at her. Under her own instruction, Robert's niece, Lady Mary Herbert, was copying out a sonnet of Sir Thomas Wyatt's on the back of an old sheet of parchment. She was an intelligent young woman, Elizabeth thought, watching her with interest. Indeed, now that her relentless child-bearing of the past few years seemed to be at an end, Lady Mary's own poetry had begun to find some admirers at court. Elizabeth had thought to enclose the sonnet with her next letter to Robert, as a reminder of happier times when they had read Wyatt's poetry together as youths. Now she thought such an act would only encourage him to write more abrupt, discourteous letters, considering her entirely in his thrall.

Helena sat at the tapestry stand, embroidering a new

scene for Elizabeth's bedchamber that depicted the young lovers Cupid and Psyche at play. A less fitting image to hang above her bed she could not imagine. Yet it seemed to amuse Helena, whose spirits had been low in recent months.

Elizabeth knew what ailed Lady Helena these days. The Swedish-born noblewoman had been so beautiful in her youth, a star of the English court. But now Helena's skin was almost as wrinkled as Elizabeth's own, and she no longer turned the courtiers' heads as she walked in the Queen's wake. And with so many of the noblemen in their prime still away at the war, the court had become a lonely place for a woman in her middle years.

There was a knock at the door and Sir Francis Walsingham entered with no formal announcement, leaning on a stick. She wondered if he was ill again. Best not to comment, though. Her own legs were too often in need of the physician's attention these days. It was never wise to draw attention to another's ailments.

Walsingham bowed gravely to the ladies, then approached her, a letter in his hand.

'Not more bad news?' she demanded. That grim look again. She dreaded it, but knew it must be faced. 'When I heard you had returned to court, I thought it was to entertain me with news of London. But I see from your face it is to frighten me with more tales of dark deeds and treachery.'

'Forgive me, Your Majesty.' He gave her an old-fashioned look. 'Would you rather walk in darkness or light?'

She sighed and settled herself at the table. 'Very well. Tell me the worst, old friend.'

'You remember young Gifford?'

Elizabeth shuddered, recalling her night-time visit to the Tower and its vile dungeons. 'Only too well. The poor boy is not back in Master Topcliffe's clutches, I trust?'

'Indeed not, Your Majesty.' Walsingham handed across the letter. 'He has played his part with great cunning and ingenuity, intercepting letters for us almost every week between your cousin Mary and the conspirators. That information has allowed me to plant a select few of my own men among them, and so to watch these plotters more closely. But it has not been easy to infiltrate their ranks. They are clever and know their business. Some would appear to have taken training from Thomas Morgan in Paris, and to have studied with other such traitors here in England, all men skilled in the art of political intrigue. Their letters are written in a new code, which took us some time to break. But as you can see, they have now been decoded into plain English.'

'So you believe this is another letter from my cousin to these men you have been watching, these Catholic plotters?'

The letter was several sheets thick. Elizabeth frowned, unrolling them and holding the parchment a little away from her so the crabbed letters did not dance in front of her eyes. Her eyesight was no longer good for close reading, but she would not have everything read out to her as though she were blind.

'Beyond any doubt, Your Majesty. The original is here, if you wish to verify your cousin's signature.'

Slowly, she read over the decoded letter with growing unease, then took up the original and studied the signature. It was indeed Mary's hand. There was a short postscript with, inserted above it, this damning command: 'Fail not to burn this privately and quickly.'

'Who is this Anthony Babington to whom she writes so intimately? Apart from a traitor to my throne, that is.' Elizabeth scanned her cousin's incriminating postscript, then threw the sheets down with a sudden vehemence. 'Is Babington her lover, that Mary addresses him at such length and with such disregard for her own discovery?'

'I do not believe so, Your Majesty. I suspect merely that your cousin grows weary of captivity, and weariness makes her reckless. In her earlier responses to Catholic conspirators, she was cautious, almost diffident. Yet now she makes no effort to hide her interest in this plot, and all but condones your assassination at the end.' He picked up the letters and showed her the last sheet of the decoded one himself, lowering his voice so her ladies-in-waiting should not overhear. 'Did you note her postscript, Your Majesty, in which Mary asks for details of how these men intend to do away with you?'

'I did note it, yes,' she said curtly. 'And felt sick.'

'Is this letter not enough to condemn her—'

Elizabeth stood up, knocking her chair backwards with a clatter. Her ladies looked up in wonder, but at one freezing look from Elizabeth they bowed their heads again to their work.

'No, a thousand times no!' she exclaimed, then had to snatch a breath, leaning over the table as pain shot through her stomach. 'I have told you before, Walsingham, I will not have the sacred blood of a queen on my hands. You may bring me a dozen such letters every year, and still I shall not order my cousin's death.'

Walsingham stood silent while she recovered, watching her. 'Should I send for your physicians, Your Majesty?'

'No, I shall be better in a moment.' She stood waiting for the fit to pass, her jaw clenched. She would not show further weakness by sitting down or allowing him to summon help. Her leg ulcer throbbed but she ignored it. 'Besides, my physicians would only bleed me, and then I would be in no fit state to govern. It is bad bile, nothing more. An imbalance of the humours. A momentary spasm. Call it what you will, it soon passes.'

'Brought on by too many unnecessary worries,'

Walsingham said, and there was genuine concern in his voice. 'Allow me to remove this source of worry for you, Your Majesty, and launch an inquiry into the contents of this treasonous letter. We can draw our own conclusions here in this room, but to act upon those conclusions will involve more sturdy measures. Your cousin Mary will need to be properly questioned over her dealings with these plotters, and the various letters we have intercepted should be examined by a jury of trusted gentlemen. Only then can we be sure of the truth.'

Elizabeth closed her eyes. The pain in her stomach had begun to abate. She thought fleetingly of her mother's trial and execution at the hands of her father, and shook her head.

'Put a queen on trial, you mean?'

'An exiled queen without a throne,' he pointed out mildly. 'Nor should you allow such considerations to sway your judgement. Once your cousin's perfidy is made public, no one in Europe will blame you for ordering her execution.'

'King Philip will blame me,' Elizabeth said bitterly, looking up at him. 'As he blamed me when my sister died, and then when I would not marry him myself. Why, even the Pope will no doubt let it be known that whomsoever brings him my severed head on a platter, a golden seat will be reserved for that murderer in heaven.'

Walsingham's smile was grim. 'I believe His Holiness has already issued just such a bloody invitation to English Catholics, Your Majesty.'

'Damn him,' she muttered. But again she shook her head. 'I shall not order Mary's execution. That is my final word on the matter, Walsingham, so do not test my patience with it again. However, it is clear that this conspiracy has gone on undisturbed long enough. It cannot be allowed to continue to its natural end, which would be my death. Arrest the men involved and rack them to see what names they spill. No man has ever worked against my throne alone; there has always been a greater name behind.'

Tired, she gestured him to leave. 'Go now, I am far from well and must rest.'

Still her spymaster hovered on the other side of the table, frowning.

'Well, what is it now?' she demanded impatiently.

'Was your food properly tasted today, Your Majesty?'

Elizabeth stared, suddenly cold. 'The same as every day since this latest business began. You fear poison?'

'While your cousin lives, I fear every shadow.'

'You feared poison before Mary even came to England,' she reminded him in a testy voice, though she knew it would not be beyond the conspirators to have poison slipped into her food or drink. 'But it is true I feel unwell. I dislike being so close to London during the summer months. Why will you not allow me to remove to the country?'

'If it will comfort you, Your Majesty, I will tell Lord Burghley that he may accommodate you in Kent. His house is not too far from London and is well enough defended. His lordship would be honoured by a royal visit, I am sure, and with his daughter expecting a child it will be a comfort for him to return home.'

'Yes,' Elizabeth managed, struggling against the cramps in her belly. 'I shall travel into Kent with the court, and return to London once the worst of the summer heat has passed. I always enjoy my visits to Lord Burghley's exquisite gardens at Theobalds.'

Her ladies had come to her side unbidden. Now they picked up her toppled chair and eased her back into it. Helena poured fresh wine into her glass and placed a tempting dish of sweetmeats in front of her. Elizabeth closed her eyes and allowed the women to tend to her, rather than upsetting herself further by dwelling on her many disappointments. She sighed as they cooled her flushed cheeks with lace-trimmed fans and wafted scented pomanders under her nose. But her calm did not last long.

'Enough, enough. This is a bellyache, that is all. I did not sleep well last night, and now I must suffer for my hours of wakefulness.' A sudden rage seized hold of Elizabeth as she considered how often she was ill these days, and why. She raised a ring-swollen finger and pointed at her secretary in open accusation. 'And is it any surprise I cannot sleep when you have made me so afraid for my life, trapped in this palace with all my protectors gone off to the war? Where is Robert when I need him? Where is Sir Philip Sidney? My court holds nothing but boys and old men leaning on sticks. If the Spanish were to send a party of invaders up the Thames tomorrow, who would beat them off from the doors of Richmond Palace? You, Sir Francis? My women? Or must I take up a sword and protect this country myself?'

Walsingham bowed and rolled the letters up again. 'Forgive me, Your Majesty, I must send out arrest warrants to my agents in London,' he murmured, discreetly ignoring her outburst. 'They will supervise the apprehension of Anthony Babington and his fellow conspirators in my absence. Though we must tread carefully and be sure we can bring each man safely to trial on the evidence thus far. If we move too quickly, some may yet escape justice and attempt to carry out their plans.' He paused in the doorway. 'I shall give orders for the court to remove to Kent as soon as Lord Burghley can ride ahead to prepare for your visit. Meanwhile, will you undertake not to wander about the estate unguarded, Your Majesty?'

'Yes, very well.'

Her temples throbbing with a headache, Elizabeth

watched him leave the chamber. Why must she always do as others bid her rather than her own will? Was she not Queen?

She sucked gloomily on a sweetmeat, then called for a quill, ink and new parchment.

Drawing the sheet towards her, she wrote the date with a bold flourish.

Robert, I am afraid you will suppose by my wandering writings that a midsummer moon has taken possession of my brains this month, but you must take things as they come into my head.

Elizabeth smiled, dipping her quill in the ink and continuing to write. Already the cramping pain in her belly had eased and she felt able to sip her wine without sickness. She would not reply to her dearest Robert in the same cross, abrupt vein in which he had written to her from abroad, demanding yet more money from the royal coffers and all but accusing her of withholding her support. Instead, she would soothe him with soft and flattering words.

It was the first time in many years that the two of them had been apart for so long and under such trying circumstances.

She wrote Robert an intimate letter over several pages, reassuring him of the full support of the English court and of her own affection for him. Yes, he had hurt her feelings. But poor Rob was a long way from home, she reminded herself compassionately, and had more reason to be afraid in the filth and screaming frenzy of a battlefield than she could ever have in England.

I pray God keep you from all harm and save you from all foes, with my million and legion of thanks, for all your pains and cares. As you know, ever the same, Elizabeth R.

Ten

'*CORPUS CHRISTI*,' THE PRIEST ANNOUNCED SOLEMNLY, turning from his makeshift altar with the Blessed Host still held aloft on its silver platter.

Goodluck raised his head as the priest approached. 'Amen,' he murmured, opening his mouth for the Host. A year ago, he had undertaken this part of the Mass with the greatest reluctance, fearing for his immortal soul. But he had spoken and acted and worshipped as a Catholic for so long now, it felt almost natural to close his mouth on the blessed body of Christ, bowing his head again in a muttered Latin prayer.

The priest moved along the row to the new man, Robert Pooley, whose London house they were visiting, and then on to Babington and Ballard. A row of traitors, lined up together as though for the gallows. Goodluck hid his expression of grim satisfaction. It had taken many months of hard work to bring them together like this. Now at last the end was in sight. And not too soon, for every day brought him closer to danger and discovery as a spy in their midst.

Each communicant muttered, 'Amen,' and crossed himself with unusual fervour. The days of summer would soon be running into autumn. Their long wait was nearly over. Letters of confirmation had been sent and received. They had been informed that King Philip's army waited only for their instruction.

Plans for the Queen's assassination could no longer be put off.

Goodluck hid his smile, knowing how each man secretly feared his own part in the conspiracy while boldly crying, 'Death to Elizabeth!' among each other. Nor were they even competent conspirators. They had not been brought up to spy and plot. They trusted too easily and spoke too openly. A friend was not a potential threat to them, but someone to be confided in, to carry treasonous letters for them without question. The only reason they had not yet been taken by the London magistrates was that Walsingham wished to play Babington along a little further, in the hope he might reveal the names of any courtiers who had involved themselves in this, though Goodluck suspected that to delay much longer might endanger the life of the Queen.

Their prayers continued as the priest moved softly to extinguish the candles on the altar, until the only light was from the torch illuminating the stairs back up to the house.

Ballard's new friend, Pooley, had arranged for them to take Mass that evening in the cellar of his home. Goodluck could have wished for a more comfortable few hours, but these Catholics seemed to delight in mortifying their flesh. The air of the cellar was chill and damp, and despite the padded cloth he had been handed on descending the stairs, to be used as a kneeler during Mass, the stony mud floor still pressed painfully into his knees. He could hardly wait to return to the tiny scented garden above, a few yards of formal greenery at the back of Pooley's town house, but drenched in hot sunshine when he had arrived earlier that day. It felt, he thought bitterly, as though they had been buried alive down here.

But Babington was taking full precautions against discovery. Each of them had been asked to arrive separately, disguised and using different routes into the city, and even Pooley's servants had been excluded from their initial meeting, the outer door guarded by a ferocious-looking wolfhound.

In the smoky, incense-thick gloom, the priest threw back his hood and came to shake hands with them all as the service came to an end.

He was a young man with watery grey eyes, but his handshake was firm enough. 'May the Lord be with you,' he said to each in turn, 'and guide you on your mission.'

Ballard bowed his head over the priest's hand. 'God be with you too, Father,' he replied fervently.

Ballard had proved a difficult quarry to hunt, Goodluck thought, watching him covertly. Stubborn, passionate, a man of great faith and determination, the priest was no fool when it came to the constant danger of conspiracy. He took few chances. It had taken Goodluck a long time to get Ballard to trust him. Even now he knew the Catholic priest was ready to sink a dagger in his belly at the merest hint that he might be a Protestant and a traitor to their cause. He was still not sure which of those two sins was worse in Ballard's eyes.

'You need not fear damnation for the deed you must do, Father Ballard,' the priest muttered, and passed him a ring. 'By token of this ring, the Holy Father sends his blessing from Rome. He prays that you may be delivered from all enemies of the True Church.'

Ballard flushed and stared down at the crested papal ring. He seemed genuinely moved by this gift from Rome. Then he slipped it into the leather pocket hanging from his belt.

'You must bear our thanks to His Holiness,' he replied, his voice shaking with intensity, 'and reassure him that we think nothing of our souls when set against the great good we do in ridding England of Elizabeth Tudor.'

The priest nodded, shaking all their hands again with solemn significance. 'Now if you will forgive me, gentlemen, I must return to Whitehall before I am missed.'

Goodluck watched him go, a frown on his face. When the priest had disappeared through the low door at the top, he turned to Anthony Babington.

'Whitehall?'

Babington smiled grimly. 'This city is riddled with loyal Papists, my friend. When the Queen is finally dead, you will see them rise up to ring the bells and rejoice, for Elizabeth Tudor is a blight on our land, a vile disease that must be cut out before we can be healthy again.'

'Amen,' Goodluck replied, and the others echoed him. 'The smoke is choking here. Shall we go up to the garden?'

'Too many ears to hear us outside in the air,' Ballard muttered, shaking his head. 'First, let us open our hearts to each other. I have news from the north.'

'Speak,' Babington encouraged him. 'Tell us first what happened to Maude. You said he left you in Yorkshire.'

They stood together in the dark cellar, four men shoulder to shoulder, almost whispering now.

'I fear that Maude was never one of us,' Ballard admitted shortly. 'While we were travelling in the north, I received an anonymous note warning me that my companion was not a Catholic. I had meant to keep Maude close until we returned to London, so we could have a chance to question him in a secure place.' He grimaced. 'But Maude must have realized my suspicions. One evening, he went out for a walk, claiming some discomfort after his meal, and did not return.'

Goodluck frowned, uncomfortable at the turn this

conversation was taking. Could sharp-eyed Maude also have been working for Walsingham? It would not surprise him to learn that his wily master had placed more than one spy undercover in this business. 'You are sure Maude was not arrested?' he asked. Ballard's eyes narrowed on his face, and Goodluck shrugged and added, 'I am told the north is as riddled with the Queen's spies as London is with the faithful.'

'Maude was not loyal to the cause.' Ballard's gaze was cold. 'I had suspected for some time that one of our number had been feeding information about us back to the Queen's men. I knew we were being watched up in the north, and I'm sure our rooms were searched when we stopped in York. And Maude was always asking questions: wanting to know the names of my contacts in Paris and Rome, with whom I had studied at Rheims, and how our secret letters were able to reach Her Majesty, Queen Mary, when she is still so closely guarded.' Babington's eyes widened at this last, and Ballard laid a reassuring hand on his shoulder. 'Luckily, I was sparing with the information I gave him. When Maude disappeared, I knew we had been wrong to take him into our confidence so trustingly. From now on, we must be sure of any newcomer's loyalty before we speak of our plans before him, even in the most private chamber.'

Babington looked alarmed. 'But Maude knows where I live. He has been at my house several times.'

'Yes, I wished to warn you, but did not want to place such secret information in a letter. Who knows who we can trust?' Ballard hesitated. 'I fear none of us can return home until after the deed is done and the country saved for God. But we are not wholly betrayed. Pooley can accommodate us instead. His name was not known to Maude. There can be no danger of discovery here.'

They all looked at their host, Pooley, who had been

telling over his rosary beads while he listened to this exchange.

Surprised by their scrutiny, Pooley nodded and muttered, 'You are all most welcome to sleep here, of course,' then returned to his prayers. '*Ave Maria, gratia plena, Dominus tecum . . .*'

Babington turned back to Ballard, frowning. 'And our plan to kill the Queen?'

'I do not see that Maude's betrayal can hurt us, if indeed he has betrayed us. The Queen is always well-guarded. Foreknowledge of our attempt will not change that. But one man can still have at her with a dagger if he is brave enough, perhaps while she is with her ladies in her bed-chamber or walking in her palace gardens. As long as there are times when she is not guarded on all sides, one of us alone should be able to come upon her and kill her face to face.'

Babington seemed convinced by this dubious argument. 'But despite Maude's disappearance, your mission was successful? We have been so eager for news here. How many men did you raise for the Catholic cause in the north?'

'Very few,' Ballard admitted.

'What?'

'It would appear the northern Catholics have lost their taste for rebellion, though many there still follow the true faith.' Ballard smiled bitterly. 'I said Mass in many rich houses in the north, with little fear of discovery by the authorities. I was told they turn a blind eye to the Catholics there, so long as certain dues are paid. But when talk turned to the possibility of the Queen's death, I was met with silence and refusal.'

Pooley looked astonished. 'They will not aid us?'

'Not even if the Queen were to die tomorrow,' Ballard told them. 'I found a small handful of nobles who were willing to fight, and could raise an army of maybe a few hundred common soldiers between them. But they have neither armour nor good weaponry, and would need to be supplied out of France or Spain. The rest claim to be happy with the way things are in England, and will not risk an uprising even for the chance of a return to the true faith. The exiled Scottish Queen is not much regarded there, I fear.'

Goodluck nodded. 'This is just as I anticipated it would be. I expect the landowners fear an influx of the Scottish over the northern border if Queen Mary takes the English throne. Land is poor there, and they would not wish to give any of it up to families who have been their natural enemies for centuries.'

'*When* Queen Mary takes the throne,' Ballard corrected him quietly, 'not *if*.'

'Forgive me, sir,' Goodluck said formally, and bowed his head.

Babington sighed. 'Come, friends, let us not lose hope or fall out over this blow. We have had bad news from the north, but it cannot deter us in our task. Even if we are the only true Catholics left in the kingdom, our fellowship in Christ must be enough to sustain us.'

'Amen, and bravely said,' Pooley commented, having finished his prayers, and tucked his rosary away inside his robe. 'I am new to at least one of your number,' he continued, looking pointedly at Goodluck, 'and I know this marks me out as a man not to be trusted. But I came to you from the start with credentials and letters from trusted friends and Catholics both here in England and on the Continent, and I am as true a man as any who ever worshipped the Holy Virgin. You are very welcome to use this house as your own until the Queen is dead. Which must be soon, I fear, from what we have heard here today.'

Babington gripped Pooley's hand, smiling. 'I trust you, Pooley. You speak so much good sense.'

'May that always be the case, my good friend.' Pooley smiled back at him. 'Now, much has been said here that must be dwelt upon in silence and solitude. Shall we each take to our rooms, and pray alone until supper time?'

They agreed to meet again at supper, and each man went his separate way for prayer and private reflection. Goodluck visited the room he was sharing with Ballard for a few moments, to write a quick note and change his priest's robe – badly in need of a wash, for it reeked of smoke and incense – for a clean shirt and a russet-brown doublet. Then he walked about Pooley's now-shady garden in the cool of the late afternoon, listening to the passing traffic in the street behind the high garden wall and muttering over his rosary beads in case he was observed from the house.

After half an hour's restless pacing, Goodluck heard the sound he had been waiting for, a street hawker's cry selling oranges.

He paused by the studded door in the garden wall and surreptitiously drew back the bolt.

The street was still busy, though the sun would soon be setting. He watched a young dark-skinned girl hurry past, her white cap concealing an unruly mop of hair, and his heart jerked, remembering Lucy. His ward must be certain he was dead by now, it had been so long since Walsingham had insisted that he infiltrate the plotters. He only hoped Lucy's privileged position at court would be enough to keep her from harm. Then, just as suddenly, his mind returned to the business at hand, for he had seen a possible contact.

A young boy stood with his back to the gate, calling out his wares to every passer-by while a man nearby – his father or uncle, perhaps – tried to interest the busy shopkeeper opposite in taking a box of oranges for his shop.

'Fresh oranges, you say?' Goodluck asked.

'Aye, master,' the hawker's boy said, turning eagerly at his voice, and coming to the gate with a tray of fragrant fruit hanging from a rope about his neck. 'Fresh off the boat this morning. A penny each, they are, and you will not find any oranges so fine this side of the Spanish main.'

Goodluck smiled, hearing the password 'Spanish main', and accepted an orange from the boy. He sniffed and squeezed the large, dimpled fruit, then tossed it in the air like a ball.

'Yes, that will quench my thirst,' he agreed. As though satisfied by its freshness, he felt in his purse for a penny. There was a narrow rolled-up slip of parchment inside, and both this and the coin he dropped on to the tray. 'For our master, and quickly. It must reach him tonight at Richmond, or tomorrow at the earliest.'

The boy showed no sign of having heard these muttered words, but turned away without even looking at Goodluck again.

'Good day to you, master,' he said idly. He continued to cry out, 'Oranges for sale! Fresh oranges for sale!' as he threaded his way through a group of passing youths.

Goodluck closed the garden gate, hoping that his urgent message would indeed reach Sir Francis Walsingham that same night, and turned to find their host, Robert Pooley, watching from an upper window.

As soon as he realized he had been seen, Pooley raised a hand in friendly greeting. Then he took several moments over closing the shutters, as though to explain why he had been at the window in the first place.

Goodluck threw his orange up in the air – as a way of giving Pooley an innocent reason for his venture into the street – and recommenced walking about the garden, his head bent once more in assiduous prayer. Yet whenever he passed the shut gate, he could not help glancing at it with a frown for his own clumsiness.

Had Robert Pooley seen and understood the exchange between him and the boy? Was he no longer safe here?

Eleven

'LUCY! LUCY!'

Lucy groped under her pillow for the dagger which was always kept there, then slipped out of bed and hurried to the window. She threw the shutters open and leaned over the wooden sill, peering down into the reeking warmth of a summer night. She had not seen Will Shakespeare for some time, and had sent his letters back unopened, but it seemed he was still unwilling to let her go.

'Will?'

Like a ghost, Will Shakespeare came out of the shadows of the houses opposite and into the moonlight. His face was pale and haggard as he stared up at her, his clothing dishevelled, no cap on his head, his dark hair tumbled and wild.

'Lucy,' was all he seemed able to say, his voice hoarse.

'You can't come here in the middle of the night,' she told him, forcing herself to sound angry, though the sight of his anguished face struck at her heart. 'My neighbours will make a complaint to the magistrate and I will be fined. Go away, I don't want to see you any more.'

Lucy glanced anxiously about the dark street. No one was stirring yet. She was afraid of what might happen if one of her neighbours did as they had threatened at his last visit and set the Watch on him.

Will did not obey her command but stayed to plead with her, his words slurred and disjointed.

'Lucy, Lucy. Your eyes are like . . .' He tailed off, confused. 'Please open the door and let me in. I need you. Can't you see I'm in agony?'

'I only see that you are drunk.'

'My letters! Did you not read any of my letters to you? I sent you sonnets too. I must have written them in my own blood, for I'm so weak now I can hardly stand.' His gaze seemed to devour her. 'Oh, Lucy, I've missed you so badly.'

She averted her gaze. 'Go home to bed, Will.'

'What, home to my cold bed? Let me into yours instead and we shall burn there together. Is your friend still there? I shall be civil to her, if that's what you're afraid of.'

'Cathy's gone. Her child began to sicken in the foul air, so she took him home to Norfolk.' She realized her mistake when Will's face brightened and he staggered to the foot of the house, staring up at her window. 'No, Will. You must stop this. What we had before . . . It's not enough for me. Don't you understand?'

'Lucy, my love, my sweetest.' He took a misstep, falling awkwardly against the wall. 'Words . . .'

'Go home, Will,' she repeated, though she desperately wanted to run down the stairs and unbolt the door to him. Yet how could she let him in again? Had he not done enough damage here?

She had known for some days that the worst had occurred. Her monthly course of blood had failed to arrive. Her breasts tingled and were fuller than before, and she felt nauseous on waking. Every woman at court knew what this meant, for these were the signs most avidly watched for by those set to safeguard the honour of the Queen's maids.

319

Like a fool, Lucy had given herself to Will Shakespeare in blind desire. Now she was with child.

She could not bear to demand that he marry her. He had already shown beyond all doubt that he would no more think of marrying her than he would wed one of the tavern whores who gave themselves for a few shillings to any stranger. To tell him that was what she wanted would merely invite further humiliation, and make it more shameful when she had to slip away into the country before she grew too large to hide her condition.

Her good friend Cathy would shelter her until the child was born, she felt sure of it. Though after that, Lucy could not see what path would support both her and a child, except one that led to ruin.

'Flay me alive rather, but do not say . . .' Will belched loudly, fell silent for a moment, then stumbled forward and beat on the door with his fists. 'Love!'

One of her neighbours' wives called out, 'For Christ's sake, let the drunken fool in or tell him to go on his way!'

'Why would you not marry me? Tell me the truth now, while you are too drunk to lie.' The words slipped out before Lucy could stop them. She stared down at him. 'Was I not good enough for you?'

He fell back from the door, one arm raised across his face. 'Do not ask me that. You must not ask.'

Slamming the shutters, Lucy climbed back into her narrow cot and sat there in the darkness. So this was what her life had become. Long nights of fear. The prospect of ruination. An unmarried woman with a child in her belly was as good as dead in this city without a protector. What was she to do? She turned the dagger over in her hands, running a finger along the blade. It was temptingly sharp, a deadly instrument she had been taught to use as a child. A swift cut of the throat and there would be silence. Yet since she was neither a murderer nor a coward, after a few moments Lucy tucked the dagger under her pillow again and tried to settle herself to sleep.

Will called out her name a few more times before weaving away into the night.

Twelve

'I AM SICK OF THIS HOUSE,' BALLARD COMPLAINED, THEN waited in impatient silence until Pooley's housekeeper had carried away the remains of their breakfast trenchers. Despite the sunny August morning, it was dim inside the low-ceilinged room, and a fire had been lit so they could more closely study the maps and plans laid out on the table. 'We do nothing here but discuss old letters and wait for a propitious moment that never comes. Meanwhile the summer lengthens and our allies beg for news. When can we move against the Queen?'

'When we are sure of the promised support from Spain and the Duke of Guise,' Goodluck reminded him drily.

He walked to the window of Pooley's front parlour and stood there, hands behind his back, gazing out at the busy London street.

'The dispatch of Queen Elizabeth is not our only concern,' Goodluck continued, covertly studying each man who passed by the window. 'Happy though her end would be, we cannot risk achieving it before our preparations for invasion are complete. After her death, we can expect half the country to rebel against Mary seizing the throne. Any rebellion will need to be put down by forces loyal to the

Catholic cause, which have been promised by the Spanish King but only in the vaguest terms. I would rather have some solid confirmation from the Spanish before we move ahead with the assassination of the Queen. Talking of which, has anyone heard back yet from Mendoza?'

His view of the street was restricted, and often blocked by passers-by. Nonetheless, Goodluck watched discreetly for signs that the house was under observation. But if it was, the agents watching them were either highly skilled or else secreted away in one of the houses opposite, for Goodluck never saw so much as a shadow out of place. Indeed, the street looked much as it had done every day since they had arrived there roughly three nights before.

Carts rumbled past in the sunshine, each time narrowly missing a shrieking gang of ragamuffins playing tag in the street. Traders called out their wares at the market corner a short distance from the house, many standing in the cool of overhanging houses or under their own makeshift shades as noon approached. Two pretty young whores wandered past with their skirts raised above the filth, showing their ankles above their clogs. Only once did a passer-by strike Goodluck as suspicious, but although the man had paused as though to check his purse for change, glancing over his shoulder at Pooley's house as he did so, he moved on swiftly, and Goodluck had not yet seen him return. There was certainly no indication that his message to Walsingham, giving the location of the house and the names of the conspirators within, had ever been received.

'Anthony sent several letters to the French ambassador last month, while visiting his family home in Staffordshire. But he should have heard back by now, I agree.' Ballard sounded impatient. 'I begin to fear Mendoza's reply may have gone up to Staffordshire and not his London house.'

Seated at the head of the table, Pooley sighed and shook his head. 'Gentlemen, this business is a mess.'

'But all is not yet lost,' Goodluck reassured him, turning from the window. 'Let us be patient until the worst of the summer's heat recedes. For myself, I find it no surprise that Mendoza has not yet written with news of the Spanish fleet. It is only August. The courts of Europe will be empty until the autumn, and all the nobles will be at their country estates. No army marches at the height of the summer, and without the army on board, the Spanish fleet will not set sail.'

Pooley seemed much struck by the truth of this statement. He nodded vigorously in Goodluck's direction, though without meeting his gaze. He had barely looked at Goodluck since the incident with the orange-seller. But perhaps Pooley had seen nothing suspicious. Just a man buying an orange on a hot evening.

'Brother Weatherley is right, of course,' Pooley agreed, referring to Goodluck by the priestly name he used when with the conspirators. 'Foolish of us not to think of that.'

Ballard stared. 'You think we have come to London too soon? That we should wait until September?'

'It's frustrating,' Goodluck commented, 'yet what else can we do but wait without further guidance from Paris or Rome? Unless you would have us strike too soon and lose all advantage after the Queen's death?'

'I would have the Queen safely executed and her cousin Mary installed on the throne before we lose the few allies we have. I have heard nothing but complaints from those men who so stoutly set their names to this letter back in June,' Ballard said, picking up the sheet on the table before him and reading it aloud. 'Robert Barnwell, John Charnock, Henry Dunne, Charles Pilney, Edward Jones, Robert Gage, and so on. These are men who have pledged their lives and fortunes to this cause, and who now ask why we delay so long.' He sounded bitter. 'And where is Anthony this morning? Is he not well?'

Pooley looked up from his contemplation of the fire. 'He is still in bed, with a headache. He will join us as soon as it is cleared.'

'Oh yes, God forbid any of us should be called upon to rebel against the state with a headache!' Ballard muttered angrily, then sat up with a start as someone hammered on the front door. 'Who the hell can that be? Pooley, are you expecting anyone this morning?'

Pooley had hurried to the window and was staring out. He whirled around, his eyes wide with terror.

'Five men, with papers in their hands. Queen's guards too, armed with pikes. They have come to arrest us.'

Ballard was already on his feet. He drew the dagger from his belt, a look of consternation on his face as one of the men at the door called out, 'Open up, in the name of the Queen!'

Pooley's servant came to the parlour door, clearly terrified, and asked in a quavering voice what he should do. But Pooley merely shook his head and stared out of the window again, his wits apparently wandering. The hammering stopped, then they heard a series of loud thuds as the men outside attempted to force the heavy oaken door.

'Some bastard has betrayed us!' Ballard swore, and looked from Pooley to Goodluck, then up at the ceiling in disbelief, as if wondering whether Babington himself had alerted the authorities to their presence there.

Goodluck stood with his back to the wall and waited, carefully not drawing his own dagger. To be arrested with as little fuss as possible was his aim, and then to ask privately for Walsingham once he was apart from the other men. It might prove useful to still seem an ally to the conspirators even after this arrest, for some of the others might need to be smoked out of hiding with cunning and false friendship rather than brute force.

If only he had the paper about his person that Walsingham had given him, to be handed over in the event of his arrest! That would have made his mind easier. But that secret paper was sewn into the lining of his old cloak hanging in the chamber above. He had intended to retrieve it before now, but had not been left alone long enough over the past few days.

They heard the crash as the oak door to the house finally gave way. Sweat on his forehead, Ballard gathered together the incriminating maps and documents, including the letter with its list of names, and thrust them into the fire. Then he turned to face the parlour door, dagger in hand.

Goodluck saw the resolute determination in Ballard's eyes and realized that the Catholic priest intended to make a fight of it. A brave man, then. Perhaps the bravest of them all, and steadfast in his faith. Watching him, Goodluck almost hoped the priest would die here, for the agonizing death that must await Ballard and his friends on the scaffold was too horrible to be contemplated.

One of the guards kicked open the door to the parlour and levelled his pike at Ballard. 'They're here, sirs,' he called over his shoulder.

Walsingham's men came trooping in and ordered them to be taken away at once. 'Master Ballard to Seething Lane, the others and their servants to the Tower to await questioning,' the leader announced.

So Ballard was to be given a chance to betray his friends before being acquainted with the horrors of the Tower, Goodluck thought wryly. Though he doubted that Ballard was the kind of man who would avail himself of such clemency, for he would know that death awaited him either way, even if he escaped the torture chamber.

Goodluck recognized none of the five men who had come to arrest them, and reconciled himself to an uncomfortable few hours until he could prove his identity.

There was a brief, undignified scuffle between Ballard and several of the guards, then the priest was overpowered and forced to his knees. While his hands were being secured behind his back, one of the men began reading out the warrants for their arrests, 'In the name of Her Majesty the Queen.' Two men approached Goodluck with drawn daggers, looking at him speculatively, for he was a large man and could have made their lives difficult if he had chosen to resist. But he shrugged, gave his name as 'Brother Weatherley', and allowed them to bind his wrists behind his back without comment, and once this had been done, followed the bound Pooley and Ballard from the room.

'Here's another still in his nightshirt,' called one of the guards from the top of the stairs, producing a frightened-looking Anthony Babington with bare legs and untidy hair, clearly just dragged from his bed.

The men below laughed, except the leader, who asked, 'What is his name?'

'Anthony Babington, so he says,' the guard replied.

The leader consulted the parchment in his hand, then shook his head. 'Send the sluggard back to bed and tell him this is his lucky day. There is no Babington upon the warrant.' He waved the others out into the street. 'Come on, or you will miss the tide with these traitors. Convey them to the Tower. I shall escort Master Ballard to Seething Lane myself.'

'Sir, if I could just fetch my cloak from upstairs,' Goodluck began outside, addressing the leader, but one of the guards hit him across the back of the head with his pike and Goodluck fell heavily to the ground, unable to save himself.

'Shut your mouth, Catholic!' the guard insisted, striking him across the back for good measure. 'You'll not need a cloak where you're going.' His fellows laughed, jeering as

Goodluck stumbled clumsily to his feet again, his hands still bound. 'Now let Jackson pull you up on to the cart. The tide was already on the turn when we left the river.'

But Goodluck had frozen, staring across the street in disbelief. In the shade of a doorway stood a familiar figure. His cap was pulled low over his face, his beard dyed bright ginger and tweaked to a point like a young man's, and his arm was about the waist of a buxom whore, her cheap gown mussed as though the two had been kissing there in the street.

To a casual observer, he would look like any young Londoner with money to spend.

But it was John Twist, all right. Goodluck would have known him anywhere.

As he watched, John nodded openly to the leader of Walsingham's men, then slouched away down the street with his whore, not even looking at Goodluck.

'Are you deaf?' the guard demanded, and cracked him about the head again. 'Up on the cart with you!'

'Babington!' Standing in the other cart, his hands now secured to the wooden frame, Ballard was shouting hoarsely up at the shuttered windows of Pooley's house. 'Show yourself, you coward! How could you betray your friends like this?'

Not surprisingly, Ballard seemed to believe that young Anthony Babington had given away their location, for he alone of their number had not been arrested. But Goodluck knew it was more likely to have been his note to the orange-seller the other night that had brought about their arrest. Though why Babington had been spared, he could not understand. Unless Walsingham had struck some kind of deal with the young man?

The cart into which Goodluck had been dragged started off with a jerk. He fell to the floor and stayed there this time, staring up at the timbered façades of houses in dazzling sunshine as the cart began to rumble down towards the river. Pooley knelt beside him, praying under his breath with remarkable composure for a man almost certainly facing a hideous death. Two of Pooley's servants were pushed in behind them, loudly protesting their innocence and calling on their master to exonerate them. But he continued to pray, raising his eyes to the other cart as Ballard was driven in the opposite direction.

Why had John Twist been at Pooley's house for their arrest, and what secret dealings did he have with the leader of Walsingham's men?

John had not looked at him. But it was impossible that he had not recognized Goodluck. So what was he up to? If Twist had thought Goodluck dead before, he certainly knew that to be a lie now.

Perhaps that was why John had been there, he thought, and for the first time felt a twinge of fear. What better way to do away with a troublesome rival than to deliver him up to the state as a traitor?

Soon Goodluck could smell the river, such a powerful and familiar smell that he made the effort to kneel up and peer through the poles of the cart. As the road descended bumpily to the quay, he caught glimpses of the River Thames between houses, flecked with tiny scum-whitened waves in the mid-channel, a thick bluish-black along the mudbanks, dotted with boats and rafts constantly crossing between the north and south.

A small boat awaited them at the jetty, a rough-looking skiff but handled with skill through the fast-flowing currents and eddies between the bridge supports. Chucking pitch-blackened barrels from boat to boat, the watermen glanced up curiously as they passed, their distinctive round-bottomed Thames skiffs tied up along the many quays and bankside jetties between Whitefriars and the Tower. Country visitors crossing the great bridge at

Southwark peered over to see the boat pass by with its cargo of liveried guards, gentlemen and prisoners on their way to the threatening mass of the Tower of London.

Taken in through the water-gate and up the steps, Goodluck was relieved to find himself separated from Pooley and his servants. Perhaps his true identity was known to the guards, after all?

'This way,' a gruff voice told him, and he was prodded through a narrow corridor in the darkness, then down a short flight of steps into the bowels of the Tower.

Hearing the soul-wrenching cries and groans from cells to either side of the corridor, Goodluck knew instantly where he was. His blood ran cold and he came to a halt, turning to look at the guard behind him.

'Sir,' he said earnestly, 'I am no traitor but one of Sir Francis Walsingham's own men. My name is not Brother Weatherley but Master Goodluck. If you would allow me to write him a note, I am sure Sir Francis will confirm this before the end of the day.'

The guard laughed and pushed him on with the sharp point of his pike. 'I like your wit, fellow. But it will avail you nothing. The other who came in with you already asked the same and was granted his freedom, for his name was on the list. Yours was not, so walk!'

'My name is Master Goodluck.'

'Not on the list,' the guard repeated and shoved him between the shoulder blades. 'Next door on the left.'

Turning into the torchlit room, Goodluck came face to face with a man whose dark, weasel-like face he instantly recognized.

Richard Topcliffe!

He had never met the famous torturer before. But Goodluck had frequently seen him on execution days, watching the grisly deaths of traitors and applauding with undisguised relish when their genitals were hacked off –

the prisoner often still alive and writhing in agony – and held up bleeding to the crowd.

Topcliffe was standing by a brazier, untying a blood-stained leather apron from about his waist. He glanced at Goodluck, then spoke briefly to the guard over his shoulder. 'He'll be too heavy for the bar. Better strip him and put him in the chair instead.' Throwing the soiled apron aside, he washed his hands fastidiously in a deep copper water bowl, then wiped them on a square of white linen. 'I need the privy. Watch him until I return.'

'Aye, Master Topcliffe,' the guard muttered, awed terror in his voice.

Goodluck heard Topcliffe leave the room and knew with a sudden cold clarity that he had only moments in which to save himself. It might be too late to avoid torture, but there was still a chance he could live through this if he acted swiftly enough.

His numb wrists had been unfastened. Now he was stripped naked and forced to sit in a high-backed chair, his neck and forearms manacled so he could not move.

'Sir,' he murmured as the guard secured him in place, 'I do not ask anything which might put you in poor standing with Master Topcliffe. But in a secret pocket in my left shoe is a small jewel. I beg you to take that jewel in return for your good service, and to carry a message to a friend for me.'

Breathing hard, sweat on his forehead, the man glanced over his shoulder at the open cell door. He was clearly terrified of Topcliffe, but crouched to examine Goodluck's discarded shoe nonetheless.

'Perhaps I will take the jewel,' the man whispered hoarsely, feeling about inside the patterned leather shoe, 'and not carry your message. You are a traitor to the Queen and destined for the gallows. You could not stop me.'

'You will not do that because it is not in your nature,'

Goodluck replied. 'You are an honest man, and I trust you to do what is right.'

The guard had found the secret pocket in Goodluck's shoe, a cunning slit where a small object or slip of paper could be hidden. He dropped the shoe and held the jewel up to the torchlight, turning it between his fingers. It was a modest but well-cut ruby which Goodluck kept for just such moments of extreme danger, where a substantial bribe could make the difference between life and death.

He shrugged. 'The name of your friend?'

Goodluck hesitated, considering. A man like this would not risk taking a message to Walsingham, in case it came out that he had accepted a bribe. But he might deliver a message to someone of no consequence. 'Mistress Lucy Morgan. You will find her with the court at Richmond Palace. If not, ask where she is living and deliver my message there instead. She will know what to do.'

The guard had turned to stare at him. 'You want me to carry this message to a woman?' he asked in disbelief.

'Yes.'

The guard looked at him doubtfully. Then they both heard the squelch of footsteps in the muddy corridor, and a man whistling a popular hymn as though on his way to church.

Richard Topcliffe was returning from the privy with the clear conscience of a sadist.

The guard's smile vanished. He slipped the ruby into the grimy black pocket hanging from his belt.

'The message? Quickly, man.'

'Tell her Master Goodluck is not dead. Tell her where I am and why. She will know what to do.'

As Topcliffe came back into the room, Goodluck knew a moment of lightheadedness and recognized it as terror. Hazily, he tried to see his situation from a distance, to gain some understanding of what had happened. If Pooley was one of Walsingham's spies, he would have been arrested at the house to make him appear innocent of duplicity in the eyes of the other conspirators, and then released so he could make his secret report to Walsingham.

But why had Goodluck's name not been on the list of men to be let go, too?

Perhaps someone had suggested to Walsingham that Goodluck was now too close to the Catholic conspirators, and had become one of them. Such conversions had been known to happen even to the best spies.

Or perhaps his name had been on the list, but had been crossed out.

He remembered John Twist, his cap pulled low and his beard dyed to look like a young man's, and that meaningful nod he had given the leader.

John Twist had betrayed him. He had changed the list of those in Walsingham's pay or had paid the leader to pretend his name was *not* on it. Somehow he had discovered that Goodluck was not dead, as he had no doubt supposed, but very much alive, and now wished to rectify that situation as soon as possible. And by ensuring that Goodluck would be handed over to Topcliffe on arrival at the Tower, he might yet have his wish.

Time seemed to pass very slowly, voices echoing in the narrow, torchlit cell.

Then everything sharpened again so that Goodluck felt he was seeing the room through a crystal. His mind cleared. He must focus now on his survival. The guard had been dismissed and Richard Topcliffe stood in front of him, a fresh apron tied about his waist. The torturer reached with gloved hands into the red heart of the brazier and extracted a glowing iron.

'As God is my witness, I am one of Walsingham's own men and should not be here,' Goodluck managed, ashamed to hear how his voice shook at the sight of that hot iron. 'I am no Catholic, but a Protestant spy.'

'Now, my good sir,' Topcliffe murmured, as though he had not even heard him, 'first we shall see of what stuff God has made you, and then we shall talk.'

The iron seared Goodluck's chest with a horrendous agony, held there longer than it seemed possible to bear, the pain so exquisite it was almost beyond feeling.

He smelt his own flesh burning, and sagged in the chair. He felt an uncontrollable weakness in all his limbs, and knew from the warmth trickling down his bare legs that he had pissed himself.

He felt no shame, for he had been tortured before and knew there could be no shame in fear.

The only shame lay in betrayal.

'Lucy,' Goodluck mumbled, not knowing what he was saying or even whether he had spoken any coherent word or merely groaned.

He watched as the iron was thrust into the brazier to heat again, then came resolutely back to sear his flesh, upon which his mumble became a trembling scream.

'Lucy!'

Thirteen

Lucy hadn't long been asleep when she woke with a start, hearing a knocking at the door below. Will Shakespeare again, she thought bitterly. She lay a moment, her heart thudding fast, then felt under the pillow for her dagger.

She crept down the stairs in the dark and listened. The knocking came again, not loud but insistent.

Fumbling for the tinderbox, she lit a half-burned spill and balanced it on the stone lip of the hearth. It gave out a ghostly half-light, but was better than darkness.

'Who's there?' she demanded, her ear pressed to the door.

'A friend,' a man's voice replied.

Instantly on her guard, she drew back. A friend? What friend? She had no friends in this city. Some of the women along her street had begun to spit as she passed. They thought her a whore. Small wonder too. Shakespeare's visits were to blame for that.

Yet there was something familiar about the man's voice. Did she know him?

Her skin prickled, gooseflesh on her arms under the thin

nightshift. Some fresh danger come to my door, she thought, and weighed the dagger in her hand.

'What is your name, friend?'

'I bear a message from Master Goodluck,' he replied, his voice muffled. 'Let me in before I am seen by the Watch.'

Master Goodluck? Her heart squeezed shut like a fist. Goodluck? It hurt to breathe. That was a name she had put away, blocked from her mind. She could not bear to hear it spoken, to think of his death. What evil trick was this?

'Master Goodluck is dead,' she whispered, staring at the door as though she could see through it.

'Let me in,' the man repeated, more urgently.

She was shaking but could not deny him. He might kill her, whoever he was. But his words . . .

Master Goodluck's name was like a charm, letting in light where she had walked so long in darkness.

Gripping the dagger between her teeth, Lucy slid back the heavy bolts that held the door firmly shut at night. Then she took a step back, set her feet wide and gripped the dagger in her right hand.

Master Goodluck is dead, she told herself. Believe nothing else. If her guardian had been alive, he would have come to find her himself by now. But could he have left some final message for her with a friend? And knowing Goodluck's friends as she did, it was also possible this was the first chance one had found to deliver it.

Whoever was on the other side of the door, she was prepared to listen to his message. But she would take no chances.

The latch lifted and she saw a man's hand reach inside the crack of the door, as though groping for her in the half-light. On his smallest finger was a thick gold ring which she recognized. That foul man, John Twist!

With a cry, she sprang forward and bore down on the door with all her weight.

'Get out!'

He swore and pushed violently against the door. 'Lucy, don't be a fool. You need me. You can't live here alone for ever. I won't hurt you, let me in!'

Lucy strained to keep him out, but he was strong. I can't hold him off much longer, she realized, and despaired. Why did none of her neighbours come to help? A dog was barking hysterically somewhere down the street. She heard a man shout at it to be quiet. The Watch must have heard the noise by now. Did they despise her so much they would see her murdered in the night? Was this how her life would end?

Twist's hand curled around the door frame. It looked like a giant spider. She took the dagger from between her teeth, slashed at his nearest finger and heard him shriek. The hand was withdrawn, and for a few seconds the pressure of his weight against the door slackened.

Lucy gave a tremendous shove and the door clicked shut. She slammed the top bolt home, then the bottom one, then slumped against the door, panting. Her blood roared in her ears. Was there any other way into the house? Only by climbing up the outside and through her bedroom window.

'That hurt,' John Twist exclaimed. She listened to him breathing hard as he leaned against the other side of the door. 'You shouldn't have done that, Lucy. I'll be back, and next time you'll open this door of your own accord or I'll smash it down.'

'No, you won't.'

'How are you planning to stop me, Lucy?' John Twist waited for an answer, then laughed. 'You should never have left court. You have no man to protect you here, no one to come running if you scream in the night. No one here would bestir himself for a black whore in the house of a dead spy.' He was calmer now, more sure of himself.

Don't get too sure, she thought furiously, and imagined sinking her blade into him. 'But I'll protect you, Lucy. All I ask is to share your bed and taste a little of what you were giving Goodluck.'

'Don't say his name,' she hissed.

'I'd rather hear you say mine.' He scratched what sounded like the point of a dagger down the door. 'Think about it, Lucy. This can be a rape or you can give yourself freely. But your door will open next time I come calling, and on that you have my word.'

His footsteps retreated along the street. The wax-dipped spill burned to the end and went out, smoking gently. Lucy stared long into the darkness, listening for John Twist to come back. But he didn't. Nonetheless, she sat with her back against the door for the rest of the night, barefoot and wearing nothing but her nightshift, dagger cradled in her lap. When the first light of dawn began to creep between cracks in the door, she shifted uncomfortably, realizing that she had fallen asleep.

She crawled to her feet, stiff and aching, and was on her way back up the stairs when there was another knock at the door.

Lucy stared at it. What now? she thought wearily. The knock came again, quiet and discreet. It did not sound like Jack Twist's hand behind it. Nor, though, did it sound like Will Shakespeare's light, confident rap.

She crept into the kitchen and listened, standing a few inches away from the door. Nothing. The knock was repeated, this time a little louder.

'Who is it? What do you want?' she demanded, feet set apart. Better to sound shrill than uncertain.

Perhaps Twist had paid one of his cronies to trick her into opening the door. Well, she had been a fool last night, but she would not be one again.

'I bring a message from a Master Goodluck,' a man

whispered through the door. He sounded nervous. 'It is a private message. For a Lucy Morgan.'

Lucy put her eye to one of the cracks in the door. It was a tall, pale-looking man she did not recognize, his cheek scarred and his cap pulled down, broad shoulders swathed in a dark cloak as though he did not wish to be seen on the street.

Who was this now? And bearing another message from her dead guardian? She shivered, cold and exhausted, more ready for her bed than to fend off another attacker. Yet surely if this was one of Twist's men, he would have come up with a different approach. That line about Goodluck had served well enough in the night, but in the chill light of dawn . . .

Over the stranger's shoulder she caught glimpses of early risers on their way to the market or down to the river, some with covered baskets over their arms, others pulling handcarts laden with goods to sell. The sun was rising and the city of London, always busiest in the mornings, was beginning to stir itself.

'I'm Lucy Morgan.' She tightened her grip on the dagger. 'Did John Twist tell you to come here?'

'I don't know a John Twist.'

'What is your message, then?'

'I told you, it's a private message. I don't wish to give it on the street for anyone to hear. Will you open the door?'

'No,' she said bluntly. 'Speak now, or go away.'

The man stood silent for a moment, as though un-decided. Then he shuffled closer to the door, so she could no longer see his face.

'Very well. Master Goodluck wants you to know that . . . that he is not dead,' he whispered hoarsely through the crack. 'Last night he was in the Tower under the care of Master Topcliffe. He says you will know what to do with this information.'

'Who are you?'

'I have delivered my message as promised, mistress. I bid you good day,' he finished, and she heard him turn away.

Lucy stood for a long while in front of the closed door after he had gone, not quite able to believe what she had heard. Her scalp prickled, and her body felt as though it had been struck by lightning, still shuddering from the blow.

Goodluck was still alive and in the Tower?

Could this be another of Master Twist's tricks? He could be trying to lure her out of the house. Yet it was daylight now. Even such a villain as Twist would hardly dare to snatch her in the street. Slowly she turned from the door, frowning as she puzzled it out. Perhaps if Twist planned to sneak inside when she was safely out of the house and hide himself upstairs . . .

Fool!

Spinning on her heel, she threw the dagger point-first into the door and watched it quiver.

Twist had lied that terrible day at Nonsuch when he had told her Master Goodluck was dead, and she, like an idiot, had believed him.

Master Goodluck is not dead, she thought. Wonder burst inside her as she realized the truth. He is not dead!

Running upstairs, Lucy lifted her nightshift over her head and dragged a low-cut court gown from the chest at the end of her bed. Shaking out the creases, she dressed herself as quickly as she could and tweaked her bodice until her breasts showed prettily over the top. Then she tidied her wayward hair and pinned it up under a French hood with lace trim. She hesitated over the remaining pieces of her jewellery, before choosing a sapphire pin and a gold chain Lord Leicester had given her, slipping them both into her purse. She did not know what horrors might await her at the Tower, but it would be foolish to arrive there empty-handed.

Much to her relief, Twist was not in the street when she finally ventured outside. She had brought the dagger, but kept it hidden under a cloth in the small basket hooked over her arm, walking nonchalantly down the sunlit street as though on her way to buy food. Several of her neighbours turned to stare as she passed in her old court gown, for she had worn only plain gowns and sombre caps since coming to live at Goodluck's house. She did not look at them but gazed straight ahead, wishing she could have afforded to keep her maidservant when she had left court.

Not that she could have taken her maid on this particular walk, Lucy thought drily. Still, it stung to know how little her neighbours thought of her.

She had intended to walk down to the banks of the Thames and buy herself a passage to the Tower from one of the skippers moored up there. But when she reached the end of the street, she hesitated, looking down at the flash of sunlight on the river, then instinctively turned left instead, heading away from the water and towards Seething Lane. She had heard Goodluck mention that address often enough.

Seething Lane.

The name had always made her shiver as a young girl; it sounded like a pot boiling over on the hearth or a cat with its back arched. But it was where Sir Francis Walsingham lived when not at court, the house where he met and spoke privately with his spies. If any man alive knew why Goodluck was in the Tower, and how to get him out, it would be Sir Francis. Though if Goodluck had somehow betrayed the Queen – a treachery of which she did not believe her guardian to be capable – there would be no saving him from the gallows.

*   *   *

It seemed to be her court gown which persuaded Walsingham's new secretary to admit Lucy to his study – or perhaps the low bodice, for he was a younger man than the one Lucy remembered from court, and gazed at her curiously when she asked to see Sir Francis Walsingham. The room into which she was shown was plainly furnished but clearly that of a wealthy and sophisticated man. She trod softly about it, admiring his shelf of gilt-edged, calf-bound books, a carved oak chest and a large portrait above the ornate fireplace of Walsingham's daughter Frances, whose secret marriage to Sir Philip Sidney had angered the Queen for many months. 'Mistress Morgan?'

She turned from her contemplation of the portrait and sank into a curtsy, seeing Sir Francis Walsingham on the threshold. Sombre in his customary black, a single diamond star pinned to his chest, winking like an eye, Walsingham looked across at her in mild surprise. No doubt he did not often find lone women in his private chambers. Words failed her for a moment. Why had she come to such a great man over what might be nothing more than a cruel trick?

Then Lucy gathered herself. Speak up, she thought sternly. This is no time to stare and gape like a witless fool. Goodluck's life was at stake. Besides, Walsingham had told her once that he would help her if ever she needed it. Well, now was his chance to prove he had meant it. She had asked little enough of him before now.

'Thank you for agreeing to speak with me, Sir Francis,' she began, picking her words carefully. 'A man came to my door today. He brought word that Master Goodluck is not dead, as I had been told, but is in the Tower. I thought you might be able to advise me whether or not . . .'

She faltered, suddenly fearing he would tell her it was not true and that Goodluck was indeed dead.

Walsingham went to his desk, frowning delicately. He

walked more slowly than she remembered. But then he was getting older – as was she. It seemed another age since she had first stood before him in the castle at Kenilworth, a child frightened by the Queen's great spymaster himself.

'Master Goodluck? Certainly he is not dead. I apologize that it was necessary for you to believe that. But in the Tower? That is news to me.' He bent to search through the scattered papers there. 'It's good to see you again, Lucy. I have often thought of you since you left court. I trust you have not given up hope of returning to your position. The Queen's favour is fickle, and it may be that she will miss your voice soon and command you back.'

Be forgiven by the Queen? Lucy said nothing, not wishing to offend such an important man, though she found him difficult to understand. Why had it been necessary for her to think Goodluck was dead? And there was more chance of her sprouting wings than returning to court. The Queen's dislike of her had been growing for years, and there were many young women at court with strong voices and feet light enough to enthrall Queen Elizabeth. The only reason Lucy had lasted so long among her ladies was that visiting ambassadors were often charmed by the novelty of her black skin and hair.

'Here we are,' he muttered, extracting a sheet and glancing over it, 'a list of those to be released in the event of their arrest this week. Master Goodluck. He is clearly named. Yet you say he is in the Tower?'

She nodded. 'Could this be the work of Master Twist, sir? He is no friend to Master Goodluck these days.'

'So Goodluck told me.' Walsingham raised his uncomfortably direct gaze to her face. 'It could be that his other suspicions were well-founded, and our Master Twist will prove himself no friend to the Queen, either.' He unclipped the ornate glass lid of his inkwell and dipped his quill. With a few careful strokes, he scratched out a note, stamped it with his seal ring, and handed it to her. 'This will free Master Goodluck from the Tower. Do you know where he is being kept?'

Lucy curtsied, accepting the note with relief. 'I believe a Master Topcliffe has care of him.'

Walsingham looked grim. 'Then God speed you to the Tower, child. I pray your guardian still lives.'

The Tower was only a short walk from Walsingham's home. Due to the crowds milling about as they waited for an execution, though, it was almost noon before she managed to deliver his note. The day was hot and there was no shade under the grey-white stone walls of the outer defences. Lucy waited a little away from the gate, her gaze on the entrance to the guardroom. She was in a frenzy of impatience but knew better than to draw attention to herself by asking for them to hurry. Being there on her own was dangerous enough. The liveried Tower guards stared down at her on their patrols about the battlements. Two or three jeered openly as they passed, their contempt undisguised.

She ignored them as best she could, tightening her grip on the basket and bending her head to avoid unfriendly looks from passers-by. A poor woman staggered away from the Tower holding out her husband's bloodstained rags, shrieking, 'Dead! Dead!' The noonday sun beat down on the entrance yard, its glare bouncing off the high white tower above until Lucy had to cover her face with her hands, suddenly dizzy. Trying not to consider what she would do if Goodluck was already dead, she listened to the gulls screaming overhead, and the shouts from the river traders selling fresh eels and whelks from handcarts outside the Tower gates.

Eventually, the captain came to the gate and beckoned her over. 'This way, mistress,' he said, not unkindly, and drew her aside so they could speak more privately. The captain's neatly trimmed beard was grey, but he had the look of a younger man, not much given to idleness. Lucy took an instant liking to him and curtsied, managing a smile. 'I've given orders for your man to be brought up from the cells. You can be thankful Master Topcliffe was not with him long, for he had many suspected traitors under his charge last night. You may take him away, but you'll need a cart.'

She stared, not understanding. 'Sir?'

'You won't find him as you left him, so to speak,' the captain told her, his manner restrained. 'Did you bring a cart? I can call for one to carry your man home, but it won't come cheap. Can you pay?'

Lucy showed him the sapphire pin and he stared at it, surprised.

'It won't cost that much. Here,' he said, and handed her two shillings from his own pouch. 'I'll not have you pay the cart-man twenty times his hire. You have an honest face. Pay me back when you can.'

'Thank you, sir,' she whispered.

Lucy did not have to wait long before an old cart-man with a pipe in his mouth pulled up at the gate. He listened to her directions without seeming to hear them, then pocketed his two shillings fare without a word. He was just relighting his pipe when the gate opened to reveal Master Goodluck, barely conscious, being dragged across the threshold by two guards.

Goodluck was barefoot and wore no shirt nor cap, his hose stained so badly it looked as though he had soiled himself. But it was his chest and belly which caught Lucy's horrified attention first. Scored with shiny red burns, his torso looked as though he had leaned against a brazier. His face too was bruised and battered, his bottom lip split, his forehead and nose scaly with dried blood.

She resisted the urge to shriek his name, remembering the woman she had seen sobbing in the yard. Instead, she pointed to the cart and watched in silence as the guards grunted, heaving and pushing him up there with little attempt at gentleness.

His eyes closed as though dead, Goodluck lay sprawled on a pile of rotten old sacking that stank of fish. Lucy bent over him and felt for a pulse. He had not moved, but he was still alive. Just.

'Goodluck, it's me, Lucy. I've come to take you home to Cheapside,' she whispered.

He did not stir.

Straightening, Lucy nodded curtly to the cart-man. 'Go carefully,' she instructed him, and wiped her damp cheek with the back of her hand. 'There's no hurry.'

Fourteen

ELIZABETH HELD UP HER HAND. 'HUSH,' SHE INSTRUCTED THE party of ladies and gentlemen at her back. 'Look, a deer. And see how tame she is? Not afraid of us at all.'

She turned to Lord Burghley in sudden excitement. 'Do you have a sweetmeat, my lord? In your pocket, perhaps? Or a piece of dried fruit, something to tempt the creature nearer? I stroked a deer once, when I was being held at the old manor of Woodstock. They are as tame there as hounds, and will come to your call. Though that was many years ago, of course, when my sister Mary was on the throne.'

Elizabeth watched as the hind took another delicate step towards them, regarded her rich gown of red damask with wide liquid eyes, then turned and fled silently across the formal lawns of Richmond Palace towards the woodland.

'There, too late.' Elizabeth sighed. 'I suppose the deer must be quite wild at Woodstock now, for the palace was in ruins even then.'

Lord Burghley bowed, apologizing. 'Alas, my pocket was empty, Your Majesty.'

'Like my coffers these days,' Elizabeth responded tartly, and moved on, resting her hands on the broad foreskirt of her gown. Her leg ulcer seemed much improved these days, though the doctors had warned her this would alter if her ladies did not continually change the dressings on her tortured flesh and bathe her leg in some strong-smelling milky solution they had prescribed. It was a nuisance, and the stench of the dressings left her uncomfortable at night, but at least she was able to walk more easily and even dance the galliard without too much pain.

At her back, Lady Mary Herbert followed with a fringed canopy raised on a pole to shade her from the sun, though in truth Elizabeth enjoyed its warmth on her face after so many months spent hiding inside, in fear of assassins. Lady Mary looked sulky, her face averted. The countess had begged leave to return home to her young children this summer, and Elizabeth had refused. But she could not allow her ladies to leave court whenever the whim struck them, or she would have no one left to attend her!

They walked for a while in silence, slowly making a circuit of the large park at Richmond Palace, a few of the gentlemen in her entourage discussing the lack of rain that summer and how brown the grass looked away from the river banks. A loud crack from the woods made Elizabeth turn in that direction, abruptly on her guard, but all she could see were oak trees heavy with dark leaves, the tiny buds of acorns just beginning to show their bitter light green above the stalk and cap.

'I am glad to be out in the daylight again. I have felt like an owl this past year, rarely allowed out except under strict guard. But at least here we should be safe, with such high walls.' Elizabeth gestured to the others to fall back. It was time for them to talk more privately. 'What news from Walsingham about this latest plot to do away with me?'

'Sir Francis has been reticent on the matter in recent

weeks, Your Majesty. Though that is by no means out of character. He will be playing some deep game, I expect.'

'No doubt,' she agreed. 'With me as his pawn.'

'I sincerely hope not, Your Majesty.' Lord Burghley glanced over his shoulder at the handful of courtiers who had accompanied them out from the palace, followed by only three of Elizabeth's bodyguards. 'Perhaps it is time to walk back to the palace, Your Majesty. Even within the grounds, we are still very exposed here and the guards are too far behind. Perhaps we should summon them. Or wait for the courtiers to catch us up, at least.'

'In heaven's name, no!' she exclaimed. Yes, by all means keep her safe from would-be assassins. She understood his caution. But this was going too far. 'Pray do not spoil an excellent morning's walk by treating me like a prisoner. I wish my guards to keep a good distance, so that I do not have to be reminded at every step of the hatred in which I am held by English Catholics. I have followed Walsingham's advice to have my dishes tasted before every meal, and have suffered no more cramps or sickness since that last bout. The grounds here are walled and, I believe, well-guarded. What harm can come to me?'

They walked on. Burghley still seemed troubled, limping slightly as though he too suffered some infirmity. But he did not press his argument to wait for the guards.

'Do you fear Walsingham dangles you as bait for these men?'

'I do not fear it, I know it. Not all of them have been run to ground,' Elizabeth pointed out coolly. 'And if they can be smoked out by seeing me as a target, so much the better. Though their treasonous activities are of no concern to me. I am not afraid of such cowards. Let one of these men come before me and state his grievance to my face. I shall not flinch if he has good reason to wish me dead. But his only reason can be a treacherous one, and that is beneath my notice.' She fanned herself slowly in the heat. 'No man who can plot the murder of his prince and the elevation of a foreigner to the English throne is worthy of my attention, let alone my fear.'

'*Bene dite*,' Burghley murmured in Latin.

Elizabeth smiled, studying the delicately feathered fan in her hand with its design of a bear and ragged staff set into a golden, jewel-encrusted handle. 'Robert gave me this fan before he went abroad. A poor soldier's gift on going to the wars, he called it.' She spread the fan to its full extent and batted the air with it. 'That is a ruby in the bear's eye. It does not look very poor, does it?'

'Lord Leicester has always been a generous man, both with his gifts and his words,' Burghley remarked drily.

'Robert is a peacock and a mad popinjay,' Elizabeth corrected him, but laughed. She glanced back at her ladies-in-waiting, who had stopped by the edge of a small ornamental lake, smiling and conversing with the noblemen who had accompanied Elizabeth out on her walk. 'Luckily, I am not averse to such proud, showy birds. I spent my childhood in rags and tatters, hidden away from the pomp of the court and eating my supper with a wooden spoon. Robert understands why I ask for gold plate and silver cups at my table now, why I must wear the costliest jewels and the finest gowns, and suffer my ladies to wear nothing but sombre black and white.'

'He is not alone in that understanding,' Burghley pointed out gently. 'I, too, knew you when you were unjustly held as a prisoner of your sister, the Queen.' He bowed as the path narrowed, close to the woods, and allowed her to walk just ahead of him. 'But you do yourself wrong, Your Majesty. I have never seen you wear costly stuff for yourself alone, to satisfy some inner greed, but rather to impress the court and visiting dignitaries with an image of merry England as it was under your father.

You may drink from a silver cup, but your wine is watered down so you may attend to affairs of state while your noble courtiers doze at the table. And, if you'll pardon my impertinence, what you eat from your gold plates is hardly enough to keep a sparrow alive.'

'So I seem to live as a queen, but in truth am more like . . . what? A pauper?'

'You are a beacon of hope to your people,' Burghley supplied quietly. 'And a great prince.'

Deeply touched by this unexpected accolade, Elizabeth stopped and placed her hand on his. 'I thank you, dear Cecil. Coming from you, a man who lives as soberly as a hermit in a holy cell, that is praise indeed.'

'Your Majesty!' one of her women cried, some way behind.

Elizabeth turned. Her heart seemed to stop with a jolt. She stared in the direction that the woman had pointed.

A commoner was nearly upon them. He walked unsteadily, as though drunk. He must have come out of the woods, for his garments were dishevelled and his cap askew.

Shocked, Elizabeth instinctively began to hurry away. Do not allow this poor creature to alarm you, she told herself sternly. Yet she was alarmed, despite herself. Her chest was tight and her mouth dry. Her steps increased in speed and her mind ran wild as he closed the gap between them, ignoring Lord Burghley's loud protests.

What is this man planning to do? Is he about to kill me? Sweet Jesu, what should I do? Scream and run, or stand firm and demand his business?

She looked back over her shoulder. The man's face twisted, his eyes narrowing. Some dangerous emotion was driving him.

Elizabeth came to an abrupt halt and turned to face her would-be assailant. It felt safer not to provoke him into violent action by moving or calling out. Besides, she did not know what concealed weapons he might be carrying. He had one hand tucked behind his back, as though hiding something.

Where was Lord Burghley? Only a few steps behind her on the path. She must not allow this villain to cause him any harm.

Drawing herself up to her full height, Elizabeth looked at the stranger. 'Sir?'

He met her gaze, then looked away. Elizabeth had the impression of a torn, desperate spirit, hell-bent on his course. 'Your Majesty,' he said raggedly, and drew his hand out from behind his back.

Lord Burghley exclaimed in horror and turned towards the courtiers, shouting, 'An assassin! Summon the guards!'

'Your Majesty,' the man repeated, his voice strained. He had produced a dagger. The long blade caught the light as his hand shook and Elizabeth stared at it, imagining how it would feel to be stabbed by such a cruel instrument.

For a moment it was as though the two of them were alone on the path, Queen and would-be assassin.

'What is your name, sir?' Elizabeth demanded, and raised her eyes slowly to his face.

His hand shook more violently. He was younger than she would have expected of an assassin, his face flushed, his gaze not quite meeting hers. 'Robert,' he muttered. 'My name is Robert Barnwell.'

'I know another man by the name of Robert. The Robert I know is a brave man and true.' As Elizabeth continued to regard him, she saw anger and shame in the young man's look. 'What heinous act have you come here to perform, Master Barnwell? Is the rightful Queen of England to die at the hand of a common assassin?'

His gaze warred with hers for a moment and she

thought that he would strike at her heart, that it was all over.

Then Robert Barnwell lowered his eyes and fled, just as the deer had done, on silent feet across the lawn, back into the green shelter of the woods.

The palace guards had finally caught up with her, sweating and weighed down with their armour and weapons in the overwhelming heat. At her brusque gesture, they ran on into the woodlands, calling out to each other and making so much noise as they crashed about between the trees, searching for the intruder, that even the birds roosting in the high branches flew up with a clatter.

'Fools!' Elizabeth exclaimed.

She could stand on her own legs no longer. She staggered. Lady Helena sat down on the grass, hurriedly billowing out her silk gown, and Elizabeth lay back against her old companion like a child in her mother's lap.

Her hands were trembling. Elizabeth held them up before her face and laughed. 'I did not shake when I saw his dagger, Helena, but look now. I am like an aspen in the wind.'

'Your courage is beyond that of any woman I know, Your Majesty,' Helena murmured, taking her hands and squeezing them gently between her own.

'This is the second assassin we have faced together,' Elizabeth reminded her, thinking of the bold-faced Italian woman who had gained access to her royal apartments at Kenilworth. She too had been wielding a dagger, but had been knocked bravely down by Helena, armed with nothing but a candlestick. 'These wicked villains who would destroy a country with a single blow. We put them all to rout, do we not?'

'I was too slow, Your Majesty,' Helena pointed out, 'and cannot share the glory this time. You chased this one away on your own.'

'Indeed I did!' Elizabeth exclaimed, and laughed. 'Perhaps we should bring the men home from the Low Countries, and send none but seasoned women to fight the Spanish. That should see the war resolved within a month.'

Lord Burghley returned from his muttered discussion with the other courtiers. He seemed most agitated by the incident. 'It is not safe for you to remain here, Your Majesty. There may be others of his evil persuasion about the grounds. Men will be sent to find this Robert Barnwell's lodgings and search them for names of his accomplices. Now I beg you will go inside out of this hot sun. A litter is on its way, Your Majesty, to carry you back to your apartments under guard. Your chief physicians have also been ordered to attend, and will examine you on your return to the palace.'

'I do not need to be examined, my lord. Nor am I so frail that I cannot walk on my own two feet.'

Imperiously, Elizabeth held out her hand, and was helped to her feet by several red-faced gentlemen – none of whom, she noted, had been there to save her from Master Barnwell.

'I shall not be carried in a litter like an invalid,' she stated firmly. 'One cowardly assassin is not enough to bring this queen to her knees.'

But much to her shame her knees began to weaken and buckle after only a few steps. The ulcer on her leg throbbed viciously. One or two of the younger women in her entourage looked away, no doubt smiling behind their fans. Staggering on, Elizabeth felt her cheeks flush with rage at their mockery. Harlots! Vipers! She looked about for assistance, but Helena had walked ahead to prepare for her return to the palace, and even Lord Burghley was talking to one of his gentlemen attendants and had not noticed. Was this the English court now? Young men and women with no respect for their queen, and men too old to draw a sword in her service?

Someone pushed through to her side from the back of the staring courtiers. 'Lean on me, Your Majesty,' a male voice murmured in her ear. Good man, she thought. Excellent man. Her saviour slipped his arm impertinently about her waist and for once she did not protest. 'I have you safe.'

'Rather too safe, I fear,' she retorted, then recognized the soft burr of the man's Devon accent and looked at the courtier properly. 'Ah, Sir Walter Raleigh. So you have come back to court from your adventuring!'

'Did you miss me, Your Majesty?'

'I hardly noticed you were gone,' she told him cruelly, enjoying the hurt flash in his eyes. 'Now let me go. I can walk well enough with my hand on your shoulder.'

'You think me too forward?'

'I think you squeeze too hard, Sir Walter. I am not the rail of one of your ships.'

Many condemned Sir Walter Raleigh's intimate manner with her, and claimed he overstepped his authority both at court and in the parliamentary seat she had granted him. But the arrogant tilt of his head, the adventurer's smile as he admired her figure, and his short dark hair . . .

Walter reminded her of Robert as a young man, that was the truth of it. Handsome. Charming. Willing to dare things other men feared to do in order to win his prize. And bold, yes. But it was an honest man's boldness.

'Did you see the young man who came to kill me?' she asked as they approached the palace.

'I saw a fool blinded by the radiance of your presence, Your Majesty. You were never in any danger.'

Elizabeth smiled, though with scant humour. 'Indeed? That is not how it felt at the time. It is my opinion that I was lucky to escape with my life.'

One of the guards came running back from the woods, his chain-mail armour jangling heavily. He dropped to both knees on the grass before Elizabeth.

'Your Majesty,' he gasped, removing his helmet and wiping his wet brow, 'we have searched the woods and found a dagger among the trees, but there is no sign of the man himself. Shall we fetch the dogs?'

'The river!' Elizabeth exclaimed impatiently, waving him away. 'He will have come by the river and returned that way, too. Out of my sight! Fetch the dogs by all means, but by the time they have been brought from their kennels, Robert Barnwell will be a mile downriver and laughing at us all for fools.'

Fifteen

'HUSH,' LUCY SAID. SHE DIPPED THE CLOTH BACK INTO THE basin. Goodluck's blood reddened the water, its tiny spider's web spreading on the surface. She wrung out the cloth and reapplied it to his swollen lip. 'Don't try to speak.'

Goodluck grimaced, but obeyed. She finished with his face, which almost looked worse now the dried blood had been removed, revealing the extent of his injuries. Gently, she shifted on the edge of the bed, beginning to dab at the lesions on his chest with pig's grease, on the advice of her neighbours. The grease was slimy and it stank most vilely, but it did seem to lessen the livid look of his burns. Downstairs, someone knocked at the door, but she took no notice.

Goodluck lay a while in silence, flinching occasionally as she cleansed his hurts. Then he caught her wrist.

'I'm sorry,' Goodluck managed in a hoarse voice. 'I let you think . . . I was dead.'

'It doesn't matter,' she lied.

'You took no harm by it?' He frowned, either knowing Lucy too well to think her so heartless, or sensing something more sinister beneath her silence. 'Lucy, what is it?'

Her heart stuttered a little. 'Master Twist . . .' she began in a whisper, then could not finish.

He lay still, watching her averted face.

'That bastard. He hurt you?'

She did not want to speak of that day. But it was important that Goodluck should know of their friend's treachery. So briefly, she told him the bare facts of her encounter with Twist, leaving out the more unpleasant details.

'I managed to escape before he had his way,' she finished, and continued greasing Goodluck's wounds with a steady hand.

'I'll kill him,' he said thickly.

'Not in this state you won't.'

'Even if it takes me a year to get out of this bed, John Twist will die at my hands,' was all Goodluck's reply, but his eyes had closed again, perhaps tired by even this small effort at revenge. She worked on him in silence. Then, the wounds on his chest and belly cleansed and greased to her satisfaction, Lucy prepared to pull down his stained hose.

Stirring, he groaned and shook his head. 'No,' Goodluck said, struggling to sit up. 'Not there.'

'It must be done,' she told him firmly. 'And there is no one else to do it. Now lie still and stop hindering me.'

Once she had finished tending to his needs, she left Goodluck uneasily dozing.

Exhausted beyond even sleep, Lucy carried the basin downstairs. She threw the soiled water out into the street, then poured fresh into the basin from the covered pail she had left behind the door. After wearily casting off her filthy apron, she washed the blood off her hands, taking care to bathe her wrists too and check under her nails.

She knelt there a while on the hearth after finishing, her hands in the cool, shallow basin, her gaze on the smouldering logs.

She did not want to think about John Twist, though she knew there was a chance he might come back and try his luck with her again. Unless, of course, he had already heard that Goodluck had escaped the Tower alive and was back in his house.

Upstairs, Goodluck moaned in his sleep.

She listened, in case he needed the chamber pot again, but he fell silent after a moment. Perhaps she had done the wrong thing, telling him of Master Twist's attack. But it was better he should know the truth than still believe John to be his friend.

Just a bad dream, she thought wearily, listening to another muffled cry from upstairs.

There would be more nightmares to follow. She never wished to see him again as he had been on first recovering consciousness, crouched in the corner and weeping un-controllably, pushing her away when she tried to comfort him. Later, Lucy had persuaded him to crawl upstairs on his hands and knees, for the cart-man had not offered to help him to the bedchamber, and she knew what he desperately needed was to sleep somewhere comfortable and familiar.

'Lucy?'

She straightened and stared about herself in a daze. The house was darker than before. She had fallen asleep on the hearth.

The whisper came again. It was not Goodluck.

'Lucy?'

Her dagger was still in the basket she had taken with her to the Tower. She fetched it and stood by the door a moment, considering. If it was Twist come back to keep his promise . . .

But she knew it was not Twist either.

When she jerked open the door, Will Shakespeare stared

first at the dagger and then at her. 'Lucy, I'm so sorry about the way I behaved last night. I was mad for you. I couldn't think.'

You were drunk, she thought drily, but said nothing.

'Can you forgive me?' he continued, trying to reach for her hand. 'I know I'm a fool, but at least I'm love's fool. Please don't pull away. Were you asleep? I knocked earlier.'

'I know,' she said calmly, not letting him inside. 'I was too busy to answer. My guardian has come home and needs me to look after him.'

Will's eyes narrowed on her face. 'Goodluck? You said he was dead.'

'I was mistaken.'

He was watching her oddly, a flush in his face. 'So he's back here? Is he upstairs?' he asked, then pushed past her without waiting for an answer and took the stairs two at a time.

She put down the dagger and followed him upstairs more slowly, her body aching with tiredness.

The sun had not yet gone down and the room was bathed in a warm yellowish light. Goodluck was heavily asleep, snoring and naked on top of the bed linen, bruises and burns visible all over his body.

Will stood over the bed and stared down at Goodluck. His face was grim. 'What happened?'

'He was in the Tower,' she whispered, not bothering to lie. 'They tortured him. But he's home now, and I intend to look after him until his hurts have healed.'

Will went back down the stairs without another word, and she followed him. He stood by the fire, staring into the dying flames, then turned to look at her, an unexpected accusation in his eyes.

'You love him,' he said flatly.

Lucy did not know how to answer him. 'Of course I love him,' she said, confused. 'Goodluck is like my father.'

'No,' he insisted. 'You love him. As you love me, too.'

'Don't be ridiculous, Will. Nobody can love two people at once. And who says I love you?'

'You think love is only for one woman, one man, at a time?' he demanded. 'It is not so. The world is crueller than you think.'

Lucy laughed. 'You do not need to tell me of the world's cruelty.' She opened the door, determined to resist him. 'You'd better go. I need to sleep.'

'With him?' he asked roughly.

Horrified, she slapped his face. The blow was harder than she intended. Her palm stung and tingled afterwards. He stared back at her, his cheek beginning to redden.

'Go,' she repeated, on the verge of tears.

'Forgive me. I've barely slept for days. I can't write, Lucy. Not a bloody word. All I can think about is you. Your face, your body . . . your kiss. Sweet Christ, I don't even know what I'm saying.'

His words made her dizzy with longing, but she said in a firm voice, 'Then go home to bed,' and shoved him through the door.

Will turned as she closed it, but Lucy was too fast, forcing it shut behind him and drawing the bolts across at the top and bottom. He slammed his hand against the frame, speaking through the crack in the wood just as John Twist had done in the night.

'Lucy, I love you.'

She laughed silently and mirthlessly. Loved her but would not marry her? Loved her but would give no explanation for his absences?

'I'm tired, Will. Please go away.'

'You don't believe me, I know. And who can blame you? I can't seem to speak my mind to you. Just one look leaves me tongue-tied, green as a schoolboy with his first love. But inside I'm still a man, and I'm burning for you. I thought I knew love before I met you. But I knew nothing. All I ever felt before was a boy's lust, a shadow of love that lasted only while the sun shone.' Will groaned, his voice catching at her heart. 'For pity's sake, Lucy, I shall die at your door of this longing. Let me sleep with you tonight.'

Lucy could not stand on her feet any longer. She sank down by the fire like a hound that has run itself almost to death on the hunt, a twitch jerking at one eyelid, her heart worn out by conflict and yearning, her limbs trembling with exhaustion.

Although Will stayed long after the sun had set, speaking urgently to her through the crack in the door, Lucy let the dark tides of his voice wash over her while she slept. In her dreams, she lay curled up in the bottom of a small rudderless craft, adrift on a wide ocean, listening for the slightest creak or stirring from the stars above her head.

Sixteen

'WILL, ARE YOU DRUNK?'

Will lifted his gaze to Kit Marlowe, sitting across from him in the noisy snug of the Three Tuns. 'What makes you ask that?'

Kit looked pointedly at the scrap of parchment in front of Will. 'Well, I may be drunk myself,' he conceded, 'but reading that upside down, your sonnet would appear to be dedicated to a "Lucy Shakespeare". Have you forgotten your own wife's name? Or perhaps you have changed wives since yesterday, when you called her sweet Anne, as I recall, and praised both her breasts in turn for having nurtured your three children? Though you were certainly drunk then, for shortly afterwards you vomited into young Dick Burbage's best cap. But not before calling him a pintpot knave for having the audacity to wear velvet in defiance of his rank as an upstart whoreson. To which his father James promptly took offence, claiming his wife was no whore, unlike your own.'

Will dipped his quill in the lidded glass inkwell he had brought with him, inked out the name 'Shakespeare' next to Lucy's and wrote 'Goodluck' beneath.

Kit watched with his brows raised. 'Not Master Goodluck of the prophetic beard, surely?'

'The very same.'

'I heard the rogue was dead.'

'So did I,' Will agreed. 'Strange how some matters fall out, is it not?'

'And others in,' Kit mused. He finished his ale. 'Well, I have work to do.'

'I wish you well with it,' Will said drily.

'My thanks.' Kit stood and looked down at the debris of empty pots and scraps of torn parchment littering the table. 'Do you live here now? Should I address all future letters to you "For Master William Shapely Shaft, courtesy of the Three Tuns"?'

Will frowned over a couplet. 'Cheeks or visage?'

'Does it concern a lady?'

'I do not have room enough on this parchment to do my answer justice.'

'Ouch.' Kit grinned. 'In that case, my advice would be "visage". It is just French enough to be a touch insulting, and is a good iamb besides, to swell out a line of pentameter.'

What a blessing a Cambridge education was, Will thought, and wrote 'her cheeks' instead of 'visage'. He himself had been forced to give up school at the age of fourteen, when his father's debts had begun to mount up. After that, there had never been any question of his becoming a scholar at one of the universities.

Will glanced up curiously as Kit gathered his own papers. 'Still working on that new tragedy?'

'Yes, though the end eludes me. But I am determined to finish it this year and see it played next. It is on the theme of the mighty Tamburlaine, so should draw the crowds well enough.' Kit hesitated, an odd look on his face. 'What did you think of Kyd's new piece?'

'*The Spanish Tragedy*? An excellent play for the groundlings, but too dark for my own taste. Though I may lean that way myself if I fail to . . .' Will laughed and shook his head, putting Lucy's name aside. Kit might be young and known for his strange passions, but he was not a man with whom one shared one's heart. Some said Kit Marlowe was a spy, and indeed he had that look at times, the face of a man who had heard too much and knew his name was on the hangman's list. 'As for me, I have been paid to rewrite a merry old comedy from the days of Good King Harry.'

'The irony is amusing, if nothing else,' Kit remarked, and touched two fingers to his cap in a mock salute. '*Vale, mi amice.*'

Will watched him go, then glanced into his empty ale pot. Did he want another?

The name 'Lucy Goodluck' mocked him from the parchment.

He called out to the landlord for an eel pie and another jug of ale, hoping he had enough in his purse to cover the cost. Lucy Morgan. With those dark, exotic looks, there was not a woman in the whole of London to match her. Yet she was faithless. Did he want to see her again? It had been nine . . . no, ten days since he had found Master Goodluck naked on her bed, and Lucy herself cold and distant.

Will dipped his quill in the inkwell again and gouged a deep inky line through her name, tearing the parchment and leaving only Goodluck's behind to haunt him.

He had hoped to extinguish all thoughts of Lucy from his mind by drinking himself into a stupor every day, yet she burned on inexorably. Her name was a dark flame even in the midday sun, bringing night to noon and despair to his heart.

Meanwhile, Kit Marlowe was writing a grand new

tragedy for the playhouse, while all William Shakespeare could do was rework old comic pieces for a few shillings a week.

Furiously, Will cast about for another clean piece of parchment, but had none left. Undeterred, he pulled a small, vellum-bound volume from his bag – a new book of sonnets he had been studying – flicked it open, and began to make a fresh draft of his own poem on the blank verso sheet, correcting it as he wrote.

> My mistress' eyes are nothing like the sun;
> Coral is far more red than her lips' red;
> If snow be white, why then her breasts are dun;
> If hairs be wires, black wires grow on her head.
> I have seen roses damasked, red and white,
> But no such roses see I in her cheeks;
> And in some perfumes is there more delight
> Than in the breath that from my mistress reeks.
> I love to hear her speak, yet well I know
> That music hath a far more pleasing sound;
> I grant I never saw a goddess go;
> My mistress, when she walks, treads on the ground:
> And yet, by heaven, I think my love as rare
> As any she belied with false compare.

*　*　*

Will left the Three Tuns in the early evening, drunk and intending to head home for a sleep. Instead, he found himself threading his way through the narrow city streets as though on some vital errand. As he headed west, bathed in the warm, summery light of the setting sun, he turned over the plot of a new history play in his head, forming a plot from an excellent story he'd found in Holinshed. It would be a chronicle play concerning King Henry the Fourth and the aptly named Hotspur, with several good battle scenes to test Burbage's new cannon. Only when he came to a halt outside the dark, shuttered house in which Lucy lived with her guardian did Will realize what he intended.

He knocked but there was no answer.

Tentatively, he pushed at the door, and it swung open. Going inside, he found the downstairs room empty, the fire unlit.

Will hesitated, then crept unsteadily upstairs, not knowing whether Lucy was at home but determined to look.

She was lying on the bed in the upstairs chamber, her eyes closed in sleep, wearing a day gown and stockings but with her shoes and cap removed. One bare forearm dangled towards the floor, her hair fanned out around her head in luxurious abundance like a black halo.

There had been no sign of Master Goodluck downstairs. Perhaps he was dead. The fellow had looked half-dead the last time Will had seen him. Perhaps he'd been arrested again and taken back to the Tower. Or perhaps he had tried to make love to Lucy and she'd told him to get out.

Still a little drunk, Will stood at the foot of the bed for a few moments and stared down at her body. Lucy was dreaming. He watched her eyelids shift restlessly from side to side, and the gentle rise and fall of her chest. Apart from those tell-tale movements, this was how Lucy might look if she were dead.

The macabre nature of his thoughts disturbed him. Will knelt beside her. 'Lucy?'

She stirred, then sat up, suddenly alarmed. 'Will? What are you doing here?'

'Hush,' he said, and leaned forward to kiss her.

Lucy struggled, but he held her down, anchoring her strong thighs with his own and bearing down on her wrists to keep her safely beneath him. Her body arched as she tried to wriggle away, exposing her warm black throat. He kissed her there too, with slow intent, all the way down to her bodice.

'I need you more than the ripe wheat needs the sun,' he muttered against her throat. 'Don't fight me, Lucy. You kill me with your coldness.'

'Let me go!'

'Where is your guardian?'

'He will be back any moment. Let me go. If Goodluck catches you here—'

'Goodluck was in no fit condition to fight when I saw him last.'

She was begging him. 'Please, Will. I cannot do this.'

He drew her wrists together above her head and reached down with his right hand, slowly raising her skirt. 'Can you not?'

Lucy closed her eyes as he stroked between her thighs, as if to shut out the truth of what they were doing. But it was impossible to hide her readiness from his searching fingers.

Desire flooded him like a dark well, bringing him swiftly to erection, and it was all Will could do not to mount her there and then, like a tethered mare. But he forced himself to go carefully, leaning forward to take her mouth again, his fingers working inside her as they kissed.

She groaned.

It was the sound he had been waiting for. Releasing her wrists, Will knelt between her thighs, loosening his clothing. A moment later, he pushed inside and groaned himself, thrusting swiftly and urgently as he began to take his pleasure.

To his surprise, Lucy did not lie passive this time but moaned and rocked with him, raising her buttocks off the bed and rolling her hips to his rhythm.

She was such a beauty. All woman, too. Pleased by her response, he dragged down her bodice and sucked on her breasts. They felt fuller than he remembered, ripe like dark fruit and eager for his mouth. Her hips rose to meet his, and she moaned his name. She wanted him!

Throwing back his head, Will drove into her, the cot creaking beneath them, his body demanding, and hers answering just as forcefully.

He looked down and found her eyes open, her face shining with sweat. 'I love you,' he gasped.

It was true, too. Not just words to keep her heart willing. He did love her. Yet saying it made it somehow more true than ever before. It was a revelation and one which lifted him swiftly towards the end.

Dazed, he repeated, 'I love you,' and renewed his thrusts.

Lucy did not reply but groaned and locked her powerful thighs behind his back, grinding herself greedily against him. At last she gave a wild cry, her body suddenly stiffening, and he knew she had reached her peak.

His own desire could not be held back any longer. Will buried himself inside her, crying her name as he filled her. It was only afterwards that he realized whose name he had cried.

She sat up as soon as he rolled away. 'What did you call me?'

His eyes had been closed in ecstasy as his body climbed slowly down from that high mountain, but now Will opened them. Anne. He had called her by his wife's name. What kind of fool was he?

'What?'

Play for time, he thought. It was possible she had not heard exactly what he had said. All things were possible in love. Which poet had said that? He wiped his hot forehead with the back of his hand and shifted on the bed, wondering how to explain his way out of this mess.

Lucy was standing now, tidying her bodice where he had

369

dragged it down, her gown already hiding those beautiful thighs again. Such strong, sturdy legs, made for a man to climb up and lose himself between.

'Who is Anne?'

He felt his cheeks flush, just as though he were a small boy caught stealing from the pantry by his mother.

His lie was instinctive. 'I don't know what you're talking about.'

'You called me Anne!' Lucy half-screamed, then backed away from him as though he was somehow poisonous. She came up against the wall and stopped there, staring at him. A moment later she had snatched up her discarded cap and run down the stairs.

'Lucy, no!'

Will stumbled wildly to his feet and went after her, losing his footing on the narrow stairs and ending up on his hands and knees at the bottom.

Both hands clasped to her cheeks, Lucy was staring at the man, his face scarred and battered under a dark cap, who stood watching from beside the fire.

It was Master Goodluck.

Seventeen

LUCY'S FEET REFUSED TO MOVE. SHE SAW THE ANGER AND disappointment in her guardian's face and shrank from it. Goodluck had come home while the two of them were upstairs, and must have heard everything. And she had sworn to him that she would never lie with Will Shakespeare again. What must he think of her now?

Goodluck had seen her despair as soon as he was well enough to sit up in his bed, and she had told him what she could, hot-faced and stammering. That Will Shakespeare had come to court and tried to seduce her, that she had refused at first, then allowed him into her bed, that little by little she had fallen in love with Will, and still he had not married her.

Goodluck walked past her and looked her lover in the face. 'You are Will Shakespeare,' he said flatly.

'I am, sir.'

'Lucy has spoken of you. You were only a boy when she met you at Kenilworth. Is your father still living?'

'When last I saw him, yes.'

'Then, by Christ,' Goodluck exclaimed bitterly, 'he should have whipped you as a boy to teach you the difference between good and evil. You have shamed my ward without making her the slightest promise of marriage, and not once, but many times. Now that game is at an end, and you will marry her.'

Will looked at him steadily. 'I cannot.'

'How dare you defy me in this? You have had your way with Lucy and now you must—'

'I cannot marry her,' Will interrupted him, 'because I am already married.'

Lucy drew her breath in and turned to look at Will. Already married? He was already married?

She said nothing though, her gaze dropping before the violent intensity in his face. What was there to say to him? She had begun to suspect weeks ago that Will was not free to marry, but by then it had been too late. Already desperately in love with the man, she had lied to Cathy and even to herself, imagining other reasons why he could not marry – but never the most likely one. And now she would pay the price for her blind and trusting faith, as many women had paid it before her.

Will took a hurried step towards her but stopped, finding Goodluck barring his way. For a moment she thought Will would attack Goodluck, and wondered feverishly where her dagger was. No one would attack her guardian again, not while she still drew breath. Then he stepped back and sighed.

'I'm sorry. It was wrong of me not to tell you of my marriage when we first met again at Whitehall. But I could not help myself. I knew you would never consent even to speak with me if you knew that I was married. Nor was I lying when I said I was in love with you.'

'You called me Anne before. Is your wife's name Anne?' she asked doggedly.

'Yes,' he agreed dully.

'You have children by her?'

'Two daughters and a son.'

'Oh, three children! He has a wife and three children at home!' She gave a cracked laugh. 'How foolish of me to think I could at least bear you an illegitimate heir. Instead, I merely bear a fourth to add to your tally.'

Will stared at her like a fool.

'I am with child!' she shouted, tears of pure fury in her eyes, and saw Goodluck turn to her in horrified disbelief.

Her nerve broke at the sight of his expression. She could have faced Will's coldness a thousand times, met his wife in the street and had her hair pulled or her face slapped by that rightly offended woman, but to have Goodluck look at her like that . . .

Lucy turned and ran from the house, still in her stockings and without shoes, her hair unbound. The sun had gone down and a smoky dusk was falling through the city. Men in tavern doorways turned to shout and stare at her running figure, but Lucy paid them no heed. She did not know where she was going, but knew she could not stay under that roof a moment longer. The river, she thought. The river. And let her feet take her downhill, slapping through the muddy stink of the open ditches, running helter-skelter for the rolling Thames.

She had not gone further than the new Angel tavern on the corner when her path was blocked by a cart turning slowly up the narrow street. The horses reared up as she came running out of the twilight, and the driver swore at her for 'a fool of a whore'.

She fell backwards into one of the ditches, and lay there in the filthy water, in the shadow of the overhanging houses.

When she looked up, a man had descended from the cart and was holding out his hand. It was Sir Francis Walsingham, his face troubled as he bent towards her.

'Come,' he insisted. 'You are hurt and must let me help you home, Mistress Morgan.'

'I have no home,' she managed hoarsely.

Sir Francis helped Lucy to her feet. His brows were raised, yet he made no comment about her wild and unkempt appearance. 'Then I shall continue on foot alone and you must return to my house in Seething Lane in the care of my man.' Walsingham seemed preoccupied, indicating that she should climb up into the cart next to his secretary. She did so, too much in despair to bother that her skirts were badly stained or to take offence at the disapproving look on his secretary's face. Let the man think what he liked. She was past caring. 'I would escort you there myself. But I must speak to Master Goodluck on an urgent matter that cannot wait.'

Walsingham gave the driver his instructions, smiling reassuringly up at Lucy.

'Don't look so sad, Lucy,' he told her. 'I have worked hard on your behalf and the Queen has agreed to grant you a place at court again, if your voice is still as sweet as it was.'

Eighteen

The woods near Uxendon Hall, Middlesex,
August 1586

'HOW MANY MEN ARE THERE, WOULD YOU SAY, AND HOW
long have they been in there?' Goodluck asked, turning
to the boy who had led them silently and unerringly
through the woods. They were crouched now behind the
ancient, fallen trunk of an oak, its bark mossed and crawling
with flies in the summer heat. He wished he was still in
London, but when Walsingham cracked the whip, he had
no choice but to run. And this time it seemed he had run
straight back into the arms of his former conspirators.
Well, their time on this earth was nearly done. And then he
could return and see that his ward was properly cared for.

His blood was up as soon as he thought of Lucy. Don't
dwell on it, he told himself. Lucy is a distraction. A weakness. You will not help her by getting yourself killed today.

'Five, sir,' the boy offered. He scratched his head, the
lice in his short yellow hair clearly visible. 'Three days
now, belike. The cloaked one comes and goes, the other
four remain.'

'He brings food?'

'Aye, sir, and walnuts.'

The boy laughed, as though this was a great jest.

Goodluck frowned. 'Walnuts?'

'For the juice, sir. It stains th' hands and face, so's gentlemen may pass as country folk.'

'Where does this "cloaked one" find food hereabouts? We must be five miles from the nearest town.'

Tentatively, the boy held out his scab-covered palm. 'I . . . I forget, sir.'

Goodluck placed another shilling in his hand. 'He must have friends nearby. Where?'

The coin disappeared under the boy's ragged jerkin. 'Uxendon Hall, two mile east. They keep the old ways there.'

'Catholics, you mean?'

The boy shrugged and spat on to the leafy floor. Either he had come to the end of his knowledge, or the word 'Catholic' was enough to strike dumb fear into him. Probably the latter, Goodluck thought. With farmers back to being hanged in the marketplace again for saying the wrong prayers on a Sunday, they knew when to fall silent, these close-mouthed country folk.

'I see.' Goodluck glanced at the captain and four guardsmen who had accompanied them through the dense woodland. 'Well, it appears we outnumber them, which is good news. But only by one man.'

'We have a musket, though,' the captain pointed out, 'and enough shot for them all, if Ned can reload quickly enough.'

'What, deprive all London of a public execution?' Goodluck said drily. 'No, better let me go in first. Then threaten to shoot if they run. But only shoot over their heads to scare them into surrendering. My orders are to have none killed who could have been taken alive and brought to trial.'

The captain seemed astonished. 'You are going in alone? If they suspect you, they'll kill you.'

'Let's hope it will not come to that, then. I have a good story to spin, and they may trust me enough to tell me where the others are. No, I am determined.'

Much to the amusement of the boy, his mouth agape and eyes wide, Goodluck took up a handful of dirt from the woodland floor and rubbed it well into his hands and face, then smeared his shirt with it too, wincing when he inadvertently brushed against the tender flesh below. For good measure, he ran his sleeves along the rough green-mossed trunk of the oak and casually ruined them.

'There,' he said, pushing his hands through his hair to dishevel it. 'Now I could pass as a fugitive too. Five traitors holed up here in the woods, but as many yet un-accounted for this side of London. Sir Francis Walsingham has charged me with finding them all, and what I need more than dead men is information.'

'Yes, sir.' A note of respect in his voice, the captain fell back. 'You heard the man. We wait for the signal as arranged, and no discharging your muskets except over their heads.'

The captain sent two of his men round to the back of the narrow glade where the traitors had been camping, then nodded to Goodluck.

Crouching slightly to protect his injuries, Goodluck slipped between the creeper-thick trunks as soundlessly as he could, loosening the dagger at his belt as he crept nearer the men's hiding-place. It was nearly two weeks since his arrest at Pooley's house. He had a story ready to explain his escape from the Tower. He had been beaten by Walsingham's men for information, then released when nothing could be proved. As stories went, it was far from convincing. But these were men on the run for their lives.

Any story would be suspect, however sound, and he only had to keep their company an hour or less.

It was a hot August afternoon, a breeze occasionally stirring the leaves above the long-dried-up bed of the old stream. A young fox cub foraging in the heaped detritus of leaves under a giant beech stopped to turn a curious eye on him, then vanished quickly into its hole in the bank. Birds sang clear-throated in the branches overhead.

He thought uncomfortably again of Lucy, his own songbird. It hurt that she was no longer innocent, but unmarried and with child. He had failed her as a guardian. He had failed her as a man. Now he could not even be there to help her through her confinement. Walsingham had reassured him that she would be kept safe at his house in Seething Lane, but he could not help his dark thoughts when he considered how Lucy had been used and abandoned by that good-for-nothing whelp of a player, Will Shakespeare. Though his feelings about John Twist's personal betrayal were even more violent. One day that bastard would pay for what he had tried to do to Lucy.

Through the trees ahead, an invisible bird repeated a single sharp note of warning, its call breaking the silence.

Goodluck paused to listen to the bird then put all thoughts of Lucy aside as he identified it as a man.

Lifting his boot over a briar patch, Goodluck moved more carefully. Within another moment he saw the rough lean-to of leafy branches and sticks they had constructed for shelter. The ground was scuffed before its narrow entrance. A fire had been lit there recently, then hurriedly disguised with earth and leaves.

Goodluck cupped his hands to his mouth and gave the low wood-pigeon coo they used to recognize each other: three haunting calls, then a pause, then two more, followed by a single note.

Suddenly, Anthony Babington was there.

Tousle-haired, his clothes dishevelled and torn in places as though ripped by briars, Babington crouched in the entrance to the makeshift shelter. A dagger in his hand, he stared up at Goodluck as though he could not believe his eyes.

'Brother Weatherley,' he managed at last, his voice hoarse. 'Are you alone?'

Goodluck nodded, but did not move any nearer. It was vital he did not frighten these men, who must already be at their wits' ends.

Babington crawled out of the shelter on his hands and knees, followed by Robert Gage and Henry Dunne, two other conspirators who had occasionally frequented Babington's house while Goodluck was there. All three stood and looked at him suspiciously, then Babington nodded to Gage, who searched him with deliberately rough hands, so that Goodluck had to bite his lip not to cry out in pain. The burns Master Topcliffe had inflicted were barely scabbed over and still agonizing when touched.

There was nothing on his person to alert them to any danger. Goodluck had seen to that.

Gage shrugged, turning back to the others with Goodluck's dagger. 'Only this.'

'Give it back to him.' Babington's eyes narrowed on Goodluck's face. 'You will forgive us if we are impolite, Brother Weatherley, but our necks are at risk now because we have trusted too simply in the past. There can be no other explanation for our arrests than that one of our number betrayed us to Walsingham. I'm glad to see you at least escaped from the Tower, though. Are Ballard and Pooley still there?'

'Pooley has been freed without charge. Ballard remains under lock and key.'

'Then God have mercy on his soul.' Babington crossed

himself. 'But both you and Pooley free? How did you manage such a feat? We heard you were taken straight to Master Topcliffe.' Warily, Babington looked Goodluck up and down. 'Even the strongest of men would find it hard to walk away from an interrogation by that vicious bastard.'

'And how did you find us here in the woods, so far from London?' demanded Gage abruptly, handing back his dagger with a reluctant expression. The man would much rather, Goodluck guessed, have plunged the blade in his heart. 'Is there a sign out on the road, saying "Fugitives here"?'

'There is no mystery, my friends, I assure you. I have been walking for days to find your camp. Pooley and I left London together, hoping to meet up with you. We traced you from Westminster to St John's Woods, and then kept walking. But Pooley got himself arrested again in Harrow while I was asking directions in a wayside tavern. I hid, and since then I have been alone. Asking only at those places where I knew there to be staunch Catholics, I followed your trail from Harrow to this idyllic spot.'

Goodluck indicated his bruised face, then dragged open his shirt to show the still-raw, oozing wounds on his chest and belly. The conspirators recoiled. Now for the story he had prepared. Luckily most of it was true. It was always easier when the lie was half-truth.

'And I did not walk away from the Tower so much as was carried on a cart. I almost died that night. I was questioned for hours, and put to the rack and the hot irons, but nothing could be proved and they let me go.'

Was that the best he could come up with? Even to his ears it sounded thin.

Babington hesitated. 'You were lucky, then.'

Was that suspicion in the traitor's face? Goodluck turned the tables on him as a distraction, his eyes narrowed. 'If I had been lucky, friend, I would have escaped capture altogether. As you appear to have done.'

Now for it. Babington had stiffened angrily, sensing everyone's gaze on his face and no doubt feeling himself under suspicion. 'Do you accuse me of being a traitor to our cause because I was not arrested with you?'

'If I accuse you of anything, it's of being a lucky bastard.' The danger was past. Or would be in a moment if he could play it right. Goodluck grinned, seizing Babington's hand in a strong grip. 'Yes, it's a miracle your name was not on the warrant that day at Pooley's house. But I am glad to see you whole and hale, nonetheless.'

Henry Dunne looked at Goodluck with dark, sullen eyes. 'Did you bring food, Brother?'

That one was not so easily convinced. But all he seemed able to think about was his stomach. Soft-bellied gentlemen traitors. No doubt they had never guessed their grand rebellion would come to this, a hard bed under the stars and nothing to eat.

Pulling a fresh-baked loaf and a pouch of tobacco from under his jacket, Goodluck winked. This would do the trick. Food in their bellies and something to smoke. In another moment he would be one of them again, a trusted ally and not a suspect spy in their midst. 'The Lord looks after his own. Here, eat it in good health. No, I insist. I have already breakfasted today. Share this loaf amongst yourselves and then join me in a pipeful of tobacco.'

'I have been dreaming of a pipe these two weeks,' Babington breathed, and shook Goodluck's hand again in youthful thanks. 'Forgive my suspicions. You are welcome indeed to our little band.'

Gage looked fearfully at Babington. 'But the smoke. Will it not give us away?'

'Come, man, surely it's safe enough to smoke a pipe here in the woods?' Goodluck countered him. 'What, are we not allowed a few puffs of tobacco between long-lost friends? But let us sit inside here if you are afraid we may be seen.'

Goodluck ducked his head to enter their makeshift shelter. The others followed him after a moment's hesitation. It was cool and dry inside, everything cast in a dappled green light, their cloaks spread over the dirt and leaves to make it more habitable.

'I saw no one on the road today,' he continued blithely, 'and the woods seemed quiet enough as I came through them. Though you are right to be careful and avoid lighting a fire. If I was able to track you all the way from London, Walsingham's men may be able to as well. We should travel on soon, and keep moving so they cannot find us.'

As the men tore at the loaf with dirty fingers, Goodluck stuffed a few wads of fresh tobacco down into the bowl of his pipe and rummaged for his tinderbox.

Dunne cast him a few doubtful looks, but Goodluck ignored him. He lit the pipe and puffed on it, enjoying the pleasant fragrance of the tobacco as it burned. He only needed Babington's trust for this mission. Three men here, two missing. All he lacked was the whereabouts of the other men on Walsingham's list, and the names of any new men in the plot about whom he knew nothing.

'So, my friends,' he murmured, passing the pipe to Anthony Babington, 'where are the others who would have supported us in this push against the Queen? For we are only four here. Ballard is in the Tower. Pooley is under arrest again, poor fellow. But what of Robert Barnwell, and John Charnock, and the rest of our brave crew? Where are they? Never tell me we are all that's left to fight for Mary's throne?'

'Charnock and Barnwell are safely with us here,' Babington told him, closing his eyes as he drew rapidly on the pipe. 'Barnwell tried to kill the Queen, did you hear that? He went to Richmond Palace armed with a dagger. But Elizabeth was too well-guarded and he could not come near her. He said he was pursued and bitten badly by one of the Queen's hounds, then escaped over the wall. A brave man indeed. As for the others, I cannot tell you their fate. They may be taken already, or on the run as we are.'

Goodluck frowned, glancing around their cramped shelter. 'Surely Charnock and Barnwell do not sleep here too? There seems hardly room for one man here, let alone five. Where do they lay their heads at night?'

Henry Dunne seized Babington's arm, whispering hoarsely, 'Do not tell him too much. We do not know yet if we can trust him!'

With undisguised disdain, Babington shook Dunne's hand off his shirt sleeve. 'Father Weatherley is an honest priest,' he told him stiffly, 'and as loyal as we are to our future queen, Mary. I trust him implicitly.'

'I thank you,' Goodluck said gravely, inclining his head.

'We are all in the pot together. Not to trust each other is to ensure Mary will never reign in her cousin's place.' Reluctantly, Babington handed the pipe to Robert Gage. 'Charnock and Barnwell are safely quartered up at Uxendon Hall, never fear. Charnock could not stand the damp of the woods at night and Barnwell's wound was irking him, so both have been given a hiding-place in the big house. I know nothing more, but Barnwell's friend comes down every day or so with food and ale from the kitchens.'

'The family know they are hiding in the house, I take it?'

'Uxendon is the home of the Bellamys, as staunch a Catholic family as ever breathed. They do not have room for us all, for that would excite comment. But we're told they will arrange horses to take us further north in a day or two. There, we can meet others true to the cause and discuss what's next to be done. King Philip's army still waits for our signal. All is not lost.' Babington hesitated, looking across at him. There was a shy friendship in his face. It almost hurt to see it. 'You will come with us when we leave, Weatherley?'

'Of course.'

'I knew you would.' Babington smiled. 'With you, we will be seven. That seems a propitious number to over-throw a corrupt state.'

Goodluck agreed with this, looking round at their faces, then asked casually, 'This friend of Barnwell's, do we know him? Is he trustworthy?'

'Barnwell trusts him and that must be enough for us.' Babington shrugged. 'He is a commoner. But at a time like this, we may need such a man. He speaks stoutly of killing Queen Elizabeth if he can get close enough, and looks to be a handy man in a fight. Barnwell claims this fellow has carried messages between Mary Stuart and King Philip over the years, and has even spoken to Mary face to face.'

'His name?'

Henry Dunne looked at Goodluck suspiciously again. 'His name is Master John Twist. And he told us to beware of you.'

'John Twist?'

Goodluck repeated the name as levelly as he knew how, forcing himself not to betray the fierce surge of hatred inside as his lips formed the words. His heart beat violently and a red haze of fury dimmed his eyes. So Twist was up to his neck in this plot too? And had done his best to betray Goodluck as a Queen's man, it seemed, without also revealing himself as having been in Walsingham's pay, too. He wondered how much money Twist would earn from the Catholics for his treachery. More than Walsingham had ever paid, presumably.

'Told you to beware of me?' He pretended confusion. It

seemed his only hope. 'For what reason? I do not even know this man's name.'

'Weatherley, pay this vicious accusation no heed,' Babington told him urgently. 'Master Twist merely said he had heard a rumour that a Father Weatherley was no priest, but a spy in Walsingham's pay. But none of us believed it. Why should we, when you have travelled all over Europe with Ballard and been such a good friend to us? Let us not distrust each other when our numbers are so mean.'

A wood pigeon's low coo sounded outside the shelter, only a few hundred feet away. The men stopped talking and listened intently. The signal came again, then silence.

Dunne's dark eyes narrowed on Goodluck's face. His smile was unpleasant. 'This will be John Twist now, down from the big house with our food. You want to know why he maligned you? Come outside, big man, and you can ask him yourself.'

So the time had come to see this comedy to its end. Well, there could be no hesitating now.

Goodluck nodded. 'So I shall.'

Crawling out after the conspirators through the narrow opening of stripped beech twigs and willow wands budding with leaves, Goodluck straightened in the dappled woodland sunshine and found himself face to face with John Twist.

Twist's opening words died on his lips at the sight of Goodluck. His sword was out in an instant, the blade pointed unwaveringly at Goodluck's heart.

'I did not think to find you here,' Twist snarled. He looked at the other three men, standing nonplussed, and urged them to run. 'Go, get as far away from here as possible!'

For the first time Goodluck realized that John Twist was in truth a Catholic conspirator. He was not playing this game for money, and never had been. The revelation shocked him, though it made sense. Twist had always seemed to have more up his sleeve than he let on, though Goodluck had thought him merely close-mouthed. The kind of man who likes to keep secrets for their own sake. Instead, Twist had been on the side of the Catholics all along, hiding his plans and allegiances even from those who knew him best – Goodluck, Ned, Sos, and the other theatrical spies in London – while pretending to be a stout Protestant. No wonder their attempts to uncover Catholic plotters had so often been thwarted or sidetracked. Twist must have been feeding both sides information, but ensuring he kept his friends one step ahead of Walsingham's men.

'We heard up at the big house that soldiers had been spotted searching the woods. Now I see why. This creature,' Twist spat vehemently, indicating Goodluck with his blade, 'is a Queen's man, and has brought ruin upon us.'

'No!' Babington exclaimed. He came to stand firm at Goodluck's right side. 'You are mistaken. Brother Weatherley is a priest and a true friend to our cause.'

'Is he indeed?' Twist asked, taunting Goodluck with an insolent stare. 'I fear you have been taken in by a master player. His name is not Weatherley, but Goodluck. Nor is he a priest, but a spy and an adventurer in Walsingham's pay.'

Shaking his head, Babington looked bewildered. It was too late now, though. The cat would not be put back into the bag. 'I cannot believe he would betray us,' he insisted. Nonetheless, he was already backing away from Goodluck, his hand on his dagger hilt. 'Brother Weatherley, tell him it is not so.'

The charade was at its end. Goodluck stood back, put his fingers to his lips, and gave the piercing whistle that was the captain's signal to move in.

'I'm sorry, Anthony,' Goodluck told him, with genuine pity for the young man. A dire fate lay ahead for Anthony Babington if proven guilty of treason. Not that every one of the conspirators did not deserve death for plotting to kill the Queen and put her cousin Mary on the throne instead. But he had grown close to them all in recent months, and to contemplate their torture and death was no pleasant thing. 'For once Master Twist is speaking the truth. My name is not Weatherley but Goodluck. I do indeed work for Sir Francis Walsingham in the Queen's service. And you are all under arrest for treason.'

The other two had begun to run at his first words, tripping over in their hurry to escape the trap. Now a pale-faced Babington turned and fled after them.

'This is not finished!' Twist told Goodluck. But it seemed Twist was taking no chances over his own arrest, for he did not stay to fight it out but turned and followed his young friends into the woodlands.

Goodluck set off after them. He was already starting to feel feverish and dizzy, but even so he called over his shoulder to the guards he knew must be behind them, 'To me! To me! They are heading for the big house!'

He caught up with Twist only a few moments later. The scheming bastard had taken a tumble down a short ravine in the woods and was now clambering out the other side, panting and cursing as he climbed, for he was hampered by his sword and his feet kept slipping on the loose soil. There was no sign of the other three men, but ahead of them through the trees could be heard muffled shouts and the clash of steel. Presumably the soldiers sent by the captain to cut off their escape route had found them.

Goodluck drew his dagger and crept up the slope after Twist, taking care not to make a sound.

Coming level with Twist a few yards from the top of the

ravine, Goodluck seized him by the cloak and whirled him round.

'Stand and fight, traitor!'

Goodluck found that he was trembling with a rage so powerful that it even dimmed the pain of his wounds. When he had first heard Twist's name, he had intended to be controlled, to bring him to justice impartially, show that he was here for Walsingham and the Queen, not for himself. But when he saw Twist's face again, the mocking smile he dared to show at his capture, instinct took over. And Goodluck's instinct was to kill the man who had laid hands on Lucy.

He considered the odds in the time it took him to leap back out of the reach of that searching blade. Twist had a good sword, and it was unsheathed too, ready in his hand. Goodluck had only a short stabbing dagger to defend himself, and whatever else was to hand in the woodlands: soil, stones, tearing briars, a gnarled branch fallen from a beech.

By way of reply, Twist lunged at him with the Spanish blade. 'As you wish.'

Ducking to avoid the lunge, Goodluck snatched up a gritty handful of soil and leaves. This he threw full into Twist's face as he passed, then turned on his heel, hearing his opponent swear, momentarily blinded. Goodluck made a stab for Twist's throat, but he had underestimated him. The sword flashed up blindly, catching his left arm, and Goodluck felt the steel sear him.

He jumped back with an oath, blood dripping down his sleeve, and half-crouched as Twist ran at him. He rolled head over heels at the last second. The blade missed, but Goodluck knew he was in a poor position. He had to get back on his feet before Twist pinned him down.

Teeth gritted at the hideous pain from his oozing burns,

he scrambled to his feet just in time to see Twist's sword descend. He parried it with his dagger, but the force of the blow carried Twist's weight through to Goodluck's shoulder.

Goodluck roared, feeling the blade cut into his flesh. 'Damn you!'

In a white-hot fury now, Goodluck stabbed again at close quarters and saw Twist's eyes widen. His knife stuck in something. He pushed hard but could go no further. Had he struck the man in the belly or only torn his cloak?

Goodluck jerked the dagger back with a grunt. Twist's sword arm was crushed between them, helpless. His left hand clawed at Goodluck instead, gripping his throat and trying unsuccessfully to throttle him with one hand. For a few seconds they were joined together by a dagger's length, face to face, both staring the other down.

'I enjoyed your pretty Lucy,' Twist told him deliberately, and watched to see Goodluck stiffen. He laughed into Goodluck's face, his breath a foul stench, and disengaged with a jolting wrench.

Taking himself a few steps back to free his sword arm, Twist jumped up on a fallen trunk and taunted him again. 'These virgins do like to tease a man with their looks and smiles that mean nothing, so I decided to teach her a lesson. Lucy squealed like a sow beneath me. Did she not tell you? I could see how much she was loving every thrust, though, so I just gave it to her harder.'

Even knowing that the bastard was lying did nothing to alleviate Goodluck's rage. He threw his dagger at Twist, then hurled himself after it. In the careering madness of his charge, he felt a sudden flash of pain as Twist's sword glanced off his belly, the blade spinning to one side. With a roar, Goodluck knocked the slighter man to the ground and crouched, straddling his body. He began to throttle Twist, not daring to slacken his grip. The contest was about brute strength now. Goodluck knew he had the edge on Twist there.

'You think I'd let you live after you tried to rape her? Yes, Lucy told me.' His hold on Twist's throat tightened, his thumbs digging into the soft flesh, squeezing the life out of the man. 'You're a treacherous dog and you deserve to die.'

Twist gasped something, his blue eyes bulging with hatred and fear, and writhed beneath him as he fought for breath. A few seconds later, Goodluck felt a terrible bubbling pain in his forearm, followed by a debilitating weakness that left his right arm useless. As soon as his grip loosened, Twist rolled with him across the leafy floor, knocking him away and staggering to his feet. Gasping and doubled over, Twist clutched a bloodied knife in his hand. It was Goodluck's own dagger, which he must have groped for during their struggle.

Twist began to advance unsteadily on Goodluck, but stopped at the sound of voices just below them.

'Time to fly, old friend. Kiss Lucy for me, would you?' Twist's voice was hoarse, a vile rasp of sound, his throat dark red and bruised from Goodluck's hands. He bent to retrieve his sword. 'Unless I see her first, that is.'

Then Twist was gone, a dark shadow weaving between the trees.

Goodluck struggled bitterly to his knees, arm hanging useless by his side as he waited for the captain and his men to reach him. He cursed himself for a fool and a coward.

Unless I see her first . . .

His first impulse was to hunt his old friend down and make sure of his death this time. Twist's secret allegiance to the Roman faith had been uncovered, his friends scattered and all his hopes of a Catholic England destroyed; Goodluck knew he would be burning for revenge by the time he reached the city. Yet he could not pursue Twist back to London himself. He must make his report to Walsingham with all urgency before any more of these traitors slipped away.

Goodluck forced himself to remain calm. Lucy would be well enough hidden in London to escape notice. The net was closing in, and soon even Twist would be in the Tower with his fellow conspirators. It was only a matter of time.

Nineteen

'THEN THE PLOT IS OVER?' ELIZABETH DEMANDED thankfully. 'There is nothing more to fear?'

'We cannot be sure of that until we have them all in custody, Your Majesty.'

Sir Francis Walsingham was smiling nonetheless, a rare enough sight to make her feel more comfortable. There were dark marks under his eyes, however, as though he had not slept for several nights. Walsingham was a good servant, she thought with a sudden flush of pleasure, putting aside the uncomfortable question of what she would do when he grew too old to serve. They were all getting old these days, her servants from the old days. She and they would age together and fear nothing, God willing.

'However,' he continued, 'we do have the leaders Babington and Ballard in the Tower, and Robert Barnwell is taken, too.'

'Robert Barnwell? You say that as though I ought to know the name.'

'He is the villain who tried to attack you at Richmond.'

'Oh, him. Yes, I remember the man now. So he has been caught at last? About time too. I was beginning to think you had lost your touch.'

Elizabeth was sitting up in bed at Whitehall, propped up on pillows, her hands resting in front of her on the stiff gold-embroidered coverlet. About her shoulders had been hung a silk, burgundy-coloured robe with ermine trim. Her scalp of shorn, patchy hair had been hidden beneath an elaborate lace cap – there had been no time to fetch and arrange one of her bedchamber wigs. Beside the heavily curtained tester bed stood Helena and Anne, more simply adorned in plain white nightshifts and caps, and various other of her ladies were now gathering near the door, most still in their nightgowns too.

It was very early morning, the sky a cool blushing pink over her gardens, and at first Elizabeth had feared some terrible calamity must have overtaken the country when Walsingham had knocked at such an hour. A Spanish army has landed on the south coast, she had thought on a wave of panic, wrenching herself from sleep as Walsingham knocked at the outer doors, demanding to see her. Then she had realized the plotters had been taken. Good news, not bad. Some had been seized at the ports, slyly trying to escape England and the Queen's justice, but some had been arrested in a wood near Uxendon Hall, home to a wealthy family of Catholics whose name would be for ever anathema to her now.

Walsingham's own agents had been involved, he had told her proudly, and Elizabeth had smiled, not much caring who was responsible, but merely thanking God that she had been spared from another plot against her life.

'What will happen to Robert Barnwell and these others, and to this Babington boy who dared to dream up this plot against me?' she demanded, and looked up at Helena. 'Since I am awake, Helena, I might as well break my fast. See to it, would you? And bring a cup of ale for me, and wine for Sir Francis if he wishes.'

'Nothing for me, thank you,' Walsingham said politely, and bowed as Helena went about her business.

'Well?' Elizabeth turned to him. 'How will they be punished for this wickedness?'

'If found guilty of conspiring against Your Majesty, each man will suffer a traitor's death. He will be hanged, drawn and quartered before the crowd.'

'Yes, yes,' she said impatiently. 'But these public executioners are too lenient, are they not? They let the men hang until they are dead, or almost dead. And where is the use in that as a deterrent? Drawing and quartering can mean little to a dead man. The crowd see that, and those among them who would rebel against my throne feel no particular concern that theirs will be a hideous death if they too follow Mary.'

'I fear Mary's followers think of nothing but her release and enthronement. I have questioned many of these Catholic conspirators over the years, and their thoughts do not dwell on their punishment, but rather on the rewards if they should succeed.' Walsingham looked on wearily as Helena served Elizabeth a cup of ale, then placed a trencher of cold meats and sugared rolls on the table beside her bed. 'They are besotted with your cousin. Like lovers, they burn to see Mary in your place and to worship her there.'

'Let them burn in truth, then. Set up stakes in the marketplaces and let them be consumed by flames.' Elizabeth sipped at the ale and recoiled. 'What is this vile tasteless pap, Helena? Ale brewed from acorns? I don't care if it was a gift. Take it away at once and fetch me something more piquant.'

'Burn the traitors, Your Majesty?' Walsingham appeared horrified. 'It is not within the law to do so.'

'These Mary-worshippers are Catholics, are they not? Burn them then, and have done with it. I will not have these villains hanged by the neck until they are dead, and so miss the punishment of their drawing and quartering. Where there is such villainy, there can be no mercy.'

'Of course,' Walsingham murmured, and bowed. 'But I feel it unlikely that the courts will order these men to be burned. There is no precedent for it. Not in cases of treason.'

'Very well. Then they must hang only for a moment, to stretch their necks, then be cut down alive to face the executioner's knife.'

'Your Majesty, the crowd may take it in poor part if the traitors' deaths are too violent, too openly vengeful.' Walsingham hesitated, as though sensing her irritable mood and not wishing to provoke her into anger. 'I understand why you should demand a bloody death for each of these men. Indeed, they would not have spared your own life if their plot had succeeded. But you are a queen, and as such you should at least consider clemency in victory. Some of these conspirators are young, and others are of gentle birth. It can be too much to see and smell a man's innards pulled out on the scaffold while he is still alive and begging Your Majesty's forgiveness.'

Elizabeth shook her head stubbornly, picking at her meat without much of an appetite. 'No, I will have them cut down alive. It is within the law to demand this, is it not?'

'Indeed it is, Your Majesty.'

'Then pass on my order to the executioners. There is to be no merciful hanging to the death for these men. I will have a powerful example made of them, so that the people will see the agony of such a death and fear to rebel themselves.' She glared at him when he still did not move to obey her. 'Do I make myself clear?'

Walsingham was looking troubled, but he bent his head nonetheless. 'Perfectly clear, Your Majesty. There is to be no mercy shown.'

Now that the matter of the traitors' deaths was settled, Elizabeth felt too restless to lie in bed any longer. She signalled to Anne to bring her slippers to the bedside. The day was growing brighter now and the bloom-rich summer gardens were calling her.

'We are done here, then. I thank you for your diligence in this matter, Sir Francis. Your efforts to protect my throne will not go unrewarded. But look at this rosy-fingered dawn. Quite Homeric in its beauty, do you not think? I shall venture out into the gardens today, now there is no longer any danger, and see how my new rose beds go.' She glanced over her shoulder at Walsingham as Anne folded back the heavy gold bedclothes and Helena bent to help her out of bed. 'I am safe to go out again, you said?'

Walsingham's smile was thin and his dark gaze did not meet hers. Her spymaster was angry with her for not following his advice, Elizabeth realized. Well, she was queen here, and Walsingham was her servant. Her father would not have stood for such interference, and nor should she. She was no longer an inexperienced young woman who needed advice at every turn. It was for her to give the orders in England now, and for Walsingham – and the rest of her Privy Council – to follow them without question.

'You will never be entirely safe until your cousin Mary is dead,' Walsingham told her, then bowed when he saw her stiffen angrily at the mention of that name. 'But yes, Your Majesty, if you take your guards with you, I do not see the harm in returning to your customary habits. It will show the people you are not afraid, and that can do nothing but good.'

Twenty

Seething Lane, London, August 1586

LUCY SHOOK HER HEAD. 'I WILL NOT MARRY A STRANGER.'

'My love, my sweet, you must,' Will said, clasping her hand. His dark eyes entreated her. It hurt to be so close to him and know they would never be married. 'Besides, Jack Parker is no stranger. You have met him in my company, you know him.'

'I will not marry him,' she said stubbornly.

'You have been given a chance to return to court after the baby is born next year. But if the Queen discovers you gave birth to a child out of wedlock, there will be no return. You know how strictly Her Majesty governs the women at court. Sir Francis has said he will protect you from the Queen, and I believe him. He is an honourable man. But to prevent scandal, we have all agreed that you must be married – and today.'

She turned her mind away from the truth of that. The darkness in her heart threatened to swallow her as it was, without dwelling on how she had ruined her reputation, too.

'If I cannot marry you, I will never be married.'

Will kissed her and held her close in the small, dark antechamber in Walsingham's house where they had been left to wait while a priest was fetched to perform the nuptials. His gaze fed on her, his kisses tormented.

'Forgive me, Lucy,' he begged her in a choking voice, 'but there is no other way. I have admitted my guilt. I have told you why I cannot marry you.'

He had betrayed her. He had made her think he loved her and that eventually, when he had enough money to support a family, they would be wed. Will Shakespeare had lain with her and said nothing of the wife and children he had left behind in Stratford. No wonder she had caught the odd smirk on his friends' faces as they had walked out together on the streets of London, or sat in the taverns behind the theatres and toasted each other for love. I deserved this fall from grace, she told herself grimly. This is my reward for stupidity and wantonness. Will had never had any intention of making good his promises. It had all been a dream.

She pushed him away. 'Don't touch me. How can you kiss me? You are a married man.'

'I am married, yes,' he agreed, his voice unsteady. 'But that does not make my love for you any less true. This is my fault, so let me help you, Lucy. This marriage will save your reputation. This is what must happen. I will not see you begging on the streets with your child.'

'That will never happen. Master Goodluck will take care of me.'

'Master Goodluck is not here. He lies wounded in some tavern in the country. You call that taking care of you?'

'It is not Goodluck's fault he cannot be here, you know fever has set into his wounds,' Lucy reminded him. 'Besides, he has left me to Sir Francis's care until he is well enough to return to London. His letter made that clear.'

'And Sir Francis agrees with me that you should marry

398

swiftly, before your condition is too widely known. Otherwise you may forfeit your place at court for ever.' Will's hand dropped to her belly, warm and possessive. 'I would give the world for this not to have happened. But it has. You are with child and I cannot marry you. But my friend Jack is still unmarried and will make you a fine husband.'

'I will never let him touch me,' she insisted angrily.

'He will never try to, my love.' Will kissed her hand before she could snatch it from him. 'As I have tried to explain, Jack is not like other men. He does not enjoy the company of women as I do.'

'How can you be sure he is not lying?' Lucy asked, bewildered.

'Jack Parker has only ever lain with men, and professes a loathing for the fairer sex. So you see, you need not fear to be raped or abused at his hands. Jack will never come to your bed at night, demanding the rights of a husband, nor expect you to give him heirs once this child of ours is born.'

'Why would he agree to such a thing, if he cannot love a woman?'

'His family have disowned him as a wastrel,' Will explained soothingly. 'This way, Jack can earn their love and respect again, and be welcomed once more as their son and heir. For what mother could resist the lure of a grandchild on the way?'

Will kissed her on the mouth, and Lucy pushed him away again. Why did she have to feel such love for him still when he had betrayed her? And betrayed his wife, too. She wondered what this unknown wife looked like. Nothing like her, he had whispered when she'd pressed him, but then refused to say more. *Nothing like her.* What did that mean? Not dark, but fair? Or beautiful, not coarse-haired and plain?

'Jack is a good friend and he has given me his word you will be safe with him. I have known him ever since I came to London. We have even been neighbours, for pity's sake. He will not betray me. And he wants nothing else in return but a heavy purse.' He grimaced. 'Sir Francis is taking care of that, thank God, for I have barely a penny to spare.'

Lucy shivered and wrapped her arms about herself. So she was to be sold to a stranger to hide her shame with a married man.

Why had she not thought it might come to this when she first let Will kiss her?

Because you trusted him, a voice mocked her inside. *Because you are a fool where Will Shakespeare is concerned, and you will continue to be a fool, for you are in love with him.*

It had been a warm day, but now that night had fallen the room was chill and no fire had been lit. The only light was from the candles on the desk. 'I wish Master Goodluck was here,' she muttered.

'I know,' Will told her, going to the door and listening to sounds from downstairs. 'But we cannot wait for his hurts to heal. There, you hear that? The priest has arrived. You need wait no longer. Sir Francis has even procured a special licence so you can be married without the reading of the banns.' He came back to her side and took her hand. His eyes were intent on her face. 'I envy you such powerful friends, Lucy. Walsingham has the ear of the Queen.'

She said nothing but pulled her hand free from his. She did not want Will Shakespeare to hold her and kiss her, for he belonged to another woman. A woman whose marriage bed Lucy had already betrayed unwittingly. One day perhaps she would meet this wife face to face. The thought made her shiver. She felt nothing but shame now.

What a blind fool she had been! Now all that remained was to hide her shame, to marry this Jack Parker who would not touch her, and try to be a good wife to him at least. What else could she do? Not turn to her guardian for help, that was for sure. She had seen Master Goodluck's horror when he'd discovered she was with child. That look in his eyes. No, she would deal with this herself.

She busied herself with straightening her gown, which belonged to Lady Walsingham herself and had been let out at the seams to accommodate Lucy's expanding belly.

It was a costly and extravagant gown – though not too far above her station if Lucy had still been one of the court ladies, tasked with dancing before a visiting ambassador or foreign prince – and at any other time she would have been thrilled to wear it. But it was pitiful to borrow such a gown to be wed to a man she barely knew, and in the night, when there could be few witnesses to carry the tale to the Queen.

Someone knocked at the door and Lucy called, 'Come in,' without even thinking, though it was not her house and she was a person of no importance now, a foolish wanton with no dowry and no parents and no husband, but a child already growing in her belly.

It was one of Walsingham's serving girls, Susan, a young rosy-cheeked maid with shining eyes and a candle in her hand.

'They are ready for you downstairs,' Susan said shyly, curtsying, and stood back with an admiring gaze as Lucy came rustling past in her wide-skirted silver gown, her black hair teased about her head with combs and white ribbons. 'You look beautiful.'

She was surprised to find Sir Francis Walsingham himself present for the ceremony, although she knew her loose behaviour must have shocked and horrified him. The priest looked sternly in her direction as she entered the candlelit room where the wedding was to take place, then turned back to his Bible and holy instruments as though she was beneath any further attention.

At the front of the room stood Jack, a little more unkempt than when she had first met him in the tavern with Will, but with just as engaging a smile. He turned swaggeringly to examine her as Will led her forward.

'So you are to be my bride?' he said, then took her hand and kissed it. 'Such a dark beauty. This is the closest I shall ever get to the shores of Africa.'

Lucy looked at him sadly. 'Sir?'

'A jest, dear wife-to-be.' He glanced at Will over her shoulder. 'You have the money as we agreed?'

'When the deed is done.'

'You drive a hard bargain, Will. But it is not often I am in the home of such a fine gentleman as Sir Francis Walsingham, so I shall mind my manners and do as I am bid. Moreover, it's late and I would not wish to keep all these good people from their beds over the matter of a purse of gold.' The young man turned to face the priest, clasping Lucy's hand tightly. 'I am ready, Father.'

'And the lady?' the priest asked.

'Lady?' Jack laughed and peered about the room, as though hunting for some other woman. 'What lady?'

Will growled at him. 'Enough jests, Jack. Let the man do his work.'

'Forgive me,' Jack bent to murmur in her ear, seeming to regret his jest. 'Come, give me a smile. I shall strive to be a good husband to you. What more could any woman ask?'

Thoroughly humiliated, Lucy stood in a daze while the priest performed the ceremony. She knelt and prayed, and whispered her responses when instructed to, and stared at the priest's holy candles on the table while the service continued, imagining herself as one of the flames dancing higher and then lower, swaying as someone at the back opened the door to go out, then growing fat and hot again – until the priest finished and turned to snuff them out one by one.

Walsingham came forward to embrace her, then handed a bulging purse to her new husband. 'This should allow you to start married life without too much hardship, Master Parker.'

'I thank you, sir,' Jack said, suddenly solemn and respectful. He looked at Lucy. 'Shall we go, wife?'

Lucy was bewildered. She had a vague memory of watching the maid pack a trunk for her earlier, but had not considered what that might mean. She had thought perhaps that they would return to the house in Cheapside after the ceremony, and live there at least until Goodluck returned. With a little imagination, there would be room for the three of them. Though secretly Lucy had hoped that Master Parker would take himself off home to his own lodgings, and leave her to live as she had done before, under Goodluck's roof, a wife in name only.

'Go where?'

'Why, to live with my parents at Aldgate,' Jack told her breezily, tucking the purse inside a red leather bag which he then slung over his shoulder. 'It is a small household, but a merry one. When I am at the play, I will sleep near the theatre and you can keep company with my mother until I return.'

He turned away, apparently losing interest in his new wife, and clasped Will's hand. 'I shall see you in a few days, I expect. Up at the Tunn or one of the other theatre taverns.'

Will glanced at Lucy, then hurriedly looked away. She thought she saw pain in his expression but could not be sure. Did he care for her at all? 'Forgive me, Jack, I have to go back to Stratford for a few weeks. I'm needed at home.'

'Oh yes,' Jack said, and smiled broadly, his gaze flicking between Lucy's face and his friend's. 'Your wife and three children call, and off you trot to Stratford, all your London friends forgotten. Well, I must accustom myself to such a life. For I am a married man now. Do you not see the chains at my neck and ankles?'

When Will had disappeared into the night and Jack had gone out laughing to prepare the cart in which Lucy's trunk and other possessions would be taken to the Parkers' house at Aldgate, Lucy walked slowly upstairs to change. She stood in silence as the maid helped her remove Lady Walsingham's borrowed gown and untangle the pretty combs and ribbons from her hair. So Will was to return to his wife in Stratford now that he had tidied away all evidence of their illicit affair? What a dutiful husband he was indeed! And now she had a husband of her own. A boastful, swaggering boy who had no need, nor any respect, for women, but lay with other men to assuage his needs instead.

Susan was kneeling on the floor, adjusting the hem of Lucy's old gown. A good-natured girl, she glanced up in concern as Lucy made a sobbing sound behind her hand.

'Are you unwell, Mistress Parker?'

Mistress Parker.

The name meant nothing to her for a few horribly blank seconds. Then Lucy realized it was her own new name, and drew another sharp breath.

'Susan, have you ever kissed a girl?' Lucy asked.

'Oh, thousands of times. I have five sweet sisters, thank the Lord, and we all kiss each other, and our mother, and our aunts and cousins, too.' Susan got up from her knees, looking at Lucy in an odd way. She passed Lucy a starched linen cap with ties, bought specially for her by Sir Francis Walsingham as a wedding gift. 'Is that what you meant, Mistress Parker?'

'I don't know what I meant,' Lucy admitted, but raised her chin and fastened the ties of the sober cap beneath it. There was no glass in which to check her reflection, but it hardly mattered. 'Well, I am as ready as I will ever be,' she told herself, and turned to go downstairs to her new husband.

Part Three

One

Cheapside, London, autumn 1586

THE LEAVES TURNED RED AND GOLDEN ON THE TREES AS summer slipped warmly into autumn that year. Although Goodluck had been at home some weeks, under the care of a maid sent to him by Walsingham as a gift for his good service, it was the twentieth of September before he felt well enough to leave his house in Cheapside. The worst of the wounds he had sustained during his fight with Twist had long since healed, and no longer irked him. But his heart weighed heavy, and he could not help but feel he had made the wrong decision in allowing Lucy to be married to Jack Parker.

Yet what else could he have done? He had visited her new home at Aldgate not long after the wedding, and found Lucy silent and withdrawn. The lad Jack had not touched her, though, so she had sworn when she had spoken with Goodluck privately, and he had been forced to leave her there in the company of the young man's parents, a tight-lipped pair who seemed to loathe their new daughter for her black skin.

He had agreed with Walsingham that any marriage was

better than none, for her belly would soon be rising out of her gown, but Goodluck was both sad and relieved that he had not been able to attend the ceremony and see his darling girl handed away to another man.

Coward! You wanted her for yourself, his heart jeered, and his mind could not argue with that damning testimony. Though he could never have asked Lucy to marry him and watched the devotion in her face turn to scorn as she realized that even Goodluck, her own guardian, lusted after her like an ageing satyr.

No, however subdued she was as a new wife, Lucy was excellently placed with this Jack Parker, a younger man who would be a better father to her child than an old spy like Goodluck could ever hope to be.

Roughly an hour before dawn that September morning, Goodluck pulled on a hood and cloak, and trod wearily out through the city and across to St Giles-in-the-Fields. There a sturdy scaffold had been erected, with a gibbet on top, and already a crowd had gathered around it, several thousand strong, with more flooding in as they waited in the chill dawn light, buying apples, spicy gingerbreads, and hot handfuls of nuts from the street sellers' glowing braziers, stamping their feet and singing the hour away until execution time.

Goodluck had witnessed many executions over the years, and knew them to be foul but oddly satisfying events for the crowd. Today, however, there was a tense silence as the cart pulled up, the drums began, and the condemned men, chained at wrists and ankles, were led in a shuffling row to the scaffold steps. Everyone had heard, as Goodluck himself had done, that these men were not to hang until they were dead, but were to be cut down warm from the rope and sliced straight open, still kicking. The ones at the front had all been discussing it as the cart appeared. This savage decision, one burly man suggested, was to frighten other would-be assassins in the crowd by the extraordinary terror of their deaths. Most seemed to agree with him, and Goodluck heard many muttering 'Unjust!' and 'Too cruel!' as the men trooped on to the platform above, most stooped and pale after weeks spent under torture in the Tower cells.

Some of the traitors came up the steps bruised and sullen-faced, waiting in silence for their turn to die. Among them Goodluck recognized Dunne and Barnwell, both men determined and recalcitrant in their last hour on earth. By contrast, young Anthony Babington seemed terrified out of his wits as he gazed at the crowd of thousands who had come to watch him pay for his crime, then raised his eyes to the rough gibbet from which they would all hang.

One man at the back of the scaffold, whom Goodluck did not recognize, looked up at the gathering light of day and cried loudly, 'Save us, O blessed Mary, Mother of our Lord!' and was promptly knocked to his knees by an executioner's man.

A few laughed at this spectacle. Others called out, 'For shame!' Still others crossed themselves furtively, muttering the Lord's Prayer under their breath. Some wept openly and tore their hair, perhaps relatives or friends of the men about to die.

One red-faced, corpulent woman, whose gown and apron strained tightly over her belly, called each traitor's name aloud in a shrill voice, demanding that they should say why they had betrayed their country before they were hanged, 'So we shall understand why you would spit in the face of our good Queen Bess and plot to put a whore and a Papist on the English throne!'

Stripped of his clothes, Ballard came to the gibbet first. Naked but unbowed, he stood straight and read aloud a passage from St Augustine while the crowd jeered.

'Forget this Papist nonsense! Confess your treason like an honest man!' called one of the sheriff's men, standing not far from Goodluck.

Ballard did not reply, but handed the book to one of the others when he had finished, and sank to his knees, praying quietly to himself.

'Have you no shame, priest?' demanded the sheriff himself, who seemed delighted to have been granted the honour of dispatching such notorious traitors. 'You would have killed the Queen and laid waste to the whole of England. Surely you will not go to your death with that on your conscience?'

'I shall be with the blessed saints and angels before long,' Ballard replied. Glancing down at the crowd as though searching for someone in particular, he scanned the faces of those nearest the scaffold. His eyes narrowed slightly, pausing momentarily on Goodluck's face, then he turned to the executioner. 'I am ready.'

The chaplain, at his back, could not resist one last stab at the poor fellow. 'The angels will not receive you if you die a Papist. It is not too late to turn away from that corrupt faith before you meet your Maker.'

Stubbornly, awaiting his punishment, Ballard began to recite the Lord's Prayer in Latin, as used to be done under the old religion. The chaplain cursed him for a heretic and a fool. Bustling to the front of the platform, he held up his plain wooden cross and spoke across the Latin, reciting the same prayer in English and encouraging the crowd below to join in and drown out Ballard's voice.

His prayers finished at last, Ballard's hands were bound behind his back, the thick coil of the rope placed about his neck, and he was set upon a stool.

The stool was kicked away. Ballard's eyes bulged and his legs jerked fitfully as the rope tautened about his neck. After only a few moments, the executioner stepped forward and cut Ballard down. He lay on the platform gasping, his eyes rolling white in his head.

'So perish all traitors!' cried the sheriff to the crowd, even though the man was still plainly alive.

The executioner's knife flashed in the early-morning light. There was an agonized scream, and suddenly he was holding Ballard's penis aloft, blood spurting from a gaping wound between the man's thighs.

The crowd shouted and stamped their approval while Ballard writhed helpless, his hands still bound, gurgling incoherently in his throat.

His penis was thrown aside into a basket. Then the knife flashed again, slitting his belly straight across until it gaped like a bloodstained mouth.

Delving inside with both hands, the executioner tugged and struggled, slowly dragging Ballard's innards out. They spilt across the platform, a coiled heap of shiny, reddish-purple loops steaming in the chill September air. Then he began to hack brutally into Ballard's chest, ducking the jets of blood which soaked his leather apron. Again the crowd cheered and applauded, though those nearest the platform were holding their noses by now, repelled by the stench of the condemned man's entrails and the shit he was passing in his last moments. Ballard's legs kicked almost on their own, his bare feet slipping in his own blood, his mouth working frantically, though by now he was beyond even an attempt at speech. Then his heart was out of his chest, still pumping blood as the executioner held it up for all to see.

In a gush of blood, Ballard died.

The crowd quietened for a few moments as the body was roughly quartered and its four parts dragged away to be thrown into the grave already dug and waiting for them, close at hand. Only when Ballard's severed head had been stuck on a spike and paraded in front of the watching people did they stir again, calling, 'God save Her Majesty!' and cursing all traitors.

Then their eyes turned to the next man in line, named as a Master Tichborne, who was still weeping and begging the Queen's forgiveness as the executioner cut his heart out. Goodluck did not recognize Tichborne, but heard him blame Babington several times as he lay dying, claiming he had corrupted them all, and saw Anthony stare and shake his head, his face white with terror.

The executions continued, relentless in their violence, blood spraying the faces of those nearest the scaffold as each traitor died in choking agony, their bodies hewn apart and decapitated before being dragged to their allotted graves. Even the vast crowd, so keen at first to see the traitors punished, grew weary in the end. Some near the platform cried out to the executioner to let the last men hang until dead, 'For pity's sake!', while others turned away from the carnage in heaving disgust, or vomited where they stood. But Goodluck could see that the sheriff had no intention of deviating from his orders. His small eyes watched viciously as each man danced on the end of the hangman's rope, and his nod seemed given more quickly each time.

Eventually it was Babington's turn.

Trembling, his handsome face almost unrecognizable under the bruising and dirt, he shuffled forward to speak his last words. But his voice seemed to fail as he stared out at the crowd. His hands were bound behind his back while he gazed helplessly up at the sky, almost as though hoping to see an angel descend and save him from the agony he knew was waiting for him.

The rope having been placed about his neck, Babington cried out, '*Parce mihi, Domine Jesu!*' and then he was thrashing in mid-air, his eyes bulging in panic.

Goodluck had seen enough. He turned and elbowed his

way through the tight-packed, shouting crowd until he was clear of their madness and could breathe a sweet country air unpolluted by blood and shit and the acrid sweat of his fellow men. Suddenly queasy, he stopped to retch behind a young oak tree, then wiped his mouth and carried on more slowly through sunlit fields towards the city walls. What a sorry waste of life, he thought, and grieved for the violence of their deaths even while he knew it to be necessary. Lord Jesus had not spared Anthony Babington, despite his desperate last plea on the scaffold. For how else could this sorry charade have ended but in a traitor's death for them all? Without such dire and unspeakable punishments for rebellion against the Queen, she would have lost her throne long ago.

And if he had not managed to get word to Lucy and be released from the Tower, he too might have joined their sad band on the scaffold this morning.

Goodluck stared ahead at the smoky city, lying squat and snug between the glittering coils of the Thames. Life on this earth was short and needlessly brutal, and it sometimes seemed to him that he had little of it left to enjoy. He loved Lucy, and as more than simply the child he had been left to bring up. He owed his life to her courage. So why the hell had he allowed Walsingham to take her away and marry her off to that fool Jack Parker?

So you could not be tempted to marry her yourself, he thought savagely.

At least Parker was a boys' man. He was not interested in women. Or so Walsingham had repeatedly reassured him when he had arranged for the marriage to take place. Lucy should be safe enough at Parker's house for the time being, hidden away from John Twist, whose whereabouts were still unknown, but who was probably back in London by now.

And Lucy's reputation was safe, too. She was less likely

now to forfeit any future place at court for her mistake in lying wantonly with Will Shakespeare. That prize must be worth the weight of any rushed, clandestine marriage to a youth she neither knew nor could love.

Two

SEATED AT HIS WORKSHOP BENCH, CLAD IN AN OLD SHEEPSKIN jacket and woollen cap, his father looked up blankly as Will ducked his head through the low doorway, glad to get out of the rain which had been falling mistily all morning.

John Shakespeare did not recognize his son.

'How may I serve you, sir?' he asked politely, setting aside the rectangle of kidskin he had been stretching over the wooden shaper.

The cramped workshop was just as it had been when Will had left it, the stink of new hides soaking in buckets in the passageway, fine skins hanging from the ceiling, ready to be cut and shaped, a rack of ready-made gloves for sale on the front counter, his father's workbench cluttered with tacks, pins, several lengths of gold lace and bobbins of gold thread to match. On a separate shelf near the wall were his glover's tools, a confusing array of knives, clippers, shapers, moulds, wooden patterns, and the curved steel needles he used for threading rough cowmen's mittens in the cold season. Will remembered picking up each of these curious implements with interest, when forced to work there as a boy, and asking what they were for. Now he looked on them with nostalgia, so very

417

different from the tools he used in the theatre, the ramshackle chests of properties and costumes, the torn script rolls and the blunted knives they used for stage fights.

'Hello, Father.' He threw down his pack and stooped to embrace John Shakespeare. 'Your grey hair's turning white. Have I been away that long? Master Burbage swears by the liberal application of coal dust to ward off grey hairs. Though it never seems to work for him.'

'Will!' His father held him close. 'Yes, I've an old man's head these days. But at least it's still on my shoulders. Let me look at you, son. I did not recognize you at first, standing there in your fine clothes like a stranger from the city. I see your chest is broader . . . and you seem to have more height.'

'Perhaps I am becoming a man at last,' Will said drily.

'With three children to your name, I would have hoped you were already a man,' his father remarked, getting to his feet, a sour note to his voice.

'How is Anne?' Will enquired idly, picking up one of the half-made gloves on the workbench and examining it. Will could see it would be a ladies' glove, to be embroidered with gold thread and jewels, and stitched finely with thick gold lace at the cuff. It might fetch as much as twenty-five shillings from a noble buyer. 'And my children?'

'Much as they were when you were last in Stratford. The twins were crawling when you left, were they not? Yes, well, now they can both *walk*,' John Shakespeare told him grimly as he plucked the soft kid glove from his hands, placing it carefully back on his workbench alongside its unstitched twin. 'They create havoc wherever they go. Hamnet no longer wakes in the night though, Lord be praised. The sound of his cry through the walls . . . I swear, some nights it was all I could do not to strangle my own grandson.'

'Hamnet has been unwell?' Will asked, at once uneasy.

418

'Not unwell, but missing his father.' John turned, a quick smile on his lips as a slender, solemn-eyed child came to the door and stood nervously staring up at Will. 'Ah, Susanna! See who it is? Your father has come home at last. Go fetch your mother.' He threw out his arm as she turned to obey. 'No, wait. Kiss your father first. He has travelled a long way and will be glad of a kiss from his eldest daughter, I'm sure.'

Susanna came forward hesitantly, looking up at Will as though he might suddenly disappear again.

'Papa?'

Will went down on one knee to embrace his daughter, and felt her thin body quiver against his, narrow as a willow wand. Her wispy hair tickled his chin like feathers. There was nothing to the child but air, he thought. She was so fragile, he could have snapped her in two with his bare hands. But of course she was still only three years old.

Three years and two months.

Was it so short a time since her birth? It seemed like for ever since that hot summer's day when his mother had come to the top of the stairs with a whimpering bundle in her arms. Indeed, this whole town was a faraway world he had half-forgotten in the noise and rumble of London.

'I have missed you so much, Susanna. I left a child wailing at the door. But now I see you have grown into a beautiful and brave young lady,' he whispered in her ear, then looked into her face. 'Can you find your mother for me?'

She nodded, then turned and ran out of the workshop, her reedy voice lisping, 'Mama! Mama!'

Will frowned, glancing out of the workshop door and along the echoing passageway into the backyard. It struck him that the place seemed curiously empty. Vats and half-barrels had been stacked against the whitewashed wall, narrowing the passage into the yard so that only a handcart could have been dragged through. A cap and leather apron hung from a peg just under the lip of the thatch, beyond which a fine autumn drizzle was beginning to darken the soil of the vegetable plot. A brown-speckled house spider had spun its web across the top of the wooden peg and was sitting in the middle of it, dancing occasionally as the breeze plucked at each gossamer thread. The yard was empty, and although he could hear voices from inside the adjoining house, they were all high-pitched female ones.

'Father, where is your apprentice?' he asked, thinking of the sullen-faced youth who had watched him with such resentment on his last few visits home. 'What was the lad's name?'

'Edward Bowden,' his father supplied quietly. Having covered his work tools with a cloth, he wound the unused length of expensive gold lace about his hand, pinned it carefully through the middle, then slipped the bundle into a wicker casket on the workbench. 'He had to leave. Decided being a glover wasn't for him.'

Will's eyes narrowed. 'After all but three years served? He won't find many master craftsmen willing to take him on if that's how he behaves.'

He felt an agonizing twist of jealousy and wondered again if the lad had enjoyed dealings with Anne while he was safely out of town.

Surely, though, his father would have written to him at once if that had been the case?

But perhaps he would have sent young Edward packing and said nothing, not wishing to disrupt their home any further by bearing tales of adultery to Will.

'What's done is done,' John Shakespeare muttered, without any heat in his voice, and shut the lid of the wicker casket. 'The lad changed his mind and chose to break his apprenticeship. I pressed no charges, nor asked for compensation, but let him go at once. Where would have been the sense in trying to stop him? Besides, I still hope to see one of my own boys here in the workshop alongside me. But so far not one of you has shown any inclination to enter the gloving trade. Even though life would be much easier for us all if you would only abandon this idle dream of companies and penny plays.'

Will smiled reluctantly. 'I'm sorry, Father. I'm a disappointment to you, I know. But once I've made enough to become a sharer in one of the new London companies, you'll see it was worth the past few years of hardship.'

'Shall we go through to the house?' His father hung up his apron. 'I can hear Anne on her way. Your mother will be fussing, too, for we were to have a simple supper tonight and now it must be the fatted calf.'

Crossing the passageway into the main house, Will was brought up short by the sight of an even smaller child in a dirty smock sitting cross-legged in the doorway and chewing on a piece of rag. A dark curly head turned enquiringly in his direction, and a husky voice chanted, 'Ba-ba! Ba-ba!'

Will crouched, coming to his level. 'Master Hamnet?' He picked the boy up in his arms and laughed as the dark eyes glared at his face in brooding accusation. 'You look just like your mother, about to demand why I've been away so long!'

'And why *have* you been away so long?' his wife asked, standing behind the boy.

He looked at her, suddenly as deeply in love with her as ever, drinking in the upward curve of her brows, her pale, delicate skin. Anne's hands and apron were stained with reddish-black marks, and her face was thinner than he remembered, but she looked remarkably beautiful for a woman caught at her cooking.

'Because I am a fool,' Will said simply, and leaned forward to kiss her.

The child between them screamed in indignation, 'Ba-ba! Ba-ba!' and rocked violently.

Anne disengaged quickly from his kiss. She bent her head to tend to Hamnet instead, hushing the child with a few muttered words.

Her cheeks seemed flushed as she straightened. 'I'm glad you're back, Will. But I can't talk now. I was just making some blackberry and apple dumplings and cannot leave them to spoil. Excuse me, Father,' she murmured, addressing John Shakespeare, then turned away and disappeared back into the house.

Hamnet screamed again as soon as his mother was gone, his cheeks damp with tears, his fat lower lip trembling.

'Come, Hamnet,' John said drily, and stooped to take the child's grubby hand. 'Let's see if we can find your grandmother. She may have a slice of apple for you, or a piece of bread to chew. Would you like that?'

Will stood a while on the dim, draughty threshold where Anne had spurned him, unable to bring himself to enter the house. He felt like a child, a boy again, not sure what to do or say, lost and bewildered by Anne's cold demeanour.

Anne could not possibly know of his infidelity with Lucy Morgan. So what was this distance between them? Had Anne truly grown closer to his father's apprentice than she ought to have done?

The thought was like a knife to his groin. It had been one thing to suspect such doings in London, when she was hundreds of miles away in Warwickshire. But here she was only a few yards away in the house, close enough to be questioned, for the truth to be seen in her face. He did not want to believe it of Anne, to imagine her in bed with another man. But it would explain why John Shakespeare had sent Edward Bowden away before he had finished serving out his apprenticeship.

Will groaned and leaned his forehead against the rough wall of the passageway. He felt sick. He began to question why he could see his wife's eyes in his son's face, yet nothing of himself, and surprised a terrible anger building inside. In a moment of madness, he considered how it might feel to take Anne's slender neck between his fingers and tighten his grip until the light died in her eyes. He knew men for whom such a punishment would be just, perhaps even tacitly applauded. A man might stray from the marriage bed, and frequently did, but never a wife. Not if the woman valued her life. Yet was that how he wished this to end? For him, William Shakespeare, to lose his temper and murder his wife for her adultery? For that crime would surely follow if he allowed this seething rage to escape the confines of his mind.

His father came back. 'What is it? Are you unwell?'

He could not tell his father what was in his heart, but kept his face averted. 'I'm tired, that's all,' he lied. 'Perhaps after a sleep—'

'Talk to her,' his father advised him, never slow at understanding. He put a hand on Will's shoulder and squeezed. 'Tell Anne how much you love her and have missed her. Women are always cold after a long absence. She'll come around.'

'Is that all it is?'

His father shrugged, and now he could not lift his eyes to Will's face.

He knows the truth, Will realized. His rage began to ebb away, faced with his father's calm reason. A memory came to him of a passage in Ovid, the death of the unfortunate Actaeon, transformed into a stag for spying on the goddess Diana and torn apart by his own hunting dogs. The divine madness of love's jealousy had touched him today, but he would not become a beast. He was still a man, with reason and forgiveness at his disposal, and he would act like one.

'Just talk to her,' his father repeated, adding reluctantly, 'Don't try to sort this out in the bedroom.'

'Father!'

They both laughed, then John Shakespeare peered out under the low-hanging thatch. 'Look, the rain has almost stopped now. Take a walk along the river with her towards Shottery, like you did when you were courting, and ask Anne to speak her mind where no one but you and God can hear. That is what a woman needs most when she is troubled. A space in which to make peace with her heart.'

The River Avon was as beautiful as ever that autumn, greyish-white and swollen by rain, each overgrown clump of weeds streaming away in the fast-running current like green pennants under the water. Will and Anne walked along the river bank for half a mile in silence, not touching, though a few times her hand brushed his by accident and was instantly snatched away.

Don't try to sort this out in the bedroom, his father had told him. What had he meant by that? If Will had taken Anne straight upstairs to bed, as he had done on every previous visit home, would she have refused to grant him his conjugal rights? The thought chafed at him, and he stole little glances at her sideways as they walked, trying to gauge the depth of her disinterest.

He still wanted her. The tug of his body on seeing her again had been proof enough of that. But would he have to force Anne to lie with him tonight? And if he did, what icy and resentful looks would tomorrow hold?

The ground was sodden, so they sat to rest on a fallen trunk a little way from the ford. They had sat there before, though never in such poor weather. The sky was grey and unpromising, suggestive of more rain yet to come that evening. In the pasture opposite, they could hear the high, staccato whistle of the herdsman, who had come with his dogs to move the sheep; the animals were huddled together under the vast canopy of a chestnut, their hooves churning up the mud and debris of split conker shells as the two dogs hemmed them in, driving them down towards the ford for watering.

The fallen beech trunk on which Will and Anne were sitting was partially hollow, the wood rotting slowly into the ground. When Will prised loose a piece of bark, he discovered a colony of tiny creatures wiggling beneath, small black beetles and whitish grubs, red-headed ants and centipedes.

'A whole civilization in miniature, lurking in darkness under a bark sky,' he murmured, showing Anne what he had found. It was a sight he had often delighted in as a boy, digging down to uncover intricate ants' nests in the dirt of the backyard or peering inside hollow trees forked by lightning to see what burrowing creatures might have made their homes inside. 'A world within a world.'

She looked disgusted. 'Ugh. Cover it up before they get on my gown.'

'Look, is that a money spider?' The little spider crawled over his sleeve and away across the rotting bark. He kept his voice light. 'The auspices are good, it seems. We shall be lucky in our coffers, if not in love.'

Anne looked at him then, her arched brows level for once. 'I wondered when you would come to the point. What has your father been saying? He's such a busybody. Did he write to you about me?'

'No.' Very carefully, Will replaced the piece of bark, bringing a merciful darkness back to the world of beetles and grubs. He rubbed his gloved hands together to remove the dirt. 'Should he have done? I take it you have something to confess?'

She remained silent, her face turned away.

'Though he did tell me of Edward Bowden's departure,' he added, watching her profile.

'And can you blame me if I looked aside at times?' Anne asked, shocking him with her sudden bluntness. 'You are never here these days and I am lonely. Until Susanna was born, I was content to be your wife, to carry your children and help your mother with the household. But I am not made of stone, Will Shakespeare. Our marriage bed has been cold since you left for London. I may not have a man's needs, but I do wish for love and the warmth of my husband's body on a winter's night!'

He stared, seeing the flush in her cheeks. 'So you admit it? You have slept with this boy? This apprentice?'

Shifting on the trunk to look at him, Anne said nothing, but gripped the sides of the fallen tree with her own gloved hands as though afraid she might fall. She was breathing rapidly, her eyes fixed on his face, her mouth working silently.

Such small, delicate hands, he thought, noticing the uneven stitching on the white kidskin gloves. It was not his father's tidy work, he realized, nor his mother's either, who often helped with the sewing in the evenings.

'Did he make those for you?'

She flushed then, and he knew it for a sign of her shame and guilt. 'They were a parting gift from Edward, yes.'

'Why?' he asked simply. 'Why betray me?'

'I have already told you,' she said, and he wondered at the sudden vehemence in her voice, as though Anne blamed him for her infidelity. 'I needed to feel alive again, not shut up in that house day after day like an old widow. Edward was always there . . . smiling at me, *listening* to me. I knew what he wanted, of course, and I never meant

426

to let him have it, I swear on my life. It was just flattering to know that a man could still want me like that. And you were so far away, sometimes I felt like I'd dreamt you.'

'Did you dream our children, too?'

She looked at him, raising her chin. 'What will you do to me now that you know? You can't throw me out. It would kill your father if my shame was made public. That's why he sent Edward away, to stop the gossips talking about us in the marketplace.'

'I imagine they'll talk anyway,' he commented, knowing what Stratford was like when a salacious story went round about one of its residents.

She hesitated, then laid her hand on his. 'Not if we show them we are still together.'

Will looked down at her gloved hand, the soft white kidskin against his own coarser cowhide.

'I can understand why Edward Bowden fell in love with you and why my father sent him away,' he remarked. 'I was only a little older than him when we were first courting, do you remember? I was so insanely in love back then. You were everything to me, Anne. When I started touring with the companies, I would think of you every night and couldn't wait to come home to see you again, to lie against you at night. You were my rock that first year in London. I was so hotheaded too, I would have given my life to defend your honour if any man had dared to cast a slur on it.' He laughed. 'Me, quiet bookish Will!'

Anne bent her head. 'I'm sorry. I didn't want to hurt you.'

'Didn't you?'

She looked up then, and bit her lip. 'Maybe a little,' she admitted. 'But I didn't mean to destroy our marriage. It was done before I knew it. One minute I was telling him of how lonely I felt without you, and the next he was kissing me.'

Will pulled his hand free from hers. 'I don't want to hear about it,' he said, as evenly as he could.

The stab of jealousy had returned, thrusting deep into his gut with every word she spoke, and Will feared where that anger might lead. Yet his heart felt empty, his senses too bewildered to act. Perhaps this was how it always felt to fall out of love with one's wife.

'It's enough to know that it happened,' he continued, 'and will never happen again. You understand me? Never again, Anne, or I swear I'll kill both of you.'

Anne wiped away the last of her tears, then sat up, rigid now and straight-backed. She stared at the swollen river, where a family of swans were drifting past in their severe white plumage. The swans looked beautiful and ethereal, like ghosts on the water, though Will knew from experience that they were violent, unpredictable birds if approached too closely.

'I cannot promise you that, Will,' she told him. 'Edward has left Stratford though, and sworn to your father that he will never come back, so you're safe enough.' Her smile was cold. 'I know my place. Your parents' house is my prison, and your children my jailors. If you will not leave London and come back home to Stratford, then I must do my duty and live out my days as a player's widow.'

He stood and waited while she composed herself, then they began to walk back along the river.

'The twins,' he asked, 'are they mine or his?'

Anne seemed shocked by the directness of his question. 'Yours, of course,' she managed, but he sensed a moment's hesitancy beneath her answer and was sickened by it.

Where the channel narrowed at the next bend in the river, the family of swans came alongside them. Their long white necks craned in and out of the weed-infested river, their webbed feet paddling swiftly but with apparent effortlessness. One of the larger swans surfaced with a trail

428

of slimy weed caught in his beak, and Will guessed he had been fishing. The younger ones skirted close to the bank, smaller-chested and grey-feathered, curious to see who these visitors were, staring up at Will and Anne before swimming back to their parents again.

'There are hundreds of white swans on the Thames, most of them clustered around the arches of London Bridge all summer,' Will remarked, stopping to watch as the swans lost interest and swam slowly back downstream. 'No one dares hunt them, for they belong to the Queen. Each year dozens are caught and plucked to fill all the Queen's feather mattresses and pillows.'

'What a thing it must be,' Anne murmured at his side, 'to wake up every morning in a soft feather bed, and know you are a queen.'

Three

The Earl of Southampton's residence, London, October 1586

THE RIVERSIDE WALK OF THE OLD PALACE WAS LIT BY FLAMING torches, their thickly smoking lights reflected on the dark swell of the Thames just beyond the wall.

Elizabeth walked to the far end, gazing across to the busy south bank of the Thames, where ferry boats and small craft illuminated by single torches bobbed at anchor on the incoming tide, waiting for fares back to the city after the pleasure houses closed for the night. The gates into the city from London Bridge were locked at dusk, so a boat would be the only way for roving gentlemen to return to their wives. Elizabeth grimaced. She did not know precisely what happened in such places, but had been told that many of her own courtiers frequented the newly established 'houses of Venus' across the river. There seemed little anyone could do to discourage this practice, for the city fathers had no jurisdiction over the south bank, and the private landowners there appeared to be on friendly terms with certain members of the Privy Council.

Staring out over the water, Elizabeth raised a pomander which hung about her neck to her nose, attempting to dispel the greasy stench of the river. She ought to go back inside, she thought, knowing that the nobles would be wondering why she had fled the room. But the breeze here was refreshing after the stuffy interior of the old palace, and it was a relief to be alone with her thoughts after the usual tiresome conversations about how the conflict in the Low Countries was going. It seemed to be the court's only topic of conversation these days, with two questions paramount in everyone's mind: how the struggle against the Spanish was going – badly, though no one had yet dared venture such a perilous opinion to her face – and when it would end. Never, at this rate.

'Are you cold, Your Majesty?' Cecil, Lord Burghley, came to her side, interrupting her thoughts. 'Perhaps you would like me to escort you back to the banqueting hall?'

Elizabeth glanced at her treasurer impatiently, then realized she was indeed shivering in the chill October air. Besides, Lord Burghley was right to be concerned. Now more than ever, she should be making an effort to seem like a strong queen, able to command respect from her troops and her people. She abhorred weakness of any kind, and this desire to escape her duties was a weakness she would not tolerate.

'Yes, very well,' Elizabeth agreed, and allowed him to lead her back inside. 'You must write and thank young Henry on my behalf for his hospitality tonight. Your ward is still at Cambridge?'

'St John's College,' Lord Burghley agreed.

'Let us hope he is not tempted to fall into Roman ways like his late father. Rarely have I known a more stubborn and unruly earl.' She brooded a moment on past dis-loyalties. 'Henry must be presented at court after he has finished his studies, Cecil, and nurtured in the Protestant faith. Too many of our noblemen have been lost to that old cause.'

'I will see to it, Your Majesty.'

The old palace had belonged to one of her father's bishops before she was born, but was now the property of the wealthy young Earl of Southampton. Poor boy! His father, the second Earl of Southampton, had been accused and imprisoned for various acts of treachery over the years, and once even suspected of harbouring that tiresome priest Edmund Campion. A careful man though, he had been hard to convict, and she did not want his son Henry to follow the same path into ruin. At least under Lord Burghley's guardianship that now seemed unlikely.

While the boy was at Cambridge, she was often invited to dine at his charming residency on the Thames, its renovations currently being overseen by Cecil. New white stucco covered the cracked red brick outside, making the vast, warren-like building feel less dark and oppressive as winter approached. Yet it seemed nothing could be done about the ancient fireplace in the Great Hall, which had smoked relentlessly throughout tonight's banquet. Indeed, the hall had become so thick with smoke, Elizabeth had been forced to rise from her seat soon after the seventh course had been served, sweeping out on to the paved riverside walk to escape it.

Now she seated herself at the head of the table and waved the nobles to sit again, for they had stood and bowed as she re-entered the room. The air was clearer, and the minstrels were playing in the gallery above the banqueting table. She looked down at the creamy, frothing liquid in the cup that had been placed before her by the food taster, his solemn bow indicating that it was safe for her to eat.

'What is this?'

'Your Majesty,' Helena murmured, seated just down

from her on the left, 'it is a lemon syllabub. A little tart on the tongue, but very refreshing.'

'Well, we must enjoy the lemons while we have them,' Elizabeth told her, lifting the cup and sniffing avidly. The sharp scent of citrus filled her senses, reminding her at once of sunshine and the pleasure of warm summer evenings spent in her palace gardens. 'Winter is on its way. There is a distinct chill to the air tonight.'

There was a noise at the door. One of the nobles at the far end rose from the table and dealt with it. He came back after a moment, and bent to whisper in Lord Burghley's ear. Elizabeth felt herself shivering again, despite the warmth of the vast log fire that illuminated the banqueting table and cast shadows in every corner.

Lord Burghley came to her side. 'Your Majesty,' he said gravely, 'there is a messenger at the door. He went to Whitehall first, then came here in search of you. He bears a letter from Lord Leicester. An urgent letter, Your Majesty.'

'A letter that could not wait until the morning?' she demanded, then saw the stricken grief in his face. 'What is it, Cecil? For heaven's sake, do not keep it from me. What is the news?'

'It might be better, Your Majesty, if we were to go aside with this messenger,' Lord Burghley murmured, and stood to pull back her chair so she could rise. 'And perhaps take one or two of your ladies with you?'

Her heart contracted with fear. Clearly some terrible news had been received, so appalling that Lord Burghley dared not speak of it before the other nobles. Her mind ran feverishly ahead as she left the hall, clicking her fingers at Helena to take up her train and follow her outside. Elizabeth could see the messenger now, waiting in the corridor. Even in the darkness, his face seemed hollow with grief and pain.

Was Robert wounded? So badly perhaps that he had written to take his final leave of her . . . ?

Lord Burghley found a small candlelit library where she could receive the messenger without fear of being overheard. He ushered them all inside, closed the door, and urged the exhausted messenger to hand over the letter.

'Your Majesty,' the man breathed, sinking to his knees before her and dragging a rolled-up parchment from his dispatch bag. There was dried blood on his face, and his clothes were spattered with mud. 'This missive was written by Lord Leicester himself. He bade me hand it to no one but the Queen.'

'You have come straight from the battlefield?' she asked, taking the letter with unsteady hands.

'Yes, Your Majesty.'

'How goes it?'

Warily, the messenger looked from her to Lord Burghley, then back again. He licked his lips. 'Not well when I left, Your Majesty.'

'Take some wine before you go,' she instructed him, glad to hear how calm her voice sounded. 'And tell the steward to serve you a good supper at the Queen's command. Whatever costs you have incurred, they will be reimbursed.'

'Thank you, Your Majesty.'

She handed the parchment silently to Lord Burghley, not trusting herself to read Robert's letter without breaking down. He must have already ascertained the general gist of its contents before it was delivered to her, for Lord Burghley showed no surprise as he unrolled it and read through it by candlelight.

His face was grim as he turned back to her. 'It is the worst of news, Your Majesty. Sir Philip Sidney is dead from the wound he received last month at the battle of Zutphen.'

Elizabeth stared. 'Pip?' she faltered. 'What, dead so young? And his wife heavy with child?'

'It is a tragedy, both for England and for those of us who loved him dearly,' Burghley agreed sombrely. He glanced down at the letter. 'His brother was with him at the end, and Lady Sidney too, the poor gentlewoman. Lord Leicester is sending her back to England once her strength has returned, for he fears she may give birth prematurely after this shock. No doubt Lady Sidney will return to her father's house for her lying-in, which cannot be far off. This will be a hard blow indeed for Walsingham. He always embraced Philip as the son he never had.'

'I pray his grandson may be born safely, then,' Elizabeth said, and turned away to hide her tears.

Lord Burghley dismissed the messenger, then handed her back the letter once the door had closed behind the man. 'I am sorry to disturb you further in your distress over this news, Your Majesty. But you will see from his letter that Lord Leicester asks to return to England at once. As we suspected, the campaign has not gone well this year. He says he has supported the rebels in their fight against the Spanish, as our treaty with the Dutch demanded, but the numbers are against them. And the conditions worsen daily as the rains continue. His lordship claims the English troops will not survive another winter out there.'

'He asks to withdraw?' She was aghast, scanning the letter with only half her attention on its contents. Robert's handwriting was so familiar, the loops and slants were darts that pierced her heart. She held the parchment against her chest and closed her eyes, inhaling. This had been written hundreds of miles away on a battlefield in a foreign land, yet she fancied she could catch Robert's scent on it, that musky tang of leather and horses that always seemed to surround him.

And now dear, sweet Pip was dead. A wound taken in

battle last month that had festered and refused to heal. She read the letter again more carefully. Brave and impatient to be in battle again, the young man had not taken as much care with the wound as he should have done. After a few weeks, gangrene had set in and killed him.

Her body ached with the knowledge that she would never again see Sir Philip Sidney's handsome face at court, nor watch him dance so elegantly that his feet seemed to fly across the floor, nor hear his delightful, intelligent poetry recited in the evenings to the gentle plucking of a lute string.

But Robert was still alive. Alive and asking to be allowed to return to England, she reminded herself.

If she denied him, would his death be the next bad news to arrive from Utrecht?

She could not stand to lose Robert. The very thought of his death wrenched at her heart. It would be a loss like none other she had ever suffered.

Elizabeth signalled Helena to stand apart from them. She murmured to Lord Burghley, 'How bad is it out there, do you think? Can we afford to withdraw our troops? I do not wish England to look weak.'

'It is a matter for the Privy Council, Your Majesty.'

'Yes, yes,' she said impatiently, then pursed her lips. 'I will write to Robert myself tonight. The messenger is to be given clean clothes and a bed, and a speedy passage back to the Lowlands tomorrow. Robert must come home as soon as possible and carry Sir Philip Sidney's body with him. Let the ship be draped in mourning cloth and have black sails. There will be a state funeral for the poor boy, with a marble tomb and mourners lining the streets. He was one of our most glorious young English noblemen and deserves to be remembered as such. You and Robert can see to the arrangements between you.'

Lord Burghley stiffened, but bowed. She knew he would

wait and try to beat her down on the expense later, when her feelings were less inflamed. For now it salved her guilty conscience to think of her dearest Pip coming home wrapped in cloth-of-gold and under guard, to be laid like a young prince in a marble tomb at St Paul's Cathedral.

'Your Majesty,' he ventured, 'should you not wait for the Council to decide what is to be done before writing to Lord Leicester?'

'The Privy Council may decide whatever they wish,' Elizabeth replied coldly, and strode to the door, Helena hurrying behind to snatch up the extravagantly laced and beaded train of her gown. 'If this wasteful death of our most shining youth tells us anything, it is that life is short and we must not squander a moment of what has been granted to us by the grace of God Almighty.' She turned in the doorway, and caught him frowning. 'Oh, away with that long face, Cecil. You may deliberate on the campaign all you wish with the other councillors. But I have been without my right hand too long. I am the Queen, and I will have Robert back at my side before Christmas.'

Four

SOMEWHERE IN THE DARK, JUMBLED MAZE OF SMALL-holdings clustered against the city walls, a cock began to crow. A few moments later, another joined it. Light had begun to glimmer behind the shutters half an hour before, but Lucy had not moved, lying there with an arm over her eyes, trying not to keep dwelling on the people whose faces she missed most here in Aldgate: Will Shakespeare, her dear friend Cathy, and Master Goodluck.

The church bell tolled the hour and Jack Parker stirred beside her, half propped up on pillows. The light was stronger now, and there could be no pretending that the day had not begun in earnest. A fat black spider dropped from the roof beams on to the coverlet and began to scrabble hurriedly across the weave. Jack stared at the spider for a moment, his eyes bleary with sleep, then brushed it to the floor.

'Tell me it's not dawn yet,' he mumbled, and wiped drool from his mouth. 'My head! I don't remember coming to bed last night. I wasn't alone at the Swan though, I'm sure of it. Who did I bring home?'

'I don't know,' Lucy replied tersely, and swung her legs out of bed, desperate to relieve herself.

She knew her insensitive young husband would not leave the room while she performed this necessary function, so she contented herself with squatting over the chamber pot behind a latticed screen. When she had finished, she came out and found him out of his nightshirt but not yet dressed, bent over the washbowl with nothing on. His nudity was not a sight she had grown used to yet, nor did she wish to. Carefully, Lucy averted her eyes. It was strange to live in such intimacy with a man who never so much as looked at her breasts. But true to Will's promise, Jack Parker was oblivious to her as a woman. His reasons for marrying her did seem to be the opportunity for a reconciliation with his parents – and the generous dowry handed to him by Walsingham himself on the night of their wedding.

Squeezing into her workaday gown and apron – and finding both increasingly hard to fasten as her girth swelled ever broader – Lucy hurried down to light the fire and bake the first bread of the day. Jack came whistling down the stairs after her and went straight out of the house, stealing an apple from the barrel and munching on it as he left.

'I'll be back in time for supper,' he threw over his shoulder. 'Well, most likely.'

Laying out fresh logs and kindling on the hearth, Lucy stiffened at the tiny fluttering sensation under her apron. She had felt it a few times now, and knew it must be the baby kicking.

Hesitant, she straightened and laid a hand on the top of her hard belly. She felt the fluttering again.

'Hush,' she whispered. 'Hush, little one.'

It felt strange, talking to an invisible being who was not even in existence yet. Yet she felt sure her own mother must have done the same when Lucy herself was in the womb, for it felt like the natural thing to do.

She looked up with a start to find Jack's stout mother, Mistress Parker, watching her from the doorway. The woman's face was tight with disapproval under her wife's cap.

Mistress Parker swept forward and folded her arms across her plain bodice, shaking her head at the cold hearth. 'Not lit the fire yet? Am I to do everything for you? When Jack said he was bringing home a wife, I thought my work would be lessened. But you're always sitting down and daydreaming instead of doing your chores. And now you're talking to yourself. It seems to me you're as much of a good-for-nothing slattern as any of the whores up at the theatre. Now, look sharp and make dough for Master Parker's nuncheon!'

She shoved Lucy towards the table. 'When you've done that, you can help me with the washing.'

'Yes, Mother,' Lucy said, docilely enough, and stood to measure out the flour, yeast and water for that day's bread.

As soon as Mistress Parker had bustled outside to complain loudly about her new daughter to a passing neighbour, Lucy sat down and slipped off her wooden clogs, rubbing her swollen feet and ankles. She found it hard, carrying a baby, though she knew that once the child was born she would be less unhappy. It was not that she didn't want the child. It was just that she felt so large and cumbersome, and her new clumsiness was becoming noticeable, with chairs knocked over and bowls accidentally smashed. She was forever needing to relieve herself too, so that walking down to the marketplace was a severe trial, especially when Mistress Parker stopped every few yards to discuss her with another crowd of strangers, explaining how her son had brought home an ugly black-skinned wife with a child already heavy in her belly. 'But what is one to do when Jack is so lusty and virile?' she would ask, mock-piteously, barely able to conceal her delight that her son had finally proved his manhood by siring a child.

The delighted shock and curiosity with which the Parkers' neighbours stared at her left Lucy feeling sick, and even more like a breeding sow than ever.

Before Mistress Parker could catch her sitting, Lucy wearily stood up and went back to rolling and kneading the day's dough.

It seemed like another age when she had danced before the court, so light on her feet that visiting lords and ambassadors had gasped to see her volta and gavotte, and the Queen herself had rewarded her with jewels and gifts of rich gowns for her performances.

She was growing more rotund and slower-moving with every week that passed, anchored to the ground by the child in her belly. Though she no longer wished to dance. Indeed, she was content to sit still, for she soon became breathless when forced to climb stairs or walk to the market with her shopping basket, or even mend linen besides the Parkers' smoky hearth in the evenings.

And all because she had been fool enough to fall in love with Will Shakespeare.

'That's enough, you stupid girl!' Mistress Parker exclaimed, pinching her arm so hard that Lucy yelped. 'You'll over-knead it if you carry on. Cover the dough with a damp muslin and put it aside now, down by the hearth. Then we've to wash the household linen before it walks off down the street on its own. You must make fresh soap for a washing ball, for we've only enough left for one more washday. Then you're to clean the sheets and coverings, and hang them out from the windows to dry. I'll tend to Jack's shirts myself. They need a delicate touch.'

Lucy swallowed her resentment and dampened a thin scrap of muslin to cover the dough while it rose. Making soap, then washing the bedsheets and other linen, those were the harder tasks, yes. But at least it would ease her thoughts of Will to be working so diligently.

'Yes, Mother.'

She set about making the washing ball, an arduous process involving ash and animal fat that took several hours of mixing and boiling in a vat. Then she fetched two buckets of water from the river and began layering the household linen inside the washtub as carefully as she knew how, while Mistress Parker stood over her, arms folded, inhaling sharply through her nose.

'Not so tight, not so tight,' she muttered at one point. 'The soap cannot reach every part if you cram them all in together like that, higgledy-piggledy, nor will the dirty water have a chance to drain away properly afterwards.' She tutted, bending to show Lucy the correct way to lay the linen round the edges. 'Merciful heavens, child, did your mother never teach you how to pack a washtub?'

'My mother died when I was born,' Lucy replied shortly, fetching the first bucket. 'She taught me nothing except how to breathe.'

Mistress Parker looked at her, shaking her head. 'Well,' she sniffed, turning away as Lucy poured water into the tub. 'It will do.'

Leaving the linen to soak near the fire, Lucy took up the twiggy broom and swept the dead leaves, soiled rushes and other debris into the street. It was a task she performed at least once a week, for Mistress Parker insisted on keeping a clean house. It was late November and the air was chill, though with the sweat on her forehead she barely felt the cold.

Looking up with an aching back, Lucy saw a cloaked man with a feathered cap standing in the doorway of one of the houses across the street. He appeared to be watching her, his gaze intent under bushy eyebrows. Lucy stared back at him, suddenly remembering that she had passed the same man on the corner yesterday, coming back from the marketplace. Bearded and with a scar below his right eye, he had been smoking a pipe while his gaze wandered along the narrow row of houses. The house in whose doorway he was now sheltering stood empty; the occupants having left for the country a few weeks back. So what was his business there, and why was he watching the Parkers' home?

Unhurried, the man turned away and disappeared down the street.

Lucy went inside and shut the door. She leaned against it for a moment, considering whether or not she had imagined the man's particular interest in her. After all, there were few black women in London. Perhaps she had lived too long at court, where every whisper was a plot, and hostile eyes watched through each secret gap and crack. Then Mistress Parker called her to take the washing out of the tub, and for the next few hours she had nothing on her mind but the back-breaking task of rinsing and wringing out the linen, and hanging it from the windows and on racks about the fire to dry.

'Hurry, girl, or they will not be dry before bedtime,' Mistress Parker urged her from her fireside seat. 'Then we would have to put the second-best linen out instead, and the shame would kill me if one of my neighbours should happen to see its sorry state.'

Before Lucy had come to the Parkers' household, they had kept a young servant named Margery, but this girl had been sent away the day after Lucy arrived.

'Why pay a servant's keep when I have a daughter now?' Mistress Parker had remarked sharply when her husband had enquired after the absent girl. Then she had taken Lucy about the house, showing her the tasks Margery had been expected to do each day, and watched with un-disguised satisfaction as Lucy had laid away her old court

443

gowns in a chest. 'That's it. You will not be needing such finery here.'

Jack did not return for supper that night as he had promised; this was no longer a surprise to Lucy, for her husband rarely made his way home before midnight. At the end of their silent meal, she set his untouched trencher of spiced lamb and pulses on the hearth to keep warm, and carried the dirty pans to the sideboard to be scoured later. While Mistress Parker darned her woollen stockings by the light of the fire, Master Parker, a corpulent merchant's clerk in his late fifties, looked over the household accounts and complained that his wife was still spending too much on meat and candles.

'Be sure to take the bedlinen up when you go, Lucy,' Mistress Parker said, laying aside her needlework and yawning, 'and make up our beds.'

Exhausted, Lucy dropped a curtsy to them both and dragged herself upstairs with the guttering remains of a tallow candle stump and the stack of clean linen. She laid out and tucked in the bedsheets in a stupefied daze, then finally kicked off her clogs, and collapsed across her own bed without even unlacing her gown. A few moments later the tallow candle burned to the end of its stump, wreathing the darkness with foul smoke.

It felt like hours later when Lucy was woken by a crash from downstairs, for her body was stiff from lying in one position for so long.

She stumbled to the chamber door in the inky dark, sleepy and confused, and peered down the stairs. The Parkers had gone to bed, and the shadowy room below was lit only by the smouldering red ashes in the hearth.

'Jack?'

The door below was kicked shut, and she heard men's voices. It was Jack, she thought, with some relief. A spill was lit from the hot ashes and the room brightened a little with its sullen light. Lucy tiptoed down a few stairs and watched her husband cross to the wooden settle, then pick over his congealed lamb supper with the point of his dagger. He looked drunk but in good humour.

There was another man with him, wearing a dark hood and with his back towards the stairs, bending over the fire as though to revive it with fresh wood.

She came down and smiled warily as Jack looked up. 'I thought it must be you. It's very late. You brought a friend back?'

'Not a friend, no. I met this fellow at the Green Man,' Jack told her cheerfully, slurring his words. 'Or was it the Swan? Anyway, he was robbed in the street and his purse taken, can you believe it? The Watch are next to useless these days, they deserve to be beaten at their heels and thrown in the stocks. So my new friend here needs a bed for the night.'

Jack grinned at her horrified expression. 'Can you find him a blanket, dear wife? No need for you to stay up, I'll keep him company until the cock crows or we fall asleep on the settle. That will give my mother a rousing shock when she gets up in the morning!'

The 'fellow' turned to look at her, throwing back his hood to reveal a swarthy, familiar face, his eyes over-bright with drink, his mouth sneering.

Lucy shrank away. It was Master Twist.

'Well met, Lucy Morgan. Or should I call you Mistress Parker?' Twist grasped Jack by the arm as he tried to stagger away. 'Hold fast, my friend.'

'What are you doing here?' she asked in a despairing whisper. 'What do you want from me?'

His voice was oddly hoarse, his words more barked than spoken. 'I will admit, I was curious to visit you here. I wondered why Goodluck would marry you off at the first sign of a swollen belly when he could have kept you for himself. A cheap whore is such a luxury, I find. Then I made young Master Parker's acquaintance tonight, and Goodluck's reasoning became clear. No need for him to put up with a pregnant whore in his house, but no danger, either, of this rooster mounting his black hen.'

To her horror, Twist was slowly drawing his dagger, his left arm still entwined with Jack's.

'A cunning man indeed, your guardian,' he finished. 'But he will find me a match for his wit after this night's work.'

'Jack!' she begged her husband urgently, seeing the malice on Twist's face. 'Come away from that man, for pity's sake!'

Jack, still befuddled with drink, half-turned to look at his new friend. But he was given no chance for escape.

Slotting the dagger neatly into Jack's neck just above his white ruff, Master Twist stepped back as though to admire his handiwork.

'And so you become a widow,' he murmured. 'Forgive me, my young friend. I find you in the way. And it is a quick and relatively easy death, as deaths go.'

With a gargling, incoherent cry, Jack Parker fell to his knees, one hand trying to stem the blood spurting in great jets from the opened vein at his throat. His eyes bulged with fear and agony as he stared first at Twist, then at Lucy, his other hand flailing in her direction as though still hoping she could save him.

As Twist had predicted, it was over quickly. Jack collapsed face-forwards on to the rush-strewn floor, where blood began to pool about his head.

Lucy turned to run for the door, but Twist was already there, blocking her only escape route.

'Trying to escape your fate, my dear Lucy?' he asked with an unpleasant smile. He produced a kerchief and used it to wipe Jack's blood from his dagger. 'I fear that will not be possible. I had only intended to enjoy your body tonight. But it strikes me that if Goodluck can marry you off so easily, he will have no qualms over a simple rape. But your death, and the death of his child . . . That will send an even clearer message to your guardian that I am not a man he can betray with impunity.'

'He betrayed you?' she asked him as a distraction, glancing about the room for some kind of weapon. But even the rack of heavy cooking pans was several steps away. Twist would be able to catch and kill her before she could reach them.

'In a manner of speaking, he betrayed us both. Do you not know the story? Around the time you turned fourteen, I went to Goodluck and asked if I could marry you. I told him I was in love with you, but was prepared to wait another year or two if he did not feel you were ready for marriage. But your guardian would have none of it. He told me never to speak to you of my feelings or he would kill me.' Twist sneered. 'Before I could test that arrogant resolve, Goodluck packed you off to court. He deliberately allowed you to enter that foul circus, where I knew you would soon be debauched and your pretty innocence spoilt – and all to spite me!'

Trying not to alert Twist to her intention, Lucy took a tiny step backwards as his gaze wavered.

If she could reach the stairs and run up them quickly enough, there was a dagger under her pillow that she could use to defend herself. Her plan was unlikely to work, and Twist would stab her in the back before she could even reach the bed. But she would not stand and be slaughtered like a sheep, as poor Jack had been.

Lucy tried not to look down at the crumpled body in its bright-red pool of blood.

'I shall enjoy watching you die more slowly than your

young husband. For you to suffer pain is only right and fair, for you have injured me, as has your guardian.' He drew down his ruff a little and showed her his throat, which was red-raw and swollen. 'Goodluck tried to strangle me, and all because I wish to free this country from a heretic queen. Can you imagine that?'

She did not wait to hear more but ran for the stairs. He came easily after her, laughing. She was almost at the top when he caught her, spinning her round on the narrow stairs. Twist clamped a hand over her mouth, staring down at her malevolently.

'Don't make a sound!' he hissed in warning. 'Or I shall kill the old man and woman too. Is that what you want? A massacre?'

She shook her head, and he relaxed his suffocating grip over her mouth.

'Good girl,' he murmured. His smile was horrible. 'Now keep climbing and show me your bed. There's no one here to protect you, Lucy.'

She turned and took another step up towards her chamber. Her dagger was there. If she could reach it . . .

But what if she could not? What if he tied her up before she had a chance to find the dagger?

He was behind her on the dark stair, his breathing loud in the close space.

Lucy spun and chopped him hard in the face with the side of her hand, just as Goodluck had taught her, satisfied by the ominous crack that told her she had broken his nose.

'You bitch!'

Twist's eyes widened as he clutched his broken nose, streaming with blood, and tried to keep his balance. But it was too late. He could not save himself. As he toppled backwards, his hand snaked out to grab her wrist and he dragged her with him down the unlit stairs.

Lucy woke to screams and the sound of running feet, a chill draught on her face from the street. She could smell smoke from lit torches, and heard voices that came and went above her head, muffled in her nightmare. She tried to move and cried out in agony. It felt as though she had been kicked in the back by a horse, and there was some warm, sticky fluid under her cheek.

'This one's alive!' a man cried.

Someone put a hand to her neck, feeling for the beat of life. A deep, strong ripple of pain possessed her and Lucy groaned, her eyes closing.

'Bring a board!' the man's gruff voice ordered, and she recognized it as belonging to one of the neighbours. 'We must carry her upstairs and send for our wives to care for her.'

I am not dead yet, Lucy thought with some astonishment, and forced her eyes open in the acrid torchlight.

The house was full of neighbours running about or standing to gawp. Mistress Parker was kneeling beside her son's dead body, rocking back and forth, her face hidden in her apron as she gave vent to her noisy grief. Beyond her lay John Twist, his fury finished at last, a half-smile on his lip and his head bent back at an unnatural angle. His dead eyes stared accusingly up at the stairs.

She had killed a man.

The neighbours came back with an old plank of wood, arguing among themselves about whose wife should sit with the black girl. Lucy screamed when they lifted her on to it, mercifully passing out.

When she came to again, she was lying in her small bedchamber, a damp cloth pressed to her forehead and several scared-looking women clustered about the mattress. Jack's mother was nowhere in sight. Downstairs she could hear Master Parker's voice, raised angrily, and other men too, their arguments deep and urgent.

Lucy stared up at the women, seeing nothing but fear and hostility on their faces. Extravagantly, a new candle had been fetched up from Mistress Parker's store cupboard and lit, its meagre light illuminating their expressions.

'What's happening downstairs?' she managed to ask, her throat dry.

One of the women offered her a cup of ale. 'Only a sip, no more. That's it. The Watch has brought the coroner to certify the deaths and take away the bodies. The sergeant will want to talk to you, too,' she whispered. 'After.'

'After what?' Lucy asked her, feeling perplexed, then moaned deep in her throat as something cruel seemed to hook its claws into her womb and try to tear it out of her belly.

Lucy shook, clutching the bed for support while the ripple of pain lasted. The tearing sensation moved through her slowly and excruciatingly, leaving her shocked and trembling, no longer able even to speak. The memory of Twist's attack disappeared in that moment, leaving Lucy with nothing but the inner certainty of her own death.

The woman dipped the cloth in a basin of water and dabbed her face with it again.

'After the baby has been born,' she explained in a matter-of-fact way. 'Now lie still and let us tie your wrists to the bed. No, you'll see, it will be better this way.' Her brown eyes were wide and sorrowful. 'The child is coming earlier than it should. You must prepare yourself to be strong.'

Five

IT WAS LATE AT NIGHT WHEN ELIZABETH FINALLY HEARD THE sound she had been waiting for in the courtyard below the state apartments at Greenwich Palace. Too nervous to go to bed, she had been playing chequers with Lady Helena for the past hour, soothed a little by Anne's voice as she sang to the lute. But time had dragged as she waited, wondering if she should have her ladies make her ready for bed, for it seemed unlikely that anyone would arrive so late at court.

Jumping up, she strode to the window and looked down at the treacle-black ribbon of river between the palace walls and the north bank. There was a commotion in the yard below, shouts and running feet, but she could see only torches flaming in the darkness and a handful of round-bellied boats being tied up alongside the riverside gate.

'Is it him? I cannot see. Oh, this is useless. I cannot bear it. Anne . . . No, Helena, run down and ask if it is indeed him.'

Lady Helena pinned a cap over her shining red hair and had just gone to the door when they all heard the sound of hurrying feet on the stairs.

Her lady-in-waiting hesitated, glancing back at Elizabeth. 'Your Majesty, someone is coming.'

'Never mind then, sit down again.'

Elizabeth turned from the window and stood staring at the closed door in helpless frustration. She was shivering now, despite the thick tapestries on the wall and the fire still burning fiercely in the hearth.

It had to be Robert. Who else could it be, travelling by boat from the east and with such attendance?

She hurried back to the table and signalled Helena to join her. 'Quick, pick up a piece. Pretend it is your turn to play. If it is indeed Robert, I refuse to let him see I was waiting for him.'

A few seconds later, with barely a knock, the door was flung open and Robert stood there, flanked by yeomen of the guard, his clothes travel-stained, his boots muddied and worn, the look on his face both fierce and weary. He looked older, his face more lined than when he had left for war. Yet he seemed bolder too, more of a soldier, his hand resting on the hilt of his sword almost defiantly.

He was waiting for permission to enter, Elizabeth realized with a shock. Robert was as unsure of his welcome as she was of his loyalty to her throne.

She stood, her head high, and held out a jewelled hand. 'My lord Leicester?'

He came forward then and dropped to one knee before her, drawing her hand to his lips. 'Your Majesty.'

Elizabeth felt a flush of heat that she struggled to control. She barely glanced at her ladies and the guards at the door. 'Leave us.'

Once they were alone, she pulled her hand from his grasp and took a step back. The hurts of the past year returned to haunt her. 'They call you King of England in the Low Countries,' she said accusingly, 'and your wife the second queen.'

'No.'

Robert stood too, shaking his head as she turned away. 'They are fools. I never usurped your power there, nor your throne. And Lettice stayed at home in England, following your command not to accompany me abroad. Your spies will have told you as much.'

'Perhaps,' she conceded, but did not lower her guard.

She went to stare down at the river, where his flotilla of boats was being unloaded. Dwarfing the rapid wherries used to carry passengers across the Thames, the last boat was being brought in to dock. The others bobbed up and down on the dark tide, already tethered to posts along the wharfside. Elizabeth watched as an army of liveried servants marched on and off the narrow gangplanks under a blaze of hand-held torches; trunks and boxes balanced on their shoulders, some carrying saddles and hooded falcons, others leading out sick-looking hunting dogs joined by a single rope, no doubt in poor spirits after their long sea journey. Ranged against the wall stood a handful of helmeted guards, leaning on their pikes in a desultory fashion as they checked that none of the earl's valuable cargo went astray. In the final boat she could see horses on deck now, huddled together and pulling excitedly at their tethers.

'Yet you travel like royalty,' she remarked drily. 'I thought some foreign prince had arrived at Greenwich, so many boats accompanied you.'

'I had to ship my servants, and all my furniture and effects back from Flushing.'

'Even your horses, Robert?'

'I had no wish to sell my stable, yet could scarcely have left the horses abroad, since I have no intention of returning to the Low Countries unless commanded there by Your Majesty.' When she said nothing, Robert came to stand beside her at the window, a note of relief in his voice. Perhaps he had feared she would do precisely that. 'I must thank Your Majesty for sending Sir Francis Drake and his men to escort us home. It was heartwarming to see our own stout ships on the horizon and know we would soon be back on English soil.'

'And your unfortunate nephew's body?'

Robert's reply was steady enough, but Elizabeth could guess at the reined-in emotions beneath his calm exterior. He had loved his nephew like a son.

'We brought Pip home with us, of course.'

'And now?'

He hesitated, then straightened and turned stiffly away from the window. 'Sir Philip Sidney's last mortal remains have been conveyed to Tower Wharf, at Walsingham's suggestion. From there his coffin will be carried up to a safe resting-place until arrangements can be made for his burial and the discharge of his debts, which I understand to be considerable. His widow Frances is with child, and accompanies his body as far as her father's house. Then she is to retire into the country to prepare for her confinement.'

She did not bother to look round at him. She could see Robert reflected in the glazed window panes; the earl was watching her from the centre of the room now, a misty image floating against the darkness outside.

'I fear for her life too,' he continued, his voice becoming rough. 'Frances has taken her husband's death hard and may not survive the coming birth. It is a terrible business. I blame myself for Pip's death. He was always impetuous and foolhardy in his courageousness, and should have been guarded more carefully. To have ridden into battle without full armour . . .' Robert drew a harsh breath, coming sharply to the point. 'This entire campaign in the Low Countries has been a disaster, Your Majesty. I cannot pretend otherwise.'

'Yet you have not given up your title there, my lord,' she remarked, not bothering to disguise the acidity in her voice. 'Or should I call you "Supreme Governor"?'

'Your Majesty.' He hesitated, then came up behind her at the window. 'Elizabeth.'

His voice tugged at her, too close at hand, too intimate. She had feared never to hear his voice again. Yet now he was here in the room with her, she wished he had stayed in the Low Countries, for Elizabeth knew herself to be utterly weak where Robert was concerned. He was the one man in all the world who could bring her to ruin, for he was the one man she truly loved.

Elizabeth turned to find Robert blocking her way. She decided to play it haughtily, raising her brows at his proximity.

'My lord?'

'I cannot believe it's only a year since I last saw the glory of your face. It felt more like a lifetime when I was in the field of battle, calling out your name in the charge . . . "For England and Elizabeth!"' Robert searched her face for any signs of encouragement, his gaze swiftly dropping to her mouth. 'I've missed you so badly, Bess.'

Trapped close against his chest, she could not help staring at Robert's face too, noting the tiny changes time and war had wrought during his absence from court, his skin so much more deeply lined. Not that such changes made him less attractive to her. On the contrary, they made Robert more of a man in her eyes, and a noble soldier at that. His hair might be silver, his beard too, yet his eyes held the same dark charm she had never been able to resist.

She felt a renewed hunger for Robert that threatened to destroy her composure. But she was still Queen and he was still married to another woman.

'Don't call me that,' she said unevenly, and tried to move past him. 'I am no longer a child.'

He seized her arm and Elizabeth swore at him with sudden indignation, struggling as she tried to slap his face. Then Robert was kissing her, crushing her against the stone wall, and she felt her body quicken into desire.

'I have dreamt of this,' he muttered against her mouth, and his hand moved down over her hip, beginning to lift her skirts. 'Every night, alone in my tent on campaign. In my dreams you were like this, an angry queen to be conquered . . . or lying naked in my arms, my willing concubine.'

She gasped and pushed him away with all her strength. 'I should have you thrown in the Tower for this insolence. Men have been executed for less!'

'Call your guards, then,' Robert taunted her as she walked away. 'I am your general. The country is still under threat. Would you lose me now, with the might of Spain almost on our doorstep?'

She turned at that, staring. 'You fear an invasion?'

'Not yet. But it must come, and soon, if we cannot send a clear message to King Philip that England is not his to claim.'

'Oh, brave words!'

'Rumour has it he is preparing an invasion fleet.' Robert went to the sideboard and poured them both a glass of red wine. He held one out to her with little attempt at courtesy, his direct gaze jangling her nerves. 'Take it. You may need it once I am done. They say the best Spanish shipmasters have been ordered to build new and faster ships of war, and as quickly as possible. This is no empty threat but a real danger. Though every Englishman knows the true danger to England lies within our shores.'

She stiffened, lowering the untouched glass of wine from her lips. 'Go on.'

'You know it already,' he muttered. 'But will not act to prevent your own death, it seems.'

'Mary?'

'Your Scottish cousin will seize this throne from you if you do not remove her from existence,' he told her bluntly. 'All of Europe wonders at your reluctance to put an end to her treacherous life. She is shameless in her plotting. She has written to almost every European Catholic court to beg their help in obtaining her release, and it is rumoured that her letters have not been complimentary of the English or their queen.'

Elizabeth felt sick. She put down the glass. So all of Europe was laughing at her? Yet even that humiliation did not make her decision any easier.

'You know why I cannot order her destruction, Robert. I have argued this before and shall again, for it is the truth. Her life is sacred to God, as mine is. Tell me, what hell awaits me after death if I condemn such a neck to the axe?'

'Better her vile neck than yours,' he said roughly, then put down his glass and took her in his arms again. 'Elizabeth, my love, look at me. I know why you will not take me back into your bed, and I thank you for the honour you have done me by putting this country's safety in my charge, despite my marriage to Lettice. But accept my advice at least, which is more honest than anything else about me, and don't let your scheming cousin kill you and usurp the English throne.'

Elizabeth allowed him to kiss her for a moment, then shivered and shook her head. 'Let me go, Robert. You are no adulterer.'

'I thank heaven for it,' he whispered against her throat, 'though at times I wish I could unmarry myself and be in your good grace again.'

Elizabeth pulled away from him, crossing the room to put some distance between them. She found it hard to think clearly when Robert was so close.

'A Catholic came at me with a knife this year,' she told him. 'Now Walsingham has set men to watch my rooms constantly, and I can go nowhere without a guard of stout yeomen. Every grain of my food must be tasted before I am allowed to eat, and all my wine and ale too, for Lord Burghley fears one of Mary's devout followers may try to poison me.'

She smiled thinly, mocking herself for cowardice. 'I was even too afraid to open parliament this year, in case some plot was hatched to kill me there.'

'Yes, I heard.'

'Then you must have seen what straits I am in. I may be a queen, but I am every bit as much in prison as my cousin Mary.' She closed her eyes. 'Yet what can I do but wait and hope God takes the decision from my hands?'

Robert watched her in silence for a while. Then he went to the window and stared out at the dark. 'You cannot hope for such a thing. All you can do is act. It is the kingly thing to do, and you know it. Your father would have had no hesitation.'

'But my sister hesitated,' she pointed out. 'I was in the Tower and feared for my life. My sister chose not to act, and I only rule now because of her hesitation to take my life.'

'And do you wish your cousin to say the same thing of you in a year's time, Elizabeth, as she sits upon your throne and gloats upon your sisterly hesitation?'

His voice was harsh, almost insulting, and Elizabeth found it hard to reply without equal anger. She loved Robert, and could not bear the thought of a life without him, but his arrogance always seemed to strike sparks off the tinderbox of her temper.

'Get out!' she exclaimed.

Robert bowed at once, very stiff, his velvet, jewel-studded cap in his hand. 'Your Majesty.'

He reached the door in a few angry strides, where she stopped him.

'There will be a banquet in your honour in the coming week,' she told him, as coldly as though they had never kissed, as though they had no feelings for each other, 'with a play, and dancing, and an hour of fireworks to celebrate your safe return from the Low Countries. You will not bring your wife to court for any of these festivities but will attend them as my personal escort. Is that clear?'

He bowed again. 'Yes, Your Majesty,' he said, and Elizabeth caught a flicker of some swiftly hidden emotion in his face. Triumph? Contempt?

Still he lingered on the threshold, holding the door open. 'Will I have the pleasure of hearing Lucy Morgan sing at the banquet, Your Majesty? I was told she was no longer at court.'

Elizabeth frowned. 'Lucy Morgan left court some time ago. I grew weary of her singing, and her reputation was sullied by some ugly rumours. You know I demand the highest chastity from my ladies,' she said significantly, and raised her gaze to his face.

'I have missed her voice this past year,' Robert said lightly, looking back at her. 'And Lucy has done, as I recall, no little service for your throne in the past. Now I am back from the Low Countries, perhaps it is also time to send for Lucy Morgan to return to court? She was always one of Pip's favourites too, and her sweet voice would be welcome at his funeral.'

His smile faltered as he turned away. 'There may be difficult times ahead, Your Majesty, and music lightens even the darkest hour.'

Six

'LUCY, WAKE UP,' A LOW VOICE SAID IN HER EAR. 'A LETTER has come for you.'

Lucy opened her eyes reluctantly. In truth, she had not been asleep but lying in a heavy torpor under her sheepskin covers, as she had done most days since leaving the Parkers' house. Her daybed was sunlit, for Goodluck had set it near his open front door, where she could see the passers-by and listen to the cries of the street traders. But the sunlight was chilly, for it was late winter and there was a light sprinkling of snow on the roofs opposite.

'Here,' Goodluck murmured, and held a cup to her lips. 'Take some ale. Then you must eat or you will never recover your strength.'

Lucy obeyed, sipping at the ale and then accepting a few mouthfuls of boiled white poultry. Afterwards, feeling less groggy, she made an effort to smile at him. 'Thank you.' She glanced at the letter on the side table. 'For me?'

'It came a few days back, but you were not well enough to read it.'

She let him arrange her pillows so she could sit up and read the letter. It was from Cathy; she recognized the slanted, childish writing at once, for her friend had never learned to form her letters correctly. She broke the seal, reading through the few sparse lines in silence, then handed it to Goodluck.

'She cannot come to stay,' she remarked sadly. 'I knew there must be something wrong when she did not reply to my last letter. That young husband of hers didn't come back from the war. So now she is a widow, and the only one to care for her sick mother.' She closed her eyes. 'I shall never see Cathy again.'

'Nonsense,' Goodluck said briskly, and sat down on the edge of her bed. He smoothed a stray lock of hair from her forehead. 'Cathy writes that her mother is *very* sick, which means the woman may likely die.'

'Goodluck!'

He grinned at her indignant expression. 'Forgive me. I do not wish calamity upon the poor invalid, I merely state what is in Cathy's letter.'

'And if she dies, what of it?'

'Then I expect her long-suffering daughter will be free to return to London as soon as she may afford to hire a cart to carry her,' Goodluck commented wryly, handing her back the letter, 'which she clearly wishes to do, judging by her postscript.'

Lucy lowered her gaze again to Cathy's postscript.

I do desperately wish to see you again, Lucy, and would do anything to return to court. Norfolk is such a desolate place for a poor widow. But while my mother ails so badly, I dare not leave her side.

'I hope she is able to beg a place at court. But I cannot return there too,' she told him, and folded the letter up again.

'Why not?' He frowned, watching her face intently. 'I do not understand your hesitance. Walsingham has written twice now, cordially extending the Queen's invitation to return, and even Lord Leicester himself has demanded

461

that you should sing at Sir Philip Sidney's funeral feast.'

'But the Queen—'

'Queen Elizabeth has forgiven you,' he insisted, 'and if she has forgiven you, it is time you forgave yourself.'

Abruptly, he threw back her sheepskin covers to expose her legs. 'Now out of bed before I tip you out. I do not wish to be cruel, Lucy, but I shall not humour you any longer in this sickness. Your bruised back has healed, it is time to get up.'

Shivering in the sudden draught, Lucy tried to snatch her covers back, but he took her arm in a firm grasp.

'You are neither diseased nor injured, the physician has said it himself,' he told her sharply. 'It is merely your mind that is sick and needs to be healed. And that can only be done by beginning to walk again, and going about your business like any other woman. You can start by putting your feet on the floor.'

She looked up at him, her eyes filling with tears. 'My baby is dead,' she whispered. 'I killed him.'

Goodluck bent to kiss her on the cheek. 'Your baby was dead before he was born, my love. You did not kill him, any more than you killed Jack Parker. Both those deaths were Master Twist's doing, as were the deaths of poor Ned and Sos, and any other man or woman who stood in his way. John Twist has paid for his crimes and burns now in hell, where all murderers must come to punishment in the end. But you are still alive, and I wish to see my ward in a clean gown and not this dirty old nightshift you've been wearing ever since I brought you home.'

He put an arm about her waist and swung her legs to the floor. 'Come now, take a step.'

As soon as her bare feet touched the floor, Lucy felt a shock run up her spine. She hung on to him and protested weakly that she could not walk.

How could Goodluck expect such a thing of her? For weeks she had been in bed, barely able to eat or sleep, staring into the darkness every night like a tormented soul until he came to read to her by candlelight or sing a lullaby, something he had not done when she was a small child. The physician had prescribed various expensive remedies, and bled her several times a week; and an odd woman dressed as a boatman had come to the house a few times to burn herbs and rub stinking oils into her back and legs. But nothing had worked. Lucy had not been able to get out of bed since the night she had given birth to Will's dead child, and seen his thin, slippery body wrapped in its winding-cloth straight from her womb.

Goodluck paid no attention to her protests. He held her tight and encouraged her to lean on him. 'One step, that's all,' he urged her, and as she obeyed, he smiled. 'And another, that's it. And one more.'

Later that evening, seated on a stool with her feet in a basin of hot water and a roaring fire warming her legs, Lucy glanced across at Goodluck. He was stretched out on the settle opposite, his cap over his eyes.

'Thank you,' she said softly, not sure if he could hear her or if he was even awake.

Pushing back the brim of his cap, Master Goodluck smiled at her with that old lopsided grin she remembered from her childhood. 'My pleasure, Lucy. Though it was Sir Francis Walsingham's idea to force you out of bed in that cruel manner, so you must blame him for it when you return to court. I spoke to him of your sickness a few days ago, and he told me of another case like yours, where it was only the woman's mind that ailed and needed to be jolted back to life.'

She looked at him curiously. 'His daughter?'

Goodluck sighed. 'Yes, poor Lady Sidney. She too was

brought to bed of a dead child after her husband's death last year.'

'I shall miss Sir Philip Sidney,' Lucy murmured. She moved her bare feet cautiously in the hot water, enjoying the sensation more than she had expected. 'He had such a merry smile, and a quick wit, too.'

'Will you return to court and sing at his funeral? I'm told they plan to bury him at St Paul's soon, now his debts have been cleared.'

'I cannot,' Lucy insisted, and felt a sudden hot rush of tears. Horrified, she hid her face in her hands, not wanting Goodluck to see her shame. 'I have been such a fool. I lay with a man who was married and bore him a dead child. I had hopes, when I was young, to be a great singer at the Queen's court, and then marry a gentleman, to be his wife, and mother to his children. But now I am ruined, utterly ruined. Even if I go back to court, I am a widow with no inheritance and a voice so rusty I shall likely be turned away at the door. I cannot even hope to dance yet, I am so weak.' She rocked in her distress. 'Who will have me now? Oh, Goodluck, what have I done?'

Then his arms were about her shoulders, and Goodluck was holding her tight in his familiar bear-hug.

'Hush, child,' he murmured, letting her sob against his chest. 'I will not force you to return to court if you do not wish it. But I cannot stay here all year round, or we will have nothing to eat. I must work, and work means I must travel, and that alone. Do you understand? That is why I pushed you to ask your friend Cathy to stay with you here. But if she cannot come, I cannot take the work Walsingham offers me, for it would mean leaving you here alone.'

She listened carefully, then nodded and dried her eyes on her apron. 'Walsingham has offered you work?'

He crouched, looking up at her searchingly. 'I know no details, but yes. I was to leave next week.'

'Take me with you,' she suggested, thinking how lovely it would be to travel with Goodluck again, as she had sometimes done as a child, just the two of them together again.

'It is not possible,' he said, and took her hand.

She looked at him, and their eyes met. For a moment she could not breathe. Then she suddenly felt the fire was too hot and turned her face away to cool it.

'Tell Walsingham you will take the work he's offered you,' she said. 'I will pack my bags and go back to court. We can meet again at Christmas perhaps, if you are able to come to the palace.'

'I may be travelling,' he said roughly, and stood up.

'Then whenever you make your way back to me, I shall see you,' she told him, and managed a shaky smile. 'That fire is so hot!'

'It will soon burn out,' he muttered, then stooped and kissed her on the forehead. 'Enjoy life at court and don't think of me. Only promise me you will take better care of yourself this time.'

She touched his face. 'I promise,' she whispered, and watched him turn away.

As long as Will Shakespeare keeps his distance, I promise . . .

Seven

Whitehall Palace, London, January 1587

'I SHALL NOT SIGN,' ELIZABETH DECLARED, AND SLAMMED her hand down on the table. Her councillors looked at her warily. She glanced at Robert, who had ridden hard from his home at Wanstead to attend this meeting of the Privy Council, and saw the frown on his face. Well, let him frown, Elizabeth thought, and looked away before he could catch her eye. She would not condemn her royal cousin to death, not on the say-so of this handful of English nobles and their glorified secretaries, who could bring her nothing more damning than a few muttered rumours of plots.

'Nothing has changed,' she insisted emphatically. 'This is all nonsense.'

Lord Howard exchanged looks with Lord Burghley, then stepped forward. So he had been chosen to talk her round, she thought, and met his nervous look with defiance. He would find this queen hard to shift!

'Your Majesty,' Lord Howard began, spreading out a map on the table, 'if you will look at this map of the Low Countries, I can show you here,' he pointed to the map, at which she refused to look, 'and here, strongholds formerly held by our forces but now held by the Spanish. Parma has taken both these fortresses from us, and will soon push forward with his plans for the invasion of England. Our spies in their camps talk of new canals being dug to allow greater ease of movement about the Low Countries, and larger vessels being commandeered by the Spanish to carry soldiers and provisions to the coast. We could be only months away, perhaps even weeks, from the sighting of a Spanish fleet off our south-east coast.'

'And how is it that these strongholds of ours fell into Spanish hands in the first place?' she demanded icily.

There was an awkward silence while the councillors glanced at each other, and then at Robert.

Robert looked furious. 'By all reports, Your Majesty, they did not fall so much as opened their gates and invited the Spanish in. We cannot be sure how this surrender came about, for our reports are scanty. But my trust was clearly misplaced in the commanders I left behind in the Low Countries.' He tore off his riding gloves and threw them down on the table, as though ready to issue a challenge to anyone there who accused him of collusion with the enemy. 'If I had known Lord Stanley would fall back on his Catholic allegiances and invite the Spanish in, I should never have left him in charge of our territories there.'

'So Spain moves ever closer to England,' Elizabeth remarked, and shuddered. 'I can see why this must indicate stronger and more urgent preparations to defend our shores. But how does it change our policy on my cousin's long imprisonment?'

Lord Howard looked apologetic. Rolling up the map, he tucked it under his arm. 'While your royal cousin lives, she excites a vision in every Catholic man, woman and child of an England brought back under the yoke of Rome. Her very existence is a threat to yours, Your Majesty, and those

467

who seek to protect her would think nothing of bringing about your death to achieve that end. You have had, I believe, recent proof of this determination in a letter from His Majesty the King of Scotland.'

Elizabeth looked away uncomfortably. She knew the letter of which he spoke, an insolent and subtly threatening missive sent via Sir William Keith, no doubt in the hope that it would frighten her into obedience.

'King James feels a son's right and proper anxiety for his mother, that is all,' she commented, though she saw from her councillors' faces that none of them believed the lightness of her dismissal.

She waved away a servant who had come to her side bearing a flagon of wine. 'Bring me ale,' she told the man impatiently, then turned her head to study the councillors about the table. 'Gentlemen, my lords, I do not see that any of this brings forward a pressing need for my cousin's execution. We have had threats, plots and assassination attempts enough these past twenty years to kill a dozen queens. Yet here I am, still alive, and will remain on the throne of England until forcibly dislodged.'

Lord Howard bowed. 'Yes indeed, Your Majesty. But consider this, if I may be so bold. With your cousin alive, the English Catholics have hope of a future where they may see Mary on the throne, and so will lend their hands to any invasion force which promises such a reward. But if Mary were to die, the only Catholic contender for the throne in the event of an invasion would be King Philip of Spain. He is a Catholic, yes. But also a foreigner, and one whose rule alongside your late sister was not popular with the people.'

Elizabeth looked at him, then at her other councillors. 'So you believe the Catholics among my people will encourage an invasion by Spain if my cousin is alive, but resist if she is dead?'

'Precisely!' Sir Christopher Hatton exclaimed, bringing his hands together loudly, then caught her eye and added, 'Your Majesty has grasped the matter in a nutshell.'

Lord Burghley leaned forward and gently pushed the warrant for Mary's execution back in front of her. 'Sign, Your Majesty, I implore you. There is no need for any further action to be taken at the present moment. But at least if you have signed the warrant, her execution can be carried out in the event of an invasion without any need to prepare the document or pass it under the Great Seal. Do you see?'

Still Elizabeth hesitated, looking round the table at the solemn faces of her Privy Councillors. She saw Robert nod intently, his gaze fixed on her face as though imploring her to go ahead, and to his right-hand side Walsingham tapped the table as though in agreement. Even old Sir Francis Knollys was watching her with undisguised approbation. It seemed not one of them was prepared to argue against this terrible decision.

As she debated whether or not to put her signature to the dreaded paper, a shadow seemed to pass over the small-paned window that faced the Greenwich gardens, as though someone had walked past in the icy weather, or a cloud had briefly obscured the sun. Her lips parted, and she remembered running through a rose garden as a small child, searching desperately for someone, with her nurse calling for her to come back, and then the tears of frustration when she was dragged away.

'Not yet! Not yet!' she exclaimed, no longer able to bear what was being asked of her.

Rising from her seat, Elizabeth strode from the chamber, pausing in the doorway only to look back accusingly at her chief councillors.

As the days passed, Elizabeth began to wonder about the wisdom of not signing her cousin's death warrant. Perhaps there were some among them who secretly wished for Mary to depose her and seize the throne. She thought of each courtier in turn, and went through his smiles and flattering comments in her mind, suspecting them all, even her own beloved Robert at times. For he spent longer and longer at home with Lettice these days and not at her side, for all she had brought him safely home from war.

Was it possible that Robert too, whose hatred for the Catholics was well-known, might desire a change of queen? What poison did Lettice drip into his ear at night when they lay together at Wanstead?

Early one morning, Elizabeth walked out with her ladies in the sharp winter weather, wrapped in a fur-lined cloak and with her black velvet cap pulled down to cover her ears. She needed time and space to think, and she never thought more deeply than when walking and enjoying the beauty and order of nature.

Rounding a magnificent holly bush in the palace gardens, rich with red berries, Elizabeth came face to face with Lettice Knollys on Robert's arm.

She came to an abrupt standstill, her breath steaming on the cold air. Lettice lowered her horrified gaze at once and dropped into a deep curtsy, her head bent. Robert bowed, his own expression defiant, though Elizabeth noted how he let go of his wife's arm, taking a quick step away from her.

'Your Majesty,' he said heavily, as though bracing himself for the storm to come.

So Lettice had come to court at last, and without seeking proper permission! Elizabeth took a moment to examine her cousin in silence. The extravagant folds of her broad-skirted red velvet gown, with its simple cloth-of-gold bodice, shimmered in the grey morning like an exotic bird's plumage, her belt hung with gold and scarlet braided tassels, her cap feathered and slanted, her white ruff as broad as Elizabeth's own. Several large jewelled rings adorned her white gloves, and the golden cross about her neck sparkled with rubies. At her back knelt a young black pageboy in livery, a quivering dog in his arms, its white fur preened and a diamond-studded collar about its neck.

Lettice herself looked as vibrant as ever, as though the years had barely touched her, her face still smooth and unwrinkled as she glanced up at the Queen.

Hateful woman! Elizabeth felt her temper begin to rise and did nothing to control it.

'Red velvet, cloth-of-gold, and even diamonds about her dog's neck? What, is your wife a queen to dress herself so lavishly?' she demanded of Robert. 'I had heard rumours of your wife's excessive finery in the past, but dismissed them as malicious gossip. But now it seems your recent elevation to the governorship in the Low Countries has gone to Lady Leicester's head. I only pray she can keep it long enough to enjoy her expensive wardrobe.'

Lettice started at that threat, her lips parted, though she said nothing.

Elizabeth enjoyed her rival's discomfort as she raged on, glaring at Robert. 'Nor do I recall inviting your wife to court. Though if I had, be sure I would have expected her to dress in more sombre colours, as befits one of my ladies. Explain yourself, if you please!'

'Forgive me, Your Majesty. It was very wrong of me not to seek your permission for Lettice to visit me at court.' Robert spoke slowly and with difficulty, though the flush in his cheeks told her of his anger, too. 'Lady Leicester has come to pay her last respects to my nephew and to console his young widow in her grief. She and her servants will return to Wanstead as soon as we have buried Philip.'

'I am glad to hear it,' Elizabeth said coldly, and regarded her favourite with warning. 'There can be only one queen,

Robert, and all other pretenders to that title should beware they do not lose their heads over it.'

Returning to her state apartments in a high temper, Elizabeth called at once for a quill and ink, and also for William Davison, the new Junior Secretary of State. He came straight from the breakfast table, crumbs still in his beard, his expression alarmed.

'Fetch the warrant for my cousin's death that was given into your charge, sir,' she told him curtly. 'Before I change my mind.'

William Davison returned a short while later with the royal warrant, more presentable and with his beard hurriedly combed through, several other men at his back as though to bear witness to the event.

Elizabeth read through the wording several times, then took up the quill, dipped it in black ink and signed the death warrant with a flourish, *Elizabeth R*.

'There,' she said, and laid down the quill. 'Master Davison, you may take this document away for safe keeping. But you are not to act upon it without further instruction from me.'

Eight

ILLUMINATED BY HUNDREDS OF FLICKERING CANDLES, THE ancient nave of St Paul's stood silent as the doors at the far end, open to the thin February daylight only moments before, darkened now with a throng of men. The assembled nobles and gentry closest to the roodscreen turned to look as the funeral procession approached the door to St Paul's. Led by a black-robed priest, carrying a plain cross before him, the pallbearers entered to the slow beat of a drum. On their shoulders lay the lead-lined coffin of Sir Philip Sidney, dead these past five months but not yet interred, the arguments over his debts having been so protracted. Behind the coffin walked his brother and heir, Sir Robert Sidney, his handsome face stony as he struggled to contain his grief.

At a signal from the bishop, Lucy drew in a long breath, counted silently in her head, and launched into song. She had been given only days to learn the music chosen by the Queen, and had struggled at first with the Latin. Her greatest fear had been that, after so many months away from court, only able to sing for herself and never allowed to practise her craft as she had done before, she would not be able to hit the notes perfectly or would find her voice weak or wanting. Now, though, the nervousness she had felt earlier that morning drained away, leaving her in a state of absolute calm.

Clasping her hands before her chest, Lucy lifted her head high, and sang as though she had never been away from court. She thought of Sir Philip Sidney, so handsome and full of promise, a great soldier and scholar, a poet whose work had never failed to touch her heart. She remembered his charming smile, the way he had jousted with the other nobles to entertain the Queen on summer progresses, his shouts of triumph at his wins, his laughter and easy sportsmanship when he lost. The high, unaccompanied notes of her song haunted the ancient church like his presence, touching its sturdy rafters and beams, its stone flags and whitewashed walls, the spaces where the people stood, the ornate roodscreen behind which the priests waited to conduct the Mass.

Beyond the open door to St Paul's, massed hordes of gentry and commoners lined the city streets, some there by decree, others simply hoping for a glimpse of the young man's coffin as it passed that morning. Hundreds had stood outside the church in silence that morning as the Queen and her entourage had arrived, Lucy among them. Some had shouted the Queen's blessing and showered her ladies with the fragile petals of spring flowers; others had knelt in respectful silence, heads bowed in prayer for the dead young man whose life they had come to celebrate, their caps held in their hands.

Her song finished, Lucy stepped back and stood to one side beside the screen, suddenly trembling. She felt sick and only managed not to faint by staring hard at one of the bright stands of candles nearest her, focusing on the golden, flickering flames and breathing in the sweet scent of the dried herbs strewn among the rushes.

Daring to look up later, while the bishop was intoning

some message of hope from the high pulpit, she caught Lord Leicester's gaze on her face.

Lord Leicester nodded, giving her the faintest of smiles, then looked back at Sir Philip's coffin, his face once again grim.

After the coffin had been conveyed down into the crypt, the procession returned to Greenwich Palace by road and river, the soldiers' banners flying in the icy February weather. It seemed hard to Lucy, a chill sunshine on her face, the signs of new growth in every field and on the river bank, that Sir Philip Sidney would never see another spring nor ever grace the court again with his dancing and poetry. But then she remembered Jack Parker, who had died through no fault of his own, but simply for having agreed to marry her and conceal her shame. And her son, born dead, his tiny waxen eyelids never opening to see her face. And Cathy's young husband too, fallen in the struggle to secure the Low Countries – and Lucy wept, covering her face in her hands, for all the deaths and the misery of life.

The Queen summoned her that evening to the Privy Chamber at Greenwich. The room had emptied of courtiers except for the Queen's ladies and her royal guards, now constantly in attendance at Walsingham's command.

It was the first time Lucy had seen Queen Elizabeth face to face since leaving court, and she knew an instant of terror before entering the chamber. The Queen had sent her away on such hostile terms, Lucy could not quite believe she had been persuaded to allow her return.

With memories of the Tower looming darkly in her mind, Lucy sank to both knees before the Queen and bowed her head. 'Your Majesty.'

'I hear you were married without permission while away from my court,' the Queen remarked coldly, 'and are now a widow. That you should be known from now on as Mistress Parker.'

'Yes, Your Majesty.'

There was a long silence. The fire crackled at Lucy's back, and a log popped loudly in the flames. Finally, the Queen clicked her fingers, signalling her to rise.

'I do not like this name, Parker. It is a common one.' There was a petulant note to the Queen's voice. 'And I do not like it that a woman must take her husband's name in this slavish fashion. Lucy Morgan suited you well enough. Since your husband is dead and cannot call us to account for it, I shall know you still as Mistress Morgan. How others address you at court is your own affair.'

Lucy said nothing, but waited. She knew there must be more, or the Queen would not have summoned her.

'I am curious about you, Mistress Morgan. You owe your return to court to Lord Leicester,' Queen Elizabeth continued, her thin lips pursed as she examined Lucy's gown with apparent disapproval. 'His lordship argued most passionately on your behalf. Though I am told Sir Francis also took you under his wing on your departure from court. Is that true?'

Lucy hesitated, her gaze carefully lowered to the floor. Sir Francis had not instructed her to keep his arrangements for her marriage secret, so it seemed safe enough to comment. Besides, if she was to keep this new place at court, she must be prepared to abase herself before the Queen and tell the truth. It galled her, yet she must do it. The Queen would accept nothing less than her complete obedience. And she had no pride left to chafe her conscience, surely? Not after everything that had happened to her.

'Yes, Your Majesty. I am most grateful to Sir Francis for his kind help, which I did not deserve.'

'Indeed,' the Queen replied drily. She tapped her fingers

on the arm of her high-backed seat. 'Well, it seems you have friends at court, and so may stay while your favour lasts. Only remember to keep yourself chaste this time, Mistress Morgan, and obedient to your betters. You may be a widow now and not to be watched as closely as a virgin, but I will have no light women in my service. Is that clear?'

Lucy curtsied. 'Yes, Your Majesty.'

'Now go and seek some better gowns for yourself from the keeper of the royal wardrobe. You cannot come to court like that. And since I will need you for state occasions, a bedchamber and a servant have also been arranged for you.' As Lucy bowed out of the Privy Chamber in a display of humility, the Queen called sharply after her. 'You have been granted bouge of court again, Mistress Morgan. Do not be a fool this time and lose it through neglecting your honour.'

The next morning, having been woken by the now un-familiar sounds of a great palace stirring in the dawn light, Lucy took herself to the chambers of the royal wardrobe to be measured for a gown. She was standing in her under-shift, being presented with an array of court gowns discarded by Queen Elizabeth as worn too often or not flattering enough to her hair or figure, when there was a loud knock at the door and it began to open.

'Go away!' one of the women called, looking shocked at the intrusion.

A very young, curly-haired pageboy grinned round the door frame, ignoring cries of outrage from the other ladies present.

'Is Mistress Morgan here?' he asked in a high voice.

'Yes.' Lucy frowned, holding up a gown to conceal her semi-clad body. 'What is it?'

Then the door opened fully to reveal Cathy standing

there, flushed and smiling, still in her travelling gown and cap, her hem dirty from the road.

Lucy shrieked with joy and ran forward, forgetting to cover herself in front of the pageboy. 'Cathy!'

They embraced fiercely, while the ladies pushed the page from the room and closed the heavy door against other passers-by.

Lucy was astonished but delighted to see her old friend. 'I was so sorry to hear about your husband. You must miss him terribly. But how are you here? I thought you were nursing your mother?'

'She passed away ten days ago,' Cathy told her, and her smile was sad. 'Just after I wrote to you last. I was so distressed after we buried her, I did not know what to do with myself. Then I received a letter and a purse of coins, bidding me to court as your maid, by order of Sir Francis Walsingham himself.'

Drawing back in shock, Lucy held her at arm's length. She felt unsteady. 'My *maid*?' she repeated. 'But no, Sir Francis must have made a mistake. You . . . you are an entertainer, not a servant.'

Cathy shook her head. 'I was never a gifted singer, Lucy. Not like you. And now I cannot even dance any more. See?' She lifted her skirt to reveal that one of her shoes was built higher than the other. 'I broke my ankle falling from a roof in the autumn. My own silly fault, thinking I could mend the thatch as well as a man. But it healed poorly, for I was busy about the house and not able to let it rest. Now I walk with a limp, and they say I shall never dance again.'

'Oh, my dearest.' Lucy held her close. Her heart hurt at the thought of her lively, fair-haired Cathy unable to dance, she who had loved so much to shine at court. 'But for you to be my servant! It does not seem right.'

'I am a widow now, remember? Just as you are. You will

478

not deny me a chance to earn my keep, surely?' Cathy's face was suddenly pale. 'If you refuse my service, I will be forced to return to Norfolk and beg a crust at my father-in-law's farm, where my son is being brought up.'

Lucy stared. 'You left him behind?'

'I could not bring a young child to court. Not as a servant,' Cathy explained quietly. 'He will be well fed and cared for on the farm, and whatever I earn will be kept safe to pay for his education.'

'I'm not sure—' Lucy began, but Cathy interrupted her, her voice catching on a sob.

'Do not turn me away, Lucy, for the sake of our old friendship. I have no money left and no place else to go.'

'Mistress Morgan, please,' one of the tiring women said impatiently at their backs, holding up a dark velvet gown with a lacy bodice for Lucy to try. 'We must hurry. There are other women to be measured this morning, and we have not yet come to an agreement on which gowns you are to be allowed from the royal wardrobe.'

'Of course,' Lucy told the woman swiftly. 'I'm sorry to have kept you waiting.'

She turned to Cathy and squeezed her hands. 'Since you are so very determined to stay, then I cannot tell you no. We shall make it work, the two of us together. Now will you not take off your cloak and help me into this gown? I fear I may be too broad in the hips for it, but the velvet is so fine, I would dearly love to wear it about the court. What do you think?'

Cathy managed a smile, beginning to unfasten her cloak. 'I think Sir Francis Walsingham is a very wise man.'

Nine

Fotheringay Castle, Northamptonshire,
8 February 1587

IT WAS ALMOST DAWN WHEN GOODLUCK SHOWED HIS PAPERS
at the castle lodge and was escorted with another group of
waiting gentlemen through the castle to a chamber with no
chairs but a good fire and some cups of spiced wine set
out, to warm them in the bitter February weather.

Goodluck took a cup of wine and sipped at it, glancing
covertly about the room.

One of the other men looked at him, frowning. 'I do not
think I know you, sir.'

Goodluck inclined his head politely, but did not give his
name. 'I am here on state business, sir. You must forgive
me,' he said, and moved to stand apart.

Nobody else spoke much after that. More gentlemen
arrived under escort and soon the room was crowded, but
awkwardly silent. Then an usher appeared at the door in
livery and, after a brief announcement about the proceedings to come, led them in an orderly fashion to the
Great Hall. There, wooden chairs had been set out in
rows; these had been alloted to most of the gentlemen and

nobles present. Those without a seat allocation were told to stand about the room wherever they felt most comfortable, but not to crowd too close either to the raised platform at the centre, or to the far door, which stood closed and was guarded by stout-faced yeomen.

Goodluck took up a position near the fire, and was glad of its heat at his back. The weather was damp that morning, and the wind had cut him to the quick as he had walked in the darkness before dawn from last night's lodging-place to Fotheringay Castle.

He recognized a few faces among those seated nearest the dais. One or two seemed to glance at Goodluck with more than passing interest. He was disguised as a local gentleman that day, wearing a country suit and hat, and carrying a stout cane instead of his sword. But there had not been much he could do about his beard, presently regrown in its grey and sable splendour, and quite distinctive to friends and enemies alike.

Now that they were in the execution room itself, with its generous crackling fire and tapestry-hung walls, the assembled gentry seemed more cheerful. Men talked among themselves about the weather, or stared with frank curiosity at the raised platform that dominated the Great Hall. Some five feet high, it had been railed off on three sides from the spectators, for all the world as though for a wrestling match – except for the yards of black crêpe with which it had been hung. At one end stood a high-backed seat, presumably intended for the exiled queen, and several other seats for witnesses, set about the dais. In grim opposition to these more comfortable objects stood the block, rough and stained, where her head would soon be laid.

Standing to one side on the dais were the executioner and his assistant, both large men, their arms folded over the black gowns and white aprons of their trade. Today at

481

least, Goodluck thought darkly, there would be no dragging out the traitor's innards while she was still alive and begging for mercy. For royalty, the penalty was beheading; an easy death by comparison with that suffered by less exalted conspirators.

The guards on the door into the antechamber drew themselves up as it opened. Several sombre-looking men entered, accompanied by a small party of soldiers, and a priest holding a Bible, from which he was reading as he walked.

Behind them came Mary Stuart herself, holding herself with dignity in a black gown with a red velvet bodice, a white veil trailing down her back from her cap. Her face was ashen pale, and her eyes red from recent weeping, yet she seemed composed.

A muttering filled the room as Mary hesitated at the foot of the platform, her eyes on the block that awaited her. Then a soldier came forward, taking each arm, and firmly escorted the Queen up the steps to the dais.

Passing the low wooden block, Mary seemed to stumble but recovered herself, and was even smiling as she settled herself into the high-backed chair.

The death warrant was then read aloud to the Queen and the crowd, in case any believed the proceedings not to be legally conducted. Goodluck barely heard a word, his attention on the faces of the rapt assembly instead. If any rebel traitor was in the room that morning, he felt sure some flicker of despair would betray him now, at the death of his best hope for a Catholic England.

But although he saw pity and discomposure on many faces there, he found no outward signs of anger.

The Dean of Peterborough stood to address the Queen, asking her to accept 'the comfortable promises of Almighty God to all penitent believing Christians', but was rudely interrupted by Mary herself, who insisted in a strong French accent that she was a true Catholic and had no need of his English comforts. She had been raised at the French court, Goodluck recalled, and was still by all accounts a popular figure there – though none of her followers in Paris had ever stirred themselves to obtain her release.

'Mr Dean!' she exclaimed, when the priest ignored this shrill outburst and attempted to continue with his address. 'I beg you not to trouble yourself with the salvation of my soul. You should know that I am settled in the ancient Catholic and Roman faith, and I mean to spend my blood today in its defence.'

Rising from her seat, her face flushed with sudden indignation, Mary dropped to her knees in the centre of the platform and began to pray loudly in Latin. Her servants at once joined in, kneeling around her as though to protect their mistress from interference. One of her women handed her a white crucifix which the Queen raised first to heaven and then kissed, praying ever more passionately in Latin, and weeping as she did so.

The Dean of Peterborough stared at Mary with undisguised loathing, then stalked to the far end of the platform. There, the block waited starkly for her neck.

The dean spoke briefly with the executioner, his back turned, but the Scots Queen's gaze had followed him – and lighted on the block.

More unnecessary cruelty, Goodluck noted. His bile rose. Did the officious bastard have to wave his triumph in her face? The dean had wished to remind Mary that she might have won that particular battle, but the end of the war was in sight.

Finishing her prayers, Mary spoke with each of her weeping servants in turn, then allowed the executioners to approach and kneel before her.

'Madam,' the older one asked, whose name Goodluck

knew to be Bull, chief executioner at the Tower of London, 'will you forgive us this discharge of our duty?'

'Willingly,' Mary replied lightly to the executioner's traditional request, though her cheeks were damp and her lips trembled as she spoke. 'I forgive you both with all my heart, for I hope this death will bring an end to the troubles of my life.'

Her expression now resolute, Mary raised her arms for the masked executioners to disrobe her.

As her black gown was slowly and respectfully removed, a petticoat of crimson satin was revealed beneath.

Several men in the front seats cried out, 'For shame!' while others frowned in open consternation, shaking their heads at this last defiant gesture. Goodluck smiled grimly. The rebel Queen knew well what the effect of such a last garment would be upon those reading of her death in months and years to come. For crimson was not only the colour of blood, but also of martyrdom. Her choice today would provide a rallying cry to every secret Catholic in the land, to rise up and die a martyr to their faith.

Led to the block, Mary knelt before it on a cushion, not looking at the dreadful object but staring some way ahead, her lips moving in silent prayer.

One of her women came forward and, with badly shaking hands, folded a gilt-embroidered white cloth for a blindfold. This she placed gently over her mistress's eyes, with some whispered words of comfort, then knotted it behind Mary's head and stepped back.

The watching gentlemen in the hall were silent at last, sitting motionless as they waited for the end. Even the Dean of Peterborough had finished reading quietly from the Psalms and now closed his Bible, looking on with a sudden expression of pity.

'*In te Domine confido, non confundar in aeternum,*'

Mary declared, putting her trust in the Lord, and fumbled blindly for the block.

Finding the smooth hollow where her neck must rest, the Scottish Queen lowered herself to the block, and then, as though to make herself more comfortable there, turned her cheek slightly to face the wall where Goodluck stood.

Her face was pale again now, almost as white as the cloth binding her eyes. There was an awkward moment as the executioner's assistant bent to remove her two hands from the block, where she had been gripping on to the wood as though for very life itself. The man muttered something in her ear, and Mary stretched her arms and legs out from the block so as not to impede the blow.

The masked executioner laid aside the cloth he had been using to wipe the sweat from his hands and picked up his axe in a businesslike manner. He stepped forward, taking up a position just behind the Queen and to her left.

As though the blindfolded Mary had suddenly sensed Bull's presence behind her, Goodluck saw her outstretched arms begin to shake. Nonetheless, the Queen did not attempt to move from the block but maintained a dignified composure in her last seconds.

Goodluck steeled himself to watch the moment of execution itself, though the compassion he felt for the Queen surprised him with its intensity. Having spent the better part of a year disguised as a Catholic, Goodluck knew that the plainer English faith was at heart not that dissimilar from its Catholic roots. At the end of one's life, it was the same Jesus Christ to whom one cried *in extremis*. The Queen's desperate prayers had moved him almost to tears, and while his head knew that Mary Stuart deserved this fate for colluding with the Catholic plotters who had sought her cousin's death, his heart told him that this execution was cruel and unjust.

'Into thy hands, O Lord,' Mary cried urgently in Latin,

repeating her prayer several times in a strong voice, 'I commend my spirit.'

Lord Shrewsbury, seated close at hand on the dais, had risen slowly to his feet as Mary was led to the block. Now, with a last grim look about the hall, he raised his white staff of office to indicate that the Queen was ready to die, and nodded to Bull to perform the task.

Bull raised his axe high, with an almost interminable pause at the top of the swing, then brought it down.

'Jesu!' Mary seemed to exclaim, her lips jerked open, blood streaming from a deep gash in the back of her head, her neck still intact.

Horrified by the man's incompetence, Goodluck swore beneath his breath and crossed himself.

Undeterred, Bull widened his stance and swung the heavy axe above his head again.

This time the blow struck true, and Mary's head fell forward, not quite cut off but no longer on her shoulders. This problem was remedied after another few moments, Bull stooping above the block to hack away at the remains of her neck with his axe. Finally the deed was done and the Queen's head dropped to the platform, fully severed.

A little breathless from his efforts, Bull bent to grasp it by its white cap. He lifted the bloodied head and swung it round to show the watching crowd. 'God save the Queen!'

At that moment the cap and red hair below seemed to detach themselves. Suddenly Bull had nothing but a cap and wig in his hand, while the Queen's almost bald head went rolling like a football across the platform, leaving a gruesome trail of blood behind.

Grey-haired, it came to rest facing Goodluck, lips still jerking up and down as though in prayer.

Sickened and speechless, Goodluck looked away from the dreadful sight. Then he heard the pitiful cries of her ladies and gentlemen attendants and, glancing across the hall, saw that Lord Shrewsbury, too, was crying. It seemed nobody quite knew what to do now that the execution was complete. For a moment there was chaos, gentlemen leaping up and knocking chairs over in their hurry either to leave the hall or to get a better view of her lifeless corpse, and above it all, the Dean of Peterborough could be heard saluting Queen Elizabeth, and crying, 'So perish all the Queen's enemies!'

As the Earl of Kent began to cheer, a sudden shriek went up from the small crowd gathered below the block. Her body still slumped sideways in a pool of blood, the dead Queen's petticoats were stirring unnaturally, almost as though her bloodied trunk was about to rise and walk again to fetch its head.

Goodluck stared, wholly disconcerted. Dark tales of supernatural resurrections came back to him, and the hairs lifted on the back of his neck.

Stooping to lift the sticky petticoat, with no sign of fear or respect, the executioner's assistant reached in and dragged out a small white terrier, which must have been concealed under the Queen's skirts throughout the execution. The little dog yapped and twisted about in his grasp, clearly panicked. One of the Queen's ladies came forward, sobbing violently, to take the animal. But as soon as he released it, the terrier scampered round and tucked itself into the gory space where Mary's head had been, its white fur matting with blood.

Goodluck bowed to the gentleman next to him, who was still staring, horrified, at the Queen's twitching lips, and left the overheated hall.

That evening, as dusk was falling, Goodluck made his way slowly back up to Fotheringay Castle, heading this time for the postern gate.

The captain happened to be in the guardroom. He asked Goodluck's business curtly, no doubt having spent the day turning a steady stream of curious visitors away from the scene of the Scottish Queen's beheading. But he accepted Goodluck's note of business politely enough and bore it away inside.

Goodluck lit a pipeful of tobacco from the brazier in the guardroom and waited out of the cold, smoking and exchanging pleasantries with the guards as they played a game of dice.

When the captain returned, he was accompanied by a short balding man whom Goodluck recognized as one of the castle servants. This man looked him up and down, then invited Goodluck to walk out with him a little way along the path.

'So you are Walsingham's man. I was beginning to think you were not coming. From his letter, I expected you this afternoon,' he told Goodluck once they were out of earshot of the castle walls.

'There were still too many people about earlier in the day. Besides, these things are better done in the dark.'

The man grunted. 'That's as may be,' he remarked, with a touch of bravado, though Goodluck noticed how he glanced nervously about himself more than once in the thickening dusk. 'But I didn't like wandering the castle with such a gruesome trophy about my person, I can tell you. If I had been searched—'

'But I take it you were not,' Goodluck commented drily. He held out a hand, turning so that no one watching from inside the castle would be able to see the transaction. 'Why not let me relieve you of your burden now? Then you may go about your duties with a clear conscience.'

Hesitant, his small, dark eyes watchful, the man dug into the pocket hanging from his belt and brought out a coarse handkerchief folded very small and tied with string.

This makeshift parcel he handed to Goodluck with a dramatic shudder. 'Here you are. Though what your master wants with it, I would not like to think.'

'As well, then,' Goodluck said pleasantly, unwrapping the small handkerchief, 'that it is none of your business.' He looked down at the short grey lock of hair concealed within the cloth folds. It curled slightly, dried blood still attached to one end. 'Strange to think her hair was no longer red, but grey.'

The man made no reply, but bowed and took himself back to the castle with a muttered, 'Goodnight,' clearly uncomfortable now that his task had been discharged.

Goodluck wrapped the dead Queen's lock of hair once more in the handkerchief, secreted the grisly parcel in the lining of his jacket, and set off back to the inn where he had been staying. It was a chill night, but with only a light frost on the ground. Spring was definitely in the air. He would keep the same room at the inn tonight, then begin the ride home to London as soon as he had breakfasted.

Though there seemed little need for him to hurry back, now that Mary was finally dead. Confirmation of her death would have reached Sir Francis Walsingham tonight anyway. Which meant the chief secretary would be too busy dealing with Queen Elizabeth's anger tomorrow to wonder where Goodluck was with the requested memento of his triumph over the Catholic Queen.

Ten

ELIZABETH REINED IN HER HORSE AT THE HEAD OF A PATH, pausing under the bare-limbed trees to admire the view. The air is so fresh out here at Greenwich, she thought. Chilly, too, with a greyish icy coating to the trunks and spring not yet upon them, but not unbearably so. Anyway, it was a relief not to be constantly raising a pomander to her nose in case some foul whiff caused her to retch.

The forest at least was clean. Nothing to shrink from here. The vast wooded estate of Greenwich Palace stretched before her, a maze of narrow forest paths and bursts of meadow for the gallop. A golden place in summer, but now the woods were still wintry, most of the stark branches not yet in bud. Inviting nonetheless; a place to try and forget the troubles that pressed so closely these days. Elizabeth thought of the dirty swell of wherries and slow river barges they had passed on their way into the woods, bobbing on a scummy tide so white in places it looked like milk that had curdled. The men aboard had halted to stare as her glittering entourage passed, shielding their eyes against the sun, then bent to their tasks again. 'Haul away there!', 'Fresh fish!', 'Passage to the docks!' Their faint cries disturbed the air even now, like crows jeering in the sunshine. A man must earn his living, but all the same . . .

Suddenly irritable, her head turned. What had she heard now? Not the coarse voices of watermen, but bells. Church bells.

She held up a hand for silence as the band of accompanying courtiers came level with her, and listened for a moment, not sure whether she had imagined the sound.

Her bodyguards glanced at each other. They too had caught the echoes from the city and seemed to sense danger. They nudged their mounts closer, flanking her small party of gentlemen and ladies.

She glanced back. Robert had stopped to listen to the bells as well. He had been riding at the back of the cavalcade, deep in conversation with one of the men he had brought back from the Low Countries, a bald-headed fellow with a curt manner. More conspiracy and high intrigue, she thought. Well, if she did not ask what went on and Robert did not tell her, she need not bother her head with it. She was oddly comfortable with that tacit arrangement. It should be her new policy. Feast and dance and ride, and never ask what her closest men were planning in their 'secret' meetings that everyone knew about.

Robert had spurred his horse towards her, now hauling on the reins to bring his stallion from a brisk canter to a standstill beside her. Such a show-off. Except he must have sunk his spurs too deeply into the horse's glossy black sides, for the animal reared up madly, hooves lashing the air. Cursing under his breath, Robert kept the horse on a short rein, talking to it and gripping its flanks with thighs and knees until the stallion was calm again.

He might no longer be the vital young man she had fallen in love with as a girl, yet he had lost none of his magical touch with horses. Nor with her, truth be told.

491

Though she should not humiliate herself by admitting that, even in the privacy of her own heart.

'Listen, do you hear? Are those bells ringing in the city, do you think?' Elizabeth asked.

He listened, one hand stroking down his horse's neck. Too idly, she thought. He was not surprised.

'What is it?' she demanded. Her eyes narrowed on his face. 'What do you know?' Her mind leapt ahead to disaster. Church bells pealing out across the river. Men running, fire in the city. An old panic swamped her, all thoughts of her ride forgotten. 'Is it an invasion? Are the Spanish coming?'

'I doubt it, Your Majesty,' he reassured her, though now he was looking uncomfortable. 'We would have had better warning.'

'Nonetheless,' she told him, wheeling her horse about, 'let us ride back and discover the cause. I cannot be easy in my mind until I am sure we are not about to be set upon by a pack of Spaniards creeping out of the hedgerows.'

'Your Majesty, wait!'

Elizabeth ignored him. She urged her horse on past the confused guards and her staring women, their mounts fidgeting and tearing at the grasses in the cold sunlight.

These church bells meant something, and Robert knew it. But what? Enough of these games, she thought, and dug in her heels.

She left the woodlands and returned by way of the winding path alongside the River Thames, which was the quicker route back to the palace grounds. The sound of bells was louder there, insistent, pealing down the river. Was every church tower in London thronged with mad bell-ringers? Her anger mounted, beating in her head with wings of steel. Her councillors were hiding some momentous happening from her. They were treating her like a child who could not be trusted with the truth.

Whatever had happened, the whole of England seemed to know. Yet she, their queen, was ignorant of it.

She envisaged hordes of swarthy Spaniards setting fire to her beloved London and putting its citizens to the sword while she rode out with her ladies like a simpering fool.

'God's death, what is it?' she exclaimed in her frustration.

At her back came the sound of hooves. Robert and her guards had begun to catch up with her.

But no, no. Wait, listen again. Her mind steadied. The church bells did not sound a warning. They were not a call to arms, nor a terrified cry of 'Invasion!' The bells rang out joyfully across the city, each peal tumbling wildly over the other in celebration as they had done on the day of her coronation.

Round the next bend, she came across a group of commoners by the waterside. Several girls had already waded out into the river with their skirts tucked high into their belts and were bent over, their pale legs reflected in the murky water, searching for the eel traps that had been weighted down on the riverbed. Yet the water must be icy at this time of year, Elizabeth thought, amazed at the sight. Sure enough, the young girls gasped and shivered as they waded, their sleeveless arms red-raw with the cold. A scrawny, grey-haired woman worked on the bankside, grimly exhorting the girls to 'Keep at it!' and 'Drag 'em up!' The rolled-up sleeves of the old woman's gown revealed surprisingly muscular arms as she wrestled the captive eels into lidded buckets for market.

Elizabeth reined in her horse. 'You there! Why do the bells ring down the river?' she called out to the old woman.

Seeing who it was, the old woman looked astonished, then fell to her knees on the muddy bank. The girls turned to stare open-mouthed from the river, shielding their eyes against the low February sun as the royal party came to a halt.

'God save the Queen!' the old woman cried out with toothless patriotism. She gave a knowing nod, as though Elizabeth had been testing her with that question and she would now prove true. 'Why, the church bells ring for joy that the Scottish Queen as plotted against Your Majesty is dead.' She crossed herself piously. 'May God in His heaven bless you and preserve you from all such wicked creatures of the devil, Your Majesty.'

Stunned, Elizabeth turned to Robert as he drew rein beside her. 'I don't understand. What does the old woman mean? Robert, what does she mean?'

'I don't know,' he muttered, but again she caught that edge in his voice and her temper flared. Why was he lying to her? Could she trust no one in this world but old and toothless women, the simple poor of London?

'I must see William Davison at once. Give the old crone a penny for her tale,' she told him in a choked voice, then brought the crop down hard on her gelding's rump and felt the animal leap forward, jerking her in the saddle.

She galloped back to Greenwich, her lips tight with anger and impatience, soon leaving her guards behind as they attempted to keep up. It could not be true, she kept thinking, the reins clutched tight in her gloved hands. Mary's death warrant had been signed, yes. But she had not given the order for it to be discharged.

Yet why would the bells be ringing if not to celebrate Mary's execution? She could understand every sly-eyed courtier in the palace concealing the truth from her. Why would the old woman have lied?

By the time Elizabeth reached the palace gates, Robert had caught up with her again, the others not far behind.

He followed her inside, trying to catch at her arm. 'Your Majesty! Elizabeth, please wait!'

'Tell me it is not true!' she exclaimed hotly, and shook him off when he did not speak. Turning, she saw Sir Christopher Hatton emerge from one of the Council chambers, his face very sombre. 'Sir Christopher, what is the meaning of these church bells that are ringing all over London? Sweet Jesu, tell me my cousin still lives!'

Sir Christopher Hatton glanced at Robert over her shoulder, then bowed his head. The silence dragged on and she felt her face flush with agitation. Why did he not speak?

'You must forgive me for being the bearer of tidings that may cause you unhappiness, Your Majesty,' Sir Christopher began with slow and politic deliberation, but she interrupted him.

'The truth! Now!'

'Your Majesty, the bells ring out to celebrate the death of one who has plotted endlessly against your royal person.'

'No,' she breathed.

Sir Christopher looked at her steadily as he continued. 'Mary Stuart was executed at Fotheringay Castle yesterday.'

'Mary is dead?' She stared at them both, and could hardly speak for the blood rushing to her head. 'Whose doing was this? By whose order was my cousin executed?'

'Your Majesty, you signed the death warrant yourself.'

'But I gave no order for the warrant to be taken to Fotheringay and carried out!' Elizabeth exclaimed, then saw the dangerous direction his remark had taken. 'How dare you suggest that this is my doing? Fetch William Davison before me. He was the man to whom I entrusted the warrant. Fetch him at once. I will have an answer here today.' She tore off her gloves. 'Someone must pay for this deed with their life. To have executed a woman of royal blood . . .'

Robert tried to steer her into a private chamber, away from the courtiers who had gathered to stare. His voice muttered in her ear, 'It should not have been done in this covert way, yes. But you must see the pressing reasons for her execution. No Englishman will blame you for this. And at least the matter is finished now. You are safe.'

'*Safe*?' she repeated, trembling with fury at his stupidity. 'Do you not see how this weakens my throne? The head which bears the crown is no longer sacrosanct but open to any rebel with an axe. What, my lord, you stare and think I make too great a matter of this execution? Why not strike off my own head, then, if hers was no matter?'

'Elizabeth—' Robert began quietly, but she interrupted him.

'You will address me with the proper respect due to your queen, my lord,' she snapped at him, 'or find yourself in the Tower this night. Go do my bidding. Fetch William Davison at once.'

In the smoky damp of her state apartments, Elizabeth knelt and clasped her hands in prayer. But no words came. 'Lord God, forgive . . . forgive what has been done in my name,' she managed at last, and muttered her way through the Lord's Prayer. Her ladies prayed with her, then fussed about her person, avoiding her gaze as they began to remove her riding dress, their faces scared. They all knew what had happened. Of course they did. She was the only one in the kingdom not to have known of Mary Stuart's death when she had ridden out that morning.

At length she allowed her ladies to draw her towards a seat by the hearth, where a good fire was roaring and her dogs slept, blissfully unaware that a Scottish noblewoman with more arrogance than sense had recently bent her head to the axe. Her ladies applied lotion to her face and hands, then bathed her feet in warm rose-water until the aching cold in her bones had subsided. There was little else to do while she waited for Davison to be found. Bitterly, Elizabeth considered what vitriolic last words Mary might have written to her Catholic allies in Europe, and wondered how soon an invasion force would land on England's shores.

She had been within her rights to keep a threat to her throne under guard all these years. But to have executed a queen, even one whose treasonous activities were well-known . . .

Elizabeth could imagine the reactions of other crowned heads of Europe on hearing of Mary's death. She must now appear as ruthless and untrustworthy a ruler as Mary had ever done herself. The Lord alone knew what would follow this political disaster.

On being hesitantly told an hour later that the Junior Secretary of State was ill and no longer at court, Elizabeth finally lost her poorly kept temper. She swept a flagon of ale to the floor, turned over a table in her way, then swore at the absent Davison, condemning him as a traitor and a murderer. Her ladies scattered as she strode back and forth across the Privy Chamber, flushed and trembling at the power of her own fury. She had been duped. She should never have signed that warrant. As soon as it was done and taken from her, she had known, she had guessed . . .

Pausing undecided in the centre of the room, Elizabeth caught Lucy Morgan's eye and almost snarled at the disapproval on the black girl's face.

'Let Davison be found at once and taken to the Tower!' she insisted furiously, ignoring Sir Christopher's stuttering attempts to mollify her.

Yes, she had wanted Mary dead. But quietly, discreetly, in such a manner that no one could ever lay blame at her door. Not like this, so brazenly and openly, with all the church bells of London ringing for sheer unadulterated joy.

'I gave the death warrant into his safe keeping,' she

pointed out icily, 'and Davison allowed it to be taken to Fotheringay Castle, all the while knowing it to be without my permission. He shall be tried for my cousin's murder and, if there is any justice in this country, executed for treacherous dereliction of his duty.' When Hatton tried to speak again, she shook her head. 'I do not care how sick he may be. Let Davison be conveyed under guard to the Tower, then bring me word it has been done.'

A servant came to the door, bowing. 'Your Majesty, Lord Burghley is here.'

'I will not admit him!' she declared, and gestured to the others to leave her. 'Indeed I am sick of this company. Out, out, all of you!'

Lady Helena paused in the doorway, clearly distressed. 'But Your Majesty, it is almost time for you to take lunch.'

'I have no wish to eat,' Elizabeth told her with barely suppressed violence, and threw a bowl of sweetmeats clattering across the room. She was aware of behaving childishly, yet could not seem to control her temper. 'I will never eat again. I am too unwell. I am sick with nerves, can none of you see that? I shall be blamed at every foreign court for this murder, though it was none of my doing. Now leave me. I will not see Lord Burghley, nor any man, unless he comes with news that Davison is in the Tower.'

Robert, hesitating on the threshold, took a step towards her.

'Get out, I said!' Elizabeth could not stand to see the pity in his face. She turned away as Robert bowed and withdrew. 'I wish to be alone. Let no one be admitted. No one!'

When the door finally closed behind the last of them, Elizabeth collapsed on to her knees and wept. She rocked and tore at her face with her nails. She wept not for her cousin Mary, though, whom she had always secretly loathed and resented, but for herself, for Elizabeth, for the terrifying shadows of the past that threatened to over-whelm her.

She thought again and again of Mary. Mary kneeling for the axe. Mary's head rolling away, grisly and bloodied. Her own bold signature on the death warrant: *Elizabeth R.*

A message came about an hour later, and she rose from her bed, reluctantly putting aside her Bible. Her women, summoned to help, smoothed her gown and dressed her hair in silence. No doubt they feared the lash of her tongue. A pity Davison had not feared it more, she thought.

The Presence Chamber was crowded with hurriedly assembled courtiers, their agitated whispers falling to silence as she walked to the dais and stood to receive the man who had so flagrantly disobeyed her. Davison was eventually ushered in, his head bowed, wringing his cap in his hands like a poor burgher come to plead for his life. He had not come alone, though, but was followed by Leicester, Burghley, and even a worried-looking Hatton. Behind them she saw other councillors, their faces tense, watching her. The message was clear. Condemn Davison and you must condemn us too. For what he did was done with our knowledge and consent.

'Master Davison, Your Majesty,' Lord Burghley murmured, and came forward to stand beside her secretary, whose face was pale with fear.

Angrily, Elizabeth looked at her councillors and knew herself defeated before she had even pronounced his fate.

Davison would still go before the Star Chamber and thence to the Tower, if she had her way. She would be damned if he walked away from this act of disobedience without punishment. But these men would not allow her to execute him for what had been done by secret order of

499

the Privy Council; that much was written on their faces.

If only she had never signed Mary's death warrant!

Yet she had signed the warrant, and known in her heart that it must eventually be used to seal her cousin's fate. In that moment, she had become her father, a tyrant who thought nothing of executing a queen, of tearing a royal mother from her child. History would judge her for that. But the Spanish would judge her for it first.

Epilogue

The Curtain Theatre, London, autumn 1587

IT WAS THE FIFTH TIME WILL HAD COME TO THE CURTAIN and paid his penny to see a performance of Kit Marlowe's popular new play, *Tamburlaine the Great*. Yet he still stood breathless and entranced among the other groundlings when Ned Alleyn, splendidly exotic in red velvet breeches and a jewel-encrusted golden coat that reached almost to his knees, came charging across the stage on his chariot, whip in hand, driving a team of four kings. The 'kings' sweated before him in the autumn sunshine, overdressed in the gold-trimmed coats and pointed slippers of the East. One of them stumbled, his crown slipped forward across his temples, and the crowd jeered.

'Ye pampered jades of Asia!' Ned cried in his role as the tyrant Tamburlaine, flourishing his long-handled whip above his head, and at once a thousand eager voices called back from the smoky, crowded pit and galleries of the Curtain Theatre, 'Tamburlaine! Tamburlaine! Tamburlaine!'

Will's chest hurt. He stared, eyes narrowed to that space where Ned stood, whirling the whip, and he saw . . . not

Marlowe's play, but his own, and many others besides, stretching ahead into the misty future, with the London mob clapping and stamping their feet for more.

Backstage, Will sought out Kit Marlowe in the crowded tiring-room and embraced him, congratulating him on his first big success. 'I have never heard anything like it,' he admitted, half sick with envy.

Kit smiled. 'Why not leave off rewriting old plays and strike out with a new theme yourself?'

'I have started work on a few things. I have one piece in hand that I am calling *Titus Andronicus*.'

'The Romans are a fair theme for the groundlings.' Kit shrugged, a note of contempt in his voice. 'The commoners love to stare and point at antique spectacle, or weep openly as they did before you and I were born, when the Passion was played in the streets for them. Though we cannot blame them for it. Better be transported for a few hours by some ancient tale to a place where the winters are short and the sun ripens the grapes than look about themselves at this ugly filth and cold.'

'Aye, but it's nothing to this.' He shook his head. 'Tamburlaine. I have tried, but cannot . . . cannot reach that pitch.'

'Poor unlucky Will,' Kit murmured, looking away.

Ned Alleyn stumbled into the tiring-room, sweating as he stripped off his golden coat and shirt, then called for ale. He stood bare-chested while he drank his fill, his humorous gaze on Will's face, then wiped a hand across his mouth. 'What, are you here again, Master Shake-a-scene? I begin to suspect you must be in love with one of us.'

'You are the best player in all of London, Ned,' Will told him, enthused by the power and intelligence of Alleyn's performance. 'Perhaps the best player on earth.'

'Oh come, why stop at earth?' Kit asked. 'Ned is the best player of all those already in heaven and hell.'

'Or the best player in the cosmos, perhaps?' Ned suggested.

'Indeed. A hard thing to comprehend, but I suspect you may even be better than Tarlton,' Kit agreed soberly.

'Oh, no,' Ned said, lifting the heavy gold chain and medallion from about his neck. 'Not better than Tarlton. That would be beyond the impossible. Why, I could never make the house laugh just by pulling my breeches down.'

Kit raised his eyebrows. 'Yet I know a few whores who would swear to the opposite.'

Philip Henslowe hurried past the door to the tiring-room, then stopped, seeing Will there.

'Shakespeare?' Henslowe paused on the threshold, frowning. 'You seem to be haunting the Curtain these days. Have you come to offer me a play? Not another old work rewritten, I hope. London is crying out for the new, the new. Did you hear the crowd today, calling Tamburlaine's name? They are barbarians themselves, they love to see evil triumph and innocent blood spilt on the boards. Write me another Tamburlaine and I will pay you . . . what I am paying Kit here.'

'Which is not enough to pay the cost of parchment and ink,' Kit murmured.

'Sorry,' Will told him regretfully. 'I owe Burbage so big a purse, I've had to promise him my soul for the next few years just to clear the debt.'

When Henslowe had gone away again, Kit looked at Will speculatively. 'But you are working on something new, aren't you? This *Titus Andronicus* you mentioned.'

'Nothing on this scale.'

'Show it to me,' Kit said lightly, and turned to assist one of the other players out of his heavy costume. 'I'll help you with it, if you like.'

'Would you?' Will hesitated, torn between admitting he needed a fresh eye on the play and not wanting Marlowe

503

to know that. 'I have another idea as well. There's this piece I culled out of Holinshed. I'm going to call it *The Famous Victories of Henry the Fifth*.'

Kit frowned. 'An English history?'

'I know it's not fashionable, but—'

'Is there more to it than battle scenes and cannon?'

'Since when has death not brought in crowds?' Will sighed. 'You think me mistaken? That I should write the Roman piece instead?'

'I told you, the groundlings love a good tragedy. And if you can give it to them with some whiff of the exotic East or ancient Rome, they will love you for it.'

'You sound like Burbage.'

'Now you are trying to insult me.' But Kit was smiling. 'Bring the Roman play over to the Angel some time. We'll look at the play together, stuff it full with blood and guts as Master Kyd would do, and stick in a violent rape or two for good measure. The Romans loved to rape their women. Talking of which, I saw that beautiful Ethiop of yours up in the gallery, a great pearl in her ear, looking untouchable and like the Queen of Sheba herself.'

'Wait.' Will caught hold of Kit's hand as his friend turned away. 'You mean Lucy?'

Marlowe arched an eyebrow at Will, who was feeling sick. 'The one who married the unfortunate Jack, yes. You did not tell me she was one of the Queen's ladies. No wonder you do not bring her to the taverns any more. Such women are too expensive for a mere playwright to keep.'

Will's grip tightened. 'Forgive me, you saw Lucy at the Curtain today? In the gallery?'

'I believe so.' Kit looked at him, surprised. 'Your black mistress was seated in a private box with several other ladies of the court, all hooded or masked. You know how they love to pretend not to attend the common play. But I recognized her at once. Even now she has been married and is past her best, she is quite unmistakable.'

Will realized that he must be staring at Kit like a lunatic. He struggled for some semblance of control. 'Lucy . . . She is no longer my mistress,' he managed.

Kit's tone was dry. 'Is she not?' he asked, and glanced down. 'Then why are you breaking my hand?'

Will left Kit Marlowe with the briefest of apologies and hurried to the back door of the Curtain. The crowd outside had almost dispersed after the performance, but some of the merchants' ladies were still waiting in the shadows there, smelling of perfume and attended by their servants, no doubt hoping for a glimpse of Ned Alleyn. Feverishly, Will began to run down towards the city walls, knocking into people in his haste, and staring wildly about himself as though touched in the brain. He had heard of Jack's death, of course, but by the time he had reached the Parkers' house his friend had been long buried and Lucy vanished. He had tried at Goodluck's place many times, but not found her there either; it was locked up as though deserted. One neighbour had suggested she had gone abroad for her health. Another had claimed she was back in the Queen's favour and had returned to court, 'Good riddance to the whore!' But he had not been able to get word of her at court, lacking the nerve and funds to bribe guards as he had done before. Even if he could have paid to find her quarters, he was not sure of the welcome he would have received.

Now Kit Marlowe had seen Lucy at the Curtain, watching *Tamburlaine the Great* from a private box with the other court ladies.

Peering down every lane and alley in the dying light, Will cursed himself for a fool. What was he doing? If Lucy Morgan was in truth back in the Queen's service, surely she would have left in a grand carriage or been carried on a litter?

He came to a halt and groaned aloud, ignoring the bemused looks of passers-by. Where was the court lodging this month? At Whitehall? At Chelsea or Richmond Palace? Even if it was Whitehall, the nearest palace, Lucy would never have returned there on foot, not in this dirt, with flies everywhere, and the stench of open ditches on either side.

Then, suddenly, there she was, ahead of him in the street, turning to stare, her face half-hidden behind the protective edge of her cloak.

'Lucy!'

The other women with her looked at him in astonishment. One giggled, another shook her head. He thought he recognized her disapproving friend, Cathy, among them, though she might have been a servant in her plain gown and cap. Lucy herself stood out from the others like a black pearl dangling from a white throat, her face drawn with pain, her dark eyes accusing him of past sins, her mouth so alluring he could hardly tear his gaze from it.

Lucy took a step backwards as he lurched towards her out of the growing dusk. 'Will?' She seemed horrified to see him. 'What are you doing here?'

'Kit told me you were at the play today. I had to come after you, I had to see you again.' He grasped her gloved hand and drew it to his mouth, barely aware of what he was doing. 'My lady, my dark lady. I never thought to see you again. When I heard about Jack's murder, I went there straightaway. But the Parkers told me . . .'

She withdrew from him, flinching.

'Forgive me, forgive me. I never wished ill on you or the child.' He thought bitterly of his own son, Hamnet, and the boy's faithless mother. Perhaps Lucy's stillborn child had been his only true heir. 'They said a murderer came in the night.'

'Master Twist,' she whispered.

'And then Goodluck took you away. I tried to visit you at the house in Cheapside, but it was empty.'

Lucy nodded. 'The Queen allowed me to return to court.'

'And now?' He gazed at her in silence a moment, unable to believe she could not feel the same overwhelming desire that pricked his body just at the sight of her. 'You are more beautiful than I remembered, Lucy. My heart and soul are broken in the mere act of looking at you. I thought you were gone for ever, stolen away in the night by that pirate Goodluck. But now you are here before me, solid flesh a man may touch and kiss. I must have dreamt you back into being, for I cannot imagine waking so lucky.'

'Are you mad?'

'If it is madness to be in love, then yes. Most likely, yes,' he agreed, and saw Cathy hide her smile behind her hand.

Will became aware of other presences in the shadowy lane, men who stared at their little group as they passed. Their faces seemed to mock him. He seized Lucy's hand again. She was a woman. Perhaps she could not understand desire, or not until she was caught within its maelstrom. Yet there was no time to woo her with words. The smoky autumn afternoon was drawing in, a chill in the air. Soon night would fall and Lucy Morgan would melt back into his past as though they had never found each other again.

'Come apart with me a moment,' he said tightly. 'I need to speak to you privately.'

Lucy hesitated, then threw a pleading look at the other women. They drew aside, talking among themselves but still watching her. 'Not here,' she whispered. 'There are too many eyes . . .'

'Then come to me, Lucy. Tomorrow at midday. I must rehearse a play in the morning, but then I can be yours until about three in the afternoon. I am still at my old lodgings, though the door has been painted blue now. You remember the way?'

She was watching him. 'Yes.'

'Beg time from court,' he urged her. Would she come? Doubt hit him again, euphoria fading as she hurried back to the other women. 'Do not fail me. Tomorrow, midday.'

Lucy came late to his lodgings the next day, though she knew the way well enough. Indeed she had passed the end of this street many times and thought of his little room, the bed with the red coverlet where they had lain so often. But it had been hard to slip away from court unnoticed, and in the end it had been Cathy, disapproving but willing to help, who had distracted the guards on the gate while Lucy disappeared into the crowds beyond. It was utter madness to be here again, standing at his door like a faithful dog. Would she never learn? Yet part of her had hungered for Will Shakespeare as soon as she had seen him again in the street, that flame still burning as violently despite everything.

So she knocked at the battered door with its coat of blue paint and stood waiting, her hood pulled forward, averting her face from passers-by.

He answered the door bare-chested, his skin damp, drying his hands on a rag. 'Lucy!'

She stared. This had been a mistake. 'I should not be here. I cannot be seen with you, Will. Nor with any man. If the Queen should hear of it—'

'What does the Virgin Queen know of love?' Will stood back and reluctantly she entered his lodgings, though half wanting to run away down the street and never see him again. That would be the wise thing to do.

508

The door closed behind her and they stood alone together in the silence. He took her gloved hands and held them fiercely, looking into her eyes. 'I cannot let you disappear again, Lucy. Do you not see that we must be lovers? It was written in the stars before time began that we should be together, and it was Venus rising that led me back to you tonight. If you refuse me, I swear that I shall haunt you like a ghost at court. I shall come to your window every night, I shall never let you go.'

'Have you forgotten that you have a wife?'

'Anne does not love me,' he told her. The bitterness in his voice had the ring of truth. 'She has betrayed me with another man. Not once but many times. She admits it freely.'

Lucy could not resist pointing out the irony of this. 'Then you have been justly served.'

'It's true, I betrayed Anne first. Nor can I blame my wife for loving where she should not. That would make me a fool and a hypocrite. But I do blame Anne for not waiting for me to return. As you have waited.'

She loved his eyes. His mouth. The timbre of his voice. 'Waited? For you?'

'Yes, for me.'

Will put his arm about her shoulder and kissed her, his mouth soon reminding her of how it had been when they had lain together as lovers. She did not pull away. Nor, though, did she invite him on. She had a choice, and she was not yet sure what it would be.

'I need you by my side, Lucy,' he whispered, then stripped off her gloves and began to kiss her fingers one by one. 'Do not reject me again, or you will ruin me. You are my muse. I have so many stories in my head, they burn me from the inside out. Yet I can write none of them without you, Lucy. Your body drives the fever from my blood.' His lips dwelt on her skin. 'Do you not love me?'

Lucy studied his bent head. Did she love him? It could be love, but not as he understood it. To him, love was a physical passion that drove two people together and locked them there in chains of fire. To her, love was the decision to be with someone for ever. And how could she be with Will for ever?

'I cannot love you. We are too different.'

'No more different than two sides of the same coin. If you will not love me, then let me love you. I have a plan. A great plan. But I need you to join me in this new venture, Lucy. Last night I saw the future. It is this,' Will muttered. He dropped her hands and kissed her throat. She arched against him, seduced by the lure of physical love. It had been so long since she had been touched, she thought. Yet she had not realized until that moment how much she had missed it. 'And Tamburlaine.'

'Tamburlaine?' she repeated blankly.

'Yes.' For a moment he stared at nothing, as though seeing the playhouse before him. 'Very like Tamburlaine, but not as Ned plays him, with so much strutting and declaiming. Rather as a man might say the words to himself, alone in a dark room. That is the future.'

Was this what he had meant when he had called her his muse? Over his shoulder she could see his torn mattress, thrown carelessly before the hearth, and the pooled remains of candle stumps from where he must have been working last night. Writing, she corrected herself.

She ran a finger down his cheek, loving the far-away look in his eyes. Perhaps it would be enough to share Shakespeare's bed simply to free his imagination. Cautiously, she considered the Queen's wrath. But she had defied the Queen before, and the sky had not fallen. She thought of her promise to Goodluck. He had not wanted to see her hurt again by falling back in with Shakespeare. Yet where was Master Goodluck now? Off on his travels abroad, spying for Sir Francis, and she felt so alone some nights . . .

Was it such a terrible thing to snatch at love in passing and enjoy what could be got without promises, rather than endlessly hankering after the settled life she would never have?

'I shall give the groundlings their "pampered jades of Asia",' Will exclaimed, quoting from Marlowe's play as he drew her closer, his hands busy with the lacing of her gown, 'but on an English battlefield, with plain-speaking soldiers and kings of common clay. And that is how I'll outKit Kit, master Marlowe with my own scenes of violent destruction.'

'War,' she whispered, yet could think of nothing but love.

Will led her towards the bed, an answering passion in his face. 'Stay with me, Lucy, and you will see. When I am done with Rome's bloody past, I shall bring England's lost glories back, and the crowd will love me for it. '

Author's Note

The clandestine wedding of Lettice Knollys, the widowed Countess of Essex, and Robert Dudley, Earl of Leicester, took place in April 1578, nearly three years after the events in *The Queen's Secret*, the first novel in this trilogy. It may be that Lettice was pregnant – or thought she was at the time – and this lent a sense of urgency and secrecy to the ceremony. Despite knowing how vehemently Queen Elizabeth would oppose their match, Leicester's dearest wish had always been for a legitimate son and heir. However, if Lettice was pregnant when they married, it came to nothing. Their son Robert, Lord Denbigh, affectionately nicknamed the 'Noble Impe', was not born until 1581. This unfortunate child, who may have suffered from some kind of congenital defect, died only a few years later in July 1584, to the utter despair of his now middle-aged parents. Whatever else may be said of Lettice and Robert, they were doting and attentive parents to this last hope for the Dudley dynasty.

To suggest that Queen Elizabeth was furious when she heard of their marriage would be an understatement. However many times she might have turned down Robert's offers of marriage, he was still her court favourite, viewed by her in much the same way as a treasured possession, and to lose Robert to her cousin Lettice – especially after all the Queen's heavy-handed attempts to prevent their match – must have been a bitter blow.

Nonetheless, even this act of disobedience by Leicester – one of the worst personal betrayals of Elizabeth's life, I have little doubt – could not destroy the deep and abiding affection the Queen felt for him. Within a few months of his wedding, Robert is reported to have been back at court and presumably back in favour, too, admitted to the Queen's private chambers to tend to her during an agonizing bout of toothache – a problem with which she was to struggle for much of her reign. In my book, for structural purposes, this bridge-mending episode takes place several years on. In the same way, the French Duke Alençon's courtship of Elizabeth does not feature in this book, since it largely took place during the years between my Prologue and Chapter One. Because of this necessary gap, it would have been impractical to introduce Alençon as an actual character, so the little Frenchman's flamboyant courtship is discussed 'off stage' when relevant to the main storyline.

Moving on to the Babington plot, this is a complex story with many different characters and threads, difficult to untangle into a straight narrative. To simplify matters, I have conflated a larger number of plotters into those featured here. Master Goodluck is a character entirely of my own invention, but he represents a number of spies with whom Elizabeth's spymaster, Sir Francis Walsingham, had very carefully infiltrated this plot. Each spy would leave the conspiracy as his identity was unmasked, with another discreetly taking his place. The fact that the conspirators continued unabashed by the discovery of such traitors in their midst indicates the high levels of confusion and naivety that surrounded this rather inept plot – though if it had succeeded, England would be a very different country today. Maude was one such spy, Pooley another, and Goodluck is there as a fictitious third to bring us the narrative of the plotters' last days, which we would otherwise miss.

The return of the priest and conspirator Ballard to England and his secret visit to Anthony Babington are not invented, though I alter some of the facts. Ballard had been led to believe, by one of Walsingham's men posing as a sympathizer, that the Spanish King and the Pope supported their plans to topple Elizabeth. Ballard was persuaded that a great European army had been raised and awaited only his signal to invade. He duly passed this wonderful news on to young Babington and their enthusiastic co-conspirators. From correspondence skilfully intercepted by Walsingham's network of spies, it is clear that they were a little squeamish about the idea of executing the Queen, yet were prepared to do the deed nonetheless. To their minds, they were heroes, champions of the old faith, who would be serving God by ridding England of the heretic Elizabeth.

The last conspirators were captured much as I describe, at the home of Catholic sympathizers, and the details of their excessively cruel executions are taken from contemporaneous accounts. It was vital to Elizabeth, who must have been quite terrified of assassination by this stage, that Catholic plotters should understand, once and for all, what agonies awaited them on the scaffold. Walsingham had it put about – no doubt as an exercise in propaganda – that the Queen herself had asked for greater clemency to be shown when the second group were executed the following day. But in fact the decision appears to have been made without Elizabeth's consent, in direct response to the sickened cries of the crowd.

In the same way, the details of Mary Stuart's execution

are so well known they have passed into legend: the less-than-accurate Bull – chosen by Walsingham to be the Scottish Queen's executioner – her scarlet petticoat denoting martyrdom, the lips which continued to move after the head had finally been severed, and the little bloodstained dog shivering under her skirts. What I do invent here is Goodluck's presence at the execution – though I have no doubt that Walsingham would have planted a spy or two at Fotheringay that day – and the grisly trophy he collects later. There is a possibility that Walsingham may have asked for items to be brought to him from the castle – certain papers, for instance, to be studied or destroyed – but here I speculate that Walsingham might have required physical *proof* of Mary's death, a woman who had frustrated him for many years.

Gilbert Gifford – surely a name worthy of a character from light opera – really existed, though his torture-chamber interview with Queen Elizabeth in my account is an elaboration of the truth. Tracked early on in his dealings with Mary, Queen of Scots, Gifford was indeed arrested and taken to Walsingham. There, he was persuaded – possibly by means of torture – to become a double agent. Gifford then continued to carry coded messages between Mary and her Catholic sympathizers, but discreetly brought them to Walsingham and his codebreakers first. Walsingham must have been overjoyed by the success of this intervention. He was now one step ahead of the conspirators. What he wanted, of course, was irrefutable proof that Mary condoned an attack on the Queen herself, for he knew Elizabeth would never otherwise agree to her cousin's execution. But once Walsingham felt he had such proof, his men moved in, arresting the ringleaders – Anthony Babington was not arrested in this first raid, possibly in order for him to lead them to further conspirators – and thus setting the wheels in motion for Mary's trial.

One of his spies, Pooley, was also arrested around this time, though later released – no doubt at a nod from Walsingham. I have Goodluck go through much the same process, but without the all-important nod. For as Shakespeare would later put it, 'Confusion now hath made his masterpiece.' At this point in the conspiracy, it must have been desperately hard to tell conspirator from spy and to ensure secret orders were passed to the right men. So my invented spy Master Goodluck is mistakenly brought before the psychopathic torturer Richard Topcliffe as a conspirator, and is lucky to escape with his life. Topcliffe was the Queen's chief torturer and Catholic priest-hunter for many years, operating in darkened rooms and using the cruellest implements of the age. He was proud of his work, and although the earlier scene between Topcliffe, Elizabeth, Walsingham and Gilbert Gifford is fictitious, Topcliffe often claimed to be intimate with Queen Elizabeth. Indeed, he was clearly a deviant, raping at least one of his victims and taking a perverse pleasure in inflicting pain.*

Where William Shakespeare is concerned, I have written with a somewhat freer hand. Few historians agree on what Shakespeare was doing in what are popularly known as 'the lost years' between his early marriage and his first noted presence in London. Consequently, in this book I place him in London early on, while his wife Anne nurses their baby daughter in Stratford, and suggest an informal apprenticeship during those years, Shakespeare learning his trade as a jobbing actor and nascent playwright. He may have been with the Queen's Men in its early days, or with Lord Strange's company. Nobody seems very sure which company he joined first, nor what he did there. Consequently, I am careful not to pin Shakespeare down to

* For more on this bizarre and sinister character Topcliffe, see Robert Hutchinson's excellent *Elizabeth's Spy Master*, pp. 74–82.

one company during these uncertain years, but to have him work 'freelance', following the money from job to job. However, I put him together in several scenes with rival playwright – and possible government spy – Christopher Marlowe, but of course we have no evidence for that friendship either. London was a small city in those days though, and they would certainly have met, if not known each other fairly well.

I take greater liberties with Shakespeare's writings, and here the reader must forgive me. Since I have William Shakespeare meet his 'Dark Lady' early in the 1580s, I needed to show him musing about her at this time too, and also developing as a writer. To this end, I mention various sonnets and plays whose dates are almost certainly later, possibly even early Jacobean. Equally, I wished to show the young Shakespeare tinkering with older, extant plays – British histories in particular, which I consider an obsession of his from early on – in an attempt to restructure and rewrite these theatrical templates so he could create something entirely his own. An early *King Leir* was already being performed by the late 1580s; it is not impossible to imagine that the play had existed as a folk piece long before that, and that Shakespeare may have seen something worth developing in its repetitive, folk-tale structure. I do not mean to suggest that the *King Leir* in my story is the same play commonly considered to be among his later and most accomplished works. But I think we can expect that a natural storyteller like Shakespeare would have been automatically rewriting its scenes in his head, even as a tyro, as he watched or played the earlier piece on stage.

As for his wife Anne Hathaway and her possible dalliance with one of his glover father's apprentices, I have no evidence to support such an infamous scenario. Many men in those times were forced to work away from home – as indeed they are today – and might not have seen their wives from one year to the next. It does strike me as odd, though, that the young William Shakespeare, having married a much older bride in what seems like a whirlwind of romantic fervour, should then absent himself for years when he could have – at the very least – brought Anne and the children to live with him in London once the money was good enough. That he suspected Anne of adultery is merely one possibility among many to explain why he did not. And the woman under suspicion is a common theme in his plays, though she tends to be proved innocent in the end. My explanation for Shakespeare's lengthy absence from the marriage bed – and his courtship of the elusive 'Dark Lady' – is not based on anything more substantial than gut feeling, in other words.

I wrote at length about Lucy Morgan's origins as a character in my Author's Note for *The Queen's Secret*, so will only repeat the bare bones of that here. Lucy Morgan exists in several official documents of the time, chiefly as one of the Queen's ladies at court, but also perhaps in a more dubious role, as 'Black Luce' of Clerkenwell. This would suggest a possible fall from grace, and for one of Elizabeth's ladies, no fall would be swifter than one brought about by an illicit affair – or worse, pregnancy. Lucy Morgan appears to become Lucy Parker at some point in the 1580s, and then begins to disappear from court records. Of course, we do not even know who this Lucy Morgan was, let alone what her life was like at court. She is a figure from history shrouded in mystery, little more than a name in a few old documents, and is therefore ripe for speculation by novelists. *Caveat lector!*

The sonnet quoted in Chapter Five is Shakespeare's Sonnet 151: 'Love is too young to know what conscience is'.

Victoria Lamb
October 2012

Select Bibliography

The editions cited below are those consulted, even where earlier or revised editions exist.

Ackroyd, Peter, *Shakespeare*, Vintage, 2005

Borman, Tracy, *Elizabeth's Women: The Hidden Story of the Virgin Queen*, Jonathan Cape, 2009

Clark, John and Ross, Cathy (eds), *London: The Illustrated History*, Penguin, 2011

Cook, Judith, *Roaring Boys: Playwrights and Players in Elizabethan and Jacobean England*, Sutton Publishing, 2004

Cooper, John, *The Queen's Agent: Francis Walsingham at the Court of Elizabeth I*, Faber, 2011

Greer, Germaine, *Shakespeare's Wife*, Bloomsbury, 2007

Gristwood, Sarah, *Elizabeth and Leicester*, Bantam Press, 2007

Haynes, Alan, *Sex in Elizabethan England*, The History Press, 2010

Hutchinson, Robert, *Elizabeth's Spy Master*, Orion, 2007

Jenkins, Elizabeth, *Elizabeth and Leicester*, Phoenix Press, 2002

Robins, Nicholas, *Walking Shakespeare's London*, New Holland Publishing, 2004

Southworth, John, *Shakespeare the Player*, Sutton Publishing, 2000

Wood, Michael, *In Search of Shakespeare*, BBC, 2003

Acknowledgements

Although every novel is written alone, it is produced and helped along in its genesis by a team of people. Among those I would like to thank is my editor at Transworld, Emma Buckley, for her gentle nudgings and insightful suggestions, which made this a better book. On the same note, Lynsey Dalladay, my publicist at Transworld, has been supportive and helpful, and always enthusiastic. My literary agent, Luigi Bonomi, and his wife, Alison, have been there for me throughout: indeed, this trilogy would not exist without them.

I would also like to thank the staff at the Bodleian Library, Oxford – in particular those in the Radcliffe Camera reading room – for their unstinting help and advice. Likewise the expert staff at the Globe Theatre in London, who answered my questions so patiently and brought new insights to my understanding of early Elizabethan theatre.

Nearer to home, I thank my husband, Steve, for adjusting his mindset to accommodate life with a full-time novelist – not always the easiest thing – and my children: Dylan, Morris and Indigo, for their continuing enthusiasm, and especially Becki, on whose shoulders fell many tasks which ought to have belonged to me. I don't know how we shall cope now you have flown the nest!

Lucy Morgan's adventures continue in the final part of
Victoria Lamb's wonderful Tudor trilogy . . .

Her Last Assassin
by Victoria Lamb

LADY-IN-WAITING Lucy Morgan is once again torn between her
dangerous attraction to William Shakespeare and her loyalty
to Queen Elizabeth I.

England is facing its gravest threat yet. The Spanish have
declared war, and Elizabeth finds herself attacked by sea –
and by Catholic conspiracy from within her own court.
Master Goodluck goes undercover, tasked with discovering
the identity of this secret assassin, leaving his ward Lucy not
knowing if the spy is alive or dead.

Meanwhile Queen Elizabeth is growing old in a court of
troublesome young noblemen, while Lucy is struggling to
love a man whose duties lie elsewhere.

When the final challenge comes, these two women must be
ready to face it. But there is one last surprise in store for both
of them . . .

The Queen's Secret
Desire and power collide in the court of Elizabeth I
by Victoria Lamb

Warwickshire, 1575

Pomp, fanfare and a wealth of lavish festivities await **Elizabeth I** at Kenilworth Castle. Organised by the **Earl of Leicester**, he knows this celebration is his last chance to persuade the Queen to **marry** him. But, a fickle man, he is unable to resist the **seductive** wiles of **Lettice Knollys**.

Enraged by the couple's growing **intimacy**, Elizabeth employs a young black singer and court entertainer to keep a watch on them. Brought up by a **spy**, Lucy's observational skills are sharper than anyone at the castle realises, and she soon uncovers far more than she bargained for: Someone at Kenilworth is plotting to **kill** the queen.

Can the knowledge Lucy is gaining prevent the **death** of the monarch? Or has it put Lucy in mortal **danger** instead?